THE VIVERO LETTER

The chiclero wasn't a very big man, but his rifle made him ten feet tall. He rattled out a few words and brought the muzzle of the rifle to bear on us. "Aguarde acqui! Tenga cuidado!"

It all happened in a split second. Harry turned and cannoned into me. "Run!" he said hoarsely, and I turned and took off up the trail. There was a shot which ricocheted across the trail in front, and a shout of warning. I turned to see Harry sprawled on the ground. The chiclero stood over him and raised the rifle to ram the butt at his skull.

I had a machete in my hand, so I threw it. It struck point first, penetrating just under his rib cage, sinking in deep.

I didn't mean to kill him—but I did.

DESMOND BAGLEY

The Vivero
Letter

FONTANA / Collins

First published by Wm. Collins 1968
First issued in Fontana Books 1970
Eighteenth Impression July 1976

Made and printed in Great Britain by
William Collins Sons & Co Ltd Glasgow

*To that stalwart institution the British pub,
particularly the Kingsbridge Inn, Totnes,
and the Cott Inn, Dartington*

I would like to thank Captain T. A. Hampton of the British Underwater Centre, Dartmouth, for detailed information about diving techniques.

My thanks also go to Gerard L'E. Turner, Assistant Curator of the Museum of the History of Science, Oxford, for information on certain bronze mirrors, Amida's Mirror in particular.

Theirs the credit for accuracy; mine the fault for inaccuracy.

One

I made good time on the way to the West Country; the road was clear and there was only an occasional car coming in the other direction to blind me with headlights. Outside Honiton I pulled off the road, killed the engine and lit a cigarette. I didn't want to arrive at the farm at an indecently early hour, and besides, I had things to think about.

They say that eavesdroppers never hear good of themselves. It's a dubious proposition from the logical standpoint, but I certainly hadn't disproved it empirically. Not that I had intended to eavesdrop—it was one of those accidental things you get yourself into with no graceful exit—so I just stood and listened and heard things said about myself that I would rather not have heard.

It had happened the day before at a party, one of the usual semi-impromptu lash-ups which happen in swinging London. Sheila knew a man who knew the man who was organizing it and wanted to go, so we went. The house was in that part of Golders Green which prefers to be called Hampstead and our host was a with-it whiz kid who worked for a record company and did a bit of motor racing on the side. His conversation was divided about fifty-fifty between Marshal MacLuhan waffle and Brand's Hatchery, all very wearing on the eardrums. I didn't know him personally and neither did Sheila—it was that kind of party.

One left one's coat in the usual bedroom and then drifted into the chatter, desperately trying to make human contact while clutching a glass of warm whisky. Most of the people were complete strangers, although they seemed to know each other, which made it difficult for the lone intruder. I tried to make sense of the elliptical verbal shorthand which passes for conversation on these occasions, and pretty soon got bored. Sheila seemed to be doing all right, though, and I could see this was going to be a long session, so I sighed and got myself another drink.

Halfway through the evening I ran out of cigarettes and remembered that I had a packet in my coat so I went up to the bedroom to get it. Someone had moved the coats from the bed and I found them dumped on the floor behind a large

7

avant-garde screen. I was rooting about trying to find mine when someone else came into the room. A female voice said, 'That man you're with is pretty dim, isn't he?'

I recognized the voice as belonging to Helen Someone-or-other, a blonde who was being squired by a life-and-soul-of-the-party type. I dug into my coat pocket and found the cigarettes, then paused as I heard Sheila say, 'Yes, he is.'

Helen said, 'I don't know why you bother with him.'

'I don't know, either,' said Sheila. She laughed. 'But he's a male body, handy to have about. A girl needs someone to take her around.'

'You could have chosen someone more lively,' said Helen. 'This one's a zombie. What does he *do*?'

'Oh, he's some kind of an accountant. He doesn't talk about it much. A grey little man in a grey little job—I'll drop him when I find someone more interesting.'

I stayed very still in a ridiculous half crouch behind that screen. I certainly couldn't walk out into full view after hearing that. There was a subdued clatter from the dressing-table as the girls primped themselves. They chattered about hair styles for a couple of minutes, then Helen said, 'What happened to Jimmy What's-his-name?'

Sheila giggled. "Oh, he was *too* wolfish—not at all safe to be with. Exciting, really, but his firm sent him abroad last month.'

'I shouldn't think you find this one too exciting.'

'Oh, Jemmy's all right,' said Sheila casually. 'I don't have to worry about my virtue with him. It's very restful for a change.'

'He's not a queer, is he?' asked Helen.

'I don't think so,' said Sheila. Her voice was doubtful. 'He's never appeared to be that way.'

'You never can tell; a lot of them are good at disguise. That's a nice shade of lipstick—what is it?'

They tailed off into feminine inconsequentialities while I sweated behind the screen. It seemed to be an hour before they left, although it probably wasn't more than five minutes, and when I heard the door bang I stood up cautiously and came out from under cover and went downstairs to rejoin the party.

I stuck it out until Sheila decided to call it a night and then took her home. I was in half a mind to demonstrate to her in the only possible way that I wasn't a queer, but I tossed the idea away. Rape isn't my way of having a good time. I dropped her at the flat she shared with two other girls and bade her a cordial good night. I would have to be very hard up for company before I saw her again.

A grey little man in a grey little job.

Was that how I really appeared to others? I had never thought about it much. As long as there are figures used in business there'll be accountants to shuffle them around, and it had never struck me as being a particularly grey job, especially after computers came in. I didn't talk about my work because it really isn't the subject for light conversation with a girl. Chit-chat about the relative merits of computer languages such as COBOL and ALGOL doesn't have the glamour of what John Lennon said at the last recording session.

So much for the job, but what about me? Was I dowdy and subfusc? Grey and uninteresting?

It could very well be that I was—to other people. I had never been one for wearing my heart on my sleeve, and maybe, judging by the peculiar mores of our times, I was a square. I didn't particularly like the 'swinging' aspect of mid-sixties England; it was cheap, frenetic and sometimes downright nasty, and I could do without it. Perhaps I was Johnny-out-of-step.

I had met Sheila a month before, a casual introduction. Looking back at that conversation in the bedroom it must have been when Jimmy What's-his-name had departed from her life that she had latched on to me as a temporary substitute. For various reasons, the principal one having to do with the proverb of the burnt child fearing the fire, I had not got into the habit of jumping into bed indiscriminately with female companions of short acquaintance, and if that was what Sheila had expected, or even wanted, she had picked the wrong boy. It's a hell of a society in which a halfway continent man is immediately suspected of homosexuality.

Perhaps I was stupid to take the catty chatter of empty-headed women so much to heart, but to see ourselves as others see us is a salutary experience and tends to make one take a good look from the outside. Which is what I did while sitting in the car outside Honiton.

A thumbnail sketch: Jeremy Wheale, of good yeoman stock and strong family roots. Went to university—but red-brick—emerging with a first-class pass in mathematics and economics. Now, aged 31, an accountant specializing in computer work and with good prospects for the future. Character: introverted and somewhat withdrawn but not overly so. When aged 25 had flammatory affaire which wrung out emotions; now cautious in dealings with women. Hobbies: indoors—recreational mathematics and fencing, outdoors—scuba diving. Cash assets to present minute: £102/18/4 in current bank account; stocks and shares to the market value of £940. Other assets: one overage Ford Cortina in which sitting brooding; one hi-fi outfit of superlative quality; one set of scuba gear in boot of car. Liabilities: only himself.

And what was wrong with that? Come to think of it—what was right with that? Maybe Sheila had been correct when she had described me as a grey man but only in a circumscribed way. She expected Sean Connery disguised as James Bond and what she got was me—just a good, old-fashioned, grey, average type.

But she had done one thing; she had made me take a good look at myself and what I saw wasn't reassuring. Looking into the future as far as I could, all I could see was myself putting increasingly complicated figures into increasingly complicated computers at the behest of the men who made the boodle. A drab prospect—not to mention that overworked word 'grey'. Perhaps I *was* getting into a rut and adopting middle-aged attitudes before my time.

I tossed the stub of the third cigarette from the window and started the car. There didn't seem to be much I could do about it, and I was quite happy and contented with my lot.

Although not perhaps as happy and contented as I was before Sheila had distilled her poison.

From Honiton to the farm, just short of Totnes, is a run of about an hour and a half if you do it early in the morning to avoid the holiday traffic on the Exeter by-pass, and dead on the minute I stopped, as I always did, on the little patch of ground by Cutter's Corner where the land fell away into the valley and where there was a break in the high hedge. I got out of the car and leaned comfortably on the fence.

I had been born in the valley thirty-one years earlier, in the farmhouse which lay snugly on the valley floor looking more like a natural growth than a man-made object. It had been built by a Wheale and Wheales had lived in it for over four hundred years. It was a tradition among us that the eldest son inherited the farm and the younger sons went to sea. I had put a crimp in the tradition by going into business, but my brother, Bob, held on to Hay Tree Farm and kept the land in good shape. I didn't envy Bob the farm because he was a better farmer than I ever would have been. I have no affinity with cattle and sheep and the job would have driven me round the twist. The most I had to do with it now was to put Bob right on his bookkeeping and proffer advice on his investments.

I was a sport among the Wheales. A long line of fox-hunting, pheasant-murdering, yeoman farmers had produced Bob and me. Bob followed the line; he farmed the land well, rode like a madman to hounds, was pretty good in a point-to-point and liked nothing better than a day's rough shooting. I was the oddity who didn't like massacring rabbits with an airgun as a boy, still less with a shotgun as a grown man. My parents, when they were alive, looked on me with some perplexity and I must have troubled their uncomplicated minds; I was not a *natural* boy and got into no mischief—instead I developed a most un-Whealeish tendency to book reading and the ability to make figures jump through hoops. There was much doubtful shaking of heads and an inclination to say 'Whatever will become of the lad?'

I lit a cigarette and a plume of smoke drifted away on the crisp morning air, then grinned as I saw no smoke coming from any of the farm chimneys. Bob would be sleeping late, something he did when he'd made a night of it at the Kingsbridge Inn or the Cott Inn, his favourite pubs. That was a cheerful practice that might end when he married. I was glad he was getting married at last; I'd been a bit worried because Hay Tree Farm without a Wheale would be unthinkable and if Bob died unmarried there was only me left, and I certainly didn't want to take up farming.

I got into the car, drove on a little way, then turned on to the farm road. Bob had had it graded and resurfaced, something he'd been talking about for years. I coasted along, past the big oak tree which, family legend said, had been planted by my great-grandfather, and around the corner which led straight into the farmyard.

Then I stamped on the brake pedal hard because someone was lying in the middle of the road.

I got out of the car and looked down at him. He was lying prone with one arm outflung and when I knelt and touched his hand it was stone cold. I went cold, too, as I looked at the back of his head. Carefully I tried to pull his head up but the body was stiff with rigor mortis and I had to roll him right over to see his face. The breath came from me with a sigh as I saw it was a perfect stranger.

He had died hard but quickly. The expression on his face showed that he had died hard; the lips writhed back from the teeth in a tortured grimace and the eyes were open and stared over my shoulder at the morning sky. Underneath him was a great pool of half-dried blood and his chest was covered with it. No one could have lost that much blood slowly—it must have gushed out in a sudden burst, bringing a quick death.

I stood up and looked around. Everything was very quiet and all I heard was the fluting of an unseasonable blackbird and the grating of gravel as I shifted my feet sounded unnaturally loud. From the house came the mournful howl of a dog and then a shriller barking from close by, and a young sheepdog flung round the corner of the house and yapped at me excitedly. He was not very old, not more than nine months, and I reckoned he was one of old Jess's pups.

I held out my hand and snapped my fingers. The aggressive barking changed to a delighted yelp and the young dog wagged his tail vehemently and came forward in an ingratiating sideways trot. From the house another dog howled and the sound made the hairs on my neck prickle.

I walked into the farmyard and saw immediately that the kitchen door was ajar. Gently, I pushed it open, and called, 'Bob!'

The curtains were drawn at the windows and the light was off, so the room was gloomy. There was a stir of movement and the sound of an ugly growl. I pushed the door open wide to let in the light and saw old Jess stalking towards me with her teeth bared in a snarl. 'All right, Jess,' I said softly. 'It's all right, old girl.'

She stopped dead and looked at me consideringly, then let her lips cover her teeth. I slapped the side of my leg. 'Come here, Jess.'

But she wouldn't come. Instead, she whined disconsolately and turned away to vanish behind the big kitchen table. I followed her and found her standing drooping over the body of Bob.

His hand was cold, but not dead cold, and there was a faint

flutter of a pulse beat at his wrist. Fresh blood oozed from the ugly wound in his chest and soaked the front of his shirt. I knew enough about serious injuries not to attempt to move him; instead, I ran upstairs, stripped the blankets from his bed and brought them down to cover him and keep him warm.

Then I went to the telephone and dialled 999. 'This is Jemmy Wheale of Hay Tree Farm. There's been a shooting on the farm; one man dead and another seriously wounded. I want a doctor, an ambulance and the police—in that order.'

II

An hour later I was talking to Dave Goosan. The doctor and the ambulance had come and gone, and Bob was in hospital. He was in a bad way and Dr. Grierson had dissuaded me from going with him. 'It's no use, Jemmy. You'd only get in the way and make a nuisance of yourself. You know we'll do the best we can.'

I nodded. 'What are his chances?' I asked.

Grierson shook his head. 'Not good. But I'll be able to tell better when I've had a closer look at him.'

So I was talking to Dave Goosan who was a policeman. The last time I had met him he was a detective sergeant; now he was a detective inspector. I went to school with his young brother, Harry, who was also in the force. Police work was the Goosans' family business.

'This is bad, Jemmy,' he said. 'It's too much for me. They're sending over a superintendent from Newton Abbot. I haven't the rank to handle a murder case.'

I stared at him. 'Who has been murdered?'

He flung out his arm to indicate the farmyard, then became confused. 'I'm sorry,' he said. 'I didn't mean to say your brother had murdered anyone. But there's been a killing, anyway.'

We were in the living-room and through the window I could see the activity in the yard. The body was still there, though covered with a plastic sheet. There were a dozen coppers, some in plain clothes and others in uniform, a few seemed to be doing nothing but chat, but the others were giving the yard a thorough going over.

I said, 'Who was he, Dave?'

'We don't know.' He frowned. 'Now, tell me the story all over again—right from the beginning. We've got to get this right, Jemmy, or the super will blow hell out of me. This is the first killing I've worked on.' He looked worried.

So I told my story again, how I had come to the farm, found the dead man and then Bob. When I had finished Dave said, 'You just rolled the body over—no more than that?'

'I thought it was Bob,' I said. 'The build was the same and so was the haircut.'

'I'll tell you one thing,' said Dave. 'He might be an American. His clothes are American, anyway. Does that mean anything to you?'

'Nothing.'

He sighed. 'Ah, well, we'll find out all about him sooner or later. He was killed by a blast from a shotgun at close range. Grierson says he thinks the aorta was cut through—that's why he bled like that. Your brother's shotgun had both barrels fired.'

'So Bob shot him,' I said. 'That doesn't make it murder.'

'Of course it doesn't. We've reconstructed pretty well what happened and it seems to be a case of self defence. The man was a thief; we know that much.'

I looked up. 'What did he steal?'

Dave jerked his head. 'Come with me and I'll show you. But just walk where I walk and don't go straying about.'

I followed him out into the yard, keeping close to his heels as he made a circuitous approach to the wall of the kitchen. He stopped and said, 'Have you ever seen that before?'

I looked to where he indicated and saw the tray that had always stood on the top shelf of the dresser in the kitchen ever since I can remember. My mother used to take it down and polish it once in a while, but it was only really used on highdays and feast days. At Christmas it used to be put in the middle of the dining-table and was heaped with fruit.

'Do you mean to tell me he got killed trying to pinch a brass tray? That he nearly killed Bob because of that thing?'

I bent down to pick it up and Dave grabbed me hastily. 'Don't touch it.' He looked at me thoughtfully. 'Maybe you wouldn't know. That's not brass, Jemmy; it's gold!'

I gaped at him, then closed my mouth before the flies got in.

'But it's always been a brass tray,' I said inanely.

'So Bob thought,' agreed Dave. 'It happened this way. The museum in Totnes was putting on a special show of local bygones and Bob was asked if he'd lend the tray. I believe it's been in the family for a long time.'

I nodded. 'I can remember my grandfather telling me that *his* grandfather had mentioned it.'

'Well, that's going back a while. Anyway, Bob lent it to the museum and it was put on show with the other stuff. Then someone said it was gold, and by God, it was! The people at the museum got worried about it and asked Dave to take it back. It wasn't insured, you see, and there was a flap on about it might be stolen. It had been reported in the papers complete with photographs, and any wide boy could open the Totnes museum with a hairpin.'

'I didn't see the newspaper reports.'

'It didn't make the national press,' said Dave. 'Just the local papers. Anyway, Bob took it back. Tell me, did he know you were coming down this weekend?'

I nodded. 'I phoned him on Thursday. I'd worked out a scheme for the farm that I thought he might be interested in.'

'That might explain it. This discovery only happened about ten days ago. He might have wanted to surprise you with it.'

I looked down at the tray. 'He did,' I said bitterly.

'It must be very valuable just for the gold in it,' said Dave. 'Well worth the attention of a thief. And the experts say there's something special about it to add to the value, but I'm no antiquarian so I can't tell you what it is.' He rubbed the back of his head. 'There's one thing about all this that really worries me, though. Come and look at this—and don't touch it.'

He led me across the yard to the other side of the body where a piece of opaque plastic cloth covered something lumpy on the ground. 'This is what did the damage to your brother.'

He lifted the plastic and I saw a weapon—an antique horse pistol. 'Who'd want to use a thing like that?' I said.

'Nasty, isn't it?'

I bent down and looked closer and found I was wrong. It wasn't a horse pistol but a shotgun with the barrels cut very short and the butt cut off to leave only the hand grip. Dave said, 'What thief in his right mind would go on a job carrying a weapon like that? Just to be found in possession would send him inside for a year. Another thing—there were two of them.'

'Guns?'

'No—men. Two, at least. There was a car parked up the farm road. We found tracks in the mud and oil droppings. From what the weather's been doing we know the car turned in the road after ten o'clock last night. Grierson reckons that this man was shot before midnight, so it's a hundred quid to a pinch of snuff that the car and the man are connected. It can't have driven itself away, so that brings another man into the picture.'

'Or a woman,' I said.

'Could be,' said Dave.

A thought struck me. 'Where were the Edgecombes last night?' Jack Edgecombe was Bob's chief factotum on the farm, and his wife, Madge, did Bob's housekeeping. They had a small flat in the farmhouse itself; all the other farm workers lived in their own cottages.

'I checked on that,' said Dave. 'They're over in Jersey on their annual holiday. Your brother was living by himself.'

A uniformed policeman came from the house. 'Inspector, you're wanted on the blower.'

Dave excused himself and went away, and I stood and watched what was going on. I wasn't thinking much of anything; my mind was numbed and small, inconsequential thoughts chased round and round. Dave wasn't away long and when he came back his face was serious. I knew what he was going to say before he said it. 'Bob's dead,' I said flatly.

He nodded gravely. 'Ten minutes ago.'

'For God's sake!' I said. 'I wasted half an hour outside Honiton; it could have made all the difference.'

'Don't blame yourself, whatever you do. It would have made no difference at all, even if you had found him two hours earlier. He was too far gone.' There was a sudden snap to his voice. 'It's a murder case now, Jemmy; and we've got a man to look for. We've found an abandoned car the other side of Newton Abbot. It may not be the right one, but a check on the tyres will tell us.'

'Does Elizabeth Horton know of this yet?'

Dave frowned. 'Who's she?'

'Bob's fiancée.'

'Oh, God! He was getting married, wasn't he? No, she knows nothing yet.'

'I'd better tell her,' I said.

'All right,' he said. 'You've got a farm to run now, and cows don't milk themselves. Things can run down fast if there isn't a firm hand on the reins. My advice is to get Jack Edgecombe back here. But don't you worry about that; I'll find out where he is and send a telegram.'

'Thanks, Dave,' I said. 'But isn't that over and above the call of duty?'

'All part of the service,' he said with an attempt at lightness. 'We look after our own. I liked Bob very much, you know.' He paused. 'Who was his solicitor?'

'Old Mount has handled the family affairs ever since I can remember.'

'You'd better see him as soon as possible,' advised Dave. 'There'll be a will and other legal stuff to be handled.' He looked at his watch. 'Look, if you're here when the superintendent arrives you might be kept hanging around for hours. You'd better pop off now and do whatever you have to. I'll give your statement to the super and if he wants to see you he can do it later. But do me a favour and phone in in a couple of hours to let us know where you are.'

III

As I drove into Totnes I looked at my watch and saw with astonishment that it was not yet nine o'clock. The day that ordinary people live was only just beginning, but I felt I'd lived a lifetime in the past three hours. I hadn't really started to think properly, but somewhere deep inside me I felt the first stirring of rage tentatively growing beneath the grief. That a man could be shot to death in his own home with such a barbarous weapon was a monstrous, almost inconceivable, perversion of normal life. In the quiet Devon countryside a veil had been briefly twitched aside to reveal another world, a more primitive world in which sudden death was a shocking commonplace. I felt outraged that such a world should intrude on me and mine.

My meeting with Elizabeth was difficult. When I told her she became suddenly still and motionless with a frozen face. At first, I thought she was that type of Englishwoman to whom the exhibition of any emotion is the utmost in bad taste, but after five minutes she broke down in a paroxysm of tears and was led away by her mother. I felt very sorry for her. Both she and Bob were late starters in the Marriage Stakes and now the race had been scratched. I didn't know her very well but enough to know that she would have made Bob a fine wife.

Mr. Mount, of course, took it more calmly, death being part of the stock-in-trade, as it were, of a solicitor. But he was perturbed about the manner of death. Sudden death was no stranger to him, and if Bob had broken his neck chasing a fox that would have been in the tradition and acceptable. This was different; this was the first murder in Totnes within living memory.

And so he was shaken but recovered himself rapidly, buttressing his cracking world with the firm assurance of the law. 'There is, of course, a will,' he said. 'Your brother was having talks with me about the new will. You may—or may not—know that on marriage all previous wills are automatically voided, so there had to be a new will. However, we had not got to the point of signing, and so the previous existing will is the document we have to consider.'

His face creased into a thin, legal smile. 'I don't think there is any point in beating about the bush, Jemmy. Apart from one or two small bequests to members of the farm staff and personal friends, you are the sole beneficiary. Hay Tree Farm is yours now—or it will be on probate. There will, of course, be death duties, but farm land gets forty-five per cent relief on valuation.' He made a note. 'I must see your brother's bank manager for details of his accounts.'

'I can give you most of that,' I said. 'I was Bob's accountant. In fact, I have all the information here. I was working on a suggested scheme for the farm—that's why I came down this weekend.'

'That will be very helpful,' said Mount. He pondered. 'I would say that the farm, on valuation, will prove to be worth something like £125,000. That is not counting live and dead stock, of course.'

My head jerked up. 'My God! So much?'

He gave me an amused look. 'When a farm has been in the same family for as long as yours the cash value of the land tends to be ignored—it ceases to be regarded as invested capital. Land values have greatly appreciated in recent years, Jemmy; and you have 500 acres of prime land on red soil. At auction it would fetch not less than £250 an acre. When you add the stock, taking into account the admirable

18

dairy herd Bob built up and the amount of modernization he has done, then I would say that the valuation for the purposes of probate will be not much less than £170,000.'

I accepted this incredible thing he was telling me. Mount was a country solicitor and knew as much about local farm values as any hard-eyed unillusioned farmer looking over his neighbour's fields. He said, 'If you sold it you would have a sizeable fortune, Jemmy.'

I shook my head. 'I couldn't sell it.'

He nodded understandingly. 'No,' he said reflectively. 'I don't suppose you could. It would be as though the Queen were to sell Buckingham Palace to a property developer. But what do you intend to do? Run it yourself?'

'I don't know,' I said a little desperately. 'I haven't thought about it.'

'There'll be time to think about it,' he said consolingly. 'One way would be to appoint a land agent. But your brother had a high opinion of Jack Edgecombe. You might do worse than make him farm manager; he can run the farming side, of which you know nothing—and you can operate the business side, of which *he* knows nothing. I don't think it would be necessary to interrupt your present career.'

'I'll think about that,' I said.

'Tell me,' said Mount. 'You said you had a scheme for the farm. Could I ask what it is?'

I said, 'The Government experimental farms have been using computers to work out maximum utilization of farm resources. Well, I have access to a computer and I put in all the data on Hay Tree Farm and programmed it to produce optimum profit.'

Mount smiled tolerantly. 'Your farm has been well worked for four hundred years. I doubt if you could find a better way of working it than the ways that are traditional in this area.'

I had come across this attitude many times before and I thought I knew how to handle it. 'Traditional ways *are* good ways, but nobody would say they are perfect. If you take all the variables involved in even a smallish farm—the right mix of arable and pasture, what animals to keep, how many animals and when to keep them, what feedstuffs to plant and what to buy—if you take all those variables and put them in permutation and combination you come up with a matrix of several million choices.

'Traditional ways have evolved to a pretty high level and it

19

isn't worth a farmer's while to improve them. He'd have to be a smart mathematician and it would probably take him fifty years of calculation. But a computer can do it in fifteen minutes. In the case of Hay Tree Farm the difference between the traditional good way and the best way is fifteen per cent net increase on profits.'

'You surprise me,' said Mount interestedly. 'We will have to talk about this—but at a more appropriate time.'

It was a subject on which I could have talked for hours but, as he said, the time wasn't appropriate. I said, 'Did Bob ever talk to you about that tray?'

'Indeed he did,' said Mount. 'He brought it here, to this office, straight from the museum, and we discussed the insurance. It is a very valuable piece.'

'How valuable?'

'Now that is hard to say. We weighed it and, if the gold is pure, the intrinsic value will be about £2,500. But there is also the artistic value to take into account—it's very beautiful —and the antiquarian value. Do you know anything of its history?'

'Nothing,' I said. 'It's just been something that's been around the house ever since I can remember.'

'It will have to be valued as part of the estate,' said Mount. 'Sotheby's might be best, I think.' He made another note. 'We will have to go very deeply into your brother's affairs. I hope there will be enough . . . er . . . loose money . . . available to pay the death duties. It would be a pity to have to sell off a part of the farm. Would you have any objection to selling the tray if it proved necessary?'

'No objection at all—if it helps to keep the farm in one piece.' I thought I would probably sell it anyway; it had too much blood on it for my liking. It would be an uncomfortable thing to have around.

'Well, I don't think there's more we can do now,' said Mount. 'I'll set the legal processes in motion—you can leave all that to me.' He stood up. 'I'm the executor of the estate, Jemmy; and executors have wide latitude, especially if they know the ins and outs of the law. You'll need ready money to run the farm—to pay the men, for example—and that can be drawn from the estate.' He grimaced. 'Technically speaking, *I'm* supposed to run the farm until probate, but I can appoint an expert to do it, and there's nothing to prevent me choosing you, so I think we'll let it go at that, shall we? Or would you rather I employed a land agent until probate?'

'Give me a couple of days,' I said. 'I want to think this over. For one thing, I'd like to talk to Jack Edgecombe.'

'Very well,' he said. 'But don't leave it much later than that.'

Before leaving Mount's office I telephoned the farm as I had promised Dave Goosan and was told that Detective-Superintendent Smith would be pleased if I would call at Totnes police station at three o'clock that afternoon. I said that I would and then went out into the street, feeling a little lost and wondering what to do next. Something was nagging at me and I couldn't pin it down, but suddenly I realized what it was.

I was hungry!

I looked at my watch and discovered it was nearly twelve o'clock. I had had no breakfast and only a very light snack the night before so it wasn't really surprising. Yet although I was hungry I didn't feel like facing a set meal, so I climbed into the car and headed towards the Cott where I could get a sandwich.

The saloon bar was almost empty with just an elderly man and woman sitting quietly in one corner. I went to the bar and said to Paula, 'I'll have a pint, please.'

She looked up. 'Oh, Mr. Wheale, I'm so sorry to hear of what happened.'

It hadn't taken long for the news to get around, but that was only to be expected in a small town like Totnes. 'Yes,' I said. 'It's a bad business.'

She turned away to draw the beer, and Nigel came in from the other bar. He said, 'Sorry to hear about your brother, Jemmy.'

'Yes,' I said. 'Look, Nigel; I just want a beer and some sandwiches. I don't feel much like talking just now.'

He nodded, and said, 'I'll serve you in a private room if you like.'

'No, that doesn't matter; I'll have it here.'

He phoned the order through to the kitchen, then spoke to Paula who went into the other bar. I took a pull of beer and was aware of Nigel coming to the counter again. 'I know you don't want to talk,' he said. 'But there's something you ought to know.'

'What is it?'

He hesitated. 'Is it true that the dead man—the burglar—up at the farm was an American?'

'There's no certainty yet, but it's a probability,' I said.

He pursed his lips. 'I don't know if this is relevant, but Harry Hannaford told me a couple of days ago that an American had made Bob an offer for that tray—you know, the one they found was so valuable.'

'Where did this happen?'

Nigel flipped his hand. 'In here! I wasn't here at the time, but Harry said he heard the whole thing. He was having a drink with Bob at the time.'

I said, 'Do *you* know this American?'

'I don't think so. We get a lot of Yanks here—you run a place as old as the Cott and you're on the culture circuit. But we didn't have any Americans staying here just then. We have one here now, though; he arrived yesterday.'

'Oh! What kind of an American?'

Nigel smiled. 'Oldish—about sixty, I'd say. Name of Fallon. He must have a lot of money, too, judging by the telephone bill he's run up. But I wouldn't say he's a suspicious character.'

'Getting back to Hannaford and the other Yank,' I said. 'Can you tell me anything more?'

'There's nothing more to tell. Just that the Yank wanted to buy the tray—that's all Harry said.' He looked up at the clock. 'He'll be in soon, as like as not, for his midday pint. He usually comes in about now. Do you know him?'

'I can't place him.'

'All right,' said Nigel. 'When he comes in I'll tip you the wink.'

The sandwiches arrived and I took them to a corner table near the fireplace. When I sat down I felt suddenly tired, which wasn't surprising considering I'd been up all night and subject to a hell of a lot of tension. I ate the sandwiches slowly and drank some more beer. I was only now coming out of the shock that had hit me when I found Bob, and it was beginning to really hurt.

The pub started to fill up and I saw one or two faces I knew, but no one bothered me, although I intercepted some curious glances from eyes that were quickly averted. But there's a basic decency among countrymen which forbade them overt curiosity. Presently I saw Nigel talking to a big man in tweeds, then he crossed to me and said, 'Hannaford's here. Want to talk to him?'

I looked around the crowded bar. 'I'd rather it wasn't here. Have you a room I can use?'

'Take my office,' said Nigel promptly. 'I'll send Harry in after you.'

'You can send a couple of pints, too,' I said, and left the bar by the back door.

Hannaford joined me in a few minutes. 'Main sorry to hear about Bob,' he said in a deep voice. 'Many's the laugh we've had here. He was a good man.'

'Yes, Mr. Hannaford; he was.' It was easy to see the relationship between Hannaford and Bob. When a man is a regular caller at a pub he strikes up an easy and casual acquaintanceship in those four walls. More often than not it goes no further than that and there may be no meeting outside the pub. But for all that there need be no shallowness to it—it's just uncomplicated and friendly.

I said, 'Nigel tells me there was an American wanting to buy the tray from Bob.'

'That there was—and more'n one. Bob had two offers to my knowledge, both from Americans.'

'Did he? Do you know anything about these men, Mr. Hannaford?'

Hannaford pulled his ear. 'Mr. Gatt was a real nice gentleman—not at all pushy like a lot of these Yanks. A middle-aged man he was, and well dressed. Very keen to buy that tray from Bob was Mr. Gatt.'

'Did he offer a price—a definite price?'

'Not straight out he didn't. Your brother said it was no use him offering any price at all until he'd had the tray valued, and Mr. Gatt said he'd give Bob the valuation price —whatever it was. But Bob laughed and said he might not sell it at all, that it was a family heirloom. Mr. Gatt looked mighty put out when he heard that.'

'What about the other man?'

'The young chap? I didn't relish him much, he acted too high and mighty for me. He made no offer—not in my hearing —but he was disappointed when Bob said he wasn't set on selling, and he spoke pretty sharpish to Bob until his wife shut him up.'

'His wife!'

Hannaford smiled. 'Well, I wouldn't swear to that—he showed me no marriage lines—but I reckon it was his wife or, maybe his sister, perhaps.'

'Did he give a name?'

'That he did. Now, what was it? Hall? No, that's not it. Steadman? Nooo. Wait a minute and I'll get it.' His big face contorted with the effort of remembering and suddenly smoothed out. 'Halstead—that was it. Halstead was the name. He gave your brother his card—I remember that. He said he'd get in touch again when the tray was valued. Bob said he was wasting his time and that's when he lost his temper.'

I said, 'Anything else you remember about it?'

Hannaford shook his head. 'That's about all there was to it. Oh, Mr. Gatt did say he was a collector of pieces like that. One of these rich American millionaires, I expect.'

I thought that rich Americans seemed to be thick on the ground around the Cott. 'When did this happen?' I asked.

Hannaford rubbed his jaw. 'Let me see—it was after they printed about it in the *Western Morning News*; two days after, to my best recollection. That'ud make it five days ago, so it was Tuesday.'

I said, 'Thank you, Mr. Hannaford. The police might be interested in this, you know.'

'I'll tell them all I've told you,' he said earnestly, and put his hand on my sleeve. 'When's the funeral to be? I'd like to be there to pay my respects.'

I hadn't thought of that; too much had happened in too short a time. I said, 'I don't know when it will be. There'll have to be an inquest first.'

'Of course,' said Hannaford. 'Best thing to do would be to tell Nigel as soon as you're sure, and he'll let me know. And others, too. Bob Wheale was well liked around here.'

'I'll do that.'

We went back into the bar and Nigel caught my eye. I put my tankard on the bar counter and he nodded across the room. 'That's the Yank who is staying here now. Fallon.'

I turned and saw a preternaturally thin man sitting near to the fire holding a whisky glass. He was abouty sixty years of age, his head was gaunt and fleshless and his skin tanned to the colour of well worn leather. As I watched he seemed to shiver and he drew his chair closer to the fire.

I turned back to Nigel, who said, 'He told me he spends a

lot of time in Mexico. He doesn't like the English climate—
he thinks it's too cold.'

IV

I spent that night alone at Hay Tree Farm. Perhaps I should
have stayed at the Cott and saved myself a lot of misery, but
I didn't. Instead I wandered through the silent rooms, peopled
with the shadowy figures of memories, and grew more and
more depressed.

I was the last of the Wheales—there was no one else. No
uncles or aunts or cousins, no sisters or brothers—just me.
This echoing, empty house, creaking with the centuries, had
witnessed a vast procession down the years—a pageant of
Wheales—Elizabethan, Jacobean, Restoration, Regency, Vic-
torian, Edwardian. The little patch of England around the
house had been sweated over by Wheales for more than four
centuries in good times and bad, and now it all sharpened down
to a single point—me. Me—a grey little man in a grey little
job.

It wasn't fair!

I found myself standing in Bob's room. The bed was still
dishevelled where I had whipped away the blankets to cover
him and I straightened it almost automatically, smoothing
down the counterpane. His dressing-table was untidy, as it
always had been, and stuck in the crack up one side of the
mirror was his collection of unframed photographs—one of
our parents, one of me, one of Stalwart, the big brute of a
horse that was his favourite mount, and a nice picture of
Elizabeth. I pulled that one down to get a better look and
something fluttered to the top of the dressing-table.

I picked it up. It was Halstead's card which Hannaford had
spoken of. I looked at it listlessly. *Paul Halstead. Avenida
Quintillana* 1534. *Mexico City.*

The telephone rang, startlingly loud, and I picked it up to
hear the dry voice of Mr. Mount. 'Hello, Jeremy,' he said. 'I
just thought I'd tell you that you have no need to worry about
the funeral arrangements. I'll take care of all that for you.'

'That's very kind of you,' I said, and then choked up.

'Your father and I were very good friends,' he said. 'But I
don't think I've ever told you that if he hadn't married

your mother, then I might have done so.' He rang off and the phone went dead.

I slept that night in my own room, the room I had always had ever since I was a boy. And I cried myself to sleep as I had not done since I was a boy.

Two

It was only at the inquest that I found out the name of the dead man. It was Victor Niscemi, and he was an American national.

The proceedings didn't take long. First, there was a formal evidence of identification, then I told the story of how I had found the body of Niscemi and my brother dying in the farmhouse kitchen. Dave Goosan then stepped up and gave the police evidence, and the gold tray and the shotguns were offered as exhibits.

The coroner wrapped it up very quickly and the verdict on Niscemi was that he had been killed in self defence by Robert Blake Wheale. The verdict on Bob was that he had been murdered by Victor Niscemi and a person or persons unknown.

I saw Dave Goosan in the narrow cobbled street outside the Guildhall where the inquest had taken place. He jerked his head at two thick-set men who were walking away. 'From Scotland Yard,' he said. 'This is in their bailiwick now. They come in on anything that might be international.'

'You mean, because Niscemi was an American.'

'That's right. I'll tell you something else, Jemmy. He had form on the other side of the Atlantic. Petty thieving and robbery with violence. Not much.'

'Enough to do for Bob,' I said viciously.

Dave sighed in exasperated agreement. 'To tell you the truth, there's a bit of a mystery about this. Niscemi was never much of a success as a thief; he never had any money. Sort of working class, if you know what I mean. He certainly never had the money to take a trip over here—not unless he'd pulled off something bigger than usual for him. And nobody can see *why* he came to England. He'd be like a fish out of water, just the same as a Bermondsey burglar would be in New York. Still, it's being followed up.'

26

'What did Smith find out about Halstead and Gatt, the Yanks I turned up?'

Dave looked me in the eye. 'I can't tell you that, Jemmy. I can't discuss police work with you even if you are Bob's brother. The super would have my scalp.' He tapped me on the chest. 'Don't forget that you were a suspect once, lad.' The startlement must have shown on my face. 'Well, dammit; who has benefited most by Bob's death? All that stuff about the tray might have been a lot of flummery. *I* knew it wasn't you, but to the super you were just another warm body wandering about the scene of the crime.'

I let out a deep breath. 'I trust I'm not still on his list of suspects,' I said ironically.

'Don't give it another thought, although I'm not saying the super won't. He's the most unbelieving bastard I've ever come across. If he fell across a body himself he'd keep himself on his own list.' Dave pulled on his ear. 'I'll give you this much; it seems that Halstead is in the clear. He was in London and he's got an alibi for when he needs it.' He grinned. 'He was picked up for questioning in the Reading Room of the British Museum. Those London coppers must be a tactful lot.'

'Who is he? What is he?'

'He says he's an archeologist,' said Dave, and looked over my shoulder with mild consternation. 'Oh, Christ; here come those bloody reporters. Look, you nip into the church—they won't have the brazen nerve to follow you in there. I'll fight a rear-guard action while you leave by the side door in the vestry.'

I left him quickly and slipped into the churchyard. As I entered the church I heard the excited yelping as of hounds surrounding a stag at bay.

The funeral took place the day after the inquest. A lot of people turned up, most of whom I knew but a lot I didn't. All the people from Hay Tree Farm were there, including Madge and Jack Edgecombe who had come back from Jersey. The service was short, but even so I was glad when it was over and I could get away from all those sympathetic people. I had a word with Jack Edgecombe before I left. 'I'll see you up at the farm; there are things we must discuss.'

I drove to the farm with a feeling of depression. So that was that! Bob was buried, and so, presumably, was Niscemi, unless the police still had his body tucked away somewhere in cold storage. But for the loose end of Niscemi's hypothetical accomplice everything was neatly wrapped up and the world could get on with the world's futile business as usual.

I thought of the farm and what there was to do and of how I would handle Jack, who might show a countryman's conservative resistance to my new-fangled ideas. Thus occupied I swung automatically into the farmyard and nearly slammed into the back of a big Mercedes that was parked in front of the house.

I got out of the car and, as I did so, so did the driver of the Mercedes, uncoiling his lean length like a strip of brown rawhide. It was Fallon, the American Nigel had pointed out at the Cott. He said, 'Mr. Wheale?'

'That's right.'

'I know I shouldn't intrude at this moment,' he said. 'But I'm pressed for time. My name is Fallon.'

He held out his hand and I found myself clutching skeletally thin fingers. 'What can I do for you, Mr. Fallon?'

'If you could spare me a few minutes—it's not easy to explain quickly.' His voice was not excessively American.

I hesitated, then said, 'You'd better come inside.'

He leaned into his car and produced a briefcase. I took him into Bob's—my—study and waved him to a chair, then sat down facing him, saying nothing.

He coughed nervously, apparently not knowing where to begin, and I didn't help him. He coughed again, then said, 'I am aware that this may be a sore point, Mr. Wheale, but I wonder if I could see the gold tray you have in your possession.'

'I'm afraid that is quite impossible,' I said flatly.

Alarm showed in his eyes. 'You haven't sold it?'

'It's still in the hands of the police.'

'Oh!' He relaxed and flicked open the catch of the briefcase. 'That's a pity. But I wonder if you could identify these photographs.'

He passed across a sheaf of eight by ten photographs which I fanned out. They were glossy and sharp as a needle, evidently the work of a competent commercial photographer. They were pictures of the tray taken from every conceivable angle; some were of the tray as a whole and there was a series of close-up detail shots showing the delicate vine leaf tracery of the rim.

28

'You might find these more helpful,' said Fallon, and passed me another heap of eight by tens. These were in colour, not quite as sharp as the black and whites but perhaps making a better display of the tray as it really was.

I looked up. 'Where did you get these?'

'Does it matter?'

'The police might think so,' I said tightly. 'This tray has figured in a murder, and they might want to know how you came by these excellent photographs of my tray.'

'Not your tray,' he said gently. 'My tray.'

'That be damned for a tale,' I said hotly. 'This tray has been used in this house for a hundred and fifty years that I am aware of. I don't see how the devil you can claim ownership.'

He waved his hand. 'We are talking at cross purposes. Those photographs are of a tray at present in my possession which is now securely locked in a vault. I came here to find out if your tray resembled mine at all. I think you have answered my unspoken question quite adequately.'

I looked at the photographs again, feeling a bit of a fool. This certainly looked like the tray I had seen so often, although whether it was an exact replica would be hard to say. I had seen the tray briefly the previous Saturday morning when Dave Goosan had shown it to me, but when had I seen it before that? It must have been around when I had previously visited Bob, but I had never noticed it. In fact, I had never examined it since I was a boy.

Fallon asked, 'Is it *really* like your tray?'

I explained my difficulty and he nodded understandingly, and said, 'Would you consider selling me your tray, Mr. Wheale? I will give you a fair price.'

'It isn't mine to sell.'

'Oh? I would have thought you would inherit it.'

'I did. But it's in a sort of legal limbo. It won't be mine until my brother's will is probated.' I didn't tell Fallon that Mount had suggested selling the damned thing; I wanted to keep him on a string and find out what he was really after. I never forgot for one minute that Bob had died because of that tray.

'I see.' He drummed his fingers on the arm of the chair. 'I suppose the police will release it into your possession.'

'I don't see why they shouldn't.'

He smiled. 'Mr. Wheale, will you allow me to examine the tray—to photograph it? It need never leave the house: I have a very good camera at my disposal.'

29

I grinned at him. 'I don't see why I should.'

The smile was wiped away from his face as though it had never been. After a long moment it returned in the form of a sardonic quirk of the corner of his mouth. 'I see you are . . . suspicious of me.'

I laughed. 'You're dead right. Wouldn't you be in my place?'

'I rather think I would,' he said. 'I've been stupid.' I once saw a crack chess player make an obviously wrong move which even a tyro should have avoided. The expression on his face was comical in its surprise and was duplicated on Fallon's face at that moment. He gave the impression of a man mentally kicking himself up the backside.

I heard a car draw up outside, so I got up and opened the casement. Jack and Madge were just getting out of their mini. I shouted, 'Give me a few more minutes, Jack; I'm a bit tied up.'

He waved and walked away, but Madge came over to the window. 'Would you like a cup of tea?'

'That seems a good idea. What about you, Mr. Fallon—would you like some tea?'

'That would be very nice,' he said.

'Then that's it, Madge. Tea for two in here, please.' She went away and I turned back to Fallon. 'I think it would be a good idea if you told me what you are really getting at.'

He said worriedly, 'I assure you I have absolutely no knowledge of the events leading to your brother's death. My attention was drawn to the tray by an article and a photograph in the *Western Morning News* which was late in getting to me. I came to Totnes immediately, arriving rather late on Friday evening . . .'

'. . . and you booked in at the Cott Inn.'

He looked faintly surprised. 'Yes, I did. I intended going to see your brother on the Saturday morning but then I heard of the . . . of what had happened . . .'

'And so you didn't go. Very tactful of you, Mr. Fallon. I suppose you realize you'll have to tell this story to the police.'

'I don't see why.'

'Don't you? Then I'll tell you. Don't you know that the man who killed my brother was an American called Victor Niscemi?'

Fallon seemed struck dumb and just shook his head.

'Didn't you read the report on the inquest this morning? It was in most of the papers.'

'I didn't read the newspaper this morning,' he said weakly.

I sighed. 'Look, Mr. Fallon; an American kills my brother and the tray is involved. Four days before my brother is murdered two Americans try to buy it from him. And now you come along, an American, and also want to buy the tray. Don't you think you've got some explaining to do?'

He seemed to have aged five years and his face was drawn, but he looked up alertly. 'The Americans,' he said. 'The ones who wanted to buy the tray. What were their names?'

'Perhaps you can tell me,' I said.

'Was one of them Halstead?'

'Now you *have* got some explaining to do,' I said grimly. 'I think I'd better run you down to the police station right now. I think Superintendent Smith would be interested in you.'

He looked down at the floor and brooded for a while, then raised his head. 'Now I think you are being stupid, Mr. Wheale. Do you really think that if I was implicated in this murder I would have come here openly today? I didn't know that Halstead had approached your brother, and I didn't know the housebreaker was an American.'

'But you knew Halstead's name.'

He flapped his hand tiredly. 'I've been crossing Halstead's trail all over Central America and Europe for the last three years. Sometimes I'd get there first and sometimes he would. I know Halstead; he was a student of mine some years ago.'

'A student of what?'

'I'm an archeologist,' said Fallon. 'And so is Halstead.'

Madge came in with the tea, and there were some scones and strawberry jam and clotted cream. She put the tray on the desk, smiled at me wanly and left the room. As I offered the scones and poured the tea I reflected that it made a cosy domestic scene very much at odds with the subject of discussion. I put down the teapot, and said, 'What about Gatt? Did you know him?'

'I've never heard of the man,' said Fallon.

I pondered awhile. One thing struck me—I hadn't caught out Fallon in a lie. He'd said that Halstead was an archeologist, and that was confirmed by Dave Goosan. He'd said he arrived at the Cott on Friday, and that was confirmed by

Nigel. I thought about that and made a long arm to pull the telephone closer. Without saying anything I dialled the Cott and watched Fallon drink his tea.

'Oh, hello, Nigel. Look, this chap Fallon—what time did he arrive last Friday?'

'About half-past six in the evening. Why, Jemmy?'

'Just something that's come up. Can you tell me what he did that night?' I stared unblinkingly at Fallon, who didn't seem at all perturbed at the trend of the questions. He merely spread some cream on a scone and took a bite.

'I can tell you everything he did that night,' said Nigel. 'We had a bit of an impromptu party which went on a bit. I talked to Fallon quite a lot. He's an interesting old bird; he was telling me about his experiences in Mexico.'

'Can you put a time on this?'

Nigel paused. 'Well, he was in the bar at ten o'clock—and he was still there when the party broke up. We were a bit late—say, quarter to two in the morning.' He hesitated. 'You going to the police with this?'

I grinned. 'You weren't breaking the licensing laws, were you?'

'Not at all. Everyone there was staying at the Cott. Guests' privileges and all that.'

'You're sure he was there continuously?'

'Dead sure.'

'Thanks, Nigel; you've been a great help.' I put down the phone and looked at Fallon. 'You're in the clear.'

He smiled and delicately dabbed his fingertips on a napkin. 'You're a very logical man, Mr. Wheale.'

I leaned back in my chair. 'How much would you say the tray is worth?'

'That's a hard question to answer,' he said. 'Intrinsically not very much—the gold is diluted with silver and copper. Artistically, it's a very fine piece and the antiquarian value is also high. I daresay that at auction in a good saleroom it would bring about £7,000.'

'What about the archeological value?'

He laughed. 'It's sixteenth-century Spanish; where's the archeological value in that?'

'You tell me. All I know is that the people who want to buy it are archeologists.' I regarded him thoughtfully. 'Make me an offer.'

'I'll give you £7,000,' he said promptly.

'I could get that at Sotheby's,' I pointed out. 'Besides, Halstead might give me more or Gatt might.'

'I doubt if Halstead could go that much,' said Fallon equably. 'But I'll play along, Mr. Wheale; I'll give you £10,000.'

I said ironically, 'So you're giving me £3,000 for the archeological value it hasn't got. You're a very generous man. Would you call yourself a rich man?'

A slight smile touched his lips. 'I guess I would.'

I stood up and said abruptly, 'There's too much mystery involved in this for my liking. You know something about the tray which you're not telling. I think I'd better have a look at it myself before coming to any firm decision.'

If he was disappointed he hid it well. 'That would appear to be wise, but I doubt if you will find anything by a mere inspection.' He looked down at his hands. 'Mr. Wheale, I have made you a most generous offer, yet I would like to go further. May I take an option on the tray? I will give you a thousand pounds now, on condition that you let no one else, particularly Dr. Halstead, inspect it. In the event of your deciding to sell me the tray then the thousand pounds is in addition to my original offer. If you decide not to sell it then you may keep the thousand pounds as long as you keep your side of the bargain.'

I drew a deep breath. 'You're a real dog in the manger, aren't you? If you can't have it, then nobody else must. Nothing doing, Mr. Fallon. I refuse to have my hands tied.' I sat down. 'I wonder what price you'd go to if I *really* pushed you.'

An intensity came into his voice. 'Mr. Wheale, this is of the utmost importance to me. Why don't *you* state a price?'

'Importance is relative,' I said. 'If the importance is archeological then I couldn't give a damn. I know a fourteen-year-old girl who thinks the most important people in the world are the Beatles. Not to me they aren't.'

'Equating the Beatles with archeology hardly demonstrates a sensible scale of values.'

I shrugged. 'Why not? They're both concerned with people. It just shows that your scale of values is different from hers. But I just might state my price, Mr. Fallon; and it may not be in money. I'll think about it and let you know. Can you come back tomorrow?'

'Yes, I can come back.' He looked me in the eye. 'And

what about Dr. Halstead? What will you do if he approaches you?'

'I'll listen to him,' I said promptly. 'Just as I've listened to you. I'm prepared to listen to anyone who'll tell me something I don't know. Not that it's happened noticeably yet.'

He did not acknowledge the jibe. Instead, he said, 'I ought to tell you that Dr. Halstead is not regarded as being quite honest in some circles. And that is all I am going to say about him. When shall I come tomorrow?'

'After lunch; would two-thirty suit you?' He nodded, and I went on, 'I'll have to tell the police about you, you know. There's been a murder and you are one coincidence too many.'

'I see your point,' he said wearily. 'Perhaps it would be as well if I went to see them—if only to clear up a nonsense. I shall go immediately; where shall I find them?'

I told him where the police station was, and said, 'Ask for Detective-Inspector Goosan or Superintendent Smith.'

Inexplicably, he began to laugh. 'Goosan!' he said with a gasp, 'My God, but that's funny!'

I stared at him. I didn't see what was funny. 'It's not an uncommon name in Devon.'

'Of course not,' he said, choking off his chuckles. 'I'll see you tomorrow, then, Mr. Wheale.'

I saw him off the premises, then went back to the study and rang Dave Goosan. 'There's someone else who wants to buy that tray,' I said. 'Another American. Are you interested?'

His voice was sharp. 'I think we might be very interested.'

'His name is Fallon and he's staying at the Cott. He's on his way to see you right now—he should be knocking on your door within the next ten minutes. If he doesn't it might be worth your while to go looking for him.'

'Point taken,' said Dave.

I said, 'How long do you intend holding on to the tray?'

'You can have it now if you like. I'll have to hold on to Bob's shotgun, though; this case isn't finished yet.'

'That's all right. I'll come in and pick up the tray. Can you do me a favour, Dave? Fallon will have to prove to you who and what he is; can you let me know, too? I'd like to know who I'm doing business with.'

'We're the police, not Dun and Bradstreet. All right, I'll let you know what I can, providing it doesn't run against regulations.'

34

'Thanks,' I said, and rang off. I sat motionless at the desk for a few minutes, thinking hard, and then got out the papers concerning the reorganization of the farm in preparation to doing battle with Jack Edgecombe. But my mind wasn't really on it.

II

Late that afternoon I went down to the police station to pick up the tray, and as soon as Dave saw me he growled, 'A fine suspect you picked.'

'He's all right?'

'He's as clean as a whistle. He was nowhere near your farm on Friday night. Four people say so—three of whom I know and one who is a personal friend of mine. Still, I don't blame you for sending him down here—you couldn't pass a coincidence like that.' He shook his head. 'But you picked a right one.'

'What do you mean?'

He grabbed a sheaf of flimsies from his desk and waved them under my nose. 'We checked him out—this is the telex report from the Yard. Listen to it and cry: John Nasmith Fallon, born Massachussetts, 1908; well educated—went to Harvard and Göttingen, with post-graduate study in Mexico City. He's an archeologist with all the letters in the alphabet after his name. In 1936 his father died and left him over 30 million dollars, which fortune he's more than doubled since, so he hasn't lost the family talent for making money.'

I laughed shortly. 'And I asked him if he considered himself a rich man! Is he serious about his archeology?'

'He's no dilettante,' said Dave. 'The Yard checked with the British Museum. He's the top man in his field, which is Central America.' He scrabbled among the papers. 'He publishes a lot in the scientific journals—the last thing he did was "Some Researches into the Calendar Glyphs of Dzi . . . Dzibi . . ." I'll have to take this one slowly . . . "Dzibilchaltun." God-almighty, he's investigating things I can't even pronounce! In 1949 he set up the Fallon Archeological Trust with ten million dollars. He could afford it since he apparently owns all the oil wells that Paul Getty missed.' He tossed the paper on to the desk. 'And that's your murder suspect.'

I said, 'What about Halstead and Gatt?'

Dave shrugged. 'What about them? Halstead's an archeologist, too, of course. We didn't dig too deeply into him.' He grinned. 'Pun not intended. Gatt hasn't been checked yet.'

'Halstead was one of Fallon's students. Fallon doesn't like him.'

Dave lifted his eyebrows. 'Been playing detective? Look, Jemmy; as far as I am concerned I'm off the case as much as any police officer can be. That means I'm not specifically assigned to it. Anything I'm told I pass on to the top coppers in London; it's their pigeon now, and I'm just a messenger boy. Let me give you a bit of advice. You can do all the speculating you like and there'll be no harm done but don't try to move in on the action like some half-baked hero in a detective story. The boys at Scotland Yard aren't damned fools; they can put two and two together a sight faster than you can, they've got access to more sources than you have, and they've got the muscle to make it stick when they decide to make a move. Leave it to the professionals; there are no Roger Sherringhams or Peter Wimseys in real life.'

'Don't get over-heated,' I said mildly.

'It's just that I don't want you making a bloody idiot of yourself.' He stood up. 'I'll get the tray—it's in the safe.'

He left the office and I picked up the telex message and studied it. It was in pretty fair detail but it more or less boiled down to what Dave had said. It seemed highly improbable that a man like Fallon could have anything in common with a petty criminal like Niscemi. And yet there was the tray— they were both interested in that, and so were Halstead and Gatt. Four Americans and the tray.

Dave came back carrying it in his hands. He put it on the desk. 'Hefty,' he said. 'Must be worth quite a bit if it really is gold.'

'It is,' I said. 'But not too pure.'

He flicked the bottom of the tray with his thumbnail. 'That's not gold—it looks like copper.'

I picked up the tray and examined it closely for, perhaps, the first time in twenty years. It was about fifteen inches in diameter and circular; there was a three-inch rim all the way round consisting of an intricate pattern of vine leaves, all in gold, and the centre was nine inches in diameter and of smooth copper. I turned it over and found the back to be of solid gold.

'You'd better have it wrapped,' said Dave. 'I'll find some paper.'

'Did you take any photographs of it?' I asked.

'Lots,' he said. 'And from every angle.'

'What about letting me have a set of prints?'

He looked pained. 'You seem to think the police are general dogsbodies for Jemmy Wheale. This isn't Universal Aunts, you know.' He shook his head. 'Sorry, Jemmy; the negatives were sent to London.'

He rooted around and found an old newspaper and began to wrap up the tray. 'Bob used to run his own darkroom. You have all the gear at home for taking your own snaps.'

That was true. Bob and I had been keen on photography as boys, he more than me. He'd stuck to it and I'd let it drop when I left home to go to university, but I thought I remembered enough to be able to shoot and develop a film and make some prints. I didn't feel like letting anyone else do it. In view of the importance Fallon had attached to examining the tray I wanted to keep everything under my own hand.

As I was leaving, Dave said, 'Remember what I said, Jemmy. If you feel any inclination to go off half-cocked come and see me first. My bosses wouldn't like it if you put a spoke in their wheel.'

I went home and found Bob's camera. I daresay he could have been called an advanced amateur and he had good equipment —a Pentax camera with a good range of lenses and a Durst enlarger with all the associated trimmings in a properly arranged darkroom. I found a spool of unexposed black and white film, loaded the camera and got to work. His fancy electronic flash gave me some trouble before I got the hang of it and twice it went off unexpectedly, but I finally shot off the whole spool and developed the film more or less successfully. I couldn't make prints before the film dried, so I went to bed early. But not before I locked the tray in the safe.

III

The next morning I continued the battle with Jack Edgecombe who was putting up a stubborn resistance to new ideas. He said unhappily, 'Eighty cows to a hundred acres is too many, Mr. Wheale, sir; we've never done it like that before.'

I resisted the impulse to scream, and said patiently, 'Look, Jack: up to now this farm has grown its own feedstuff for the cattle. Why?'

He shrugged. 'It's always been like that.'

That wasn't an answer and he knew it. I said, 'We can buy cattle feed for less than it costs us to grow it, so why the devil should we grow it?' I again laid out the plan that had come from the computer, but giving reasons the computer hadn't. 'We increase the dairy herd to eighty head and we allocate this land which is pretty lush, and any extra feed we buy.' I swept my hand over the map. 'This hill area is good for nothing but sheep, so we let the sheep have it. I'd like to build up a nice flock of greyface. We *can* feed sheep economically by planting root crops on the flat by the river, and we alternate the roots with a cash crop such as malting barley. Best of all, we do away with all this market garden stuff. This is a farm, not an allotment; it takes too much time and we're not near enough to a big town to make it pay.'

Jack looked uncomprehendingly stubborn. It wasn't done that way, it never had been done that way, and he didn't see why it should be done that way. I was in trouble because unless Jack saw it *my* way we could never get on together.

We were interrupted by Madge. 'There's a lady to see you, Mr. Wheale.'

'Did she give a name?'

'It's a Mrs. Halstead.'

That gave me pause. Eventually I said, 'Ask her to wait a few minutes, will you? Make her comfortable—ask her if she'd like a cuppa.'

I turned back to Jack. One thing at a time was my policy. I knew what was the matter with him. If he became farm manager and the policy of the farm changed radically, he'd have to take an awful lot of joshing from the neighbouring farmers. He had his reputation to consider.

I said, 'Look at it this way, Jack: if we start on this thing, you'll be farm manager and I'll be the more-or-less absentee landlord. If the scheme falls down you can put all the blame on me because I'll deserve it, and you're only doing what I tell you to. If it's a success—which it will be if we both work hard at it—then a lot of the credit will go to you because you'll have been the one who made it work. You are the practical farmer, not me. I'm just the theoretical boy. But I reckon we can show the lads around here a thing or two.'

He contemplated that argument and brightened visibly—I'd offered him a way out with no damage to his self-esteem. He said slowly, 'You know, I like that bit about doing away with the garden produce; it's always been a lot of trouble—too much hand work, for one thing.' He shuffled among the papers. 'You know, sir, if we got rid of that I reckon we could work the farm with one less man.'

That had already been figured out—by the computer, not me—but I was perfectly prepared to let Jack take the credit for the idea. I said, 'Hey, so we could! I have to go now, but you stay here and go through the whole thing again. If you come up with any more bright ideas like that then let me know.'

I left him to it and went to see Mrs. Halstead. I walked into the living-room and said, 'I'm sorry to have kept you waiting.' Then I stopped dead because Mrs. Halstead was quite a woman—red hair, green eyes, a nice smile and a figure to make a man struggle to keep his hands to himself—even a grey little man like me.

'That's all right, Mr. Wheale,' she said. 'Your housekeeper looked after me.' Her voice matched the rest of her; she was too perfect to be true.

I sat opposite her. 'What can I do for you, Mrs. Halstead?'

'I believe you own a gold tray, Mr. Wheale.'

'That is correct.'

She opened her handbag. 'I saw a report in a newspaper. Is this the tray?'

I took the clipping and studied it. It was the report that had appeared in the *Western Morning News* which I had heard of but not seen. The photograph was a bit blurred. I said, 'Yes, this is the tray.'

'That picture is not very good, is it? Could you tell me if your tray is anything like this one?'

She held out a postcard-size print. This was a better picture of a tray—but not my tray. It appeared to have been taken in some sort of museum because I could see that the tray was in a glass case and a reflection somewhat ruined the clarity of the picture. Everyone seemed to be pushing photographs of trays at me, and I wondered how many there were. I said cautiously, 'It might be something like this one. This isn't the best of pictures, either.'

'Would it be possible to see your tray, Mr. Wheale?'

'Why?' I asked bluntly. 'Do you want to buy it?'

'I might—if the price were right.'

I pushed her again. 'And what would be a right price?'

She fenced very well. 'That would depend on the tray.'

I said deliberately, 'The going price has been quoted as being £7,000. Could you match that?'

She said evenly, 'That's a lot of money, Mr. Wheale.'

'It is,' I agreed. 'It was, I believe, the amount offered by an American to my brother. Mr. Gatt said he'd pay the price at valuation.'

Perhaps she was a little sad. 'I don't think that Paul . . . my husband . . . realized it would be as much as that.'

I leaned forward. 'I think I ought to tell you that I have had an even higher offer from a Mr. Fallon.'

I watched her closely and she seemed to tighten, an almost imperceptible movement soon brought under control. She said quietly, 'I don't think we can compete with Professor Fallon when it comes to money.'

'No,' I said. 'He seems to have a larger share than most of us.'

'Has Professor Fallon seen the tray?' she asked.

'No, he hasn't. He offered me a very large sum, sight unseen. Don't you find that odd?'

'Nothing that Fallon does I find odd,' she said. 'Unscrupulous, even criminal, but not odd. He has reasons for everything he does.'

I said gently, 'I'd be careful about saying things like that, Mrs. Halstead, especially in England. Our laws of slander are stricter than in your country.'

'Is a statement slanderous if it can be proved?' she asked. 'Are you going to sell the tray to Fallon?'

'I haven't made up my mind.'

She was pensive for a while, then she stirred. 'Even if it is not possible for us to buy it, would there be any objection to my husband examining it? It could be done here, and I assure you it would come to no harm.'

Fallon had specifically asked that Halstead should not be shown the tray. To hell with that! I said, 'I don't see why not.'

'This morning?' she said eagerly.

I lied in my teeth. 'I'm afraid not—I don't have it here. But it could be here this afternoon. Would that suit you?'

'Oh, yes,' she said, and smiled brilliantly. A woman has no right to be able to smile at a man like that, especially a man involved in tricking her into something. It tends to weaken his resolution. She stood up. 'I won't waste any more of your time this morning, Mr. Wheale; I'm sure you're a busy man. What time should we come this afternoon?'

'Oh, about two-thirty,' I said casually. I escorted her to the door and watched her drive away in a small car. These archeological boffins seemed to be a queer crowd; Fallon had imputed dishonesty to Halstead, and Mrs. Halstead had accused Fallon of downright criminality. The in-fighting in academic circles seemed to be done with very sharp knives.

I thought of the chemistry set I had when a boy; it was a marvellous set with lots of little bottles and phials containing powders of various hue. If you mixed the powders odd things were likely to happen, but if they were kept separate they were quite inert.

I was tired of meeting with inertness from Fallon and the Halsteads—no one had been forthright enough to tell why he wanted the tray. I wondered what odd things were likely to happen when I mixed them together at two-thirty that afternoon.

IV

I went back and had another go at Jack Edgecombe. If he hadn't actually caught fire, at least he was a bit luminous around the edges, which made arguing with him less of an uphill struggle. I chipped at him a bit more and managed to strike another spark of enthusiasm, and then packed him off to look at the farm with a new vision.

The rest of the morning was spent in the darkroom. I cut up the length of 35 mm film, which was now dry, and made a contact print just to see what I had. It didn't seem too bad and most of the stuff was usable, so I settled down and made a series of eight by ten prints. They weren't as professional as those that Fallon had shown me, but they were good enough for comparison with his.

I even printed out my failures including those that had happened when the electronic flash popped off unexpectedly. One of those was very interesting—to the point of being worthy of scrutiny under a magnifying glass. It was a real puzzler and I badly wanted to set up the tray and take more pictures, but there wasn't time to do it before my visitors arrived.

41

The Halsteads came fifteen minutes early, thus demonstrating their eagerness. Halstead was a man of about thirty-five who seemed to be living on his nerves. I suppose he was handsome in an odd sort of way if you go for the hawklike visage; his cheekbones stood out prominently and his eyes were deep sunk in dark sockets so that he looked as though he were recovering from a week's binge. His movements were quick and his conversation staccato, and I thought he'd be a wearing companion if one had to put up with him for any length of time. Mrs. Halstead seemed to manage all right and maintained a smooth outward serenity which shed a calmness over the pair of them and compensated for Halstead's nerviness. Maybe it was something she worked hard at.

She introduced her husband and there was the briefest of social chit-chat before a sudden silence. Halstead looked at me expectantly and twitched a bit. 'The tray?' he enquired in a voice which rose a bit more than was necessary.

I looked at him blandly. 'Oh, yes,' I said. 'I have some photographs here in which you might be interested.' I gave them to him and noted that his hands were trembling.

He flicked through them quickly, then looked up and said sharply, 'These are pictures of *your* tray?'

'They are.'

He turned to his wife. 'It's the right one—look at the vine leaves. Exactly like the Mexican tray. There's no doubt about it.'

She said doubtfully, 'It *seems* to be the same.'

'Don't be a fool,' he snapped. 'It is the same. I studied the Mexican tray long enough, for God's sake! Where's our picture?'

Mrs. Halstead produced it and they settled down to a comparison. 'Not an identical replica,' pronounced Halstead. 'But close enough. Undoubtedly made by the same hand—look at the veining in the leaves.'

'I guess you're right.'

'I *am* right,' he said positively, and jerked his head round to me. 'My wife said you'd let me see the tray.'

I didn't like his manner—he was too damned driving and impolite, and perhaps I didn't like the way he spoke to his wife. 'I told her there wasn't any reason why you shouldn't see it. At the same time there doesn't seem any reason why you should. Would you care to enlighten me?'

He didn't like resistance or opposition. 'It's a purely professional and scientific matter,' he said stiffly. 'It forms part of my present research; I doubt if you would understand it.'

'Try me,' I said softly, resenting his superior and condescending attitude. 'I can understand words of two syllables—maybe words of three syllables if you speak them very slowly.'

Mrs. Halstead chipped in. 'We would be very grateful if we *could* see the tray. You would be doing us a great service, Mr. Wheale.' She wouldn't apologize for her husband's unfortunate manner, but she was doing her best to drop some polite social oil into the works.

We were interrupted by Madge. 'There's a gentleman to see you, Mr. Wheale.'

I grinned at Halstead. 'Thank you, Mrs. Edgecombe; show him in, will you?'

When Fallon walked in Halstead gave a convulsive jerk. He turned to me and said in a high voice, 'What's he doing here?'

'Professor Fallon is here on my invitation, as you are,' I said sweetly.

Halstead bounced to his feet. 'I'll not stay here with that man. Come along, Katherine.'

'Wait a minute, Paul. What about the tray?'

That brought Halstead to a dead stop. He looked uncertainly at me, then at Fallon. 'I resent this,' he said in a trembling voice. 'I resent it very much.'

Fallon had been as astonished to see Halstead as Halstead had been to see him. He stood poised in the doorway and said, 'You think I don't resent it, too? But I'm not blowing my top about it like a spoiled child. You were always too explosive, Paul.' He advanced into the room. 'May I ask what you think you're doing, Wheale?'

'Maybe I'm holding an auction,' I said easily.

'Umph! You're wasting your time; this pair hasn't two cents to rub together.'

Katherine Halstead said cuttingly, 'I always thought you bought your reputation, Professor Fallon. And what you can't buy, you steal.'

Fallon whirled. 'Goddammit! Are you calling me a thief, young lady?'

'I am,' she said calmly. 'You've got the Vivero letter, haven't you?'

Fallon went very still. 'What do you know about the Vivero letter?'

'I know it was stolen from us nearly two years ago—and I know that you have it now.' She looked across at me. 'What conclusions would you draw from that, Mr. Wheale?'

I looked at Fallon speculatively. The chemicals were mixing nicely and maybe they'd brew a little bit of truth. I was all for stirring up the broth. I said, 'Do you have this letter?'

Fallon nodded reluctantly. 'I do—I bought it quite legally in New York, and I have a receipt to prove it. But, hell, these are a fine pair to talk about theft. What about the papers you stole from me in Mexico, Halstead?'

Halstead's nostrils pinched in whitely. 'I stole nothing from you that wasn't mine. And what did you steal from me—just my reputation, that's all. There are too many thieving bastards like you in the profession, Fallon; incompetents who build their reputations on the work of others.'

'Why, you son of a bitch!' roared Fallon. 'You had your say in the journals and no one took any notice of you. Do you think anyone believes that poppycock?'

They were facing each other like fighting cocks and in another minute would have been at each other's throats had I not yelled at the top of my voice, 'Quiet!' They both turned, and I said in a calmer voice, 'Sit down both of you. I've never seen a more disgraceful exhibition by two grown men in my life. You'll behave yourselves in my house or I'll turn the lot of you out—and neither of you will ever get to see this bloody tray.'

Fallon said sheepishly, 'I'm sorry, Wheale, but this man got my goat.' He sat down.

Halstead also seated himself; he glared at Fallon and said nothing. Katherine Halstead's face was white and she had pink spots in her cheeks. She looked at her husband and tightened her lips and, when he maintained his silence, she said, 'I apologize for our behaviour, Mr. Wheale.'

I said bluntly, 'You do your own apologizing, Mrs. Halstead; you can't apologize for others—not even your husband.' I paused, waiting for Halstead to say something, but he maintained a stubborn silence, so I ignored him and turned to Fallon. 'I'm not particularly interested in the ins-and-outs of your professional arguments, although I must say I'm surprised at the charges that have been made here this afternoon.'

Fallon smiled sourly. 'I didn't start the mud-throwing.'

'I don't give a damn about that,' I said. 'You people are incredible. You're so wrapped up in your tuppenny-ha'penny professional concerns that you forget a man has been murdered because of that tray. Two men are already dead, for God's sake!'

Katherine Halstead said, 'I'm sorry if we appear so heartless; it must seem peculiar to you.'

'By God, it does! Now, listen to me carefully—all of you. I seem to have been dealt a high card in this particular game— I've got the tray that's so damned important. But nobody is going to get as much as a sniff at it until I'm told the name of the game. I'm not going to operate blindfolded. Fallon, what about it?'

He stirred impatiently. 'All right, it's a deal. I'll tell you everything you want to know—but privately. I don't want Halstead in on it.'

'Not a chance,' I said. 'Anything you want to tell me, you do it here and now in this room—and that applies to you, Halstead, too.'

Halstead said in a cold rage, 'This is monstrous. Am I to give away the results of years of research to this charlatan?'

'You'll put up or you'll shut up.' I stuck out a finger. 'The door's open and you can leave any time you like. Nobody is keeping you here. But if you go, that leaves Fallon with the tray.'

Indecision chased over his face and his knuckles whitened as he gripped the arms of the chair. Katherine Halstead took the decision from him. She said firmly, 'We accept your conditions. We stay.' Halstead looked at her with a sudden air of shock, and she said, 'It's all right, Paul; I know what I'm doing.'

'Fallon—what about you?'

'I guess I'm stuck with it,' he said, and smiled slowly. 'Halstead talks about years of research. Well, I've put in quite a few years myself. It wouldn't surprise me if we both know all there is to know about the problem. Heaven knows, I've been falling over this pair in every museum in Europe. I doubt if the pooling of information is going to bring up anything new.'

'I might surprise you,' said Halstead sharply. 'You have no monopoly on brains.'

'Cut it out,' I said coldly. 'This confessional is going to be run under my rules, and that means no snide comments from anyone. Do I make myself quite clear?'

45

Fallon said, 'You know, Wheale, when I first met you I didn't think much of you. You surprise me.'

I grinned. 'I surprise myself sometimes.' And so I did! Whatever had happened to the grey little man?

Three

It was an astonishing, incredible and quite preposterous story, and, if I did not have a queer and inexplicable photograph up in the darkroom, I would have rejected it out of hand. And yet Fallon was no fool and he believed it—and so did Halstead, although I wouldn't have bet on the adequacy of *his* mental processes.

I ruled the proceedings firmly while the story was being told. Occasionally there were outbursts of temper, mostly from Halstead but with a couple of bitter attacks from Fallon, and I had to crack down hard. It was quite apparent that, while none of them liked what I was doing, they had no alternative but to comply. My possession of the tray was a trump card in this curious and involved game, and neither Fallon nor Halstead was prepared to let the other get away with it.

Fallon seemed to be the more sensible and objective of the two men so I let him open the account, asking him to begin. He pulled his ear gently, and said, 'It's hard to know where to start.'

I said, 'Begin at the beginning. Where did you come into it?'

He gave his ear a final tug, then folded one thin hand on top of the other. 'I'm an archeologist, working in Mexico mostly. Do you know anything about the Mayas?'

I shook my head.

'That's a great help,' he said acidly. 'But I don't suppose it matters at this stage because the preliminaries had nothing to do with the Mayas at all—superficially. I came across several references in my work to the de Vivero family of Mexico. The de Viveros were an old Spanish family—Jaime de Vivero, the founder, staked his claim in Mexico just after the time of Cortes; he grabbed a lot of land, and his descendants made it pay very well. They became big landowners, ranchers, owners of mines and, towards the end, industrialists. They were one of the big Mexican families that really ruled the roost. They weren't what you'd call a very public-spirited crowd and most of their money came from squeezing the peasants. They supported Maximilian in that damn-fool effort of the Hapsburgs to establish a kingdom in Mexico in the eighteen-sixties.

'That was their first mistake because Maximilian couldn't stand the pace and he went down. Still, that wasn't enough to break the de Viveros, but Mexico was in upheaval; dictator followed dictator, revolution followed revolution, and every time the de Viveros backed the wrong horse. It seems they lost their powers of judgement. Over a period of a hundred years the de Vivero family was smashed; if there are any of them still around they're lying mighty low because I haven't come across any of them.' He cocked an eye at Halstead. 'Have you come across a live de Vivero?'

'No,' said Halstead shortly.

Fallon nodded in satisfaction. 'Now, this was a very wealthy family in its time, even for Mexico, and a wealthy Mexican family was really something. They had a lot of possessions which were dispersed during the break-up, and one of these items was a golden tray something like yours, Wheale.' He picked up his briefcase and opened it. 'Let me read you something about it.'

He pulled out a sheaf of papers. 'The tray was something of a family heirloom and the de Viveros looked after it; they didn't use it except at formal banquets and most of the time it was locked away. Here's a bit of gossip from the eighteenth century; a Frenchman called Murville visited Mexico and wrote a book about it. He stayed on one of the de Vivero estates when they threw a party for the governor of the province—this is the relevant bit.'

He cleared his throat. ' "Never have I seen such a splendid table even in our French Court. The grandees of Mexico live like princes and eat off gold plate of which there was a profusion here. As a centrepiece to the table there was a magnificent array of the fruits of the country on golden trays, the most magnificent of which was curiously wrought in a pattern of vine leaves of exquisite design. I was informed by one of the sons of the family that this tray had a legend—that it was reputed to have been made by an ancestor of the de Viveros. This is unlikely since it is well known that the de Viveros have a noble lineage extending far back into the history of Old Spain and could not possibly have indulged in work of

47

this nature, no matter how artful. I was told also that the tray is supposed to hold a secret, the discovery of which will make the recipient wealthy beyond measure. My informant smiled as he communicated this to me and added that as the de Viveros were already rich beyond computation the discovery of such a secret could not possibly make them effectively wealthier." '

Fallon dropped the papers back into the briefcase. 'That didn't mean much to me at the time, but I'm always interested in any secrets concerning Mexico so I copied it out as a matter of routine and filed it away. Incidentally, that bit about the noble lineage in Old Spain is phoney; the de Viveros were social climbers, men on the make—but we'll come to that later.

'Pretty soon after that I seemed to run into the de Viveros no matter which way I turned. You know how it is—you come across a strange word in a book, one which you've never seen before, and then you come across it again twice in the same week. It was like that with the de Viveros and their tray. Coming across references to the de Viveros is no trick in Mexico—they were a powerful family—but, in the next year I came across no less than seven references to the de Vivero tray, three of which mentioned this supposed secret. It appeared that the tray was important to the de Viveros. I just filed the stuff away; it was a minor problem of marginal interest and not really in my field.'

'Which is?' I asked.

'The pre-Columbian civilizations of Central America,' he answered. 'A sixteenth-century Spanish tray didn't mean much to me at the time. I was busy working on a dig in south Campeche. Halstead was with me then, among others. When the dig was finished for the season and we'd got back to civilization he picked a quarrel with me and left. With him went my de Vivero file.'

Halstead's voice was like a lash. 'That's a lie!'

Fallon shrugged. 'That's the way it was.'

So far we hadn't reached any point at which the tray was important, but here was the first mention of the deep-rooted quarrel between these two men, and that might be of consequence so I decided to probe. 'What was the quarrel about?'

'He stole my work,' said Halstead flatly.

'The hell I did!' Fallon turned to me. 'This is one of the things that crop up in academic circles, I'm sorry to say. It happens like this; young men just out of college work in the field with older and more experienced workers—I did the same myself with Murray many years ago. Papers get written and sometimes the younger fellow reckons he's not given due credit. It happens all the time.'

'Was it true in this case?'

Halstead was about to speak up but his wife put her hand on his knee and motioned him to silence. Fallon said, 'Most certainly not. Oh, I admit I wrote a paper on some aspects of the Quetzaecoatl legend which Halstead said I stole from him, but it wasn't like that at all.' He shook his head wearily. 'You've got to get the picture. You're on a dig and you work hard all day and at night you tend to relax and, maybe, drink a bit. Now, if there's half a dozen of you then you might have a bull session—what you English call "talking shop". Ideas fly around thick and fast and nobody is ever certain who said what or when; these ideas tend to be regarded as common property. Now, it *may* be that the origin of the paper I wrote happened in such a way, and it *may* be that it was Halstead's suggestion, but I can't prove it and, by God, neither can he.'

Halstead said, 'You know damn well that I suggested the central idea of that paper.'

Fallon spread his hands and appealed to me. 'You see how it is. It might have gone for nothing if this young fool hadn't written to the journals and publicly accused me of theft. I could have sued the pants off him—but I didn't. I wrote to him privately and suggested that he refrain from entering into public controversy because I certainly wasn't going to enter into an argument of that nature in the professional prints. But he continued and finally the editors wouldn't print his letters any more.'

Halstead's voice was malevolent. 'You mean you bought the goddamn editors, don't you?'

'Think what you like,' said Fallon in disgust. 'At any rate, I found my de Vivero file had vanished when Halstead left. It didn't mean much at the time, and when it did start to mean something it wasn't much trouble to go back to the original sources. But when I started to bump into the Halsteads around every corner I put two and two together.'

'But you don't *know* he took your file,' I said. 'You couldn't prove it in a law court.'

'I don't suppose I could,' agreed Fallon.

'Then the less said about it the better.' Halstead looked pleased at that, so I added, 'You both seem free and easy in throwing accusations about. This isn't my idea of professional dignity.'

'You haven't heard the whole story yet, Mr. Wheale,' said Mrs. Halstead.

'Well, let's get on with it,' I said. 'Go ahead, Professor Fallon—or do you have anything to say, Dr. Halstead?'

Halstead gloomed at me. 'Not yet.' He said it with an air of foreboding and I knew there were some more fireworks ahead.

'Nothing much happened after that for quite a while,' said Fallon. 'Then when I was in New York, I received a letter from Mark Gerryson suggesting I see him. Gerryson is a dealer whom I have used from time to time, and he said he had some Mayan chocolate jugs—not the ordinary pottery jugs, but made of gold. They must have come from a noble house. He also said he had part of a feather cloak and a few other things.'

Halstead snorted and muttered audibly, 'A goddamn feather cloak!'

'I know it was a fake,' said Fallon. 'And I didn't buy it. But the chocolate jugs were genuine. Gerryson knew I'd be interested—the ordinary Mayan specialist doesn't interest Gerryson because he hasn't the money that Gerryson asks; he usually sells to museums and rich collectors. Well, I run a museum myself—among other things—and I've had some good stuff from Gerryson in the past.

'We dickered for a bit and I told him what I thought of his feather cloak; he laughed about that and said he was pulling my leg. The chocolate jugs were genuine enough and I bought those. Then he said he wanted my opinion on something that had just come in—it was a manuscript account by a Spaniard who had lived among the Mayas in the early sixteenth century and he wanted to know if it was genuine.'

'He was consulting you as an expert in the field?' I said. I saw Katherine Halstead lean forward intently.

Fallon nodded. 'That's right. The name of the Spaniard was de Vivero, and the manuscript was a letter to his sons.' He fell silent.

Halstead said, 'Don't stop now, Fallon—just when it's getting interesting.'

Fallon looked at me. 'Do you know anything about the conquest of Mexico?'

'Not much,' I said. 'I learned a bit about it at school—Cortes and all that—but I've forgotten the details, if I ever knew them.'

'Just like most people. Have you got a map of Mexico?'

I walked across the room and picked an atlas from the shelf. I drew up the coffee table and laid down the atlas turned to the correct page. Fallon hovered over it, and said, 'I'll have to give you some background detail or else the letter won't make sense.' He brought down his finger on to the map of Mexico close to the coast near Tampico. 'In the first couple of decades of the fifteen-hundreds the Spaniards had their eyes on what we now know as Mexico. There were rumours about the place—stories of unimaginable wealth—and they were poising themselves to go in and get it.'

His finger swept in an arc around the Gulf of Mexico. 'Hernandez de Cordoba explored the coast in 1517 and Juan de Grijalva followed in 1518. In 1519 Hernan Cortes took the plunge and mounted an expedition into the interior and we know what happened. He came up against the Aztecs and by a masterly mixture of force, statesmanship, superstition and pure confidence trickery he licked them—one of the most amazing feats any man has ever done.

'But having done it he found there were other worlds to conquer. To the south, covering what is now Yucatan, Guatemala and Honduras was another Amerind empire—that of the Mayas. He hadn't got as much gold from the Aztecs as he expected, but the Mayas were dripping with it if the reports that came up from the south were true. So in 1525 he marched against the Mayas. He left Tenochtitlan—now Mexico City—and hit the coast here, at Coatzacualco, and then struck along the spine of the isthmus to Lake Peten and thus to Coban. He didn't get much for his pains because the main strength of the Mayas wasn't on the Anahuac plateau at all but in the Yucatan Peninsula.'

I leaned over his shoulder and followed his exposition alertly. Fallon said, 'Cortes gave up personal direction at that point—he was pulled back to Spain—and the next expedition was led by Francisco de Montejo, who had already explored the coast of Yucatan from the sea. He had quite a respectable force but he found the Mayas a different proposition from the Aztecs. They fought back, and fought back hard, and Montejo was no Cortes—the Spaniards were trounced in the first few battles.

'With Montejo was Manuel de Vivero. I don't suppose Vivero was much more than a common foot soldier, but something funny happened to him. He was captured by the Mayas and they didn't kill him; they kept him alive as a sort of slave and as a mascot. Now, Montejo never did pacify Yucatan—he *never* got on top of the Mayas. Come to that, nobody ever did; they were weakened and absorbed to some extent, but they were never defeated in battle. In 1549, twenty-two years after he started out, Montejo was in control of barely half of the Yucatan Peninsula—and all this time Vivero was a captive in the interior.

'This was a rather curious time in the history of the Mayas and something happened which puzzled archeologists for a long time. They found that the Spaniards and the Mayas were living and working together side by side, each in his own culture; they found a Mayan temple and a Spanish church built next to each other and, what is more, contemporaneous —built *at the same time*. This was puzzling until the sequence of events had been sorted out as I've just described.

'In any event, there the Mayas and the Spaniards were, living cheek by jowl. They fought each other, but not continuously. The Spaniards controlled eastern Yucatan where the great Mayan cities of Chichen Itza and Uxmal are, but western Yucatan, the modern province of Quintana Roo, was a closed book to them. It's still pretty much of a closed book even now. However, there must have been quite a bit of trade going on between the two halves and Vivero, captive though he was, managed to write a letter to his sons and smuggle it out. That's the Vivero letter.'

He dug into his briefcase again. 'I have a transcription of it here if you want to read it.'

I flipped open the file he gave me—there was quite a lot of it. I said, 'Do you want me to read this now?'

'It would be better if you did,' he said. 'We'd be able to get on with the rest of our business a little faster. You can't understand anything until you read that letter.'

'All right,' I said. 'But I'll take it into my study. Can I trust you two not to kill each other in my absence?'

Katherine Halstead said coolly, 'There will be no trouble.'

I grinned at her cheerfully. 'I'll have Mrs. Edgecombe bring you tea; that ought to keep the temperature down—no one kills over the teacups, it would be downright uncivilized.'

II

To my sons, Jaime and Juan, greetings from Manuel de Vivero y Castuera, your father.

For many years, my sons, I have been seeking ways by which I could speak to you to assure you of my safety in this heathen land. Many times have I sought escape and as many times I have been defeated and I know now that escape from my captivity cannot be, for I am watched continually. But by secret stratagems and the friendship of two men of the Mayas I am able to send you this missive in the hope that your hearts will be lightened and you will not grieve for me as for a dead man. But you must know, my sons, that I will never come out of this land of the Mayas nor out of this city called Uaxuanoc; like the Children of Israel I shall be captive for as long as it pleases the Lord, our God, to keep me alive.

In this letter I shall relate how I came to be here, how God preserved my life when so many of my comrades were slain, and tell of my life among those people, the Mayas. Twelve years have I been here and have seen many marvels, for this is the Great City of the Mayas, the prize we have all sought in the Americas. Uaxuanoc is to Tenochtitlan which Hernan Cortes conquered as Madrid is to the meanest village in Huelva, the province of our family. I was with Cortes in the taking of Tenochtitlan and saw the puissant Montezuma and his downfall, but that mighty king was as a mere peasant, a man poor in wealth, when put against even the ordinary nobility of Uaxuanoc.

You must know that in the Year of Christ One Thousand, Five Hundred and Twenty Seven I marched with Francisco de Montejo into the Yucatan against the Mayas. My position in the company was high and I led a band of our Spanish soldiers. I had a voice with Cortes when I was with that subtle soldier and I was high in the councils of Francisco de Montejo, and so I know the inner reasons for the many stratagems of the campaign. Since I have lived with the Mayas I have come to know them, to speak their words and to think their thoughts, and so I know also why those stratagems came to naught.

Francisco de Montejo was—and, I hope, still is—my friend. But friendship cannot blind me to his shortcomings as a soldier and as a statesman. Brave he undoubtedly is, but his is the bravery of the wild boar or of the bull of the Basque country which charges straight without deceit or evasion and so is easily defeated. Bravery is not enough for a soldier, my sons: he must be wily and dishonest, telling lies when appearing to speak truth, even to his men when he finds this necessary; he must retreat to gain an advantage, ignoring the ignorant pleadings of braver but lesser soldiers; he must lay traps to ensnare the enemy and he must use the strength of the enemy against himself as Cortes did when he allied himself with the Tlascalans against the men of Mexico.

Hernan Cortes knew this most well. He spoke pleasantly to all and of all, but kept his counsel and went his own way. It may be that this use of lies and chicanes, the inventions of the Devil, is against the teachings of Holy Church and, indeed, would be reprehensible when fighting fellow Christians; but here we are fighting the Children of the Devil himself and turn his own weapons against him in the assurance that our cause is just and that with the help of our Lord, Jesus Christ, we can bring these ignorant savages to the One and True Faith.

Be that as it may, Francisco de Montejo was—and is—lacking in the qualities I have named and his efforts to subdue the Maya came to naught. Even now, twelve years after we marched so gaily on our Holy Crusade, the Maya is as strong as ever, though some of his cities are lost. Yet I would not lay all blame on Francisco, for this is as strange a land as any I have seen in all my journeyings in the Americas, where many strange and wondrous things are to be seen daily.

This I will tell you: the land of Yucatan is not like any other. When Hernan Cortes defeated the army of the Mayas on his journey to El Peten and the Honduras he was fighting on the uplands of Anahuac where the land is open and where all the noble resources of the art of war in which we are so advanced can be used. When we marched into Yucatan with de Montejo on the central strongholds of the enemy we found a green wilderness, a forest of trees so vast that it would cover all of Old Spain,

54

In this place, our horses, which so affright the ignorant savages, could not be used in battle; but we were not cast down, thinking to use them as pack animals. To our sore disappointment they were afflicted by disease and began to die, more each day. And those that survived were of little value, for the trees grew thickly and a man can go where a horse cannot, and from being the most valued of our possessions, they stooped to become a hindrance to our expedition.

Another misfortune of this land is the lack of water, which is very strange, for consider: how is it that there can be a growth of strong trees and bushes of divers kind where there is no water? But it is indeed so. When the rain comes, which it does infrequently but more often at certain times of year, then it is soaked direct into the solid earth so that there are no streams and rivers in this land; but sometimes there is a pool or well which the Maya calls cenote and here the water is fresh and good although it is fed not by running streams but rather issues forth from the bowels of the earth.

Because these places are few in the forest they are sacred to the Mayas who set up their temples here and give praise to their idolatrous gods for the good water. Here also they set up their castles and strong places, and so when we marched with de Montejo we had to fight for the very water for our bellies to give us strength to fight more.

The Mayas are a stubborn people who close their ears to the Word of Christ. They would not listen to Francisco de Montejo, nor to any of his captains, myself included, nor even to the good priests of God in our train who pleaded with them in the Name of our Saviour. They rejected the Word of the Lamb of God and resisted us with weapons although, in truth, since my captivity I have found them a peaceful people, very slow to wrath but in their anger terrible.

Although their weapons are poor, being wooden swords with stone edges and spears with stone tips, they resisted us mightily for their numbers were great and they knew the secret paths of the land and laid snares for us, in which ambuscades many of my comrades were slain and in one of these affrays I, your father, was taken prisoner, to my shame.

I could not fight more for my sword was knocked from my hand, nor could I run on their swords and die for I was bound with ropes and helpless. I was carried, slung on a pole, along many devious paths in the forest and so came to the encampment of their army where I was questioned to some lengths by a great Cacique. The tongue of these people is not so different from the Toltec tongue that I could not understand but I dissimulated and gave no knowledge of my understanding and so by this means was I able to keep hidden from them the place of our main force, nor could they wring it from me by means of torture because of the confusion of tongues.

I think they were going to kill me but a priest among them pointed to my hair which, as you know, is the colour of ripe grain in summer, a strange thing for a Spaniard and more natural in northern lands. And so I was taken from that camp and sent under guard to the great city of Chichen Itza. In this city there is a great cenote and chichen in the Mayan tongue means the mouth of a well. In this great pool are maidens thrown who go down to the underworld and return to tell of the mysteries they have seen in Hades. Surely these are the Devil's spawn!

In Chichen Itza I saw a Cacique even greater than the first, a noble finely dressed in an embroidered kilt and feather cloak and surrounded by papas or the priests of these people. I was again questioned but to no avail and much was made of my hair and a great cry arose among the papas that surely I was Kukulkan, he whom you will know in the Toltec tongue as Quetzaecoatl, the white god who is to come from the West, a belief among the heathen that has served us well.

In Chichen Itza I spent one month closely guarded in a stone cell but other than that I was not harmed, being served regularly with the corn of these people and some meat, together with that bitter drink called chocolatl. After one month I was sent again under guard to their main city which is Uaxuanoc and where I now am. But the guards were young nobles finely dressed in embroidered cotton armour and with good weapons of their kind. I do not think their armour as good as our iron armour, but no doubt it suffices well enough when they fight among themselves. I was fettered loosely but other than that no harm was offered and the chains were heavy, being of gold.

Uaxuanoc is a large city and there are many temples and big buildings the greatest of which is the temple to Kukulkan, decorated with the Feathered Serpent in his honour. Thither was I taken so that the papas of the temple could behold me and pass judgement whether I was indeed Kukulkan, their chief god. There was much argument among the papas: some said I was not Kukulkan because why would their chief god fight against them? Others among them asked why should not Kukulkan bring his warriors to chastise them with magical weapons if they had transgressed against the law of the gods; rather should they seek in their hearts where the transgression lay. Again, some said that this could not be Kukulkan because he spoke not their tongue, and others asked: why should the gods speak an earthly tongue when they undoubtedly spoke among themselves of things that could not be uttered by human lips?

I trembled before them but kept an outward calm, for was I not in evil straits? If I were not Kukulkan they would sacrifice me in the temple in the manner of the Aztecs of Tenochtitlan and tear the living heart from my body. But if they believed I was their god they would bow down before me and worship and I would be an abomination before Christ and damned thereafter to the pains of hell, for no mortal man is worthy of worship before God.

They resolved their disputation by taking me before their king for him to pass judgement between the divers parties in the manner of their law, he being the sole arbitrator in matters of high state and religion among them. He passed for a tall man among the Mayas though not as tall as would seem so in our eyes; he had a noble countenance and was dressed finely in a cloak of the bright feathers of humming birds and wore much gold about his person. He sat on a golden throne and above his head was a representation of the Feathered Serpent in gold and precious stones and fine enamels.

And he judged in this manner: that I should not be sacrificed but should be taken aside and taught the tongue of the Mayas so that I should be able to utter from my own lips and with their understanding what and who I was.

I was so overjoyed at the judgement of this Solomon that I nearly went on my knees before him but I caught myself up with the thought that indeed I did not know their tongue— or so they thought—and to learn it would take me many months or even years. By this stratagem I saved my life and my soul.

I was taken aside and put into the care of the eldest of the papas, who led me to the great temple where I was given lodging in the quarters of the papas. Soon I found I was free to come and go in the city as I wished although always accompanied by two noble guards and still clinking my golden fetters. Many years afterwards I discovered that the papas gave me this freedom for fear I was indeed Kukulkan and would exact vengeance at a later time if imprisoned. As for the golden chains: was not gold the metal of the gods? Perhaps Kukulkan would not be dishonoured by gold—if indeed this was Kukulkan. The king himself wore golden chains though they did not fetter him. Thus the papas reasoned in fear of disgrace should they be proved wrong in any way.

They taught me their tongue and I was slow to learn, my voice unready and my speech stumbling, and by this means passed many months to the great disappointment of the papas. During this time I saw many abominations in the great temple; young men sacrificed to Kukulkan, their bodies oiled and their heads garlanded with flowers going willingly to the blood-stained altar to have their hearts torn out by the papas and held in their sight before vision faded from their eyes. I was forced to attend these blasphemous ceremonies before the idol of the Feathered Serpent, my guards holding my arms so that I could not leave. Every time I closed my eyes and prayed to Christ and the Virgin for succour from the awful fate to which I found myself condemned.

There were other sacrifices at the great cenote in the midst of the city. A ridge of land splits the city from east to west and on the top of the ridge is the temple of Yum Chac, the god of rain, whose palace these foolish people believe to be at the bottom of the cenote. At ceremonies in honour of Yum Chac maidens are cast from the temple to the deep pool at the bottom of the cliff and disappear into the dark waters. These infidel wickednesses I did not attend.

It was during this time that I found my salvation from the terrible dilemma under which I laboured. You must know that the Mayas are great workers in stone and gold, although much of their labour is directed to making their heathen idols, a task unfitting for Christian hands. My sons, your grandfather and my father was a goldsmith in the city of Sevilla and when I was young I learned the trade at his knee. I observed that the Mayas were ignorant of the way of using wax which is common in Spain so I pleaded with the papas to give me gold and beeswax and to let me use a furnace to melt the gold.

They consulted among themselves and let me have the gold and beeswax and watched me closely to see what I did. There was a maiden, not above fourteen, who attended me in my

58

lodging and saw to my wants, and I made a little model of her in the wax while the papas looked on and frowned, for they were afraid of some bewitchment. The Mayas have none of the Parisian plaster so I was constrained to use well watered clay to put about the statue and to make the funnel on the top for the pouring of the gold.

I was allowed to use the temple smithy and the papas cried in wonder as the gold was poured into the funnel and the hot wax spurted from the vent hole, the while I sweated for fear that the clay mould would break, but it did not and I was well satisfied with my little statue which the papas took before the king and told him of its making. Thereafter I made many objects in gold but would not make idols for the temple nor any of the golden implements used therein. The king commanded I teach the royal smiths this new art of working in gold, which I did, and many of the great Caciques of the land came and had me make jewellery for them.

The day came when I could no longer hide my knowledge of the Mayan tongue and the papas took me to the king for judgement and he asked me to speak from my mouth who or what I was. I spake plainly that indeed I was not Kukulkan but a nobleman from lands to the east and a faithful subject of the great Emperor Charles V of Spain who had commanded me to come to the Mayas and spread the Word of Christ among them.

The papas murmured among themselves and prevailed upon the king, saying that the gods of the Mayas were strong and they needed none other and that I should be sacrificed in the temple of Kukulkan for blasphemy. I spake boldly straight to the king, asking him would he kill such a one as I who could teach his smiths many wonders so that his kingdom should be ornamented beyond all others?

The king smiled on me and gave orders that indeed I should not be sacrificed but should be given a house and servants and should teach my arts to all the smiths of the land to the benefit of the kingdom but that I should not teach the Word of Christ on pain of death. This last he said to please the papas of Kukulkan. And I was given a house with a smithy and many serving-maids and the smiths of the land came and sat at my feet and my chains were struck from me.

Twice thereafter I escaped and was lost in the great forest and the king's soldiers found me and took me back to Uaxuanoc and the king was lenient and punished me not. But the third time I escaped and was brought back again into the city he frowned like thunder and spoke to me, saying his patience was at an end and that if I escaped but once more I would be sacrificed in the temple of Kukulkan, so I perforce desisted and stayed in the city.

Here I have been for twelve long years, my sons, and am indeed counted now as one of their own save for the guards about my house and those that follow me when I go to the market place. I do not go to the temples but instead have made a chapel to Jesus and the Virgin in my house where I pray daily and am not hindered, for the king said: Let every man pray to the gods of his heart. But he will not let me preach the Word of Christ in the city and I do not for fear of death and am ashamed thereat.

Uaxuanoc is a great and fine city with much gold. Even the gutters which lead the rainwater from the temple roofs to the cisterns are gold and I myself use golden spoons in my kitchen, in which manner I am greater than any king in Christendom. I believe these people to have sprung from the loins of those Egyptians who kept the Israelites in captivity, for their temples are pyramids in the Egyptian manner as were described to me by a traveller who had been in those parts. But the king's palace is a square building, very great and plated with sheets of gold within and without even to the floors so that one walks on gold. And these people have the art of enamel such as I have never seen, but use the art in blasphemy to make their idols, although much fine jewellery is also made, even the common people wearing gold and enamel.

My life is easy, for I am held in much respect for my work in the smithy and because I have the friendship of the king who gives me many gifts when I please him with my work. But often in the nights I weep and wish I were back again in Spain even in a common tavern in Cadiz where there is music and singing, for these Mayas have but poor music, knowing only the pipe and drum and I have no knowledge of the musical art to teach them other.

But I say to you, my sons, God has touched this land with His Finger and surely intends it to be brought into the Fold of Christ for I have seen wonder upon wonder here and an even greater marvel which is a sign for all to behold that the gentle Hand of Christ encompasses the whole world and there is no corner which escapes Him. I have seen this sign written in burning gold upon a mountain of gold which lies not a step from the centre of the city and which shines in imperishable glory more brightly than the golden palace of the king of the Mayas; and surely this sign means that Christians shall possess this land for their own and the heathen shall be cast down and that men of Christ shall overturn the idols in the temples and shall strip the gold from the temple roofs and from the palace of the king and shall take possession of the golden mountain and the burning sign thereon which is a wonder for all eyes to see.

Therefore, my sons, Jaime and Juan, read carefully this letter for it is my wish that this glory shall come to the family of de Vivero which shall be exalted thereby. You know the de Viveros are of ancient lineage but were put upon in past time by the Moors in Spain so that the fortunes of the family were lost and the heads of the family were forced into common trade. My father was a goldsmith which, praise be to God, has been the saving of my soul in this land. When the infidel Moors were driven from Spain our family fortunes changed and by inheritance from my father I was able to buy land in the province of Huelva and became Alcalde. But I looked afar to the new lands in the West and thought that a man might hew a greater inheritance to pass to his sons, who then might become governors of provinces under the king in these new lands. So I came to Mexico with Hernan Cortes.

Whoever takes this city of Uaxuanoc shall also possess that mountain of gold of which I have written and his name shall sound throughout all Christendom and he shall sit on the right hand of Christian kings and be honoured above all other men and it is my wish that this man should be called de Vivero. But it has grieved me that my sons should be quarrelsome as was Cain unto Abel, fighting the one with the other for little reason and bringing shame upon the name of de Vivero instead of uniting for the good of the family. Therefore I charge you under God to make your peace. You, Jaime, shall beg the forgiveness of your brother for the sins you have committed against him, and you, Juan, shall do likewise, and both shall live in amity and work towards the same end and that is to take this city and the mountain of gold with its wondrous sign.

So with this letter I send you gifts, one for each, made in that marvellous manner which my father learned of that stranger from the East which the Moors brought to Cordoba many years ago and of which I have spoken to you. Let the scales of enmity fall from your eyes and look upon these gifts with proper vision which shall join you together with strong bonds so that the name of de Vivero shall echo in Christendom for all time to come.

The men who shall bring you these gifts are Mayas whom I have secretly baptized in Christ against the wishes of the king and taught our Spanish tongue for their greater aid and safety in seeking you. Look upon them well and honour them, for they are brave men and true Christians and deserve much reward for their service.

Go with God, my sons, and fear not the snares laid in this forest land by your enemies. Remember what I have told you of the qualities of the true soldier, so that you shall prosper in battle and overcome the wickedness of the heathen to possess this land and the great wonder contained therein. So the name of de Vivero will be exalted for evermore.

It may be that when this is brought to pass I will be dead, for the king of the Mayas becomes old and he who will be king looks not upon me with favour, being corrupted by the papas of Kukulkan. But pray for me and for my soul, for I fear I shall spend long in purgatory for my pusillanimity in hesitating to convert this people to Christ for fear of my life. I am but a mortal man and much afraid, so pray for your father, my sons, and offer masses for his soul.

Written in the month of April in the year of Christ, One Thousand, Five Hundred and Thirty Nine.

Manuel de Vivero y Castuera,
　　Alcalde in Spain,
　　　　Friend of Hernando Cortes
　　　　and Francisco de Montejo.

III

I put the transcription of the Vivero letter back into the file and sat for a moment thinking of that long-dead man who had lived out his life in captivity. What had happened to him? Had he been sacrificed when the king died? Or had he managed to whip up a little more ingenuity and double-talk the Mayas into letting him live?

What a mixed-up man he was—according to our modern way of thinking. He regarded the Mayas as the man regarded the lion: 'This animal is dangerous; it defends itself when attacked.' That smacked of hypocrisy but de Vivero was educated in a different tradition; there was no dichotomy involved in converting the heathen and looting them of their gold simultaneously—to him it was as natural as breathing.

He was undoubtedly a brave and steadfast man and I hoped he had gone to his death unperturbed by the mental agonies of purgatory and hell.

There was an air of tension in the living-room and it was evident that the birdies in their little nest had not been agreeing. I tossed down the file, and said, 'All right; I've read it.'

Fallon said, 'What did you think of it?'

'He was a good man.'

'Is that all?'

'You know damn well that isn't all,' I said without heat. 'I see the point very well. Would I be correct if I said that this city of . . . Uax . . . Uaxua . . .' I stumbled.

'Wash-wan-ok,' said Fallon unexpectedly. 'That's how it's pronounced.'

'. . . Anyway, that this city hasn't been uncovered by you people?'

'Score one for you,' said Fallon. He tapped the file and said with intensity, 'On Vivero's evidence Uaxuanoc was bigger than Chichen Itza, bigger than Uxmal—and those places are pretty big. It was the central city of the Mayan civilization and the man who finds it will make a hell of a name for himself; he's going to be able to answer a lot of questions that are now unanswerable.'

I turned to Halstead. 'Do you agree?'

He looked at me with smouldering eyes. 'Don't ask damn-fool questions. Of course I agree; it's about the only thing Fallon and I agree about.'

I sat down. 'And you're racing each other—splitting your guts to get there first. My God, what a commentary on science!'

'Wait a minute,' said Fallon sharply. 'That's not entirely true. All right; I agree that I'm trying to get in ahead of Halstead, but that's only because I don't trust him on something as important as this. He's too impatient, too thrusting for an important dig. He'll want to make a *quick* reputation—I know him of old—and that's the way evidence gets destroyed.'

Halstead didn't rise to the argument as I expected. Instead, he looked at me sardonically. 'There you have a fine example of professional ethics,' he said mockingly. 'Fallon is ready to run anyone's reputation into the ground if he can get what he wants.' He leaned forward and addressed Fallon directly. 'I don't suppose you want to add to your own reputation by the discovery of Uaxuanoc?'

'My reputation is already *made*,' said Fallon softly. 'I'm at the top already.'

'And you don't want anybody passing you,' said Halstead cuttingly.

I'd just about had enough of this bickering and was about to say so when Katherine Halstead interjected, 'And Professor Fallon has peculiar means of making sure he isn't passed.'

I raised my eyebrows and said, 'Could you explain that?'

She smiled. 'Well, he did steal the original of the Vivero letter.'

'So we're back at that again,' said Fallon disgustedly. 'I tell you I bought it from Gerryson in New York—and I can prove it.'

'That's enough of that,' I said. 'We've had enough of these counter-accusations. Let's stick to the point. From what I can gather old de Vivero sent the letter and gifts to his sons. You think that the gifts were two golden trays and that there is something about those trays that has a bearing on Uaxuanoc. Is that right?'

Fallon nodded and picked up the file. 'There was a hell of a lot of gold in Uaxuanoc—he mentions it time and again—and he made it quite clear that he wanted his sons to be leaders in sharing the loot. The one thing he didn't do that he might logically have been expected to do was to tell them where to find the city. Instead, he sent them gifts.'

Halstead broke in. 'I'm sure that I can figure this out just as well as Fallon. Vivero's family life wasn't too happy—it seems that his sons hated each other's guts, and Vivero didn't like that. It seems logical to me that he'd give each of them a piece of information, and the two pieces would have to be joined to make sense. The brothers would *have* to work together.' He spread his hands. 'The information wasn't in the letter so it must have been in the gifts—in the trays.'

'That's how I figured it, too,' said Fallon. 'So I went hunting for the trays. I knew the Mexican de Vivero tray was still in existence in 1782 because that's when Murville wrote about it, and I started to track it down from there.'

Halstead sniggered and Fallon said irascibly, 'All right; I

made a goddamn fool of myself.' He turned to me and said with a weak grin, 'I chased all over Mexico and finally found it in my own museum—I'd owned it all the time!'

Halstead laughed loudly. 'And I'd beaten you to it; I knew it was there before you did.' The smile left his face. 'Then you withdrew it from public exhibition.'

I shook my head irritably. 'How the devil can you own something like that and not know about it?' I demanded.

'Your family did,' pointed out Fallon reasonably. 'But my case was a bit different. I established a trust, and, among other things, the trust runs a museum. I'm not responsible personally for everything the museum buys, and I don't know every item in stock. Anyway, the museum had the tray.'

'That's one tray. What about the other?'

'That was a bit more difficult, wasn't it, Paul?' He smiled across the room at Halstead. 'Manuel de Vivero had two sons, Jaime and Juan. Jaime stayed in Mexico and founded the Mexican branch of the de Viveros—you know about them already—but Juan had a bellyful of America and went back to Spain. He took quite a bit of loot with him and became an Alcalde like his father—that's a sort of country squire and magistrate. He had a son, Miguel, who prospered even more and became a wealthy shipowner.

'Came the time when trouble rubbed up between Spain and England and Philip II of Spain decided to end it once and for all and began to build the Armada. Miguel de Vivero contributed a ship, the *San Juan de Huelva*, and skippered her himself. She sailed with the Armada and never came back—neither did Miguel. His shipping business didn't die with Miguel, a son took over, and it lasted quite a long time—until the end of the eighteenth century. Fortunately they had a habit of keeping records and I dug out a juicy bit of information; Miguel wrote a letter to his wife asking her to send him "the tray which my grandfather had made in Mexico". It was with him on the ship when the Armada sailed for England. I thought then that the whole thing was finished.'

'I got to that letter before you did,' said Halstead with satisfaction.

'This sounds like a cross between a jigsaw puzzle and a detective story,' I said. 'What did you do then?'

'I came to England,' said Fallon. 'Not to look for the tray —I thought that was at the bottom of the sea—but just for a holiday. I was staying in Oxford at one of the colleges and

I happened to mention my searches in Spain. One of the dons —a dry-as-dust literary character—said he vaguely remembered something about it in the correspondence of Herrick.'

I stared at Fallon. 'The poet?'

'That's right. He was rector of Dean Prior—that's not far from here. A man called Goosan had written a letter to him; Goosan was a local merchant, a nobody; his letter wouldn't have been preserved if it hadn't have been written to Herrick.'

Halstead was alert. 'I didn't know about this. Go on.'

'It doesn't really matter,' said Fallon tiredly. 'We know where the tray is now.'

'I'm interested,' I said.

Fallon shrugged. 'Herrick was bored to death with country life but he was stuck at Dean Prior. There wasn't much to do so I suppose he took more interest in his parishioners than the usual dull clod of a country priest. He certainly took an interest in Goosan and asked him to put on paper what he had previously said verbally. To cut a long story short, Goosan's family name had originally been Guzman, and his grandfather had been a seaman on the *San Juan*. They'd had a hell of a time of it during the attack on England and, after one thing and another, the ship had gone down in a storm off Start Point. The captain, Miguel de Vivero, had died previously of ship fever—that's typhus—and when Guzman came ashore he carried that goddamn tray as part of his personal loot. Guzman's grandson—that's the Goosan who wrote to Herrick —even showed Herrick the tray. How your family got hold of it I don't know.'

I smiled as I said, 'That's why you laughed when I told you to see Dave Goosan.'

'It gave me something of a shock,' admitted Fallon.

'I didn't know anything about Herrick,' said Halstead. 'I was just following up on the Armada and trying to discover where the *San Juan* had sunk. I happened to be in Plymouth when I saw a photograph of the tray in the newspaper.'

Fallon raised his eyes to the ceiling. 'Sheer luck!' he commented.

Halstead grinned. 'But I was here before you.'

'Yes, you were,' I said slowly. 'And then my brother was murdered.'

He blew up. 'What the hell do you mean by that crack?'

'Just making a true observation. Did you know Victor Niscemi?'

66

'I'd never heard of him until the inquest. I don't know that I like the trend of your thinking, Wheale.'

'Neither do I,' I said sourly. 'Let's skip it—for the moment. Professor Fallon: I presume you've given your tray a thorough examination. What did you find?'

He grunted. 'I'm not prepared to discuss that in front of Halstead. I've been pushed far enough.' He was silent for a moment, then he sighed. 'All right; effectively, I found nothing. I assume that whatever it is will only come to light when the trays are examined as a pair.' He stood up. 'Now, I've had just about enough of this. A little while ago you told Halstead to put up or shut up—now I'm putting the same proposition to you. How much money will you take for the tray? Name your price and I'll write you a cheque right now.'

'You haven't enough money to pay my price,' I said, and he blinked in surprise. 'I told you my price might not necessarily be in cash. Sit down and listen to what I've got to say.'

Slowly Fallon lowered himself into his chair, not taking his eyes from me. I looked across at Halstead and at his wife who was almost hidden in the gathering shadows of evening. I said, 'I have three conditions for parting with the tray. *All* those conditions must be met before I do so. Is that clear?'

Fallon grunted and I accepted that as agreement. Halstead looked tense and then inclined his head stiffly.

'Professor Fallon has a lot of money which will come in useful. He will therefore finance whatever expedition is to be made to find this city of Uaxuanoc. You can't object to that, Fallon; it is something you would do in any event. But I will be a part of the expedition. Agreed?'

Fallon looked at me speculatively. 'I don't know if you could take it,' he said a little scornfully. 'It's not like a stroll on Dartmoor.'

'I'm not giving you a choice,' I said. 'I'm giving you an ultimatum.'

'All right,' he said. 'But it's your skin.'

'The second condition is that you help me as much as possible to find out why my brother was killed.'

'Won't that interfere with your jaunt in Yucatan?' he queried.

'I'm not so certain it will,' I said. 'I think that whoever wanted the tray enough to send a man armed with a sawn-off shotgun also knew that the tray had a secret. Possibly we'll meet him in Yucatan—who knows?'

'I think you're nuts,' he said. 'But I'll play along with you. I agree.'

'Good,' I said pleasantly, and prepared to harpoon him. 'The third condition is that Halstead comes with us.'

Fallon sat bolt upright and roared, 'I'll be damned if I'll take the son of a bitch.'

Halstead jumped from his chair. 'That's twice today you've called me that. I ought to knock your—'

'Belt up!' I yelled. Into the sudden silence that followed I said, 'You two make me sick. All afternoon you've been sniping at each other. You've both done very well in your investigations so far—you've arrived at the same point at the same time and honours ought to be even. And you've both made identical accusations about each other, so you're square there, too.'

Fallon looked stubborn, so I said, 'Look at it this way. If we two join forces, you know what will happen: Halstead will be hanging around anyway. He's as tenacious as you are and he'll follow the trail wherever we lead him. But the point doesn't arise, does it? I said that all *three* of my conditions must be met and, by God, if you don't agree to this I'll *give* my tray to Halstead. That way you'll have one each and be on an even footing for the next round of this academic dog-fight. Now, do you agree or don't you?'

His face worked and he shook his head sadly. 'I agree,' he said in a whisper.

'Halstead?'

'I agree.'

Then they both said simultaneously, 'Where's the tray?'

Four

Mexico City was hot and frenetic with Olympic Gamesmanship. The hotels were stuffed to bursting, but fortunately Fallon owned a country house just outside the city which we made our headquarters. The Halsteads also had their home in Mexico City but they were more often than not at Fallon's private palace.

I must say that when Fallon decided to move he moved fast. Like a good general, he marshalled his army close to the point of impact; he spent a small fortune on telephone calls and the end result was a concentration of forces in Mexico City. I had a fast decision to make, too; my job was a good one and I hated to give it up unceremoniously, but Fallon was pushing hard. I saw my boss and told him of Bob's death and he was good enough to give me six months' leave of absence. I bore down heavily on the farm management, so I suppose I deceived him in a way, yet I think that going to Yucatan *could* be construed as looking after Bob's estate.

Fallon also used the resources that only money can buy. 'Big corporations have security problems,' he said. 'So they run their own security outfits. They're as good as the police any time, and better in most cases. The pay is higher. I'm having Niscemi checked out independently.'

The thought of it made me a bit dizzy. Like most people, I'd thought of millionaires as just people who have a lot of money but I hadn't gone beyond that to the power and influence that money makes possible. That a man was able to lift a telephone and set a private police force in motion made me open my eyes and think again.

Fallon's house was big and cool, set in forty acres of manicured grounds. It was quiet with unobtrusive service, which clicked into action as soon as the master set foot in it. Soft-footed servants were there when you wanted them and absent when not needed and I settled into sybaritic luxury without a qualm.

Fallon's tray had not yet come from New York, much to his annoyance, and he spent a lot of time arguing the archeological toss with Halstead. I was pleased to see that loss of temper was now confined to professional matters and did not take such a personal turn. I think much of that was due to Katherine Halstead, who kept her husband on a tight rein.

The morning after we arrived they were at it hammer and tongs. 'I think old Vivero was a damned liar,' said Halstead.

'Of course he was,' said Fallon crossly. 'But that's not the point at issue here. He says he was taken to Chichen Itza . . .'

'And I say he couldn't have been. The New Empire had fallen apart long before that—Chichen Itza was abandoned when Hunac Ceel drove out the Itzas. It was a dead city.'

Fallon made an impatient noise. 'Don't look at it from your viewpoint; see it as Vivero saw it. Here was an averagely ignorant Spanish soldier without the benefit of the hindsight we have. He *says* he was taken to Chichen Itza—he actually names it, and Chichen Itza is only one of two names he gives in the manuscript. He didn't give a damn whether *you* think Chichen Itza was occupied—he was taken there and he said so.' He stopped short. 'Of course, if you *are* right, it means that the Vivero letter is a modern fake, and we're all up the creek.'

'I don't think it's a fake,' said Halstead. 'I just think that Vivero was a congenital liar.'

'I don't think it's a fake, either,' said Fallon. 'I had it authenticated.' He crossed the room and pulled open a drawer. 'Here's the report on it.'

He gave it to Halstead, who scanned through it and dropped it on the table. I picked it up and found a lot of tables and graphs, but the meat was on the last page under the heading *Conclusions.* 'The document appears to be authentic as to period, being early sixteenth-century Spanish. The condition is poor—the parchment being of poor quality and, perhaps, of faulty manufacture originally. A radio-carbon dating test gives a date of 1534 A.D. with an error of plus or minus fifteen years. The ink shows certain peculiarities of composition but is undoubtedly of the same period as the parchment as demonstrated by radio-carbon testing. An exhaustive linguistic analysis displays no deviation from the norm of the sixteenth century Spanish language. While we refrain from judgement on the content of this document there is no sign from the internal evidence of the manuscript that the document is other than it purports to be.'

I thought of Vivero curing his own animal skins and making his own ink—it all fitted in. Katherine Halstead stretched out her hand and I gave her the report, then turned my attention back to the argument.

'I think you're wrong, Paul,' Fallon was saying. 'Chichen Itza was never wholly abandoned until much later. It was a religious centre even after the Spaniards arrived. What about the assassination of Ah Dzun Kiu?—that was in 1536, no less than nine years *after* Vivero was captured.'

'Who the devil was he?' I asked.

'The chief of the Tutal Kiu. He organized a pilgrimage to Chichen Itza to appease the gods; all the pilgrims were massacred by Nachi Cocom, his arch-enemy. But all that is immaterial—what matters is that we know *when* it happened, and that it's consistent with Vivero's claim to have been taken to Chichen Itza—a claim which Paul disputes.'

'All right, I grant you that one,' said Halstead. 'But there's a lot more about the letter that doesn't add up.'

I left them to their argument and walked over to the window. In the distance light reflected blindingly from the water of a swimming pool. I glanced at Katherine Halstead. 'I'm no good at this sort of logic chopping,' I said. 'It's beyond me.'

'It's over my head, too,' she admitted. 'I'm not an archeologist; I only know what I've picked up from Paul by a sort of osmosis.'

I looked across at the swimming pool again—it looked very inviting. 'What about a swim?' I suggested. 'I have some gear I want to test, and I'd like some company.'

She brightened. 'That's a good idea. I'll meet you out there in ten minutes.'

I went up to my room and changed into trunks, then unpacked my scuba gear and took it down to the pool. I had brought it with me because I thought there might be a chance of getting in some swimming in the Caribbean somewhere along the line and I wasn't going to pass up that chance. I had only swum in clear water once before, in the Mediterranean.

Mrs. Halstead was already at the pool, looking very fetching in a one-piece suit. I dumped the steel bottles and the harness by the side of the pool and walked over to where she was sitting. A flunkey in white coat appeared from nowhere and said something fast and staccato in Spanish, and I shrugged helplessly and appealed to her. 'What's he saying?'

She laughed. 'He wants to know if we'd like something to drink.'

'That's not a bad idea. Something long and cold with alcohol in it.'

'I'll join you.' She rattled away in Spanish at the servant who went away. Then she said. 'I haven't thanked you for what you've done for Paul, Mr. Wheale. Everything has happened so quickly—I really haven't had time to think.'

'There's nothing to thank me for,' I said. 'He just got his due.' I refrained from saying that the real reason I had brought Halstead into it was to keep him close where I could watch him. I wasn't too happy about husband Paul; he was too free with his accusations and his temper was trigger-quick. Somebody had been with Niscemi when Bob had been killed and though it couldn't have been Halstead that didn't mean he had nothing to do with it. I smiled pleasantly at his wife. 'Nothing to it,' I said.

'I think it was very generous—considering the way he behaved.' She looked at me steadily. 'Don't take any notice of him if he becomes bad-tempered again. He's had . . . had disappointments. This is his big chance and it plays on his nerves.'

'Don't worry,' I said soothingly. Privately I was certain that if Halstead became unpleasant he would get a quick bust on the snoot. If I didn't sock him then Fallon would, old as he was. It would be better if I did it, being neutral, then this silly expedition would be in less danger of breaking up.

The drinks arrived—a whitish concoction in tall frosted glasses with ice tinkling like silver bells. I don't know what it was but it tasted cool and soothing. Mrs. Halstead looked pensive. She sipped from her glass, then said tentatively, 'When do you think you will leave for Yucatan?'

'Don't ask me. It depends on the experts up there.' I jerked my head towards the house. 'We still don't know where we're going yet.'

'Do you think the trays have a riddle—and that we can solve it?'

'They have—and we will,' I said economically. I didn't tell her I thought I had the solution already. There was an awful lot I wasn't telling Mrs. Halstead—or anybody else.

She said, 'What do you think Fallon's attitude would be if I suggested going with you to Yucatan?'

I laughed. 'He'd blow his top. You wouldn't have a chance.'

She leaned forward and said seriously, 'It might be better if I went. I'm afraid for Paul.'

'Meaning what?'

She made a fluttery gesture with her hand. 'I'm not the catty kind of woman who makes derogatory statements about her own husband to other men,' she said. 'But Paul is not an ordinary man. There is a lot of violence in him which he can't control—alone. If I'm with him I can talk to him; make him see things in a different way. I wouldn't be a drag on you—I've been on field trips before.'

She talked as though Halstead were some kind of a lunatic needing a nurse around him all the time. I began to wonder about the relationship between these two; some marriages are awfully funny arrangements.

She said, 'Fallon would agree if you put it to him. You could *make* him.'

I grimaced. 'I've already twisted his arm once. I don't think I could do it again. Fallon isn't the man who likes to be pushed around.' I took another pull at the drink and felt the coolness at the back of my throat. 'I'll think about it,' I said finally.

But I knew then that I'd put the proposition to Fallon—and make him like it. There was something about Katherine Halstead that got at me, something I hadn't felt about a woman for many years. Whatever it was, I'd better keep it bottled up, this was no time for playing around with a married woman —especially one married to a man like Paul Halstead.

'Let's see what the water's like,' I suggested, and got up and walked to the edge of the pool.

She followed me. 'What have you brought that for?' she asked, indicating the scuba gear.

I told her, then said, 'I haven't used it for quite some time so I thought I'd check it. Have you done any scuba diving?'

'Lots of times,' she said. 'I spent a summer in the Bahamas once, and spent nearly every day in the water. It's great fun.'

I agreed and settled down to checking the valves. I found that everything was working and put on the harness. As I was swilling the mask out with water she dived into the pool cleanly, surfaced and splashed at me. 'Come in,' she called.

'Don't tell me—the water's fine.' I sat on the edge of the pool and flopped in—you don't dive with bottles on your back. As usual, I found it difficult to get into the correct rhythm of breathing; it's something that requires practice and I was short of that. Because the demand valve is higher in the water than the lungs there is a difference of pressure to be overcome which is awkward at first. Then you have to breathe so as to be economical of air and that is a knack some divers never find. But pretty soon I had got it and was breathing in the irregular rhythm which feels, at first, so unnatural.

I swam around at the bottom of the pool and made a mental note to change the belt weights. I had put on a little flesh since the last time I wore the harness and it made a difference to flotation. Above, I could see Katherine Halstead's sun-tanned limbs and I shot upwards with a kick of the flippers and grabbed her ankles. As I pulled her under I saw the air dribbling evenly from her mouth in a regular line of bubbles rising to the surface. If I had surprised her it certainly didn't show; she had had sense enough not to gasp the air from her lungs.

73

She jack-knifed suddenly and her hands were on my air pipe. With a sudden twitch she pulled the mouthpiece away and I swallowed water and let go of her ankles. I rose to the surface gasping and treading water to find her laughing at me. I spluttered a bit and said, 'Where did you learn that trick?'

'The beach-bums in the Bahamas play rough,' she said. 'A girl learns to look after herself.'

'I'm going down again,' I said. 'I'm out of practice.'

'There'll be another drink waiting when you come out,' she said.

I dropped to the bottom of the pool again and went through my little repertoire of tricks—taking the mouthpiece out and letting the pipe fill with water and then clearing it, taking the mask off and, finally, taking off the whole harness and climbing into it again. This wasn't just a silly game; at one time or another I'd *had* to do every one of those things at a time when it would have been positively dangerous not to have been able to do them. Water at any depth is not man's natural element and the man who survives is the man who can get himself out of trouble.

I had been down about fifteen minutes when I heard a noise. I looked up and saw a splashing so I popped to the surface to see what was going on. Mrs. Halstead had been smacking the water with the palm of her hand, and Fallon stood behind her. I climbed out, and he said, 'My tray has arrived—now we can compare them.'

I shucked off the harness and dropped the weight belt. 'I'll be up as soon as I've dried off.'

He regarded the scuba gear curiously. 'Can you use that—at depth?'

'It depends on what depth,' I said cautiously. 'The deepest I've been is a little over a hundred and twenty feet.'

'That would probably be enough,' he said. 'You might come in useful after all, Wheale; we might have to explore a cenote.' He dismissed the subject abruptly. 'Be as quick as you can.'

Near the pool was a long cabin which proved to be change-rooms. I showered and dried off, put on a terry-towelling gown and went up to the house. As I walked in through the French windows Fallon was saying '. . . thought it was in the vine leaves so I gave it to a cryptographer. It could be the number of veins on a leaf or the angle of the leaves to the stem or any combination of such things. Well, the guy did a
74

run-through and put the results through a computer and came up with nothing.'

It was an ingenious idea and completely wrong. I joined the group around the table and looked down at the two trays. Fallon said, 'Now we've got two trays, so we'll have to go through the whole thing again. Vivero might have alternated his message between them.'

I said casually, 'What trays?'

Halstead jerked up his head and Fallon turned and looked at me blankly. 'Why, these two here.'

I looked at the table. 'I don't see any trays.'

Fallon looked baffled and began to gobble. 'Are . . . are you nuts? What the hell do you think these are? Flying saucers?'

Halstead looked at me irefully. 'Let's not have any games,' he said. 'Murville called this one a tray; Juan de Vivero called that one a tray, and so did Goosan in his letter to Herrick.'

'I don't give a damn about that,' I said frankly. 'If everyone calls a submarine an aeroplane, it still can't fly. Old Vivero didn't call them trays and he made them. He didn't say, "Here, boys, I'm sending you a couple of nice trays." Let's see what he *did* say. Where's the transcription?'

There was a glint in Fallon's eye as he held out the sheaf of papers which were never far from him. 'You'd better make this good.'

I flipped the sheets over to the last page. 'He said, "I send you gifts made in that marvellous manner which my father learned of that stranger from the East." He also said, "Let the scales of enmity fall from your eyes and look upon these gifts with proper vision." Doesn't that mean anything to you?'

'Not much,' said Halstead.

'These are mirrors,' I said calmly. 'And just because everyone has been using them as trays doesn't alter the fact.'

Halstead made a sound of irritation, but Fallon bent and examined them. I said. 'The bottom of that "tray" isn't copper—it's speculum metal—a reflective surface and it's slightly convex; I've measured it.'

'You could be right at that,' said Fallon. 'So they're mirrors! Where does that get us?'

'Take a closer look,' I advised.

Fallon picked up one of the mirrors and Halstead took the other. After a while Halstead said, 'I don't see anything except the reflection of my own face.'

'I don't do much better,' said Fallon. 'And it's not a good reflective surface, either.'

'What do you expect of a metal mirror that's had things dumped on it for the last four hundred years? But it's a neat trick, and I only came upon it by accident. Have you got a projection screen?'

Fallon smiled. 'Better than that—I have a projection theatre.'

He would have! Nothing small about millionaire Fallon. He led us into a part of the house where I had never been, and into a miniature cinema containing about twenty seats. 'I find this handy for giving informal lectures,' he said.

I looked around. 'Where's the slide projector?'

'In the projection room—back there.'

'I'll want it out here,' I said.

He looked at me speculatively, and shrugged. 'Okay, I'll have it brought in.'

There was a pause of about ten minutes while a couple of his servants brought in the projector and set it on a table in the middle of the room, acting under my instructions. Fallon looked interested; Halstead looked bored; Mrs. Halstead looked beautiful. I winked at her. 'We're going to have a fine show,' I said. 'Will you hold this mirror, Mrs. Halstead?'

I puttered around with the projector. 'I'm using this as a very powerful spotlight,' I said. 'And I'm going to bounce light off the mirror and on to that screen up there. Tell me what you see.'

I switched on the projector light and there was a sharp intake of breath from Fallon, while Halstead lost his boredom in a hurry and practically snapped to attention. I turned and looked at the pattern on the screen. 'What do you think it is?' I asked. 'It's a bit vague, but I think it's a map.'

Fallon said, 'What the hell! How does it . . .? Oh, never mind. Can you rotate that thing a bit, Mrs. Halstead?'

The luminous pattern on the screen twisted and flowed, then steadied in a new orientation. Fallon clicked his tongue. 'I think you're right—it *is* a map. If that indentation on the bottom right is Chetumal Bay—and it's the right shape—then above it we have the bays of Espiritu Santo and Ascension. That makes it the west coast of the Yucatan Peninsula.'

Halstead said, 'What's that circle in the middle?'

'We'll come to that in a minute,' I said, and switched off the light. Fallon bent down and looked at the mirror still held by Mrs. Halstead and shook his head incredulously. He looked at me enquiringly, and I said, 'I came across this bit of trickery by chance. I was taking photographs of my tray—or mirror—and I was a bit ham-handed; I touched the shutter button by accident and the flash went off. When I developed the picture I found that I'd got a bit of the mirror in the frame but most of the picture was an area of wall. The light from the flash had bounced off the mirror and there was something bloody funny about its reflection on the wall, so I went into it a bit deeper.'

Halstead took the mirror from his wife. 'This is impossible. How can a reflection from a plane surface show a selectively variable pattern?' He held up the mirror and moved it before his eyes. 'There's nothing here that shows.'

'It's not a plane mirror—it's slightly convex. I measured it; it has a radius of convexity of about ten feet. This is a Chinese trick.'

'Chinese!'

'Old Vivero said as much. ". . . that stranger from the East which the Moors brought to Cordoba." He was Chinese. That stumped me for a bit—what the hell was a Chinaman doing in Spain in the late fifteenth century? But it's not too odd, if you think about it. The Arab Empire stretched from Spain to India; it's not too difficult to imagine a Chinese metal worker being passed along the line. After all, there were Europeans in China at that date.'

Fallon nodded. 'It's a plausible theory.' He tapped the mirror. 'But how the hell is this thing done?'

'I was lucky,' I said. 'I went to the Torquay Public Library and there it was, all laid out in the ninth edition of the Encyclopaedia Britannica. I was fortunate that the Torquay Library is a bit old-fashioned because that particular item was dropped from later editions.'

I took the mirror from Halstead and laid it flat on the table. 'This is how it works. Forget the gold trimmings and concentrate on the mirror itself. All early Chinese mirrors were of metal, usually cast of bronze. Cast metal doesn't give a good reflective surface so it had to be worked on with scrapers to give a smooth finish. Generally, the scraping was done from the centre to the edge and that gave the finished mirror its slight convexity.'

Fallon took a pen from his pocket and applied it to the mirror, imitating the action of scraping. He nodded and said briefly, 'Go on.'

I said, 'After a while the mirrors began to become more elaborate. They were expensive to make and the manufacturers began to pretty them up a bit. One way of doing this was to put ornamentation on the *back* of the mirror. Usually it was a saying of Buddha cast in raised characters. Now, consider what might happen when such a mirror was scraped. It would be lying on its back on a solid surface, but only the raised characters would be in contact with that surface—the rest of the mirror would be supported by nothing. When scraper pressure was applied the unsupported parts would give a little and a fraction more metal would be removed over the supported parts.'

'Well, I'll be damned!' said Fallon. 'And that makes the difference?'

'In general you have a convex mirror which tends to diffuse reflected light,' I said. 'But you have plane bits where the characters are which reflects light in parallel lines. The convexity is so small that the difference can't be seen by the eye, but the short wavelengths of light show it up in the reflection.'

'When did the Chinese find out about this?' queried Fallon.

'Some time in the eleventh century. It was accidental at first, but later they began to exploit it deliberately. Then they came up with the composite mirror—the back would still have a saying of Buddha, but the mirror would reflect something completely different. There's one in the Ashmolean in Oxford—the back says "Adoration for Amida Buddha" and the reflection shows Buddha himself. It was just a matter of putting a false back on the mirror, as Vivero has done here.'

Halstead turned over the mirror and tapped the gold back experimentally. 'So under here there's a map cast in the bronze?'

'That's it. I rather think Vivero re-invented the composite mirror. There are only three examples known; the one in the Ashmolean, another in the British Museum, and one somewhere in Germany.'

'How do we get the back off?'

'Hold on,' I said. 'I'm not having that mirror ruined. If you rub a mercury amalgam into the mirror surface it improves the reflection a hundred per cent. But a better way would be to X-ray them.'

'I'll arrange it,' said Fallon decisively. 'In the meantime we'll have another look. Switch on that projector.'

I snapped on the light and we studied the vague luminous lines on the screen. After a while Fallon said, 'It sure looks like the coast of Quintana Roo. We can check it against a map.'

'Aren't those words around the edge?' asked Katherine Halstead.

I strained my eyes but it was a bit of a blurred mish-mash nothing was clear. 'Might be,' I said doubtfully.

'And there's that circle in the middle,' said Paul Halstead. 'What's that?'

'I think I've solved that one,' I said. 'Old Vivero wanted to reconcile his sons, so he gave them each a mirror. The puzzle can only be solved by using both mirrors. This one gives a general view, locating the area, and I'll lay ten to one that the other mirror gives a blown-up view of what's in that little circle. Each mirror would be pretty useless on its own.'

'We'll check on that,' said Fallon. 'Where's my mirror?'

The two mirrors were exchanged and we looked at the new pattern. It didn't mean much to me, nor to anyone else. 'It's not *clear* enough,' complained Fallon. 'I'll go blind if we have much more of this.'

'It's been knocked about after four hundred years,' I said. 'But the pattern on the back has been protected. I think that X-rays should give us an excellent picture.'

'I'll have it done as soon as possible.'

I turned off the light and found Fallon dabbing at his eyes with a handkerchief. He smiled at me. 'You're paying your way, Wheale,' he said. 'We might not have found this.'

'You would have found it,' I said positively. 'As soon as your cryptographer had given up in disgust you'd have started to wonder about this and that—such as what was concealed in the bronze-gold interface. What puzzles me is why Vivero's sons didn't do anything about it.'

Halstead said thoughtfully, 'Both branches of the family regarded these things as trays and not mirrors. Perhaps Vivero's rather obscure tip-off just went over their heads. They may have been told the story of the Chinese mirrors as children, when they were too young to really understand.'

'Could be,' agreed Fallon. 'It could also be that the quarrel between them—whatever it was—couldn't be reconciled so easily. Anyway, they didn't do anything about it. The Spanish branch lost their mirror and to the Mexican branch it was reduced to some kind of a legend.' He put his hands on the

79

mirror possessively. 'But we've got them now—that's different.'

II

Looking back, I think it was about this time that Fallon began to lose his grip. One day he went into the city and when he came back he was gloomy and very thoughtful, and from that day on he was given to sudden silences and fits of absent-mindedness. I put it down to the worries of a millionaire—maybe the stock market had dropped or something like that—and I didn't think much about it at the time. Whatever it was it certainly didn't hamper his planning of the Uaxuanoc expedition into which he threw himself with a demoniac energy. I thought it strange that he should be devoting *all* his time to this; surely a millionaire must look after his financial interests—but Fallon wasn't worried about anything else but Uaxuanoc and whatever else it was that had made him go broody.

It was in the same week that I met Pat Harris. Fallon called me into his study, and said, 'I want you to meet Pat Harris—I borrowed him from an oil company I have an interest in. I'm fulfilling my part of the bargain; Harris has been investigating Niscemi.'

I regarded Harris with interest although, on the surface, there was little about him to excite it. He was average in every way; not too tall, not too short, not too beefy and not too scrawny. He wore an average suit and looked the perfect average man. He might have been designed by a statistician. He had a more than average brain—but that didn't show.

He held out his hand. 'Glad to meet you, Mr. Wheale,' he said in a colourless voice.

'Tell Wheale what you found,' ordered Fallon.

Harris clasped his hands in front of his average American paunch. 'Victor Niscemi—small time punk,' he said concisely. 'Not much to say about him. He never was much and he never did much—except get himself rubbed out in England. Reform school education leading to bigger things—but not much bigger. Did time for rolling drunks but that was quite a while ago. Nothing on him in the last four years; he never appeared on a police blotter, I mean. Clean as a whistle as far as his police record goes.'

'That's his official police record, I take it. What about unofficially?'

Harris looked up at me approvingly. 'That's a different matter, of course,' he agreed. 'For a while he did protection for a bookie, then he got into the numbers racket—first as protection for a collector, then as collector himself. He was on his way up in a small way. Then he went to England and got himself shot up. End of Niscemi.'

'And that's all?'

'Not by a hell of a long way,' said Fallon abruptly.

'Go on, Harris.'

Harris moved in his chair and suddenly looked more relaxed. 'There's a thing you've got to remember about a guy like Niscemi—he has friends. Take a look at his record; reform school, petty assault and so on. Then suddenly, four years ago, no more police record. He was still a criminal and still small time, but he no longer got into trouble. He'd acquired friends.'

'Who were . . .?'

'Mr. Wheale, you're English and maybe you don't have the problems we have in the States, so what I'm going to tell you now might seem extraordinary. You'll just have to take my word for it. Okay?'

I smiled. 'After meeting Mr. Fallon there's very little I'll find unbelievable.'

'All right. I'm interested in the weapon with which Niscemi killed your brother. Can you describe it?'

'It was a sawn-off shotgun,' I said.

'And the butt was cut down. Right?' I nodded. 'That was a lupara; it's an Italian word and Niscemi was of Italian origin or, more precisely, Sicilian. About four years ago Niscemi was taken into the Organization. Organized crime is one of the worse facts of life in the United States, Mr. Wheale; and it's mostly run by Italian Americans. It goes under many names—the Organization, the Syndicate, Cosa Nostra, the Mafia—although Mafia should strictly be reserved for the parent organization in Sicily.'

I looked at Harris uncertainly. 'Are you trying to tell me that the Mafia—the Mafia, for God's sake!—had my brother killed?'

'Not quite,' he said. 'I think Niscemi slipped up there. He certainly slipped up when he got *himself* killed. But I'd better describe what goes on with young punks like Niscemi when they're recruited into the Organization. The first thing he's told is to keep his nose clean—he keeps out of the way of the cops and he does what his capo—his boss—tells him, and nothing else. That's important, and it explains why Niscemi suddenly stopped figuring on the police blotter.' Harris pointed a finger at me. 'But it works the other way round, too. If Niscemi was up to no good with regard to your brother it certainly meant that he was acting under orders. The Organization doesn't stand for members who go in to bat on their own account.'

'So he was *sent*?'

'There's a ninety-nine per cent probability that he was.'

This was beyond me and I couldn't quite believe it. I turned to Fallon. 'I believe you said that Mr. Harris is an employee of an oil company. What qualifications has he for assuming all this?'

'Harris was in the F.B.I.,' said Fallon.

'For fifteen years,' said Harris. 'I thought you might find this extraordinary.'

'I do,' I said briefly, and thought about it. 'Where did you get this information about Niscemi?'

'From the Detroit police—that was his stamping-ground.'

I said, 'Scotland Yard is interested in this. Are the American police collaborating with them?'

Harris smiled tolerantly. 'In spite of all the sensational stuff about Interpol there's not much that can be done in a case like this. Who are they going to nail for the job? The American law authorities are just glad to have got Niscemi out of their hair, and he was only small time, anyway.' He grinned and came up with an unexpected and parodied quotation. ' "It was in another country and, besides, the guy is dead." '

Fallon said, 'It goes much further than this. Harris is not finished yet.'

'Okay,' said Harris. 'We now come to the questions: Who sent Niscemi to England—and why? Niscemi's capo is Jack Gatt, but Jack might have been doing some other capo a favour. However, I don't think so.'

'Gatt!' I blurted out. 'He was in England at the time of my brother's death.'

Harris shook his head. 'No, he wasn't. I checked him out on that. On the day your brother died he was in New York.'

'But he wanted to buy something from Bob,' I said. 'He made an offer in the presence of witnesses. He *was* in England.'

'Air travel is wonderful,' said Harris. 'You can leave London at nine a.m. and arrive in New York at eleven-thirty a.m.—local time. Gatt certainly didn't kill your brother.' He pursed his lips, then added, 'Not personally.'

'Who—and what—is he?'

'Top of the heap in Detroit,' said Harris promptly. 'Covers Michigan and a big slice of Ohio. Original name, Giacomo Gattini—Americanized to Jack Gatt. He doesn't stand very tall in the Organization, but he's a capo and that makes him important.'

'I think you'd better explain that.'

'Well, the Organization controls crime, but it's not a centralized business like, say, General Motors. It's pretty loose, in fact; so loose that sometimes pieces of it conflict with each other. That's called a gang war. But they're bad for business, attract too much attention from the cops, so once in a while all the capos get together in a council, a sort of board meeting, to iron out their difficulties. They allocate territory, slap down the hotheads and decide when and how to enforce the rules.'

This was the raw and primitive world that had intruded on Hay Tree Farm, so far away in Devon. I said, 'How do they do that?'

Harris shrugged. 'Suppose a capo like Gatt decided to ignore the top bosses and go it on his own. Pretty soon a young punk like Niscemi would blow into town, knock off Gatt and scram. If he failed then another would try it and, sooner or later, one would succeed. Gatt knows that, so he doesn't break the rules. But, while he keeps to the rules, he's capo—king in his own territory.'

'I see. But why should Gatt go to England?'

'Ah,' said Harris. 'Now we're coming to the meat of it. Let's take a good look at Jack Gatt. This is a third-generation American mafioso. He's no newly arrived Siciliano peasant who can't speak English, nor is he a half-educated tough bum like Capone. Jack's got civilization; Jack's got culture. His daughter is at finishing school in Switzerland; one son is at a good college in the east and the other runs his own business—a legitimate business. Jack goes to the opera and ballet; in fact I hear that he's pretty near the sole support of one

83

ballet group. He collects pictures, and when I say collects I don't mean that he steals them. He puts up bids at the Parke-Bernet Gallery in New York like any other millionaire, and he does the same at Sotheby's and Christie's in England. He has a good-looking wife and a fine house, mixes in the best society and cuts a fine figure among the best people, none of whom know that he's anything other than a legitimate businessman. He's that, too, of course; I wouldn't be surprised if he wasn't one of your biggest shareholders, Mr. Fallon.'

'I'll check on it,' said Fallon sourly. 'And how does he derive his main income? The illegitimate part?'

'Gambling, drugs, prostitution, extortion, protection,' reeled off Harris glibly. 'And any combination or permutation. Jack's come up with some real dillies.'

'My God!' said Fallon.

'That's as maybe,' I said. 'But how did Niscemi suddenly pitch up at the farm? The photograph of the tray only appeared in the Press a few days before. How did Gatt get on to it so fast?'

Harris hesitated and looked at Fallon enquiringly. Fallon said glumly, 'You might as well have the whole story. I was upset at Halstead's accusation that I stole the Vivero letter from him, so I put Harris on to checking it.' He nodded to Harris.

'Gatt had men following Mr. Fallon and probably Halstead, too,' said Harris. 'This is how it came about.

'Halstead *did* have the Vivero letter before Mr. Fallon. He bought it here in Mexico for $200. Then he took it home to the States—he lived in Virginia at the time—and his house was burgled. The letter was one of the things that were stolen.' He put the tips of his fingers together and said, 'The way I see it, the Vivero letter was taken by sheer chance. It was in a locked briefcase that was taken with the other stuff.'

'What other stuff?' I asked.

'Household goods. TV set, radios, a watch, some clothing and a little money.'

Fallon cocked a sardonic eye at me. 'Can you see me interested in second-hand clothing?'

'I think it was a job done by a small-time crook,' said Harris. 'The easily saleable stuff would be got rid of fast—there are plenty of unscrupulous dealers who'd take it. I daresay the thief was disappointed by the contents of the briefcase.'

'But it got to the right man—Gerryson,' I said. 'How did he get hold of it?'

'I wondered about that myself,' said Harris. 'And I gave Gerryson a thorough going-over. His reputation isn't too good; the New York cops are pretty sure he's a high-class fence. One curious thing turned up—he's friendly with Jack Gatt. He stays at Jack's house when he's in Detroit.'

He leaned forward. 'Now, this is a purely hypothetical reconstruction. The burglar who did the Halstead residence found himself with the Vivero letter; it was no good to him because, even if he realized it had some value, he wouldn't know how much and he wouldn't know where to sell it safely. Well, there are ways and means. My guess is, it was passed along channels until it came to someone who recognized its value—and who would that be but Jack Gatt, the cultured hood who owns a little museum of his own. Now, I don't know the contents of this letter, but my guess is that if Gatt was excited by it then he'd check back to the source—to Halstead.'

'And what about Gerryson?'

'Maybe that was Gatt's way of getting a second opinion,' said Harris blandly. 'Mr. Fallon and I have been talking about it, and we've come to some conclusions.'

Fallon looked sheepish. 'Er . . . it's like this . . . I . . . er . . . I paid $2,000 to Gerryson for the letter.'

'So what,' I said.

He avoided my eyes. 'I knew the price was too low. It's worth more than that.'

I grinned. 'You thought it might be . . . is the word *hot*, Mr. Harris?'

Harris winked. 'That's the word.'

'No,' said Fallon vehemently. 'I thought Gerryson was making a mistake. If a dealer makes a mistake it's his business —they take us collectors to the cleaners often enough. I thought I was taking Gerryson, for a change.'

'But you've changed your mind since.'

Harris said, 'I think Mr. Fallon got took. I think Gatt fed the letter to him through Gerryson just to see what he'd do about it. After all, he couldn't rely on Halstead who is only another young and inexperienced archeologist. But if he gave the letter to Mr. Fallon, who is the top man in the business, and then Mr. Fallon started to run around in the same circles as Halstead, Gatt would be certain he was on the right track.'

'Plausible, but bloody improbable,' I said.

'Is it? Jack Gatt is no dumb bunny,' said Harris earnestly. 'He's highly intelligent and educated enough to see a profit in things that would be right over any other hood's head. If there's any dough in this Gatt will be after it.'

I thought of the golden gutters of the roofs of Uaxuanoc and of the king's palace plated with gold within and without. I thought of the mountain of gold and the burning sign of gold which Vivero had described. Harris could very well be right.

He said, 'I think that Halstead and Mr. Fallon have been trailed wherever they've been. I think that Niscemi was one of the trailers, which is why he was on the spot when your golden tray was discovered. He tipped off Gatt, and Gatt flew across and made your brother an offer for it. I've investigated his movements at the time and it all checks out. When your brother turned him down flat he told Niscemi to get the tray the hard way. That wasn't something that would worry Jack Gatt, but he made damned sure that he wasn't even in the country when the job was pulled. And then Niscemi—and whoever else was with him—bungled it, and he got himself killed.'

And Gatt was the man whom that simple Devonshire farmer, Hannaford, had liked so much. I said, 'How can we get at the bastard?'

'This is all theoretical,' said Harris. 'It wouldn't stand up in a law court.'

'Maybe it's too theoretical,' I said. 'Maybe it didn't happen like that at all.'

Harris smiled thinly, and said, 'Gatt has this house under observation right now—and Halstead's house in the city. I can show you the guys who are watching you.'

I came to attention at that and looked at Fallon, who nodded. 'Harris is having the observers watched.'

That put a different complexion on things. I said, 'Are they Gatt's men?'

Harris frowned. 'Now that's hard to say. Let's say that someone in Mexico is doing Gatt a favour—the Organization works like that; they swap favours all the time.'

Fallon said, 'I'll have to do something about Gatt.'

Harris asked curiously, 'Such as?'

'I swing a lot of weight,' said Fallon. 'A hundred million dollars' worth.' He smiled confidently. 'I'll just lean on him.'

Harris looked alarmed. 'I wouldn't do that—not to Jack Gatt. You might be able to work that way with an ordinary business competitor, but not with him. He doesn't like pressure.'

'What could he do about it?' asked Fallon contemptuously.

'He could put you out of business—permanently. A bullet carries more weight than a hundred million dollars, Mr. Fallon.'

Fallon suddenly looked shrunken. For the first time he had run into a situation in which his wealth didn't count, where he couldn't buy what he wanted. I had given him a slight dose of the same medicine but that was nothing to the shock handed him by Harris. Fallon wasn't a bad old stick but he'd had money for so long that he tended to handle it with a casual ruthlessness—a club to get what he wanted. And now he had come up against a man even more ruthless who didn't give a damn for Fallon's only weapon. It seemed to take the pith out of him.

I felt sorry for him and, more out of pity than anything else, I made conversation with Harris in order to give him time to pull himself together. 'I think it's time you were told what's at stake here,' I said. 'Then you might be able to guess what Gatt will do about it. But it's a long story.'

'I don't know that I want to know,' said Harris wryly. 'If it's big enough to get Jack Gatt out of Detroit it must be dynamite.'

'Is he out of Detroit?'

'He's not only out of Detroit—he's in Mexico City.' Harris spread his hands. 'He says he's here for the Olympic Games —what else?' he said cynically.

Five

As I dressed next morning I reflected on the strange turns a man's life can take. Four weeks previously I had been a London accountant—one of the bowler hat brigade—and now I was in exotic Mexico and preparing to take a jump into even more exotic territory. From what I could gather from Fallon the mysteriously named Quintana Roo was something of a hell hole. And why was I going to Quintana Roo? To hunt for a lost city, for God's sake! If, four weeks before, anyone had offered that as a serious prediction I would have considered him a candidate for the booby-hatch.

I knotted my tie and looked consideringly at the man facing me in the mirror: Jemmy Wheale, New Elizabethan, adventurer at large—*have gun, will travel*. The thought made me smile, and the man in the mirror smiled back at me derisively. I didn't have a gun and I doubted whether I could use one effectively, anyway. I suppose a James Bond type would have unpacked his portable helicopter and taken off after Jack Gatt long ago, bringing back his scalp and a couple of his choicest blondes. Hell, I didn't even look like Sean Connery.

So what was I supposed to do about Jack Gatt? From what Pat Harris had said Gatt was in an unassailable position from the legal point even if he had given the word to Niscemi. There wasn't a single charge to be brought against him that would stick. And for me to tackle Gatt on his own terms would be unthinkably stupid—the nearest analogy I could think of was Monaco declaring war on Russia and the United States.

What the devil was I doing in Mexico, anyway? I looked back on the uncharacteristic actions of my recent past and decided that the barbed words of that silly little bitch, Sheila, had probably set me off. Many men have been murdered in the past, but their brothers haven't run around the world thirsting for vengeance. Sheila's casual words had stabbed me in the ego and everything I had done since then had been to prove to myself that what she had said wasn't true. Which only went to show I was immature and probably a bit soft in the head.

Yet I had taken those actions and now I was stuck with the consequences. If I quit now and went back to England, then I suppose I'd regret it for the rest of my life. There would always be the nagging suspicion that I had run out on life and somehow betrayed myself, and that was something I knew I couldn't live with. I wondered how many other men did stupidly dangerous things because of a suspected assault on their self-respect.

For a short period I had talked big. I had browbeaten a millionaire into doing what I wanted him to do, but that was only because I had a supreme bargaining counter—the Vivero mirror. Now Fallon had the mirror and its secret and I was thrown back on my own resources. I didn't think he'd break his promises, but there wasn't a thing I could do if he reneged.

The grey little man was still around. He was dressed in some pretty gaudy and ill-fitting clothes and he wore his disguise with panache, but he wished to God he wore his conservative suit and his bowler hat and carried his rolled umbrella instead of this silly lance. I pulled a sour face at the man in the mirror; Jemmy Wheale—sheep in wolf's clothing.

My mood was uncertain and ambivalent as I left the room.

I found Pat Harris downstairs wearing a stethoscope and carrying a little black box from which protruded a shiny telescopic antenna. He waggled his hand at me frantically and put his finger to his lips, elaborately miming that I should be quiet. He circled the room like a dog in a strange place, crisscrossing back and forwards, and gradually narrowed his attention to the big refectory table of massive Spanish oak.

Suddenly he got down on to his hands and knees and disappeared beneath the table, completing his resemblance to a dog. All I could see were the seat of his pants and the soles of his shoes; his pants were all right, but his shoes needed repairing. After a while he backed out, gave me a grin, and put his finger to his lips again. He beckoned, indicating that I should join him, so I squatted down, feeling a bit silly. He flicked a switch and a narrow beam of light shot from the little torch he held. It roamed about the underside of the table and then held steady. He pointed, and I saw a small grey metal box half hidden behind a crossbeam.

He jerked his thumb and we climbed out from under the table and he led me at a quick walk out of the room, down the passage, and into Fallon's study which was empty. 'We've been bugged,' he said.

I gaped at him. 'You mean, that thing is . . .'

'. . . a radio transmitter.' He took the stethoscope from his ears with the air of a doctor about to impart bad news. 'This gadget is a bug finder. I sweep the frequencies and if there's a transmitter working close by this thing howls at me through the earphones. Then, to find it, all I have to do is watch the meter.'

I said nervously, 'Hadn't you better shut up about it?' I looked about the study. 'This place . . .'

'It's clean,' he said abruptly. 'I've checked it out.'

'Good God!' I said. 'What made you think there even might be anything like that?'

He grinned. 'A nasty suspicious mind and a belief in

human nature. I just thought what I'd do if I were Jack Gatt and wanted to know what goes on in this house. Besides, it's standard procedure in my business.' He rubbed his chin. 'Was anything said in that room—anything important?'

I said cautiously, 'Do you know anything about what we're trying to do?'

'It's all right—Fallon filled me in on everything. We stayed up pretty late last night.' His eyes lit up. 'What a hell of a story—if true!'

I cast my mind back. 'We were all standing around that table talking about the trays. It was then I broke the news that they were really mirrors.'

'That's not too good,' said Harris.

'But then we went into the projection room,' I said. 'And I demonstrated what would happen when you bounced a light off the mirrors. Everything else was said in there.'

'Show me this projection room,' said Harris. So I showed him, and he donned his stethoscope and spent a few minutes twiddling the knobs on his gadget. At last he unclipped the earphones. 'Nothing here; so there's a good chance that Gatt knows only that these things are mirrors but can't know the particular significance.'

We went back into the study and found both Fallon and Halstead. Fallon was unsealing a large envelope, but stopped dead when he heard what Harris had to say. 'The conniving bastard!' he said in some wonder. 'Rip out the goddamn thing.'

'Hell, no!' objected Harris. 'I want that transmitter left where it is. It will be useful.' He looked at us with a slow smile. 'Do any of you gentlemen fancy yourselves as radio actors? I think we can feed Jack Gatt quite a line. All you have to remember is to say nothing important in that room.'

Fallon laughed. 'You're quite a conniver yourself, Harris.'

'I'm a professional,' said Harris easily. 'I don't think we'll make it a live show; there'd be too much chance of a slip-up. This calls for a nicely edited tape which we can feed into that microphone.' He paused. 'I'll keep an eye on that room. Someone will have to change the batteries; they won't last for ever.'

'But where is it transmitting to?' asked Halstead.

'Probably the car that's parked up the road a piece. Those two guys have been staked out there for a couple of days now. My guess is that they have a receiver linked to a tape-recorder. I won't bother them until they've swallowed the story we're going to concoct, and maybe not even then. It's one thing knowing something, but it's even better when the opposition doesn't know that you know it. My advice is to come the innocent bit. You're not supposed to know that Jack Gatt even exists.'

Fallon was right about Harris; he was the most deceitful man I've ever met, and an accountant is no stranger to wool-pulling. When I came to know him better I'd trust him with my life, but I wouldn't trust him not to know more about me than I did myself. His business was information and he gathered it assiduously, on the job and off it. He had a mind like a well-organized computer memory but, unlike a good computer, he tended to play tricks with what he knew.

Fallon ripped open the envelope. 'Let's get down to business. These are the X-ray prints—life size.' He sorted them out and gave us each two prints, one of each mirror.

They were very good, startling in clarity of details that had only been hinted at in the screened reflections. I said, 'Mrs. Halstead was right; these are words around the circumference.' I looked closer. 'I can't read Spanish.'

Fallon took a reading glass and mumbled a bit to himself. 'As near as I can make out it goes something like this. On your mirror it says: "The path to true glory leads through the portals of death." And on my mirror: "Life everlasting lies beyond the grave." '

'Morbid!' commented Harris.

'Not very precise instructions,' said Halstead ironically.

'It *may* mean something,' said Fallon doubtfully. 'But one thing is certain; this is definitely the coast of Quintana Roo.' He moved the magnifying glass over the print. 'And, by God, cities are indicated. See those square castle-like things?'

I sensed the air of rising excitement. 'Those two at the top must be Coba and Tulum,' said Halstead tensely. 'With Chichen Itza to the west.'

'And there's Ichpatuun on Chetumal Bay. And what's that south of Tulum? Would that be Chunyaxche?' Fallon lifted his head and stared into the middle distance. 'A city was discovered there not long ago. There's a theory it was the centre of the seaboard trade on the coast.'

Halstead's hand stabbed down. 'There's another city indicated just inland of it—and another here.' His voice cracked. 'And here's another. If this map is accurate we'll be discovering lost cities by the bushel.'

'Take it easy,' said Fallon and laid the print aside. 'Let's have a look at Uaxuanoc.' He took the other print and stared at it. 'If this corresponds to the small circle on the large-scale map then we ought to be able to pinpoint the position.'

I looked at my copy. Hills were indicated but there was no scale to tell how high they were. Scattered over the hills were crude representations of buildings. I remembered that Vivero had said in his letter that the city was built on a ridge lying east and west.

Halstead said, 'The layout looks like a mixture of Chichen Itza and Coba—but it's bigger than either. A lot bigger.'

'There's the cenote,' said Fallon. 'So this place would be the temple of Yum Chac—if Vivero is to be believed. I wonder which is the king's palace?' He turned and grasped a large cardboard tube from which he took a map. 'I've spent a lot of time on this map,' he said. 'A lifetime.'

He unrolled it and spread it on the desk, weighing down the corners with books. 'Everything the Mayas ever built is marked here. Do you notice anything odd about it, Wheale?'

I contemplated the map and said at last, 'It looks crowded in the south.'

'That's the Peten—but that was the Old Empire which collapsed in the eleventh century. The Itzas moved in later—new blood which gave the Mayas a shot in the arm like a transfusion. They reoccupied some of the old cities like Chichen Itza and Coba, and they built some new ones like Mayapan. Forget the south; concentrate on the Yucatan Peninsula itself. What looks funny about it?'

'This blank space on the west. Why didn't they build there?'

'Who says they didn't?' asked Fallon. 'That's the Quintana Roo. The local inhabitants have a rooted objection to archeologists.' He tapped the map. 'They killed an archeologist here, and built his skeleton into a wall facing the sea as a sort of decoration—and as a warning to others.' He grinned. 'Still want to come along?'

The grey little man inside me made a frightened squawk but I grinned back at him. 'I'll go where you go.'

He nodded. 'That was a while ago. The indios sublevados have shot their bolt. But it's still not a pleasure trip. The inhabitants tend to be hostile—both the chicleros and the Chan

92

Santa Rosa Indians; and the land itself is worse. That's the reason for this big blank space—and Uaxuanoc is plumb in the middle.'

He bent over the map, and compared it with the print. 'I'd put it about there—give or take twenty miles. Vivero didn't have the benefit of a trigonometric survey when he did this scrawl; we can't rely on it too much.'

Halstead shook his head. 'It's going to be one hell of a job.' He looked up and found me smiling. I couldn't see what was going to be difficult about it. I'd been browsing through Fallon's library and studying the pictures of Mayan cities; there were pyramids the size of the Washington Pentagon, and I didn't see how you could miss seeing one of those.

Halstead said coldly, 'Take a circle twenty miles across— that's over three hundred square miles to search. You can walk within ten feet of a Mayan structure and not see it.' His lips drew back in a humourless smile. 'You can even be walk- ing *on* it and not know it. You'll learn.'

I shrugged and let it pass. I didn't believe it was as bad as that.

Fallon said worriedly, 'What I don't know is why this man Gatt should be so interested. I can't see any conceivable motive for his interference.'

I regarded Fallon in astonished silence, then said, 'The gold, of course! Gatt is a treasure hunter.'

Fallon had a baffled look on his face. 'What gold?' he said dimly.

It was my turn to be baffled. 'You've read the Vivero letter, damn it! Doesn't he describe the king's palace as being plated with gold? Doesn't he go on and on about gold? He even men- tions a mountain of gold!'

Halstead gave a shout of laughter and Fallon looked at me as though I had gone out of my mind. 'Where would the Mayas get the gold to cover a building?' he demanded. 'Use a bit of common sense, Wheale.'

For a moment I thought I *had* gone crazy. Halstead was laughing his head off and Fallon was looking at me with an air of concern. I turned to Harris who spread his hands and shrugged elaborately. 'It beats me,' he said.

Halstead was still struggling to contain himself. It was the first time I'd seen him genuinely amused at anything. 'I don't see what's funny,' I said acidly.

'Don't you?' he said, and wiped his eyes. He broke into

93

chuckles. 'It's the funniest thing I've heard in years. Tell him, Fallon.'

'Do you really think Uaxuanoc is dripping in gold—or that it ever was?' Fallon asked. He too was smiling as though an infection had spread to him from Halstead.

I began to get angry. 'Vivero said so, didn't he?' I picked up the prints and thrust them under Fallon's nose. 'You believe in these, don't you? Vivero placed cities where you *know* there are cities, so you believe him that far. What's so bloody funny about the rest of his story?'

'Vivero was the biggest liar in the western hemisphere,' said Fallon. He looked at me in wonder. 'I thought you knew. I told you he was a liar. You've heard us discussing it.'

I told myself to relax, and said slowly, 'Would you mind spelling it out again in words of one syllable?' I glanced at Harris who, by his expression, was as puzzled as I was. 'I'm sure that Mr. Harris would like to be let in on the joke, too.'

'Oh, I see,' said Fallon. 'You really took the Vivero letter at its face value.' Halstead again broke into laughter; I was getting pretty tired of that.

Fallon said, 'Let's take one or two points in the letter. He said the de Viveros were of ancient lineage and had been hammered by the Moors so that the family fortunes were lost. He was a goddamn liar. His father was a goldsmith— that's true enough—but his grandfather was a peasant who came from a long line of peasants—of nobodies. His father's name was Vivero, and it was Manuel himself who added on the aristocratic prefix and changed it to de Vivero. He did that in Mexico—he would never have got away with it in Spain. By the time Murville visited the Mexican branch of the family the myth had really taken hold. That's why he couldn't believe that a de Vivero had actually made the tray.'

'So he was a liar on that point. Lots of people lie about themselves and their families. But how do you know he was lying about the gold? And why should he spin a yarn like that?'

'All the gold the Mayas ever had was imported,' said Fallon. 'It came from Mexico, from Panama and from the Caribbean islands. These people were neolithic, they weren't metal workers. Look at Vivero's description of their weapons— wooden swords with stone edges. He was right there, but the stone would be obsidian.'

'But the Mayas *had* gold,' I objected. 'Look what they found

94

when the cenote at Chichen Itza was dredged.' I'd read about that.

'So what did they find? A hell of a lot of gold objects—all imported,' said Fallon. 'Chichen Itza was an important religious centre and the cenote was sacred. You find sacred wells all over the world in which offerings are made, and cenotes are particularly important in Yucatan because water is so precious. There were pilgrimages made to Chichen Itza over a period of hundreds of years.'

Harris said, 'You can't put up a public fountain in New York without people throwing money into it.'

'Exactly,' said Fallon in a pleased voice. 'There seems to be a primitive attraction to water in that sense. Three Coins in the Fountain—and all that kind of thing. But the Mayas had no gold of their own.'

I was confused. 'Then why the hell should Vivero say they had?'

'Ah, that puzzled me at first, but Halstead and I discussed it and we've come up with a theory.'

'I'd be pleased to hear it,' I said sourly.

'Vivero found *something*—there's no doubt about that. But what it was, we don't know. He was cryptic about it because no doubt, he didn't want to give the secret away to anyone who might read that letter. The one thing he was quite clear about was that he wanted to reserve the honour of discovery for his sons—for the de Vivero family. So if he couldn't actually tell his sons this mysterious secret then he had to find some other way of attracting them—and that was what they would confidently expect to find. Gold!'

I slumped in my chair dejectedly. 'And why would the Spaniards be expecting to find gold where there wasn't any? You've got me going round in circles.'

'It's simple enough. The Spaniards came to Mexico looking for plunder—and they found it. They raided the Aztecs and found gold in plenty in the temple treasuries and in Montezuma's palace. What they failed to realize was that it wasn't a *continuing* supply. They weren't deep-thinking men and it never occurred to them that this hoard of gold which they had looted from the Aztecs had been built up over centuries, a little year by year. They thought there must be a major source, a huge mine, perhaps. They gave it a name, They called it Eldorado—and they never stopped looking for it. It didn't exist.

'Consider these Spanish soldiers. After they had looted the Aztecs Cortes divided the spoils. When he had received and swindled his captains, and the captains had put their sticky fingers into what was left, there was little enough for the common soldiers. A gold chain, perhaps—or a wine cup. These men were soldiers, not settlers, and always on the other side of the hill was Eldorado. So they attacked the Mayas, thinking this was Eldorado and, after the Mayas, Pizarro attacked the Incas of Peru. They brought down whole civilizations because they weren't prepared to sweat and dig the gold from the ground themselves. It was there, right enough, but it certainly wasn't in Yucatan. The Mayas, like the Aztecs, certainly had plenty of gold, but not in such quantities that they could cover buildings or make rainwater gutters from the stuff. The nobles wore small pieces of gold jewellery and the temple priests used certain gold implements.'

Harris said, 'So all this talk about gold by Vivero was just a come-on to get his boys moving?'

'It seems so,' said Fallon. 'Oh, I daresay he did surprise the Mayas by melting gold and casting it. That was something they hadn't seen before. I'll show you a piece of genuine Mayan goldwork and you'll see what I mean.' He went to a safe, unlocked it, and returned with a small gold disk. 'This is a plate, probably used by a noble. You can see it's very nicely chased.'

It was very thin and flimsy looking. The design was of a warrior holding a spear and a shield with other figures bearing odd shaped objects. Fallon said, 'That probably started out as a nugget found in a mountain stream a long way from Yucatan. The Mayas beat it flat into its present shape and incised that design with stone tools.'

I said, 'What about the mountain of gold? Was that another of Vivero's lies? Couldn't there have been a mine?'

'Not a chance,' said Fallon decisively. 'The geology is dead against it. The Yucatan Peninsula is a limestone cap—not auriferous at all. No other metals, for that matter—that's why the Mayas never got out of the Stone Age, smart though they were.'

I sighed. 'All right, I accept it. No gold.'

'Which brings us back to Gatt,' said Fallon. 'What the hell is he after?'

'Gold,' I said.

'But I've just told you there is no gold,' said Fallon exasperately.

'So you did,' I said. 'And you convinced me. You convinced Harris, too.' I swung round to face Harris. 'Before you heard this explanation did you believe there was gold in Yucatan?'

'I thought that was what this was all about,' he said. 'Buried treasure in ruined cities.'

'There you are,' I said. 'What makes you think Gatt believes any different? He may be an educated man, but he's no archeological expert. I'm not an illiterate myself, and I believed in buried treasure. I didn't have the technical knowledge to know Vivero was lying, so why should Gatt? Of course he's after the gold. He has the same mentality as the Conquistadores—just another gangster unwilling to sweat for his money.'

Fallon looked surprised. 'Of course. I hadn't allowed for the lay mind. He must be told the truth.'

Harris wore a crooked smile. 'Do you think he'd believe you?' he asked sardonically. 'Not after reading the Vivero letter, he wouldn't. Hell, I can still see that king's palace all shiny in the sun, even though I know it's not true. You'd have a whale of a job convincing Gatt.'

'Then he must be a stupid man,' said Fallon.

'No, Gatt's not stupid,' said Harris. 'He just believes that men who spend as much time as you have on this thing, men who are willing to spend time in the jungle looking for something, are looking for something very valuable. Gatt doesn't believe that scientific knowledge is particularly valuable, so it must be dough. He just measures you by his own standards, that's all.'

'Heaven forbid!' said Fallon fervently.

'You're going to have trouble with Jack,' said Harris. 'He doesn't give up easily.' He nodded to the prints on the table. 'Where did you have those made?'

'I have an interest in an engineering company in Tampico. I had the use of a metallurgical X-ray outfit.'

'I'd better check up on that,' said Harris. 'Gatt might get on to it.'

'But I've got the negatives here.'

Harris looked at him pityingly. 'What makes you think those are the only negatives? I doubt if they'd get it right first time—they'd give you the best of a series. I want to see what has happened to the others and have them destroyed before Gatt starts spreading palm-oil among your ill-paid technicians.'

Harris was a professional and never gave up. He had a total disbelief in the goodness of human nature.

II

Fallon's way of organizing an archeological expedition was to treat it like a military operation—something on the same scale as the landing on Omaha Beach. This was no penurious egghead scratching along on a foundation grant and stretching every dollar to cover the work of two. Fallon was a multimillionaire with a bee in his bonnet and he could, and did, spend money as though he had a personal pipeline to Fort Knox. The money he spent to find Uaxuanoc would have been enough to build the damn place.

His first idea was to go in by sea, but the coast of Quintana Roo is cluttered up with islands and uncharted shoals and he saw the difficulties looming ahead so he abandoned the idea. He wasn't troubled about it; he merely chartered a small fleet of air freighters and flew his supplies in. To do this he had to send in a construction crew to build an airstrip at the head of Ascension Bay. This eventually became his base camp.

As soon as the airstrip was usable he sent in a photographic reconnaissance aircraft which operated from the base and which did an aerial survey, not only of the area in which Uaxuanoc was suspected to be, but of the entire provinces of Quintana Roo and Yucatan. This seemed a bit extravagant so I asked him why he did it. His answer was simple: he was co-operating with the Mexican Government in return for certain favours—it seemed that the cartographic department of the State Survey was very short on information about those areas and Fallon had agreed to supply a photo-mosaic.

'The only person who ever took aerial photographs of Quintana Roo was Lindbergh,' he said. 'And that was a long time ago. It will all come in very useful professionally.'

From Ascension Bay helicopters set up Camp Two in the interior. Fallon and Halstead spent quite a lot of time debating where to set up Camp Two. They measured the X-ray prints to the last millimetre and transferred reading to Fallon's big map and eventually came to a decision. Theoretically, Camp Two should have been set up smack on the top of the temple of Yum Chac in Uaxuanoc. It wasn't, of course; but that surprised nobody.

Halstead favoured me with one of his rare smiles, but there didn't seem to be much real humour in it. 'A field trip is like being in the army,' he said. 'You can use all the mechanization you like, but the job gets done by guys using their own feet. You're still going to regret coming on this jaunt, Wheale.'

I had the distinct impression that he was waiting for me to fall flat on my face when we got out in the field. He was the kind of man who would laugh himself silly at someone slipping on a banana skin and breaking his leg. A primitive sense of humour! Also, he didn't like me very much.

While all this was going on we stayed at Fallon's place outside Mexico City. The Halsteads had given up their own place and had moved in, so we were all together. Pat Harris was around from time to time. He departed upon mysterious trips without warning and came back just as unexpectedly. I suppose he reported to Fallon but he said nothing to the rest of us for the quite simple reason that everyone was too busy to ask him.

Fallon came to me one day, and said, 'About your skin-diving experience. Were you serious?'

'Quite serious. I've done a lot of it.'

'Good,' he said. 'When we find Uaxuanoc we'll want to investigate the cenote.'

'I'll need more equipment,' I said. 'The stuff I have is good enough for an amateur within reach of civilization but not for the middle of Quintana Roo.'

'What kind of equipment?'

'Oh, an air compressor for recharging bottles is one of the biggest items.' I paused. 'If the dives are more than a hundred and fifty feet I'd like a stand-by recompression chamber in case anyone gets into trouble.'

He nodded. 'Okay; get your equipment.'

He turned away and I said gently, 'What do I use in place of money?'

He stopped. 'Oh, yes. I'll ask my secretary to arrange all that. See him tomorrow.'

'Who is going down with me?'

'You need someone else?' he asked in surprise.

'That's a cardinal rule—you don't dive alone. Especially into the murky depths of a hole in the ground. Too many things can go wrong underwater.'

'Well, hire somebody.' he said a little irritably. This was a minor part of the main problem and he was only too eager to get rid of it.

So I went shopping and bought some lovely expensive equipment. Most of it was available locally, but the recompression chamber was more difficult. I saw Fallon's secretary about that and a few telephone calls to the States produced a minor flap in the far-flung Fallon empire; it also produced a recompression chamber on the first available air freighter. Maybe that piece of equipment was an extravagance, but it's one thing getting the bends in England where the port hospitals are equipped to handle it and where the Navy will give a hand in an emergency, and it's quite another thing to have nitrogen bubbling in your blood like champagne in the middle of a blasted wilderness. I preferred to play safe. Besides, Fallon could afford it.

I ended up with enough gear to outfit an average aqualung club, and normally I should have been full of gloating at the opportunity to handle and use all those efficient and well-designed tools of the diver's trade—but I wasn't. It had come too easy. This wasn't something I'd sweated for, something I'd saved up to buy, and I began to see why rich people became bored so easily and began to indulge in way-out entertainments. Not that Fallon was like that, to give him his due; he was all archeologist and very professional.

Then I rounded up Katherine Halstead and took her down to the pool. 'All right,' I said. 'Show me.'

She looked at me in surprise. 'Show you what?'

I pointed to the scuba harness I had brought down. 'Show me that you can use that thing.'

I watched her as she put it on and made no attempt to help her. She seemed familiar enough with it and chose the belt weights with care, and when she went into the water she did it the right way without any fuss. I put on my own gear and followed her and we drifted around the bottom of the pool while I tested her on the international signals which she seemed to understand. When we came out, I said, 'You're hired.'

She looked puzzled. 'Hired for what?'

'As second string diver on the Uaxuanoc Expedition.'

Her face lit up. 'You really mean that?'

'Fallon told me to hire someone—and you can't come along as a passenger. I'll tell him the bad news.'

He blew up as predicted, but I argued him into it by saying that Katherine at least knew something about archeology and that he wouldn't get an archeological diver this side of the Mediterranean.

She must have worked on her husband because he didn't object, but I caught him looking at me speculatively. I think it was then that he was bitten by the bug of jealousy and began to have the idea that I was up to no good. Not that I cared what he thought; I was too busy drilling his wife into the routine of learning how to use the air compressor and the recompression chamber. We got pretty matey and soon we were on first name terms. Up to then I'd always called her Mrs. Halstead, but you can hardly stick to that kind of thing when you're both ducking in and out of a pool. But I never laid a finger on her.

Halstead never called me anything but Wheale.

III

I liked Pat Harris. As a person he was slow and easy-going, no matter how mistrustful and devious he was when on the job. Just before we were due to leave for Quintana Roo he seemed to be spending more time at the house and we got into the habit of having a noggin together late at night. Once I asked him, 'What exactly is your job, Pat?'

He ran his finger down the outside of his beer glass. 'I suppose you could call me Fallon's trouble-shooter. When you have as much dough as he's got you find an awful lot of people trying to part you from it. I run checks on guys like that to see if everything is on the up and up.'

'Did you run a check on me?'

He grinned, and said easily, 'Sure! I know more about you than your own mother did.' He drank some cold beer. 'Then one of his corporations sometimes has security trouble and I go and see what's going on.'

'Industrial espionage?' I queried.

'I guess you'd call it that,' he agreed. 'But only from the security angle. Fallon doesn't play dirty pool, so I stick to counter-espionage.'

I said, 'If you investigated me, then you must have done the same with Halstead. He seems a pretty odd type.'

Pat smiled into his beer. 'You can say that again. He's a guy who thought he had genius and who has now found out that all he has is talent. That really disappoints a man—settling for second best. The trouble with Halstead is that he hasn't come to terms with it yet; it's really griping him.'

'You'll have to spell it out for me,' I said.

Pat sighed. 'Well, it's like this. Halstead started out as a boy wonder—voted the graduate most likely to succeed and all that kind of crap. You know, it's funny how wrong guys can be about other guys; every corporation is stuffed full to the brim with men who were voted most likely to succeed, and they're all holding down second-rate jobs. The men at the top—the guys who really have the power—got there the hard way by clawing their way up and wielding a pretty sharp knife. There are a hell of a lot of corporation presidents who never went to college. Or you have guys like Fallon—he started at the top.'

'In his business,' I said. 'But not in archeology.'

'I'll give you that,' said Pat. 'Fallon would succeed in anything he put his hand to. But Halstead is a second-rater; he knows it but he won't admit it, even to himself, and it's sticking in his craw. He's eaten up with ambition—that's why he was going solo on this Uaxuanoc thing. He wanted to be the man who discovered Uaxuanoc; it would make his name and he'd salvage his self-respect. But you twisted his arm and forced him in with Fallon and he doesn't like that. He doesn't want to share the glory.'

I contemplated that, then said cautiously, 'Both Fallon and Halstead were free in throwing accusations at each other. Halstead accused Fallon of stealing the Vivero letter. Well, we seem to have cleared up that one, and Fallon is in the clear. But what about Fallon's charge that Halstead pinched the file he'd built up?'

'I think Halstead is guilty of that,' said Pat frankly. 'Look at the timetable. Fallon, out of interest's sake, built up a dossier of references to the Vivero secret; Halstead knew about it because Fallon told him—there wasn't any need to keep it under wraps because it didn't seem all that important. Fallon and Halstead came back to civilization after a dig, and Halstead found the Vivero letter. He bought it up in Durango for two hundred dollars from an old guy who didn't know its value. But Halstead did—he knew it could be the key to the Vivero secret, whatever that was. And apart from that it was archeological dynamite—a city no one had even heard of.'

He reached out and opened another bottle of beer. 'I checked on the date he bought it. A month later he picked a quarrel with Fallon and went off in a huff, and Fallon's Vivero dossier disappeared. Fallon didn't think much of it at the time. As I say, the Vivero file didn't seem so important, and he thought Halstead might have made a genuine error and mixed up some of Fallon's papers with his own. And he didn't think it worth his while to add to the grief that Halstead was stirring up just about that time. He thinks differently now.'

I said slowly, 'It's all very circumstantial.'

'Most evidence is,' said Pat. 'Crimes are usually committed without witnesses. Another thing that inclines me to think he did it is his general reputation in the profession.'

'Not good?'

'A bit smelly. He's under suspicion of faking some of his results. Nothing that anyone can pin on him, and certainly not enough to justify him being drummed out of the profession publicly. But certainly enough for anything he produces in the future to be inspected mighty carefully. There's nothing new in that, of course; it's been done before. You had a case in England, didn't you?'

'That was in anthropology,' I said. 'The Piltdown man. Everyone wondered why it didn't fit in to the main sequence and there was a lot of theory-twisting to jam it in. Then science caught up with it when they developed radio-carbon date testing and discovered it was a fake.'

Pat nodded. 'Some guys do that kind of thing. If they can't make a reputation the straight way, they'll make it the crooked way. And they're usually like Halstead—second-raters who want to make a quick name.'

'But it's still circumstantial,' I said stubbornly. I didn't want to believe this. To me, science was equated with truth, and I didn't want to believe that any scientist would stoop to fraud. And maybe I didn't want to believe that Katherine

Halstead was the kind of woman who would marry a man like that.

'Oh, he hasn't been found with dirty hands,' said Pat. 'But I guess it's just a matter of time.'

I said, 'How long have they been married?'

'Three years.' The hand holding his glass suddenly hovered halfway to his lips. 'If you're thinking what I think you're thinking, my advice is—don't! I know she's quite a dish, but keep your hands off. Fallon wouldn't like it.'

'Quite a thought-reader, aren't you?' I said sarcastically. 'Mrs. Halstead is safe from me, I assure you.' Even as I said it I wondered how far that was true. I was also amused at the way Harris had put it—*Fallon wouldn't like it*. Pat's first loyalty was to his boss and he didn't give a damn about how Halstead might react. I said, 'Do you think she knows what you've told me—about her husband's reputation?'

'Probably not,' said Pat. 'I can't see anyone going up to her and saying, "Mrs. Halstead, I have to tell you your husband's reputation is lousy." She'd be the last person to find out.' He regarded me with interest. 'What made you push her on to Fallon in this diving caper? That's twice you've made the boss eat crow. Your credit's running out fast.'

I said slowly, 'She can control her husband where other people can't. You know the foul temper he has. I've no intention of spending my time in Quintana Roo keeping those two from assaulting each other. I'll need some help.'

Pat cocked his head on one side, then nodded abruptly. 'You just might be right. Trouble won't come from Fallon, but Halstead might stir something up. I'm not saying he's nuts, but he's very unstable. You know what I think? I think if he gets a fraction too much pressure on him one of two things will happen—either he'll split right open like a rotten egg, or he'll blow up like a bomb. Now, if you're in a pressure situation, either way brings you grief. I wouldn't rely on him in a jam, and I'd trust him as far as I could throw the Empire State Building.'

'Quite a recommendation. I'd hate to have you write out a testimonial for me, Pat.'

He grinned. 'Yours might be a bit better. All you have to do, Jemmy, to get a hundred per cent score is to stop being so goddamn unobtrusive and neutral. I know you English have a reputation for being quiet, but you push it too far. Do you mind if I speak frankly?'

'Can I stop you?'

He snorted with laughter. 'Probably not.' He lifted his glass. 'I'm probably just cut enough to tell the truth—it's a failing of mine which has earned me a couple of black eyes in my time.'

'You'd better go ahead and tell me the worst. I promise not to sock you.'

'Okay. You've got some iron in you somewhere, or you wouldn't have been able to strongarm Fallon the way you have. He can be a tough guy to handle. But what have you done since? Fallon and Halstead are running things now and you're sitting on the sidelines. You've twisted Fallon's arm again over Mrs. Halstead—something that doesn't matter a damn, and he'll remember it. What the hell are you doing on this jaunt, anyway?'

'I had a crazy idea I might be able to do something about my brother.'

'That you can forget,' said Pat briefly.

'So I've found out,' I said gloomily.

'I'm glad you realize it,' he said. 'Gatt would swat you like a fly and never give it another thought. Why don't you quit and go home, Jemmy; go back to that little farm of yours? You've found out there's no treasure to be hunted, and you don't give two cents for all the lost cities in Latin America, do you? Why stick around?'

'I'll stick around as long as Gatt does,' I said. 'He might leave himself open long enough for me to get at him.'

'Then you'll wait until hell freezes over. Look, Jemmy: I've got fifteen operatives on to him now, and I'm no nearer finding out what he's up to than when I started. He's a smart cookie and he doesn't make mistakes—not those kind of mistakes. He keeps himself covered all the time—it's a reflex with him.'

'You'll agree he'll be interested in what we'll be doing in Quintana Roo?'

'Apparently so,' said Pat. 'He's certainly keeping tabs on this operation.'

'Then he'll have to follow us there,' I said. 'He can't do anything from Mexico City. If he's so bloody interested in hypothetical treasure in Uaxuanoc, he'll have to go to Uaxuanoc to pick up the loot. Do you agree with that?'

'It's feasible,' said Pat judiciously. 'I can't see Jack being so trusting as to send anyone else—not with what he thinks is at stake.'

'He won't be on his home ground, Pat. He's a civilized city type—he'll be out of his depth. From what I can gather Quintana Roo is as unlike New York City as Mars is. He might make a mistake.'

Pat looked at me in astonishment. 'And what makes you think you're any different? I grant you that Gatt is a city type, but civilized he is not. Whereas you are a city type *and* civilized. Jemmy, you're a London accountant; you'll be just as much out of your depth in the Quintana Roo as Gatt.'

'Exactly,' I said. 'We'll be on equal terms—which is more than can be said right now.'

He drained his glass and slammed it down on to the table with a bang. 'I think you're nuts,' he said disgustedly. 'You talk a weird kind of sense, but I still think you're nuts. You're as batty as Halstead.' He looked up. 'Tell me, can you handle a gun?'

'I've never tried,' I said. 'So I don't know.'

'For Christ's sake!' he said. 'What are you going to do if you do come up against Gatt on even terms, as you call it? Kiss him to death?'

'I don't know,' I said. 'I'll see when the time comes. I believe in handling situations as they happen.'

He passed his hand over his face in a bemused way and looked at me for a long time without saying anything. He took a deep breath. 'Let me outline a hypothetical situation,' he said mildly. 'Let us suppose that you've managed to separate Jack from his bodyguards, and that's a pretty foolish supposition in the first place. And let us suppose that there the two of you are, a pair of city slickers, babes in the wood.' He stuck out a rigid finger. 'The first—and last—thing you'd know was that Jack had bush-whacked you with a lupara, and you'd be in no condition to handle *any* situation.'

'Has Gatt ever killed anyone himself?' I asked.

'I'd guess so. He came up through the ranks in the Organization. Served his apprenticeship, you might say. He'll have done a killing or two in his younger days.'

'That's a long time ago,' I observed. 'Maybe he's out of practice.'

'Agh, there's no talking to you,' said Pat in a choked voice. 'If you have any brains you'll go back where you came from. I *have* to stick around, but at least I know what the score is, and I get paid for it. But you're the kind of guy that Kipling wrote about—"If you can keep your head while all about you are losing theirs, then maybe you don't know what the hell is going on."'

I laughed. 'You have quite a talent for parody.'

'I'm not as good as Fallon,' he said gloomily. 'He's turned this whole operation into a parody of security. I used the bug Gatt planted on us to feed him a queer line, and what does Fallon do? He stages a goddamn TV spectacular, for God's sake! I wouldn't be surprised, when you fly down to that airstrip he's built, if you don't find the CBS cameras already rolling and hooked up into a coast-to-coast broadcast—and a line of Rockettes from Radio City to give added interest. Every paisano in Mexico knows what's going on. Gatt doesn't have to bug us to find out what we're doing; all he has to do is to ask at any street corner.'

'It's a tough life,' I said sympathetically. 'Does Fallon usually behave like this?'

Harris shook his head. 'I don't know what's got into him. He's turned over control of his affairs to his brother—given him power of attorney. His brother's a nice enough guy, but I wouldn't trust *anyone* that far with a hundred million bucks. He's thinking of nothing else but finding this city.'

'I don't know about that,' I said thoughtfully. 'He seems to be worried about something else. He goes a bit dreamy at unexpected moments.'

'I've noticed that, too. Something's bugging him, but he hasn't let me in on it.' Harris seemed resentful at the idea that something was being kept from him. He rose to his feet and stretched. 'I'm going to bed—there's work to do tomorrow.'

IV

So there it was again!

First Sheila, and now Pat Harris. He hadn't said it as bluntly as Sheila, but he'd said it nevertheless. Apparently, my exterior appearance and mannerisms gave a good imitation of Caspar Milquetoast—the nine-to-fiver, the commuter par excellence. The trouble was that I wasn't at all sure that the interior didn't match the exterior.

Gatt, from Pat's description, was lethal. Maybe he wouldn't shoot anyone just to make bets on which way he'd fall, but he might if there was a dollar profit in it. I began to feel queasy at the thought of going up against him, but I knew I couldn't turn back now.

Pat's assessment of Halstead was quite interesting, too, and I wondered how much Katherine knew about her husband. I think she loved him—in fact, I was sure of it. No woman in her right mind would tolerate such a man otherwise, but maybe I was prejudiced. At any rate, she consistently took his side in any argument he had with Fallon. The very picture of a faithful wife. I went to sleep thinking about her.

Six

We went to Camp One in Fallon's flying office—a Lear executive jet. Pat Harris didn't come with us—his job was to keep tabs on Gatt—so there were just four passengers, Fallon, the Halsteads and myself. Fallon and Halstead engaged in another of their interminable professional discussions, and Katherine Halstead read a magazine. Halstead had done a bit of manoeuvring when we entered the plane and Katherine was sitting on the other side of him and as far from me as it was possible to get. I couldn't talk to her without shouting across a technical argument so I turned my attention to the ground.

Quintana Roo, seen from the air, looked like a piece of mouldy cheese. The solid vegetative cover was broken only occasionally by a clearing which showed as a dirty whitish-grey among the virulent green of the trees. I did not see a single water-course, no rivers and not even a stream, and I began to appreciate Halstead's point of view about the difficulties of archeological exploration in the tropics.

At one point Fallon broke off his discussion to speak with the pilot on the intercom, and the plane wheeled slowly and began to descend. He turned to me and said, 'We'll have a look at Camp Two.'

Even from a thousand feet the forest looked solid enough to walk on without touching ground. There could have been a city the size of London under that sea of green and you'd never see it. I reminded myself not to be so bloody cocky in the future about things I knew nothing about. Halstead
108

might be a faker, if what Pat Harris said was true, but a faker, of all people, must have a knowledge of his field. He had been right when he had said that this was going to be a tough job.

Camp Two came and went before I had a chance to get a good look at it, but the plane banked and turned and we orbited the site, standing on one wingtip. There wasn't much to see: just another clearing with half a dozen prefabricated huts and some minuscule figures which waved their arms. The jet couldn't land there, but that wasn't the intention. We straightened on course and rose higher, heading for the coast and Camp One.

About twenty minutes and eighty miles later we were over the sea and curving back over the white surf and gleaming beaches to touch down at the airstrip at Camp One. The jet bumped a bit in the coastal turbulence but put down gently and rolled to a stop at the further end of the strip, then wheeled and taxied to a halt in front of a hangar. As I left the plane the heat, after the air-conditioned comfort of the flight, was like the sudden blow of a hammer.

Fallon didn't seem to notice the heat at all. Years of puttering about in this part of the world had already dried the juices from him and he had been thoroughly conditioned. He set off at a brisk walk along the strip, followed by Halstead, who also didn't seem to mind. Katherine and I followed along more slowly and, by the time we got to the hut into which Fallon had disappeared she was looking definitely wilted and I felt a bit brown around the edges myself.

'My God!' I said. 'Is it always like this?'

Halstead turned and gave me a smile which had all the elements of a sneer. 'You've been spoiled by Mexico City,' he said. 'The altitude up there takes the edge off. It's not really hot here on the coast. Wait until we get to Camp Two.' His tone implied that I'd feel bloody sorry for myself.

It was cooler in the hut and there was the persistent throb of an air-conditioning unit. Fallon introduced us to a big, burly man. 'This is Joe Rudetsky; he's the boss of Camp One.'

Rudetsky stuck out a meaty hand. 'Glad to meet you, Mr. Wheale,' he boomed.

I later found out how Fallon had managed to organize the whole operation so quickly. He had merely appropriated the logistics unit from one of his oil exploration teams. Those boys were used to operating in rough country and under

109

tropical conditions, and this job was very little different from a score of others they had done in North Africa, Saudi Arabia and Venezuela. When I explored the camp I admired the sheer efficiency of it all. They certainly knew how to make themselves comfortable—even to ice-cold Coca-Cola.

We stayed in Camp One all that day and slept there the night. Fallon and Halstead checked the mountain of equipment they evidently thought they needed, so Katherine and I did the same with the scuba gear. We weren't going to take it to Camp Two because that would be pointless; Camp Two was a mere centre of exploration and if and when we discovered Uaxuanoc it would be abandoned and Camp Three would be set up on the city site.

We worked until lunchtime and then stopped for something to eat. I wasn't very hungry—the heat affected my appetite—but I relished the bottle of cold lager that Rudetsky thrust into my hand. I'd swear it hissed going down.

Katherine and I had completed our inspection and found everything present and in working order, but Fallon and Halstead still had quite a way to go. I offered to give them a hand, but Fallon shook his head. 'It's mostly instrument checking now,' he said. 'You wouldn't know how to do that.' His gaze wandered over my shoulder. 'If you turn round you'll see your first Maya.'

I twisted in my chair and looked across the strip. On the other side of the flattened ground and standing within easy running distance of the trees were two men. They were dressed in rather baggy trousers and white shirts and stood quite still. They were rather too far away for me to distinguish their features.

Fallon said, 'They don't know what to make of us, you know. This is an unprecedented invasion.' He looked across at Rudetsky. 'Have they given you any trouble, Joe?'

'The natives? No trouble at all, Mr. Fallon. Those guys are from up the coast; they have a two-bit coconut plantation.'

'A cocal,' said Fallon. 'These people live entirely isolated lives, cut off from everything. The sea on one side—the forest on the other. There'll be just the one family—the cocal won't support two—and they're dependent entirely on their own resources.'

That seemed a grim life. 'What do they live on?' I asked.

Fallon shrugged. 'Fish, turtles, turtle eggs. Sometimes they're lucky enough to shoot a wild pig. Then twice a year they'll sell their copra and that gives them a little ready money to buy clothing and needles and a few cartridges.'

'Are those the indios sublevados you talked about?'

Fallon laughed. 'These boys aren't rebels—they wouldn't know how to start. We'll meet the indios sublevados in the interior, and the chicleros, too.' He switched to Rudetsky. 'Have you had any chicleros round here?'

Rudetsky nodded grimly. 'We ran the bastards off. They were stealing us blind.' He looked across at Katherine who was talking to Halstead, and lowered his voice. 'They murdered a native last week; we found his body on the beach.'

Fallon didn't seem perturbed. He merely picked up his pipe and said, 'You'd better keep a good watch, and don't let them in the camp on any account. And you'd better have the men stay in the camp and not go wandering around.'

Rudetsky grinned. 'Where is there to go?' he asked.

I began to wonder what kind of a country I was in where a murder could be taken so casually. Hesitantly, I said, 'Who or what are chicleros?'

Fallon pulled a sour face. 'The result of an odd penal system they have here. There's a tree which grows in the forest, the zapote; it grows only here, in Guatemala and in British Honduras. The tree is tapped for its sap and that's called chicle— it's the basic material of chewing gum. Now, no man in his right mind will go into the forest to gather chicle; the Maya certainly won't because he's too intelligent to risk his skin. So the government dumps its convicts in here to do the job. It's a six months' season but a lot of the chicleros stay all the year round. They're a local scourge. Mostly they kill each other off, but occasionally they'll knock off an outsider or an Indian.' He drew on his pipe. 'Human life isn't worth much in Quintana Roo.'

I thought that over. If I heard Fallon aright then this forest was deadly. If the Mayas whose native land it was wouldn't work in the forest then it must be positively lethal. I said, 'Why the devil don't they grow the trees in plantations?'

His face twisted into a wry grin. 'Because of the same argument that's been used for slavery ever since one man put a yoke on another. It's cheaper to continue using convicts than to start plantations. If the people who chew gum knew how it was produced, every stick would make them sick to their stomachs.' He pointed the stem of his pipe at me. 'If you ever meet any chicleros, don't do a damn thing. Keep your hands to your sides, don't make any sudden moves and like as not they'll just pass you by. But don't bet on it.'

I began to wonder if I was still in the twentieth century. 'And where do the indios sublevados come into all this?'

'That's quite a story,' said Fallon. 'The Spaniards took two hundred years to get on top of the Mayas, and the Lakondon tribe they *never* licked. The Mayas were kept down until 1847 when they rose in rebellion here in Quintana Roo. It was more populated in those days and the Mayas gave the Mexicans, as they now were, a hell of a trouncing in what was known as the War of the Castes. Try as they might the Mexicans could never get back in again. In 1915 the Mayas declared an independent state; they dealt with British Honduras and made business deals with British firms. The top Maya then was General Mayo; he was a really tough old bird; but the Mexicans got at him through his vanity. They signed a treaty with him in 1935, made him a general in the official Mexican army and invited him to Mexico City where they seduced him with civilization. He died in 1952. After 1935 the Mayas seemed to lose heart. They'd had a tough time since the War of the Castes and the land was becoming depopulated. On top of famine, which hit them hard, the Mexicans started to move colonists into Chan Santa Cruz. There are not more than a few thousand of the indios sublevados left now, yet they still rule the roost in their own area.' He smiled. 'No Mexican tax collectors allowed.'

Halstead had broken off his conversation with his wife. 'And they don't like archeologists much, either,' he observed.

'Oh, it's not as bad as it was in the old times,' said Fallon tolerantly. 'In the early days of General Mayo any foreigner coming into Quintana Roo was automatically a dead man. Remember the story I told of the archeologist whose bones were built into a wall? But they've lost a lot of steam since then. They're all right if they're left alone. They're better than the chicleros.'

Halstead looked at me and said, 'Still glad to be along with us, Wheale?' He had a thin smile on his face.

I ignored him. 'Why isn't all this common knowledge?' I asked Fallon. 'A government running a species of slavery and a whole people nearly wiped out surely calls for comment.'

Fallon knocked out his pipe on the leg of the table. 'Africa is popularly known as the Dark Continent,' he said. 'But there are some holes and corners of Central and South America
112

which are pretty black. Your popular journalist sitting in his office in London or New York has very limited horizons; he can't see this far and he won't leave his office.'

He put the pipe in his pocket. 'But I'll tell you something. The trouble with Quintana Roo isn't the Indians or the chicleros; they're people, and you can always get along with people somehow.' He stretched out his arm and pointed. 'There's your trouble.'

I looked to where he was pointing and saw nothing unusual—just the trees on the other side of the strip.

'You still don't understand?' he asked, and swung round to Rudetsky. 'What kind of a job did you have in clearing this strip?'

'The hardest work I've ever done,' said Rudetsky. 'I've worked in rain forest before—I was an army engineer during the war—but this one beats all hell.'

'That's it,' said Fallon flatly. 'Do you know how they classify the forest here? They say it's a twenty-foot forest, or a ten-foot forest, or a four-foot forest. A four-foot forest is getting pretty bad—it means that you can't see more than four feet in any direction—but there are worse than that. Add disease, snakes and shortage of water and you realize why the chicleros are among the toughest men in the world—those of them that survive. The forest is the enemy in Quintana Roo, and we'll have to fight it to find Uaxuanoc.'

II

We went to Camp Two next day, travelling in a helicopter which flew comparatively slowly and not too high. I looked down at the green tide which flowed beneath my feet and thought back to the conversation I'd had with Pat Harris about Jack Gatt and our hypothetical encounter in Quintana Roo. While I had envisaged something more than Epping Forest I certainly hadn't thought it would be this bad.

Fallon had explained the peculiarities of the Quintana Roo forest quite simply. He said, 'I told you the reason why there is no native gold in Yucatan is because of the geology of the area—there's just a limestone cap over the peninsula. That explains the forest, too, and why it's worse than any other.'

'It doesn't explain it to me.' I said. 'Or maybe I'm particularly stupid.'

'No; you just don't have the technical knowledge,' he said. 'The rainfall is quite heavy, but when it falls it sinks right into the ground until it meets an impermeable layer. Thus there is a vast reservoir of fresh water under Yucatan, but a shortage of water because there are no rivers. The water is quite close to the surface; on the coast you can dig a hole on the beach three feet from the sea and you'll get fresh water. In the interior sometimes the limestone cap collapses to reveal the underground water—that's a cenote. But the point is that the trees always have water available at their roots. In any other rain forest, such as in the Congo, most of the water is drained away into rivers. In Quintana Roo it's available to the trees and they take full advantage.'

I looked down at the forest and wondered if it was a twenty-foot forest or a four-footer. Whatever it was, I couldn't see the ground and we were less than five hundred feet high. If Jack Gatt had any sense he wouldn't come anywhere near Quintana Roo.

Camp Two was much simpler than Camp One. There was a rough hangar for the helicopter—a wall-less structure looking something like a Dutch barn; a dining-room-cum-lounge, a store hut for equipment and four huts for sleeping quarters. All the huts were factory-made prefabs and all had been flown in by helicopter. Simpler it might have been but there was no lack of comfort; every hut had an air-conditioning unit and the refrigerator was full of beer. Fallon didn't believe in roughing it unless he had to.

Apart from the four of us there were the cook and his helper to do the housekeeping and the helicopter pilot. What he was going to do, apart from flying us back and forward between camps, I didn't know; in the search for Uaxuanoc the helicopter would be about as much use as a bull's udder.

All around lay the forest, green and seemingly impenetrable. I walked to the edge of the clearing and inspected it, trying to assess it by the rating Fallon had given. As near as I could tell this would be a fifteen-foot forest—a rather thin growth by local standards. The trees were tall, pushing and fighting in a fiercely competitive battle for light, and were wreathed and strangled by an incredible variety of parasitic plant life. And apart from the purely human sounds which came from the huts everything was deathly silent.

I turned to find Katherine standing near me. 'Just inspecting the enemy,' I said. 'Have you been here before—in Quintana Roo, I mean?'

'No,' she said. 'Not here. I was on digs with Paul in Campeche and Guatemala. I've never seen anything like this before.'

'Neither have I,' I said. 'I've lived a sheltered life. If Fallon had taken the trouble to explain things when we were back in England as he explained them at Camp One I doubt if I'd be here at all. This is a wild-goose chase if ever there was one.'

'I think you underestimate Fallon—and Paul,' she said. 'Don't you think we'll find Uaxuanoc?'

I jerked my thumb at the green wall. 'In this? I wouldn't trust myself to find the Eiffel Tower if someone dumped it down here.'

'That's just because you don't know how to look and where to look,' she said. 'But Paul and Fallon are professionals; they've done this before.'

'Yes, there are tricks to ever trade,' I admitted. 'I know there are plenty in mine, but I can't see much use for an accountant here. I feel as out of place as a Hottentot at a Buck House garden party.' I looked into the forest. 'Talk about not being able to see the wood for the trees—I'll be interested to see how the experts go about this.'

I soon found out because Fallon called a conference in the big hut. There was a huge photo-mosaic pinned to a cork board on the wall and the table was covered with maps. I was curious to know why the helicopter pilot, a Texan called Harry Rider, was included in the discussion, but it soon became clear.

Fallon broke open the refrigerator and served beer all round, then said succinctly, 'The key to this problem is the cenotes. We know Uaxuanoc was centred on a cenote because Vivero said so, and there was no reason for him to lie about *that*. Besides, it's the most likely occurrence—a city must have water and the only water is at the cenotes.'

He took a pointer and stepped up to the photo-mosaic. He laid the tip of the pointer in the centre, and said, 'We are here, next to a very small cenote on the edge of the clearing.' He turned to me. 'If you want to see your first Mayan structure you'll find it next to the cenote.'

I was surprised. 'Aren't you going to investigate it?'

'It's not worth it; it won't tell me anything I don't know already.' He swept the pointer around in a large circle. 'Within ten miles of this point there are fifteen cenotes, large and small, and around one of them *may* be the city of Uaxuanoc.'

I was still trying to clarify in my mind the magnitude of the problem. 'How *big* would you expect it to be?' I asked.

Halstead said, 'Bigger than Chichen Itza—if we can believe Vivero's map.'

'That doesn't mean much to me.'

'The centre of Copan is over seventy-five acres,' said Fallon. 'But you mustn't confuse a Mayan city with any other city you've seen. The centre of the city—the stone structures we are looking for—was the religious and administrative centre, and probably the market-place. Around it, for several square miles, lived the Mayas of the city. They didn't live in neat little houses built into streets as we do but in an immense system of small-holdings. Each family would have its own little farm, and the household buildings were very little different from the huts that the Mayas now build, although probably more extensive. There's nothing wrong with the Mayan hut—it's ideally suited to this climate.'

'And the population?'

'Chichen Itza was about 200,000 according to Morley,' said Halstead. 'Uaxuanoc might run upwards of a quarter-million.'

'That's a devil of a lot of people,' I said in astonishment.

'To build the immense structures they did required a lot of hands,' said Fallon. 'These were a neolithic people, remember, using stone tools to carve stone. I expect the centre of Uaxuanoc will be about one hundred acres, if we can rely on Vivero's map, so the outer city would have been populous, with more people in it than in the whole of Quintana Roo now. But there'll be no trace left of the outer city; timber buildings don't last in this climate.'

He tapped with the pointer again. 'Let's get on with it. So we have fifteen cenotes to look at, and if we don't find what we're looking for we'll have to go further afield. That will be unfortunate, because within twenty miles of here there are another forty-nine cenotes and it's going to take a long time if we have to investigate them all.'

He waved the pointer at the pilot. 'Fortunately we have Harry Rider and his helicopter so we can do it in reasonable comfort. I'm getting too old to tackle the forest.'

Rider said, 'I've already had a look at some of those water-holes, Mr. Fallon; in most of them there's no place to put down—not even my chopper. It's real thick.'

Fallon nodded. 'I know; I've been here before and I know what it's like. We'll run a preliminary photo survey. Colour film might show up differences in vegetation due to underlying structures, and infra-red might show more. And I'd like to do some flights early morning and late evening—we might get something out of the shadows.'

He turned and regarded the photo-mosaic. 'As you can see, I've numbered the cenotes under consideration. Some are more likely than others. Vivero said there was a ridge running through Uaxuanoc with a temple at the top and a cenote at the bottom. Cenotes and ridges seem to be associated in this area, which is bad luck; but it cuts the possibles down to eleven. I think we can forget numbers four, seven, eight and thirteen for the time being.' He turned to Rider. 'When can we start?'

'Any time you like—I'm fuelled up,' said Rider.

Fallon consulted his watch. 'We'll fix up the cameras, and leave directly after lunch.'

I helped to load the cameras into the helicopter. There was nothing amateurish or snapshottery about this gear; they were professional aerial cameras and I noticed that the helicopter was fitted with all the necessary brackets to receive them. My respect for Fallon's powers of organization grew even more. Allowing for the fact that he had more money to chuck about than appeared decent, at least he knew how to spend it to the best advantage. He was no playboy of the jet-set circuit spilling his wealth into some casino owner's pocket.

After a quick lunch Fallon and Halstead made for the helicopter. I said, 'What do I do?'

Fallon rubbed his chin. 'There doesn't seem to be anything you can do,' he said, and over his shoulder I saw Halstead grinning widely. 'You'd better rest up this afternoon. Stay out of the sun until you're used to this heat. We'll be back in a couple of hours.'

I watched the helicopter take off and disappear over the trees feeling a little silly and like an unwanted spare part. Katherine was nowhere to be seen—I think she'd gone into the hut she shared with Halstead to unpack their personal gear. I wondered what to do and wandered disconsolately to the far end of the clearing to look at the Mayan building Fallon had mentioned.

The cenote was about thirty feet in diameter and the water lay about fifteen feet down in the pit. The sides of the

117

pit were almost sheer, but someone had cut rough steps so as to get to the water. I was startled by the sudden noisy throb of an engine close by and found a small pump run by a petrol engine which had apparently come into operation automatically. It was pumping water from the cenote up to the camp—another bit of Fallonese efficiency.

I didn't find a building although I looked hard enough, and after half an hour of futile searching I gave up. I was about to go back to the camp when I saw two men on the other side of the cenote looking at me. All they wore were ragged white trousers and they stood as still as statues. They were small, sinewy and brown, and a stray sunbeam falling through the leaves reflected in a coppery sheen from the naked chest of the nearest man. They regarded me solemnly for the space of thirty seconds and then turned and vanished into the forest.

III

The helicopter came back and Fallon dumped a load of film spools on the table in the big hut. 'Know anything about film processing?' he asked.

'In an amateur sort of way.'

'Umph! That might not be good enough. But we'll do the best we can. Come with me.' He led me into another hut and showed me his photographic department. 'You should be able to get the hang of this,' he said. 'It's not too difficult.'

There was no dabbling in trays of hypo for Fallon; he had the neatest darkroom set-up I'd ever seen—and he didn't need a darkroom. I watched him as he demonstrated. It was a big box with a sliding, light-tight door at one side and a slot at the other. He slid open the door, put a spool of undeveloped film into a receptacle and threaded the leader through sprockets. Then he closed the door and pressed a button. Fifteen minutes later the developed colour film uncoiled through the slot on the other side, dry and ready for screening.

He took the cover off the box and showed me the innards —the sets of slowly turning rollers and baths of chemicals, and the infra-red dryer at the end—and he explained which chemicals went where. 'Think you can handle it? It will save time if we have someone who can process the film as quickly as possible.'

'I don't see why not,' I said.

'Good! You can carry on with these, then. There's something I want to talk over with Paul.' He smiled. 'You can't really carry on a sensible conversation in a whirlybird—too noisy.' He held up a spool. 'This one consists of stereo pairs; I'll show you how to cut it and register it accurately into frames when it's developed.'

I got stuck in to developing the films, pleased that there was something I could do. All it took was time—the job itself was so simple it could have been contracted out to child labour. I developed the last spool—the stereos—and took it to Fallon, and he showed me how to fit the images into the double frames, which was easy if finicky.

That evening we had a magic-lantern show in the big hut. Fallon put a spool into the film strip projector and switched on. There was just a green blur on the screen and he chuckled. 'I seem to have got the focus wrong on that one.'

The next frame was better and the screen showed an area of forest and a cenote reflecting the blue of the sky. It just looked like any other bit of forest to me, but Fallon and Halstead discussed it for quite a while before moving on to the next frame. It was a good two hours before all the pictures were shown and I'd lost interest long before that, especially when it seemed that the first cenote had proved a bust.

Fallon said at last, 'We still have the stereo pictures. Let's have a look at those.'

He changed the projectors and handed me a pair of polaroid glasses. The stereo pictures were startlingly three-dimensional; I felt that all I had to do was lean forward to pluck the topmost leaf from a tree. Being aerial shots, they also gave a dizzying sense of vertigo. Fallon ran through them all without result. 'I think we can chalk that one off our list,' he said. 'We'd better go to bed—we'll have a heavy day tomorrow.'

I yawned and stretched, then I remembered the men I had seen. 'I saw two men down at the cenote.'

'Chicleros?' asked Fallon sharply.

'Not if chicleros are little brown men with big noses.'

'Mayas,' he decided. 'They'll be wondering what the hell we're doing.'

I said, 'Why don't you ask them about Uaxuanoc? Their ancestors built the place, after all.'

'They wouldn't know about it—or if they did, they wouldn't

tell us. The modern Maya is cut off from his history. As far as he is concerned the ruins were made by giants or dwarfs and he steers clear of them. They're magical places and not to be approached by men. What did you think of that building down there?'

'I couldn't find it,' I said.

Halstead gave a suppressed snort, and Fallon laughed. 'It's not so hidden; I spotted it straight away. I'll show you to-morrow—it will give you some idea of what we're up against here.'

IV

We established a routine. Fallon and Halstead made three flights a day—sometimes four. After each flight they would hand me the films and I would get busy developing them and every night we would screen the results. Nothing much came of that except the steady elimination of possibilities.

Fallon took me down to the cenote and showed me the Mayan building and I found that I had passed it half a dozen times without seeing it. It was just by the side of the cenote in thick vegetation, and when Fallon said, 'There it is!' I didn't see a thing except another bit of forest.

He smiled, and said, 'Go closer,' so I walked right to the edge of the clearing and saw nothing except the dappled dazzle-pattern of sun, leaves and shadows. I turned around and shrugged, and he called, 'Push your hand through the leaves.' I did as he said and rammed my fist against a rock with an unexpected jolt.

'Now step back a few paces and have another look,' said Fallon.

I walked back, rubbing my skinned knuckles and looked again at the vegetation through narrowed eyes. It's a funny thing—one moment it wasn't there and a split second later it was, like a weird optical illusion, but even then it was only the ghostly hint of a building made up imperfectly of shadows. I lifted my hand and said uncertainly, 'It starts there—and ends . . . there?'

'That's right; you've got it.'

I stared at it, afraid it would go away again. If any army staff in the world wants to improve its camouflage units I would strongly advise a course in Quintana Roo. This natural camouflage was just about perfect. I said. 'What do you think it was?'

'Maybe a shrine to Chac, the Rain God; they're often associated with cenotes. If you like you can strip the vegetation from it. We might find something of minor interest. But watch out for snakes.'

'I might do that, if I can ever find it again.'

Fallon was amused. 'You'll have to develop an eye for this kind of thing if you contemplate archeological research in these parts. If not, you'll walk right through a city and not know it's there.'

I could believe him.

He consulted his watch. 'Paul will be waiting for me,' he said. 'We'll be back with some film in a couple of hours.'

The relationship between the four of us was odd. I felt left out of things because I didn't really know what was going on. The minutiae of research were beyond me and I didn't understand a tenth of what Fallon and Halstead were talking about when they conversed on professional matters, which is all they ever spoke to each other about.

Fallon rigidly confined his relationship with Halstead to the matter in hand and would not overstep it by an inch. It was obvious to me that he did not particularly like Paul Halstead, nor did he trust him overmuch. But then, neither did I, especially after that conversation with Pat Harris. Fallon would have received an even more detailed report on Halstead from Harris and so I understood his attitude.

He was different with me. While regarding my ignorance of archeological fieldwork with a tolerant amusement, he did not try to thrust his professional expertise down my throat. He patiently answered my questions which, to him, I suppose, were simple and often absurd, and let it go at that. We got into the habit of sitting together in the evening for an hour before going to bed, and we yarned on a wide variety of topics. Apart from his professional work he was well read and a man of wide erudition. Yet I was able to interest him in the application of computers to farming practice and I detailed what I was doing to Hay Tree Farm. It seemed that he owned a big ranch in Arizona and he saw the possibilities at once.

But then he shook his head irritably. 'I'll pass that on to my brother,' he said. 'He's looking after all that now.' He stared blindly across the room. 'A man has so little time to do what he really wants to do.'

Soon thereafter he became abstracted and intent on his own thoughts and I excused myself and went to bed.

Halstead tended to be morose and self-contained. He ignored me almost completely, and rarely spoke to me unless it was absolutely necessary. When he did volunteer any remarks they were usually accompanied by an ill-concealed sneer directed at my abysmal ignorance of the work. Quite often I felt like taking a poke at him, but I bottled up my temper for the sake of the general peace. In the evenings, after our picture show and discussion, he and his wife would withdraw to their hut.

And that leaves Katherine Halstead, who was tending to become a tantalizing mystery. True, she was doing what she said she would, and kept her husband under tight control. Often I saw him on the edge of losing his temper with Fallon —he didn't lose his temper with me because I was beneath his notice—and be drawn back into semi-composure by a look or a word from his wife. I thought I understood him and what made him tick, but I'm damned if I could understand her.

A man often sees mystery in a woman where there is nothing but a yawning vacuity, the so-called feminine mystery being but a cunning façade behind which lies nothing worthwhile. But Katherine wasn't like that. She was amusing, intelligent and talented in a number of ways; she sketched competently in a better than amateur way, she cooked well and alleviated our chuckwagon diet, and she knew a hell of a lot more about the archeological score than I did, although she admitted she was but a neophyte. But she would never talk about her husband in any way at all, which is a trait I'd never come across in a married woman before.

Those I had known—not a few—always had something to say about their mates, either in praise or blame. Most would be for their husbands, with perhaps a tolerant word for their weaknesses. A few would praise incessantly and not hear a word against the darling man, and a few, the regrettable bitches, would be acid in esoteric asides meant for one pair of ears but understood by all—sniping shots in the battle of the sexes. But from Katherine Halstead there was not a cheep, one way or the other. She just didn't talk about him at all It was unnatural.

122

Because Fallon and Halstead were away most of the day we were thrown together a lot. The camp cook and his assistant were very unobtrusive; they cooked the grub, washed the dishes, repaired the generator when it broke down, and spent the rest of their time losing their wages to each other at gin rummy. So Katherine and I had each other for company during those long hot days. I soon got the film developing taped and had plenty of time on my hands, so I suggested we do something about the Mayan building.

'We might come up with an epoch-making discovery,' I said jocularly. 'Let's give it a bash. Fallon said it would be a good idea.'

She smiled at the idea that we might find anything of importance, but agreed that it would be something semi-constructive to do, so we armed ourselves with machetes and went down to the cenote to hew at the vegetation.

I was surprised to see how well preserved the building was once it was denuded of its protective cover. The limestone blocks of which it was built were properly cut and shaped, and laid in a workmanlike manner. On the wall nearest the cenote we found a doorway with a sort of corbelled arch, and when we looked inside there was nothing but darkness and an angry buzz of disturbed wasps.

I said, 'I don't think we'd better go in there just yet; the present inhabitants might not like it.'

We withdrew back into the clearing and I looked down at myself. It had been hard work cutting the creepers away from the building and I'd sweated freely, and my chest was filthy with bits of earth turned into mud by the sweat. I was in a mess.

'I'm going to have a swim in the cenote,' I said. 'I need cleaning up.'

'What a good idea,' she said. 'I'll get my costume.'

I grinned. 'I won't need one—these shorts will do.'

She went back to the huts and I walked over to the cenote and looked down into the dark water. I couldn't see bottom and it could have been anything between six inches and sixty feet deep, so I thought it was inadvisable to dive in. I climbed down to water level by means of the steps, let myself into the water and found it pleasantly cool. I splashed about for a bit but I didn't find bottom, so I dived and went down to look for it. I must have gone down thirty feet and I still hadn't found it. It was bloody dark down there, which gave me a good indication of conditions if I had to dive for Fallon. I let myself up slowly, dribbling air from my mouth, and came up to sunlight again.

'I wondered where you were,' Katherine called, and I looked up to see her poised on the edge of the cenote, silhouetted against the sun fifteen feet above my head. 'Is it deep enough for diving?'

'Too deep,' I said. 'I couldn't find bottom.'

'Good!' she said, and took off in a clean dive. I swam slowly around the cenote and became worried when she didn't come up, but suddenly I felt my ankles grabbed and I was pulled under.

We surfaced laughing, and she said, 'That's for pulling me under in Fallon's pool.' She flicked water at me with the palm of her hand, and for two or three minutes we had a splashing match like a couple of kids until we were breathless and had to stop. After that we just floated around feeling the difference between the coolness of the water and the heat of the direct sun.

She said lazily, 'What's it like down there?'

'Down where?'

'At the bottom of this pool.'

'I didn't find it; I didn't go down too far. It was a bit cold.'

'Weren't you afraid of meeting Chac?'

'Does he live down there?'

'He has a palace at the bottom of every cenote. They used to throw maidens in, and they'd sink down to meet him. Some of them would come back with wonderful stories.'

'What about those who didn't come back?'

'Chac kept them for his own. Sometimes he'd keep them all and the people would become frightened and punish the cenote. They'd throw stones into it and flog it with branches. But none of the maidens would ever come back because of that.'

'You'd better be careful, then,' I said.

She splashed water at me. 'I'm not exactly a maiden.'

I swam over to the steps. 'The chopper should be coming back soon. Another batch of film to be processed.' I climbed halfway up and stopped to give her a hand.

At the top she offered me a towel but I shook my head. 'I'll dry off quickly enough in the sun.'

'Suit yourself,' she said. 'But it's not good for your hair.' She spread the towel on the ground, sat on it, and started to rub her hair with another towel.

I sat down beside her and started to flip pebbles into the cenote. 'What are you *really* doing here, Jemmy?' she asked.

'I'm damned if I know,' I admitted. 'It just seemed a good idea at the time.'

She smiled. 'It's a change from your Devon, isn't it? Don't you wish you were back on your farm—on Hay Tree Farm? Incidentally, do you always make hay from trees in Devon?'

'It doesn't mean what you think. It's a dialect word meaning a hedge or enclosure.' I flicked another pebble into the pool. 'Do you think that annoys Chac?'

'It might, so I wouldn't do it too often—not if you have to dive into a cenote. Damn! I don't have any cigarettes.'

I got up and retrieved mine from where I had left them and we sat and smoked in silence for a while. She said, 'I haven't played about like that in the water for years.'

'Not since the carefree days of the Bahamas?' I asked.

'Not since then.'

'Is that where you met Paul?'

There was the briefest pause before she said, 'No. I met Paul in New York.' She smiled slightly. 'He isn't the type you find on the beach in the Bahamas.'

I silently agreed; it was impossible to equate him with one of those Travel Association carefree holiday advertisements—all teeth, sun glasses and suntan. I probed deeper, but went about it circuitously. 'What were you doing before you met him?'

She blew out a plume of smoke. 'Nothing much; I worked at a small college in Virginia.'

'A school teacher!' I said in surprise.

She laughed. 'No—just a secretary. My father teaches at the same college.'

'I thought you didn't look like a schoolmarm. What does your father teach? Archeology?'

'He teaches history. Don't imagine I spent *all* my time in the Bahamas. It was a very short episode—you can't afford more on a secretary's salary. I saved up for that vacation for a long time.'

I said, 'When you met Paul—was that before or after he'd started on this Vivero research?'

'It was before—I was with him when he found the Vivero letter.'

'You were married then?'

'We were on our honeymoon,' she said lightly. 'It was a working honeymoon for Paul, though.'

'Has he taught you much about archeology?'

She shrugged. 'He's not a very good teacher, but I've picked up quite a lot. I've tried to help him in his work—I think a wife should help her husband.'

'What do you think of this Vivero thing—the whole caper?'

She was silent for a time, then said frankly, 'I don't like it, Jemmy, I don't like anything about it. It's become an obsession with Paul—and not only him. Look at Fallon. My God, take a good look at yourself!'

'What about me?'

She threw her cigarette away half-smoked. 'Don't you think it's ridiculous that you should have been jerked out of a peaceful life in England and dumped in this wilderness just because of what a Spaniard wrote four hundred years ago? Too many lives are being twisted, Jemmy.'

I said carefully, 'I wouldn't say I'm obsessional about it. I don't give a damn about Vivero or Uaxuanoc. My motives are different. But you say that Paul is obsessed by it. How does his obsession take him?'

She plucked nervously at the towel in her lap. 'You've seen him. He can think or talk of nothing else. It's changed him; he's not the man I knew when we were married. And he's not only fighting Quintana Roo—he's fighting Fallon.'

I said shortly, 'If it weren't for Fallon he wouldn't be here now.'

'And that's a part of what he's fighting,' she said passionately. 'How can he compete with Fallon's reputation, with Fallon's money and resources? It's driving him crazy.'

'I wasn't aware that this was any kind of competition. Do you think Fallon will deny him any credit that's due to him?'

'He did before—why shouldn't he do it again? It's really Fallon's fault that Paul is in such a bad state.'

I sighed. Pat Harris was dead right. Katherine didn't know about Halstead's bad reputation in the trade. The advertising boys had got it down pat—*even her best friend wouldn't tell her!* I debated for a moment whether or not to tell her all about Pat Harris's investigations, but to tell a woman that her husband was a liar and a faker was certainly not the best way of making friends and influencing people. She would become more than annoyed and would probably tell Halstead—and what Halstead would do in his present frame of mind might be highly dangerous.

I said, 'Now, look, Katherine: if Paul has an obsession it has nothing to do with Fallon. I think Fallon is eminently fair, and will give Paul all the credit that's coming to him. That's just my own personal opinion, mind you.'

'You don't know what that man has done to Paul,' she said sombrely.

'Maybe he had it coming to him,' I said brutally. 'He doesn't make it easy for anyone working with him. I'm not too happy about his attitude to me, and if he keeps it up he's going to get a thick ear.'

'That's an unfair thing to say,' she burst out.

'What the hell's unfair about it? You asked to come on this jaunt on the grounds that you could control him. Well, you just do that, or I'll do a bit of controlling in my own way.'

She scrambled to her feet. 'You're against him, too. You're siding with Fallon.'

'I'm not siding with anyone,' I said tiredly. 'I'm just sick to death of seeing a piece of scientific research being treated as though it were a competitive sporting event—or a war. And I might tell you that *that* attitude is one sided—it doesn't come from Fallon.'

'It doesn't have to,' she said viciously. 'He's on top.'

'On top of what, for God's sake? Both Fallon and Paul are here doing a job of work, and why Paul doesn't get on with it and await the outcome is beyond me.'

'Because Fallon will . . .' She stopped. 'Oh, what's the use of talking? You wouldn't understand.'

'That's right,' I said sarcastically. 'I'm so dumb and stupid I can't put two and two together. Don't be so bloody patronizing.'

It's said that some women appear more beautiful when angry, but for my money it's a myth probably bruited about by constitutionally angry women. Katherine was in a rage and she looked ugly. With one quick movement she brought up her hand and slapped me—hard. She must have played a lot of tennis in her time because that forehand swing of hers really jolted me.

I just looked at her. 'Of course that solves a lot of problems.' I said quietly, 'Katherine, I admire loyalty in a wife, but you're not just loyal—you've been brainwashed.'

There was a sudden throb in the air and then a roar as the helicopter appeared over the trees and passed overhead. I looked up and saw Paul Halstead's head twist around to watch us.

Seven

Every three days a big helicopter came in from Camp One bringing drums of fuel for the diesel generators and cylinders of gas for the camp kitchen as and when necessary. It also brought in the mail which had been flown from Mexico City by Fallon's jet, so I could keep in touch with England. Mount wrote to me telling me that probate was going through without much difficulty, and Jack Edgecombe had taken fire at last and was enthusiastic about the new plan for the farm. He was going ahead in spite of acid comments from the locals and was sure we were on to a good thing.

Reading those letters from Devon while in that stinking hot clearing in the middle of Quintana Roo made me home-sick and I debated once again whether or not to quit. This business had got nothing to do with me and I was feeling more on the outside than ever because there was a distinct coolness now between Katherine and myself.

On the day of the quarrel there had been raised voices from the Halsteads' hut quite late into the night and, when Katherine appeared next morning, she wore a shirt with a high collar. It wasn't quite high enough to hide the bruise on the side of her throat and I felt an odd tension in the pit of my stomach. But how a man and his wife conducted their marriage had nothing to do with me, so I left it at that. Katherine, for her part, pointedly ignored me, but Halstead didn't change at all —he just went on his usual bastardly way.

I was just on the point of quitting when Fallon showed me a letter from Pat Harris who had news of Gatt. *'Jack is making the rounds of Yucatan,'* he wrote. *He has been to Merida, Valladolid and Vigio Chico, and is now in Felipe Carillo Puerto. He seems to be looking for something or someone— my guess is someone, because he's talking to some of the weirdest characters. Since Jack prefers to spend his vacations in Miami and Las Vegas I think this is a business trip—but it sure is funny business. It's not like him to sweat when there is no need, so whatever he is doing must be important.'*

'Felipe Carillo Puerto used to be called Chan Santa Cruz,' said Fallon. 'It was the heart of the Mayan revolt, the capital of the indios sublevados. The Mexicans changed the name of the town when they got on top of the rebels in 1935. It's not very far from here—less than fifty miles.'

'It's obvious that Gatt's up to something,' I said.

'Yes,' agreed Fallon pensively. 'But what? I can't understand the man's motives.'

'I can,' I said, and laid it all out for Fallon's inspection—gold, gold, and again gold. 'Whether or not there is any gold doesn't matter as long as Gatt thinks there is.' I had another thought. 'You once showed me a plate of Mayan manufacture. How much would the gold in that be worth?'

'Not much,' he said derisively. 'Maybe fifty or sixty dollars.'

'How much would the plate be worth at auction?'

'That's hard to say. Most of those things are in museums and don't come on the open market. Besides, the Mexican Government is very strict on the export of Mayan antiquities.'

'Make a guess?' I urged.

He looked irritated, and said, 'These things are priceless—no one has ever tried to put a price on them. Any unique work of art is worth what someone is willing to pay.'

'How much did you pay for that plate?'

'Nothing—I found it.'

'How much would you sell it for?'

'I wouldn't,' he said definitely.

It was my turn to get exasperated. 'For God's sake! How much would you be willing to pay for that plate if you didn't have it already? You're a rich man and a collector.'

He shrugged. 'Maybe I'd go up to $20,000—maybe more, if pushed.'

'That's good enough for Gatt, even if he is clued up on the gold fallacy—which I don't think he is. Would you expect to find any similar objects in Uaxuanoc?'

'It's likely,' said Fallon. He frowned. 'I think I'd better have a word with Joe Rudetsky about this.'

'How are things coming along?' I asked.

'We can't get anything more out of the air survey,' he said.

'Now we've got to get down on the ground.' He pointed to the photo-mosaic. 'We've cut down the probables to four.' He looked up. 'Ah, here's Paul.'

Halstead came into the hut, the usual glower on his face. He dumped two belts on the table, complete with scabbarded machetes. 'These are what we'll need now,' he said. His tone implied—*I told you so!*

'I was just talking about that,' said Fallon. 'Will you ask Rider to come in?'

'Am I a messenger boy now?' asked Halstead sourly.

Fallon's eyes narrowed. I said quickly, 'I'll get him.' It wasn't to anyone's advantage to bring things to a boil, and *I* was quite willing to be a messenger boy—there are less dignified professions.

I found Rider doing a polishing job on his beloved chopper. 'Fallon's calling a conference,' I said. 'You're wanted.'

He gave a final swipe with a polishing rag. 'Right away.' As he walked with me to the hut, he asked, 'What's with that guy, Halstead?'

'What do you mean?'

'He's been trying to order me around; so I told him I work for Mr. Fallon. He got quite sassy about it.'

'He's just like that,' I said. 'I wouldn't worry about it.'

'I'm not worried about it,' said Rider with elaborate unconcern. 'But he'd better worry. He's liable to get a busted jaw.'

I put my hand on Rider's arm. 'Not so fast—you wait your turn.'

He grinned. 'So it's like that? Okay, Mr. Wheale; I'll fall in line right behind you. But don't wait too long.'

When Rider and I walked into the hut there seemed to be some tension between Fallon and Halstead. I thought that maybe Fallon had been tearing into Halstead for his uncooperative attitude—he wasn't the man to mince his words—and Halstead looked even more bloody-minded than ever. But he kept his mouth shut as Fallon said shortly, 'Let's get to the next step.'

I leaned against the table. 'Which do you tackle first?'

'That's obvious,' said Fallon. 'We have four possibles, but there's only one at which we can put down the helicopter. That's the one we explore first.'

'How do you get to the others?'

'We winch a man down,' said Fallon. 'I've done it before.'

So he might have, but he wasn't getting any younger. 'I'll give that a go,' I offered.

Halstead snorted. 'With what object in mind?' he demanded. 'What do *you* think you could do when you got on the ground? This needs a man with eyes in his head.'

Regardless of the unpleasant way in which he phrased it, Halstead was probably right. I had already seen how difficult it was to spot a Mayan ruin which Fallon had seen casually, and I could certainly miss something which might prove of the utmost importance.

Fallon made a quick gesture with his hand. 'I'll go down—or Paul will. Probably both of us.'

Rider said hesitantly, 'What about Number Two—that one's real tricky.'

'We'll consider that if and when it's necessary,' said Fallon. 'We'll save it until the last. When will you be ready to leave?'

'I'm ready now, Mr. Fallon.'

'Let's go, then. Come on, Paul.'

Fallon and Rider walked out and I was about to follow when Halstead said. 'Just a minute, Wheale; I want to talk to you.'

I turned. There was something in his voice that made my short hairs prickly. He was buckling a belt around his middle and adjusting the machete at his side. 'What is it?'

'Just this,' he said in a strained voice. 'Stay away from my wife.'

'What the hell do you mean by that?'

'Exactly what I said. You've been hanging around her like a dog around a bitch in heat. Don't think I haven't seen you.' His deeply sunken eyes looked manic and his hands were trembling slightly.

I said, 'The choice of phrase was yours—you called her a bitch, not me.' His hand clutched convulsively at the hilt of the machete, and I said sharply, 'Now just listen to me. I haven't touched Katherine, nor do I intend to—nor would she let me if I tried. All that's gone on between us is all that goes on between reasonable people in our position, and that's conversation of varying degrees of friendliness. And I must say we're not too friendly right at this minute.'

'Don't try to pull that on me,' he said savagely. 'What were you doing with her down at the pool three days ago?'

'If you want to know, we were having a flaming row,' I said.

'But why don't you ask her?' He was silent at that, and looked at me hard. 'But, of course, you did ask her, didn't you? You asked her with your fist. Why don't you try asking me that way, Halstead? With your fists or with that oversized carving knife you have there? But watch it—you can get hurt.'

For a moment I thought he was going to pull the machete and cleave my skull, and my fingers closed around one of the stones that Fallon used to weigh the maps on the table. At last he expelled his breath in a whistling sound and he thrust home the machete into its sheath the half inch he had withdrawn it. 'Just stay away from her,' he said hoarsely. 'That's all.'

He shouldered past me and left the hut to disappear into the blinding sunlight outside. Then came the sudden rhythmical roar from the chopper and it took off, and the sound faded quickly as it went over the trees, just as it always did.

I leaned against the table and felt the sweat break out on my forehead and at the back of my neck. I looked at my hands. They were trembling uncontrollably, and when I turned them over I saw the palms were wet. What the flaming hell was I doing in a set-up like this? And what had possessed me to push at Halstead so hard? The man was obviously a little loose in the brainbox and he could very well have cut me down with that damned machete. I had a sudden feeling that this whole operation was sending me as crazy as he obviously was.

I pushed myself away from the table and walked outside. There was no one to be seen. I strode over to the Halsteads' hut and knocked on the door. There was no reply, so I knocked again, and Katherine called, 'Who is it?'

'Who were you expecting? It's Jemmy, damn it!'

'I don't want to talk to you.'

'You don't have to,' I said. 'All you have to do is listen. Open the door.'

There was a long pause and then a click as the door opened not too widely. She didn't look very well and there were dark smudges below her eyes. I leaned on the door and swung it open wider. 'You said you could control your husband,' I said. 'You'd better start hauling on the reins because he seems to think that you and I are having a passionate affair.'

'I know,' she said tonelessly.

I nodded. 'You know, of course. I wonder how he could

have got that impression? You couldn't have led him on a bit—some women do.'

She flared. 'That's a despicable thing to say.'

'Very likely it is; I'm not feeling too spicable right now. That nutty husband of yours and I nearly had a fight not five minutes ago.'

She looked alarmed. 'Where is he?'

'Where do you think he is? He's gone with Fallon in the chopper. Look, Katherine; I'm not too sure that Paul shouldn't pull out of this expedition.'

'Oh, no,' she said quickly. 'You couldn't do that.'

'I could—and I will—if he doesn't bloody well behave himself. Even Rider is threatening to hammer him. You know that he is only here because of my say-so; that I forced him down Fallon's throat. One word from me and Fallon will be only too glad to get rid of him.'

She grabbed my hand. 'Oh, please, Jemmy; please don't do that.'

'Get up off your knees,' I said. 'Why the hell should you have to plead for him? I told you a long time ago, back in England, that you can't apologize for another person—not even your husband.' She was looking very blue, so I said, 'All right, I won't push him out—but see that he stays off my neck.'

'I'll try,' she said. 'I really will try. Thanks, Jemmy.'

I blew out my cheeks. 'If I'm accused of it, and if I'm going to get into a fight because of it, this passionate affair might not be such a bad idea. At least I'll get myself half-killed because of something I did.'

She stiffened. 'I don't think that's funny.'

'Neither do I,' I said wearily. 'With me the girl has to be willing—and you're not exactly panting hotly down the back of my neck. Forget it. Consider I made a pass and got slapped down. But, Katherine, how you stand that character, I don't know.'

'Maybe it's something you wouldn't understand.'

'Love?' I shrugged. 'Or is it misplaced loyalty? But if I were a woman—and thank God I'm not—and a man hit me, I'd walk right out on him.'

Pink spots showed in her cheeks. 'I don't know what you mean.'

I lifted a finger and smoothed down her collar. 'I suppose you got that bruise walking into a door.'

She said hotly, 'How I get my bruises is none of your damned business.'

The door slammed in my face.

I contemplated the sun-seared woodwork for quite a while, then sighed and turned away. I went back to the big hut and opened the refrigerator and looked at the serried rows of beer cans, all nicely frosted. Then I slammed it shut and went into Fallon's hut where I confiscated a bottle of his best Glenlivet whisky. I needed something stronger than beer right then.

An hour later I heard the chopper coming back. It landed and taxied into the hangar and out of the sun and, from where I was sitting, I could see Rider refuelling and I heard the rhythmic clank of the hand pump. I suppose I should have gone to help him but I didn't feel like helping anyone, and after three stiff whiskies the idea of going into the sun struck me as being definitely unwise.

Presently Rider came into the hut. 'Hot!' he said, stating the obvious.

I looked up at him. 'Where are the brains?'

'I dropped them at the site. I'll go back in four hours to pick them up.' He sat down and I pushed the whisky bottle at him. He shook his head. 'Uh-uh—that's too strong for this time of day. I'll get me a cold beer.'

He stood up, got his beer, and came back to the table. 'Where's Mrs. Halstead?'

'Sulking in her tent.'

He frowned at that, but his brow cleared as he drank his beer. 'Ah, that's good!' he sat down. 'Say, what happened between you and Halstead? When he climbed into the chopper he looked as though someone had rammed a pineapple up his ass.'

'Let's say we had a slight altercation.'

'Oh!' He pulled a pack of cards from his shirt pocket and and riffled them. 'What about a game to pass the time?'

'What would you suggest?' I enquired acidly. 'Happy Families!'

He grinned. 'Can you play gin?'

He beat the pants off me.

II

There was nothing at the site. Fallon came back looking tired and drawn and I thought that his years were catching up with him. The forest of Quintana Roo was no place for a man in his sixties, or even for a man in his thirties as I had recently discovered. I had taken a machete and done a bit of exploring and I hadn't left the clearing for more than ten minutes before I was totally lost. It was only because I had the sense to take a compass and to make slash marks on trees that I managed to get back.

I gave him a glass of his own whisky which he accepted with appreciation. His clothes were torn and blood caked cuts in his hands. I said, 'I'll get the first-aid kit and clean that up for you.'

He nodded tiredly. As I cleaned the scratches, I said, 'You ought to leave the dirty work to Halstead. '

'He works hard enough,' said Fallon. 'He's done more than me today.'

'Where is he?'

'Getting cleaned up. I suppose Katherine is doing the same to him as you've done to me.' He flexed his fingers against the adhesive dressings. 'It's better when a woman does it, somehow. I remember my wife bandaging me up quite often.'

'I didn't know you are married.'

'I was. Very happily married. That was many years ago.' He opened his eyes. 'What happened between you and Halstead this morning?'

'A difference of opinion.'

'It often happens with that young man, but it's usually of a professional nature. This wasn't, was it?'

'No, it wasn't,' I said. 'It was personal and private.'

He caught the implication—that I was warning him off—and chose to ignore it. 'For anyone to interfere between man and wife is very serious,' he said.

I drove the cork into the bottle of antiseptic. 'I'm not interfering; Halstead just thinks I am.'

'I have your word for that?'

'You have my word—not that it's any business of yours,' I said. As soon as I had said it I was sorry. 'It is your business, of course; you don't want this expedition wrecked.'

'That wasn't in my mind,' he said. 'At least, not as far as you are concerned. But I am becoming perturbed about Paul; he is proving very awkward to work with. I was wondering if I could ask you to release me from my promise. It's entirely up to you.'

I pounded at the cork again. I had just promised Katherine that I wouldn't get Halstead tossed out on his ear, and I couldn't go back on that. 'No,' I said. 'Other promises have been made.'

'I understand,' said Fallon. 'Or, at least, I think I do.' He looked up at me. 'Don't make a fool of yourself, Jemmy.'

That piece of advice was coming a bit too late. I grinned and put down the antiseptic bottle. 'It's all right; I'm not a home wrecker. But Halstead had better watch himself or he'll be in trouble.'

'Pour me another whisky,' said Fallon. He picked up the antiseptic bottle, and said mildly, 'We're going to have trouble getting that cork out again.'

The Halsteads had another quarrel that night. Neither of them appeared for supper and, after dark, I listened to the raised voices coming from their hut, rising and falling but never distinguishable enough to make sense. Just raw anger coming from the darkness.

I half expected Halstead to stomp over to my hut and challenge me to a duel, but he didn't and I thought that maybe Katherine must have argued him out of it. More probably, the argument I had put up had a lot of weight behind it. Halstead couldn't afford to be ejected from the expedition at this stage. It might be a good idea to pass on Fallon's attitude to Katherine just to make sure that Halstead realized that I was the only person who could prevent it.

As I went to sleep it occurred to me that if we did find Uaxuanoc I'd better start guarding my back.

III

Four days later there was only one site to be investigated. Fourteen out of the fifteen in Fallon's original list had proved to be barren; if this last one proved a bust then we would have to extend our radius of exploration and take in another forty-seven sites. That would be a bind, to say the least of it.

We had an early-morning conference before the last site was checked and nobody was happy about it. The cenote lay below a ridge which was thickly covered in trees and Rider was worried about the problem of getting in while coping with air currents. Worse still, there was no possible place for a man to drop from the winch; the vegetation was thick and extended right to the edge of the cenote without thinning in any way.

Fallon studied the photographs and said despondently, 'This is the worst I've seen anywhere. I don't think there's a chance of getting in from the air. What do you think, Rider?'

'I can drop a man,' said Rider. 'But he'd probably break his neck. Those trees are running to 140 feet and tangled to hell. I don't think a man could reach the ground.'

'The forest primeval,' I commented.

'No,' contradicted Fallan. 'If it were, our work would be easier. All this ground has been cultivated at one time—all over Quintana Roo. What we have here is a second growth; that's why it's so goddamn thick.' He switched off the projector and walked over to the photo-mosaic. 'It's very thick for a long way around this cenote—which is archeologically promising but doesn't help us in getting in.' He laid his finger on the photograph. 'Could you put us down there, Rider?'

Rider inspected the point Fallon indicated, first with the naked eye and then through a magnifying glass. 'It's possible,' he said.

Fallon applied a ruler. 'Three miles from the cenote. In that stuff we couldn't do more than half a mile an hour—probably much less. Say a full day to get to the cenote. Well, if it must be done, we'll do it.' He didn't sound at all enthusiastic.

Halstead said, 'We can use Wheale now. Are you good with a machete, Wheale?' He just couldn't get out of the habit of needling me.

'I don't have to be good,' I said. 'I use my brains instead. Let me have another look at those photographs.'

Fallon switched on the projector and we ran through them again. I stopped at the best one which showed a very clear view of the cenote and the surrounding forest. 'Can you get down over the water?' I asked Rider.

'I guess I could,' said Rider. 'But not for long. It's goddamn close to that hillside at the back of the pool.'

I turned to Fallon. 'How did you make this clearing we have here?'

'We dropped a team in with power saws and flame-throwers,' he said. 'They burned away the ground vegetation and cut down the trees—then blasted out the stumps with gelignite.'

137

I stared at the photograph and estimated the height from water-level to the edge of the pit of the cenote. It appeared to be about thirty feet. I said, 'If Rider can drop me in the water, I can swim to the edge and climb out.'

'So what?' said Halstead. 'What do you do then? Twiddle your thumbs?'

'Then Rider comes in again and lowers a chain saw and a flame-thrower on the end of the winch.'

Rider shook his head violently. 'I couldn't get them anywhere near you. Those trees on the edge are too tall. Jesus, if I get the winch cable tangled in those I'd crash for sure.'

'Supposing when I went into the water I had a thin nylon cord, say about a couple of hundred yards, with one end tied to the winch cable. I pay it out as I swim to the side, then you haul up the cable and I pay out some more. Then you take up the chopper, high enough to be out of trouble, and I pay out even more line. When you come down again over the cenote with the stuff dangling on the end of the cable, I just haul it in to the side. Is that possible?'

Rider looked even more worried. 'Hauling a heavy weight to one side like that is going to have a hell of an effect on stability.' He rubbed his chin. 'I reckon I could do it though.'

'What would you reckon to do once you got down?' asked Fallon.

'If Rider will tell me how much clear ground he needs to land the chopper, I'll guarantee to clear it. There might be a few stumps, but he'll be landing vertically, so they shouldn't worry him too much. I'll do it—unless someone else wants to volunteer. What about you, Dr. Halstead?'

'Not me,' he said promptly. He looked a bit shamefaced for the first time since I'd met him. 'I can't swim.'

'Then I'm elected,' I said cheerfully, although why I was cheerful is hard to say. I think it was the chance of actually doing something towards the work of the expedition that did it. I was tired of being a spare part.

I checked on the operation of the saw and the flame-thrower and saw they were fully fuelled. The flame-thrower produced a satisfactory gout of smoky flame which shrivelled the undergrowth very nicely. 'I'm not likely to start a forest fire, am I?' I asked.

'Not a chance,' said Fallon. 'You're in a rain forest and these aren't northern conifers.'

Halstead was coming with me. There was so much weight to be put into the helicopter that there could be only two passengers, and since it was going to be a job for a strongish man to attach the gear to the winch cable and get it out of the helicopter Halstead was chosen in preference to Fallon.

But I wasn't too happy about it. I said to Rider, 'I know you'll be busy jockeying this chopper at the critical moment, but I'd be obliged if you'd keep half an eye on Halstead.'

He caught the implication without half trying. 'I operate the winch. You'll get down safely.'

We took off and were over the site within a very few minutes. I waggled my hand in a circle to Rider and he orbited the cenote at a safe height while I studied the situation. It's one thing to look at photographs on solid ground, and quite another to look at the real thing with the prospect of dangling over it on the end of a line within the next five minutes.

At last I was satisfied that I knew where to aim for once I was in the water. I checked the nylon cord which was the hope of the whole operation and stepped into the canvas loops at the end of the cable. Rider brought the helicopter lower, and I went cautiously through the open door and was only supported by the cable itself.

The last thing I saw of Rider was his hand pulling on a lever and then I was dropping away below the helicopter and spinning like a teetotum. Every time I made a circuit I saw the green hillside behind the cenote coming closer until it was too damned close altogether and I thought the blades of the rotor were going to chop into projecting branches.

I was now a long way below the helicopter, as far as the winch cable would unreel, and my rate of spin was slowing. Rider brought the chopper down gently into the chimney formed by the surrounding trees and I touched the water. I hammered the quick-release button and the harness fell away and I found myself swimming. I trod water and organized the nylon cord, then struck out for the edge of the cenote, paying out the cord behind me, until I grasped a tree root at water-level.

The sides of the cenote were steeper than I had thought and covered with a tangle of creeper. I don't know how long it took me to climb the thirty feet to the top but it was much longer than I had originally estimated and must have seemed a lifetime to Rider, who had a very delicate bit of flying to do.

But I made it at last, bleeding from a score of cuts on my arms and chest, yet still holding on to that precious cord.

I waved to Rider and the helicopter began to inch upwards, and slowly the cable was reeled in. I paid out the cord, and when the helicopter was hovering at a safe height, five hundred feet of cord hung down in a graceful catenary curve. While Halstead was no doubt struggling to get the load on to the end of the winch cable I got my breath back and prepared for my own struggle.

It was not going to be an easy task to haul over a hundred pounds of equipment sixty feet sideways. I took off the canvas belt that was wrapped around my middle and put it about a young tree. It was fitted with a snap hook with a quick release in case of emergencies. There was very little room to move on the edge of the cenote because of the vegetation— there was one tree that must have been ninety feet high whose roots were exposed right on the rim. I took the machete and swung at the undergrowth, clearing space to move in.

There was a change in the note of the chopper's engine, the pre-arranged signal that Rider was ready for the next stage of the operation, and, slowly it began to descend again with the bulk of the cargo hanging below on the winch cable. Hastily I began to reel in the cord hand over hand until the shapeless bundle at the end of the winch cable was level with me, but sixty feet away and hanging thirty feet above the water of the cenote.

I wrapped three turns of the cord around the tree to serve as a friction brake and then began to haul in. At first it came easily but the nearer it got the harder it was to pull it in. Rider came lower as I pulled which made it a bit easier, but it was still back-breaking. Once the chopper wobbled alarmingly in the air, but Rider got it under control again and I continued hauling.

I was very glad when I was able to lean over and snap the hook of the canvas belt on to the end of the winch cable. A blow at the quick-release button let the cargo fall heavily to the ground. I looked up at the chopper and released the cable, which swung in a wide arc right across the cenote. For a moment I thought it was going to entangle in the trees on the other side, but Rider was already reeling it in fast and the chopper was going up like an express lift. It stopped at a safe height, then orbited three times before leaving in the direction of Camp Two.

I sat on the edge of the cenote with my feet dangling over the side for nearly fifteen minutes before I did anything else. I was all aches and pains and felt as though I'd been in a wrestling match with a bear. At last I began to unwrap the gear. I put on the shirt and trousers that had been packed, and also the calf-length boots, then lit a cigarette before I went exploring.

At first I chopped around with the machete because the tank of the flame-thrower didn't hold too much fuel and the thing itself was bloody wasteful, so I wanted to save the fire for the worst of the undergrowth. As I chopped my way through that tangle of leaves I wondered how the hell Fallon had expected to travel half a mile in an hour; the way I was going I couldn't do two hundred yards an hour. Fortunately I didn't have to. All I had to do was to clear an area big enough for the helicopter to drop into.

I was flailing away with the machete when the blade hit something with a hell of a clang and the shock jolted up my arm. I looked at the edge and saw it had blunted and I wondered what the devil I'd hit. I swung again, more cautiously, clearing away the broad-bladed leaves, and suddenly I saw a face staring at me—a broad, Indian face with a big nose and slightly crossed eyes.

Half an hour's energetic work revealed a pillar into which was incorporated a statue of sorts of a man elaborately dressed in a long belted tunic and with a complicated head-dress. The rest of the pillar was intricately carved with a design of leaves and what looked like over-sized insects.

I lit a cigarette and contemplated it for a long time. It began to appear that perhaps we had found Uaxuanoc, although being a layman I couldn't be certain. However, no one would carve a thing like that just to leave it lying about in the forest. It was a pity in a way, because now I'd have to go somewhere else to carve my helicopter platform—the chopper certainly couldn't land on top of this cross-eyed character who stood about eight feet tall.

I went back to the edge of the cenote and started to carve a new path delimiting the area I wanted to clear, and a few random forays disclosed no more pillars, so I got busy. As I expected, the flame-thrower ran out of juice long before I had finished but at least I had used it to the best advantage to leave the minimum of machete work. Then I got going with

141

the chain saw, cutting as close to the ground as I could, and there was a shriek as the teeth bit into the wood.

None of the trees was particularly thick through the trunk, the biggest being about two and a half feet. But they were tall and I had trouble there. I was no lumberjack and I made mistakes—the first tree nearly knocked me into the cenote as it fell, and it fell the wrong way, making a hell of a tangle that I had to clean up laboriously. But I learned and by the time darkness came I had felled sixteen trees.

I slept that night in a sleeping-bag which stank disgustingly of petrol because the chain saw around which it had been wrapped had developed a small leak. I didn't mind because I thought the smell might keep the mosquitoes away. It didn't.

I ate tinned cold chicken and drank whisky from the flask Fallon had thoughtfully provided, diluting it with warmish water from a water-bottle, and I sat there in the darkness thinking of the little brown people with big noses who had carved that big pillar and who had possibly built a city on this spot. After a while I fell asleep.

Morning brought the helicopter buzzing overhead and a man dangling like a spider from the cable winch. I still hadn't cleared up enough for it to land but there was enough man-oeuvring space for Rider to drop a man by winch, and the man proved to be Halstead. He dropped heavily to the ground at the edge of the cenote and waved Rider away. The helicopter rose and slowly circled.

Halstead came over to me and then looked around. 'This isn't where you'd intended to clear the ground. Why the change?'

'I ran into difficulties,' I said.

He grinned humourlessly. 'I thought you might.' He looked at the tree stumps. 'You haven't got on very well, have you? You should have done better than this.'

I waved my arm gracefully. 'I bow to superior knowledge. Be my guest—go right ahead and improve the situation.'

He grunted but didn't take me up on the offer. Instead he unslung the long box he carried on his shoulder, and extended an antenna. 'We had a couple of walkie-talkies sent up from Camp One. We can talk to Rider. What do we need to finish the job?'

'Juice for the saw and the flamer; dynamite for the stumps

—and a man to use it, unless you have the experience. I've never used explosives in my life.'

'I can use it,' he said curtly, and started to talk to Rider. In a few minutes the chopper was low overhead again and a couple of jerrycans of fuel were lowered to us. Then it buzzed off and we got to work.

To give Halstead his due, he worked like a demon. Two pairs of hands made a difference, too, and we'd done quite a lot before the helicopter came back. This time a box of gelignite came down, and after it Fallon descended with his pockets full of detonators. He turned them over to Halstead, and looked at me with a twinkle in his eye. 'You look as though you've been dragged through a bush backwards.' He looked about him. 'You've done a good job.'

'I have something to show you,' I said and led him along the narrow path I had driven the previous day. 'I ran across Old-Cross-eyes here; he hampered the operation a bit.'

Fallon threw a fit of ecstatics and damned near clasped Cross-eyes to his bosom. 'Old Empire!' he said reverently, and ran his hands caressingly over the carved stone.

'What is it?'

'It's a stele—a Mayan date stone. In a given community they erected a stele every katun—that's a period of nearly twenty years.' He looked back along the path towards the cenote. 'There should be more of these about; they might even ring the cenote.'

He began to strip the clinging creepers away and I could see he'd be no use anywhere else. I said, 'Well, I'll leave you two to get acquainted. I'll go help Halstead blow himself up.'

'All right,' he said absently. Then he turned. 'This is a marvellous find. It will help us date the city right away.'

'The city?' I waved my hand at the benighted wilderness. 'Is *this* Uaxuanoc?'

He looked up at the pillar. 'I have no doubt about it. Stelae of this complexity are found only in cities. Yes, I think we've found Uaxuanoc.'

IV

We had a hell of a job getting Fallon away from his beloved pillar and back to Camp Two. He mooned over it like a lover who had just found his heart's desire, and filled a notebook with squiggly drawings and pages of indecipherable scribblings. Late that afternoon we practically had to carry him to the helicopter, which had landed precariously at the edge of the cenote, and during the flight back he muttered to himself all the way.

I was very tired, but after a luxurious hot bath I felt eased in body and mind, eased enough to go into the big hut and join the others instead of falling asleep. I found Fallon and Halstead hot in the pursuit of knowledge, with Katherine hovering on the edge of the argument in her usual role of Halstead-quietener.

I listened in for a time, not understanding very much of what was going on and was rather surprised to find Halstead the calmer of the two. After the outbursts of the last few weeks, I had expected him to blow his top when we actually found Uaxuanoc, but he was as cold as ice and any discussion he had with Fallon was purely intellectual. He seemed as uninterested as though he'd merely found a sixpence in the street instead of the city he'd been bursting a gut trying to find.

It was Fallon who was bubbling over with excitement. He was as effervescent as a newly opened bottle of champagne and could hardly keep still as he shoved his sketches under Halstead's nose. 'Definitely Old Empire,' he insisted. 'Look at the glyphs.'

He went into a rigmarole which seemed to be in a foreign language. I said, 'Ease up, for heaven's sake! What about letting me in on the secret?'

He stopped and looked at me in astonishment. 'But I'm telling you.'

'You'd better tell me in English.'

He leaned back in his chair and shook his head sadly. 'To explain the Mayan calendar would take me more time than I have to spare, so you'll have to take my word for a lot of this. But look here.' He pushed over a set of his squiggles which I recognized as the insects I had seen sculpted on the pillar. 'That's the date of the stele—it reads: "9 Cycles, 12 Katuns, 10 Tuns, 12 Kins, 4 Eb, 10 Yax", and that's a total of 1,386,112 days, or 3,797 years. Since the Mayan datum from which all time measurement started was 3113 B.C., then that gives us a date of 684 A.D.'

He picked up the paper. 'There's a bit more to it—the

Mayas were very accurate—it was 18 days after the new moon in the first cycle of six.'

He had said all that very rapidly and I felt a bit dizzy. 'I'll take your word for it,' I said. 'Are you telling me that Uaxuanoc is nearly thirteen hundred years old?'

'That stele is,' he said positively. 'The city is older, most likely.'

'That's a long time before Vivero,' I said thoughtfully. 'Would the city have been occupied that long?'

'You're confusing Old Empire with New Empire,' he said. 'The Old Empire collapsed about 800 A.D. and the cities were abandoned, but over a hundred years later there was an invasion of Toltecs—the Itzas—and some of the cities were rehabilitated like Chichen Itza and a few others. Uaxuanoc was one of them, very likely.' He smiled. 'Vivero referred often to the Temple of Kukulkan in Uaxuanoc. We have reason to believe that Kukulkan was a genuine historical personage; the man who led the Toltecs into Yucatan, very much as Moses led the Children of Israel into the Promised Land. Certainly the Mayan-Toltec civilization of the New Empire bore very strong resemblances to the Aztec Empire of Mexico and was rather unlike the Mayan Old Empire. There was the prevalence of human sacrifice, for one thing. Old Vivero wasn't wrong about that.'

'So Uaxuanoc was inhabited at the time of Vivero? I mean, ignoring his letter and going by the historical evidence.'

'Oh, yes. But don't get me wrong when I talk of empires. The New Empire had broken up by the time the Spaniards arrived. There were just a lot of petty states and warring provinces which banded together into an uneasy alliance to resist the Spaniards. It may have been the Spaniards who gave the final push, but the system couldn't have lasted much longer in any case.'

Halstead had been listening with a bored look on his face. This was all old stuff to him and he was becoming restive. He said, 'When do we start on it?'

Fallon pondered. 'We'll have to have quite a big organization there on the site. It's going to take a lot of men to clear that forest.'

He was right about that. It had taken three man-days to clear enough ground for a helicopter to land, piloted by a very skilful man. To clear a hundred acres with due archeological care was going to take a small army a hell of a long time.

He said, 'I think we'll abandon this camp now and pull back to Camp One. I'll get Joe Rudetsky busy setting up Camp Three on the site. Now we can get a helicopter in it shouldn't prove too difficult. We'll need quarters for twenty men to start with, I should think. It will take at least a fortnight to get settled in.'

'Why wait until then?' asked Halstead impatiently. 'I can get a lot of work done while that's going on. The rainy season isn't far off.'

'We'll get the logistics settled first,' said Fallon sharply. 'It will save time in the long run.'

'The hell with that!' said Halstead. 'I'm going to go up there and have a look round anyway. I'll leave you to run your goddamn logistics.' He leaned forward. 'Can't you see what's waiting to be picked up there—right on the ground? Even Wheale stumbled over something important first crack out of the box, only he was too dumb to see what it was.

'It's been there thirteen hundred years,' said Fallon. 'It will still be there in another three weeks—when we can go about the job properly.'

'Well, I'm going to do a preliminary survey,' said Halstead stubbornly.

'No, you're not,' said Fallon definitely. 'And I'll tell you why you're not. Nobody is going to take you—I'll see to that. Unless you're prepared to take a stroll through the forest.'

'Damn you!' said Halstead violently. He turned to his wife. 'You wouldn't believe me, would you? You've been hypnotized by what Wheale's been telling you. Can't you see he wants to keep it to himself; that he wants first publication?'

'I don't give a damn about first publication,' said Fallon energetically. 'All I want is for the job to be done properly. You don't start excavating a city in the manner of a grave-robber.'

Their voices were rising, so I said, 'Let's keep this quiet, shall we?'

Halstead swung on me, and his voice cracked. 'You keep out of this. You've been doing me enough damage as it is—crawling to my wife behind my back and turning her against me. You're all against me—the lot of you.'

'Nobody's against you,' said Fallon. 'If we were against you, you wouldn't be here at all.'

I cut in fast. 'And any more of this bloody nonsense and

you'll be out right now. I don't see why we have to put up with you, so just put a sock in it and act like a human being.'

I thought he was going to hit me. His chair went over with a crash as he stood up. 'For Christ's sake!' he said furiously, and stamped out of the hut.

Katherine stood up. 'I'm sorry,' she said.

'It's not your fault,' said Fallon. He turned to me. 'Psychiatry isn't my forte, but that looks like paranoia to me. That man has a king-size persecution complex.'

'It looks very like it.'

'Again I ask you to release me from my promise,' he said.

Katherine was looking very unhappy and disturbed. I said slowly, 'I told you there had been other promises.'

'Maybe,' said Fallon. 'But Paul, being in the mood he is, could endanger all of us. This isn't a good part of the world for personal conflicts.'

I said slowly, 'Katherine, if you can get Paul to see sense and come back and apologize, then he can stay. Otherwise he's definitely out—and I mean it. That puts it entirely in your hands, you understand.'

In a small voice she said, 'I understand.'

She went out and Fallon looked at me. 'I think you're making a mistake. He's not worth it.' He pulled out his pipe and started to fill it. After a moment he said in a low voice, 'And neither is she.'

'I've not fallen for her,' I said. 'I'm just bloody sorry for her. If Halstead gets pushed out now, her life won't be worth living.'

He struck a match and looked at the flame. 'Some people can't tell the difference between love and pity,' he said obscurely.

v

We flew down to the coast and Camp One early next morning. Halstead had slept on it, but not much, because the connubial argument had gone on long into the night. But she had evidently won because he apologized. It wasn't a very convincing apology and came as haltingly as though it were torn from him by hot pincers, but I judged it politic to accept it. After all, it was the first time in my experience that he had apologized for anything, so perhaps, although it came hesitantly, it was because it was an unaccustomed exercise. Anyway, it was a victory of sorts.

We landed at Camp One, which seemed to have grown larger in our absence; there were more huts than I remembered. We were met by Joe Rudetsky who had lost some of his easy imperturbability and looked a bit harried. When Fallon asked him what was the matter, he burst into a minor tirade.

'It's these goddamn poor whites—these chiclero bastards! They're the biggest lot of thieves I've ever seen. We're losing equipment faster than we can fly it in.'

'Do you have guards set up?'

'Sure—but my boys ain't happy. You jump one of those chicleros and he takes a shot at you. They're too goddamn trigger-happy and my boys don't like it; they reckon this isn't the job they're paid for.'

Fallon looked grim. 'Get hold of Pat Harris and tell him to ship in some of his security guards—the toughest he can find.'

'Sure, Mr. Fallon, I'll do that.' Rudetsky looked relieved because someone had made a decision. He said, 'I didn't know what to do about shooting back. We thought we might wreck things for you if we got into trouble with the local law.'

'There isn't much of that around here,' said Fallon. 'If anyone shoots at you, then you shoot right back.'

'Right!' said Rudetsky. 'Mr. Harris said he'd be coming along today or tomorrow.'

'Did he?' said Fallon. 'I wonder why.'

There was a droning noise in the sky and I looked up. 'That sounds like a plane. Maybe that's him.'

Rudetsky cocked his head skywards. 'No,' he said. 'That's the plane that's been flying along the coast all week—it's back and forward all the time.' He pointed. 'See—there it is.'

A small twin-engined plane came into sight over the sea and banked to turn over the airstrip. It dipped very low and howled over us with the din of small engines being driven hard. We ducked instinctively, and Rudetsky said, 'It's the first time he's done that.'

Fallon watched the plane as it climbed and turned out to sea. 'Have you any idea who it is?'

'No,' said Rudetsky. He paused. 'But I think we're going to find out. It looks as though it's coming in for a landing.'

The plane had turned again over the sea and was coming in straight and level right at the strip. It landed with a small bounce and rolled to a stop level with us, and a man climbed out and dropped to the ground. He walked towards us and, as he got nearer, I saw he was wearing tropical whites, spotlessly cleaned and pressed, and an incongruous match to the clothing worn by our little party after the weeks at Camp Two.

He approached and raised his Panama hat. 'Professor Fallon?' he enquired.

Fallon stepped forward. 'I'm Fallon.'

The man pumped his hand enthusiastically. 'Am I glad to meet you, Professor! I was in these parts and I thought I'd drop in on you. My name is Gatt—John Gatt.'

Eight

Gatt was a man of about fifty-five and a little overweight. He was as smooth as silk and had the politician's knack of talking a lot and saying nothing. According to him, he had long admired Professor Fallon and had regretted not being able to meet him before. He was in Mexico for the Olympic Games and had taken the opportunity of an excursion to Yucatan to visit the great Mayan cities—he had been to Uxmal, Chichen Itza and Coba—and, hearing that the great Professor Fallon was working in the area, he had naturally dropped in to pay his respects and to sit at the feet of genius. He name-dropped like mad—apparently he knew everyone of consequence in the United States—and it soon turned out that he and Fallon had mutual acquaintances.

It was all very plausible and, as he poured out his smoke-screen of words, I became fidgety for fear Fallon would be too direct with him. But Fallon was no fool and played the single-minded archeologist to perfection. He invited Gatt to stay for lunch, which invitation Gatt promptly accepted, and we were all set for a cosy chat.

As I listened to the conversation of this evidently cultured man I reflected that, but for the knowledge gained through Pat Harris, I could have been taken in completely. It was almost impossible to equate the dark world of drugs, prostitution and extortion with the pleasantly spoken Mr. John Gatt, who talked enthusiastically of the theatre and the ballet

149

and even nicked Fallon for a thousand dollars as a contribution to a fund for underprivileged children. Fallon made out a cheque without cracking a smile—a tribute to his own acting ability but even more a compliment to the fraudulent image of Gatt.

I think it was this aura of ambivalence about Gatt that prevented me from lashing out at him there and then. After all, this was the man who had caused the death of my brother and I ought to have tackled him, but in my mind there lurked the growing feeling that a mistake had been made, that this could not be the thug who controlled a big slice of the American underworld. I ought to have known better. I ought to have remembered that Himmler loved children dearly and that a man may smile and be a villain. So I did nothing—which was a pity.

Another thing which puzzled me about Gatt and which was a major factor contributing to my indecision was that I couldn't figure out what he was after. I would have thought that his reason for 'dropping in' would be to find out if we had discovered Uaxuanoc, but he never even referred to it. The closest he got to it was when he asked Fallon, 'And what's the subject of your latest research, Professor?'

'Just cleaning up some loose ends,' said Fallon noncommittally. 'There are some discrepancies in the literature about the dating of certain structures in this area.'

'Ah, the patient spadework of science,' said Gatt unctuously. 'A never-ending task.' He dropped the subject immediately and went on to say how impressed he had been by the massive architecture of Chichen Itza. 'I have an interest in city planning and urban renewal,' he said. 'The Mayas certainly knew all about pedestrian concourses. I've never seen a finer layout.'

I discovered later that his interest in city planning and urban renewal was confined to his activities as a slum landlord and the holding up of city governments to ransom over development plans. It was one of his most profitable sidelines.

He didn't concentrate primarily on Fallon; he discussed with Halstead, in fairly knowledgeable terms, some aspects of the Pueblo Indians of New Mexico, and talked with me about England. 'I was in England recently,' he said. 'It's a great country. Which part are you from?'

'Devon,' I said shortly.

'A very beautiful place,' he said approvingly. 'I remember

when I visited Plymouth I stood on the very spot from which the Pilgrim Fathers set sail so many years ago to found our country. It moved me very much.'

I thought that was a bit thick coming from a man who had started life as Giacomo Gattini. 'Yes, I rather like Plymouth myself,' I said casually, and then sank a barb into him. 'Have you ever been to Totnes?'

His eyes flickered, but he said smoothly enough, 'I've never had the pleasure.' I stared at him and he turned away and engaged Fallon in conversation again.

He left soon after lunch, and when his plane had taken off and headed north, I looked at Fallon blankly and said, 'What the devil do you make of that?'

'I don't know what to make of it,' said Fallon. 'I expected him to ask more questions than he did.'

'So did I. If we didn't know he was up to something I'd take that visit as being quite above board. Yet we know it wasn't—he must have been after *something*. But what was it? And did he get it?'

'I wish I knew,' said Fallon thoughtfully.

II

Pat Harris turned up in the jet during the afternoon and didn't seem surprised that we had had a visit from Gatt. He merely shrugged and went off to have a private talk with Fallon, but when he came back he was ruffled and exasperated. 'What's wrong with the Old Man?' he asked.

'Nothing that I know of,' I said. 'He's just the same as always.'

'Not from where I stand,' said Pat moodily. 'I can't get him to listen to me. All he's concerned with is pushing Rudetsky. Anything I say just bounces off.'

I smiled. 'He's just made the biggest discovery of his life. He's excited, that's all; he wants to get moving fast before the rains break. What's worrying you, Pat?'

'What do *you* think?' he said, staring at me. 'Gatt worries me—that's who. He's been holed up in Merida, and he's collected the biggest crowd of cut-throats assembled in Mexico since the days of Pancho Villa. He's brought in some of his own boys from Detroit, and borrowed some from connections in Mexico City and Tampico. And he's been talking to the chicleros. In my book that means he's going into the forest—he must have the chicleros to help him there. Now you tell me—if he goes into the forest, where would he be going?'

'Camp Three,' I said. 'Uaxuanoc. But there'll be nothing there for him—just a lot of ruins.'

'Maybe,' said Pat. 'But Jack evidently thinks differently. The thing that gripes me is that I can't get Fallon to do anything about it—and it's not like him.'

'Can't you do anything yourself? What about the authorities—the police? What about pointing out that there's a big build-up of known criminals in Merida?'

Pat looked at me pityingly. 'The fix is in,' he said patiently, as though explaining something to a small child. 'The local law has been soothed.'

'Bribed!'

'For Christ's sake, grow up!' he yelled. 'These local cops aren't as upright as your London bobbies, you know. I did what I could—and you know what happened? I got tossed in the can on a phoney charge, that's what! I only got out yesterday by greasing the palm of a junior cop who hadn't been lubricated by the top brass. You can write off the law in this part of the world.'

I took a deep breath. 'Accepting all this—what the hell would you expect Fallon to do about it?'

'He has high-level connections in the government; he's well respected in certain circles and can set things going so that the local law is short-circuited. But they're personal connections and he has to do it himself. I don't swing enough weight myself—I can't reach up that high. '

'Would it do any good if I talked to him?' I asked.

Pat shrugged. 'Maybe.' He shook his head dejectedly. 'I don't know what's got into him. His judgement is usually better than this.'

So I talked to Fallon and got a fast brush-off. He was talking to Rudetsky at the time, planning the move to Camp Three, and all his attention was on that. 'If you find anything in the preliminary clean-up, don't touch it,' he warned Rudetsky. 'Just leave it and clear round it.'

'I won't mess around with any stones,' said Rudetsky reassuringly.

Fallon looked tired and thinner than ever, as though the

flesh was being burned from his bones by the fire glowing within him. Every thought he had at that time was directed solely to one end—the excavation of the city of Uaxuanoc—and nothing else was of the slightest importance. He listened to me impatiently and then cut me off halfway through a sentence. 'All this is Harris's job,' he said curtly. 'Leave it to him.'

'But Harris says he can't do anything about it.'

'Then he's not worth the money I'm paying him,' growled Fallon, and walked away, ignoring me, and plunged again into the welter of preparations for the move to Camp Three.

I said nothing of this to the Halsteads; there was no point in scaring anyone else to death. But I did have another conversation with Pat Harris before he left to find out what Gatt was doing. I told him of my failure to move Fallon and he smiled grimly at Fallon's comment on his worth, but let it go.

'There's one thing that puzzles me,' he said. 'How in hell did Gatt know when to pitch up here? It's funny that he arrived just as soon as you'd discovered the city.'

'Coincidence,' I suggested.

But Pat was not convinced of that. He made me tell him of everything that had been said and was as puzzled as I had been about Gatt's apparent disinterest in the very thing we knew he was after. 'Did Gatt have the chance to talk to any-one alone?' he asked.

I thought about it and shook my head. 'He was with all of us all the time. We didn't let him wander around by himself, if that's what you mean.'

'He wasn't alone with anyone—not even for a minute?' Pat persisted.

I hesitated. 'Well, before he went to his plane he shook hands all round.' I frowned. 'Halstead had lagged behind and Gatt went back to shake hands. But it wasn't for long—not even fifteen seconds.'

'Halstead, by God!' exclaimed Pat. 'Let me tell you some-thing. You can pass along a hell of a lot of information in a simple handshake. Bear that in mind, Jemmy.'

With that cryptic remark he left, and I began to go over all the things I knew about Halstead. But it was ridiculous to suppose he had anything to do with Gatt. Ridiculous!

Harry Rider was a very busy man during the next few days. He flew Rudetsky and a couple of his men to Camp Three at Uaxuanoc, dropped them and came back for equipment. Rudetsky and his team hewed a bigger landing area out of the forest, and then the big cargo-carrying helicopter could go in and things really got moving. It was like a well-planned military operation exploiting a beach-head.

It would have been a big disappointment all round if this wasn't the site of Uaxuanoc, but Fallon showed no worry. He urged Rudetsky on to greater efforts and complacently watched the helicopters fly to and fro. The cost of keeping a big helicopter in the air is something fantastic and, although I knew Fallon could afford it, I couldn't help but point it out.

Fallon drew his pipe from his mouth and laughed. 'Damn it, you're an accountant,' he said. 'Use your brains. It would cost a lot more if I didn't use those choppers. I have to pay a lot of highly skilled men a lot of money to clear that site for preliminary investigation, and I'm damned if I'm going to pay them for hacking their way through the forest to get to the site. It's cheaper this way.'

And so it was from a cost-effectiveness point of view, as I found out when I did a brief analysis. Fallon wasn't wasting his money on that score, although some people might think that the excavation of a long-dead city was a waste of money in the first place.

Four more archeologists arrived—young men chock-full of enthusiasm. For three of them this was their first experience of a big dig and they fairly worshipped at the feet of Fallon, although I noticed they all tended to walk stiff-legged around Halstead. If his notoriety had spread down to the lower ranks of the profession then he was indeed in a bad way. I'm surprised Katherine didn't see it, although she probably put it down to the general effect of his prickly character on other people. But what a hell of a thing to have to live with!

Ten days after Fallon had made the big decision we went up to Camp Three and, circling over the cenote, I looked down upon a transformed scene quite different from what I had seen when dangling on the end of that cable. There was a little village down there—the huts were laid out in neat lines and there was a landing area to one side with hangars for the aircraft. All this had been chopped out of dense forest, in just over a week; Rudetsky was evidently something of a slave driver.

We landed and, as the rotor flapped into silence, I heard the howl of power saws from near by as the assault on the forest went on. And it was hot—hotter even than Camp Two; the sun, unshielded by the cover of trees, hammered the clearing with a brazen glare. Perspiration sprang out all over my body and by the time we had reached the shelter of a hut I was dripping.

Fallon wasted no time. 'This is not a very comfortable place,' he said. 'So we might as well get on with the job as quickly as we can. Our immediate aim is to find out what we have here in broad detail. The finer points will have to wait for the years to come. I don't intend to excavate any particular buildings at this time. Our work now is to delimit the area, to identify structures and to clear the ground for our successors.'

Halstead stirred and I could see he wasn't happy about that, but he said nothing.

'Joe Rudetsky has been here for nearly two weeks,' said Fallon. 'What have you found, Joe?'

'I found eight more of those pillars with carvings,' said Rudetsky. 'I did like you said—I just cleared around them and didn't go monkeying about.' He stood up and went to the map on the wall. Most of it was blank but an area around the cenote had been inked in. 'Here they are,' he said. 'I marked them all.'

'I'll have a look at them,' said Fallon. 'Gentlemen, Mr. Rudetsky is not an archeologist, but he is a skilled surveyor and he will be our cartographer.' He waved his hand. 'As the work goes on I hope this map will become filled in and cease to be terra incognita. Now, let's get on with it.'

He set up five teams, each headed by an archeologist who would direct the work, and to each team he gave an area. He had had the Vivero map from the mirror redrawn and used it as a rough guide. Then he turned to me. 'You will be an exception, Jemmy,' he said. 'I know we aren't going for detailed exploration at this time, but I think the cenote might provide some interesting finds. The cenote is yours.' He grinned. 'I think you're very lucky to be able to splash about in cool water all day while the rest of us sweat in the heat.'

I thought it was a good idea, too, and winked at Katherine. Halstead caught that and favoured me with a stony glare.

155

Then he turned to Fallon, and said, 'Dredging would be quicker—as Thompson did at Chichen Itza.'

'That was a long time ago,' said Fallon mildly. 'Dredging tends to destroy pottery. It would be a pity not to use the advanced diving techniques that have been developed since Thompson's day.'

This was so true archeologically that Halstead could not object further without looking a damned fool, and he said no more; but he spoke in a low tone to Katherine and shook his head violently several times. I had a good idea what he was telling her but I didn't interrupt—I'd find out soon enough.

The discussion continued for another half hour and then the meeting broke up. I went along with Rudetsky who was going to show me where the diving gear was and he led me to a hut that had been erected right on the edge of the cenote. 'I thought you'd like to be on the spot,' he said.

Half of the hut was to be my living quarters and contained a bed with mosquito netting, a table and chair and a small desk. The other half of the hut was filled with gear. I looked at it and scratched my head. 'I'd like to get that air compressor out of here,' I said. 'And all the big bottles. Can you build a shack by the side of the hut?'

'Sure: that's no trouble at all. I'll have it fixed by to-morrow.'

We went outside and I looked at the cenote. It was roughly circular and over a hundred feet in diameter. Behind it, the ridge rose sharply in almost a cliff, but easing off in steepness towards the top where Vivero had placed the Chac temple. I wondered how deep it was. 'I'd like a raft,' I said. 'From that we can drop a shot line and anchor it to the bottom—if we can get down that far. But that can wait until I've done a preliminary dive.'

'You just tell me what you want and I'll fix it,' said Rudetsky. 'That's what I'm here for—I'm Mr. Fixit in person.'

He went away and I tossed a pebble into the dark pool. It plopped in the middle of the still water and sent out a widening circle of ripples which lapped briefly at the edge, thirty feet below. If what I had been told was correct, many people had been sacrificed in this cenote and I wondered what I'd find at the bottom.

I went back to the hut and found Katherine waiting for me. She was looking dubiously at the pile of equipment and seemed appalled at the size of it. 'It's not as bad as that,' I said. 'We'll soon get it sorted out. Are you ready to go to work?'

She nodded. 'I'm ready.'

'All the air bottles are full,' I said. 'I saw to that at Camp One. There's no reason why we shouldn't do a dive right now and leave the sorting until later. I wouldn't mind a dip—it's too bloody hot here.'

She unbuttoned the front of her shirt. 'All right. How deep do you think it is?'

'I wouldn't know—that's what we're going to find out. What's the deepest you've ever gone?'

'About sixty-five feet.'

'This might be deeper,' I said. 'When we find out how deep I'll make out a decompression table. You stick to it and you'll be all right.' I jerked my thumb at the recompression chamber. 'I don't want to use that unless I have to.'

I tested it. Rudetsky's electricians had wired it up to the camp supply and it worked all right. I pumped it up to the test pressure of ten atmospheres and the needle held steady. It was highly unlikely that we'd ever have to use it at more than five atmospheres though.

When one is making a dive into an unknown hole in the ground you find you need an awful amount of ancillary equipment. There was the scuba gear itself—the harness, mask and flippers; a waterproof watch and compass on the left wrist —I had an idea it would be dark down there and the compass would serve for orientation: and a depth meter and a decompression meter on the right wrist. A knife went in the belt and a light mounted on the head—by the time we were through kitting ourselves out we looked like a couple of astronauts.

I checked Katherine's gear and she checked mine, then we clumped heavily down the steps Rudetsky had cut in the sheer side of the cenote and down to the water's edge. As I dipped my mask into the water, I said, 'Just follow me, and keep your light on all the time. If you get into trouble and you can't attract my attention make for the surface, but try to stay a few minutes at the ten-foot level if you can. But don't worry—I'll be keeping an eye on you.'

'I'm not worried,' she said. 'I've done this before.'

'Not in these conditions,' I said. 'This isn't like swimming in the Bahamas. Just play it safe, will you?'

'I'll stick close,' she said.

I gave the mask a final swish in the water. 'Paul didn't seem too happy about this. Why did he want to dredge?'

She sighed in exasperation. 'He still has the same stupid idea about you and me. It's ridiculous, of course.'

'Of course,' I said flatly.

She laughed unexpectedly and indicated the bulky gear we were wearing. 'Not much chance, is there?'

I grinned at the idea of underwater adultery as I put on the mask. 'Let's call on Chac,' I said, and bit on the mouthpiece. We slipped into the water and swam slowly to the middle of the cenote. The water was clear but its depth made it dark. I dipped my head under and stared below and could see nothing, so I surfaced again and asked Katherine, by sign, if she was all right. She signalled that she was, so I signed that she was to go down. She dipped below the surface and vanished and I followed her, and just before I went down I saw Halstead standing on the edge of the cenote staring at me. I could have been wrong, though, because my mask was smeared with water—but I don't think I was.

It wasn't so bad at first. The water was clear and light filtered from the surface, but as we went deeper so the light failed rapidly. I had dived often off the coast of England and it is quite light at fifty feet, but diving into a comparatively small hole is different; the sheer sides of the cenote cut off the light which would otherwise have come in at an angle and the general illumination dropped off sharply.

I stopped at fifty feet and swam in a circle, checking to see if the compass was in order. Katherine followed, her flippers kicking lazily and the stream of bubbles from her mask sparkling in the light of the lamps like the fountaining eruption of a firework. She seemed all right, so I kicked off again and went down slowly, looking behind from time to time to see if she followed.

We hit bottom at sixty-five feet, but that was at the top of a slope which dropped into darkness at an angle of about twenty degrees. The bottom consisted of a slimy ooze which stirred as I casually handled it and rose into a smokescreen of sorts. I saw Katherine's light shining through the haze dimly, and thought that this was going to make excavation difficult.

It was cold down there, too. The hot sun merely warmed the surface of the water and, since the warm water was less dense, it stayed at the top of the pool. The water at the bottom came from the pores in the limestone all about, and was never exposed to the sun. I was beginning to get chilled as it sucked the heat from my body.

I signalled to Katherine again, and cautiously we swam down the slope to find that it ended in a solid wall. That was the absolute bottom of the cenote and I checked it at ninety-five feet. We swam about for a while, exploring the slope. It was smooth and level and nothing broke its surface. The ooze of which it was composed was the accumulated detritus of hundreds of years of leaf droppings from the surface and anything that was to be found would have to be discovered by digging.

At last I signalled that we were going up, and we rose from the bottom of the slope up past the vertical wall of limestone. About thirty feet up from the bottom I discovered a sort of cave, an opening in the sheer wall. That deserved to be explored, but I didn't feel like doing it then. I was cold and wanted to soak some hot sun into my bones.

We had been underwater for half an hour and had been down nearly a hundred feet, and so we had to decompress on the way up. That meant a five-minute wait at twenty feet, and another five-minute wait at ten feet. When we began diving in earnest we'd have the shot line to hold on to at these decompression stops, but as it was we just circled in the water while I kept an eye on the decompression meter at my wrist.

We surfaced in the welcome sun and swam to the side. I heaved myself out and gave Katherine a hand, then spat out the mouthpiece and took off the mask. As I closed down the valve on the tank, I said, 'What did you think of that?'

Katherine shivered. 'You're right; it's not like the Bahamas. I didn't think I could feel so cold in Quintana Roo.'

I took off the harness and felt the hot sun striking my back. 'It seems bloody silly, but we're going to have to wear thermal suits, otherwise we'll freeze to death. What else struck you about it?'

She pondered. 'The ooze down there is going to be bad. It's dark enough without having to work in the muck we're going to stir up.'

I nodded. 'A suction pump is going to come in useful. The pump itself can be at the surface and we'll pump the mud ashore—with a filter in the line to catch any small objects. That'll cut down on the fog down there.' Now that I'd seen the

159

situation, ideas were beginning to come thick and fast. 'We can drop our shot line from the raft, and anchor it to the bottom with a big boulder. We're going to have to have two lines to the bottom, because one will have to be hauled up every day.'

She frowned. 'Why?'

'Come up to the hut and I'll show you.'

We arrived at the hut to find Rudetsky and a couple of his men building a lean-to shelter against one end of it. 'Hi!' he said. 'Have a nice dip?'

'Not bad. I'd like that raft now if you can do it.'

'How big?'

'Say, ten feet square.'

'Nothing to it,' he said promptly. 'Four empty oil drums and some of that lumber we're cutting will make a dandy raft. Will you be using it in the evenings?'

'It's not very likely,' I said.

'Then you won't mind if the boys use it as a diving raft. It's nice to have a swim and cool off nights.'

I grinned. 'It's a deal.'

He pointed to the air compressor. 'Will that be all right just there?'

'That's fine. Look, can you lead that exhaust pipe away—as far away from the intake of the air pump as possible. Carbon monoxide and diving don't go together.'

He nodded. 'I'll get another length of hose and lead it round the other side of the hut.'

I joined Katherine in the hut and dug out my tattered copy of the Admiralty diving tables. 'Now I'll tell you why we have to have two lines to the bottom,' I said. I sat down at the table and she joined me, rubbing her hair with a towel. 'We're going down about a hundred feet and we want to spend as much time as possible on the bottom. Right?'

'I suppose so.'

'Say we spend two hours on the bottom—that means several decompression stops on the way up. Five minutes at fifty feet, ten at forty feet, thirty at thirty feet, forty at twenty feet and fifty at ten feet—a total of . . . er . . . one hundred and thirty-five minutes—two and a quarter hours. It's going to be a bit of a bind just sitting around at these various levels, but it's got to be done. Besides the weighted shot rope from the raft, we'll have to have another with slings fitted at the various levels to sit in, and with air bottles attached, because your harness bottles will never hold enough. And the whole lot will have to be pulled up every day to replenish the bottles.'

'I've never done this kind of thing before,' she said. 'I've never been so deep nor stayed so long. I hadn't thought of decompression.'

'You'd better start thinking now,' I said grimly. 'One slip-up and you'll get the bends. Have you ever seen that happen to anyone?'

'No, I haven't.'

'Fizzy blood doesn't do you any good. Apart from being terrifyingly painful, once a nitrogen embolism gets to the heart you're knocking at the Pearly Gates.'

'But it's so long,' she complained. 'What do you *do* sitting at ten feet for nearly an hour?'

'I haven't done this too often myself,' I confessed. 'But I've used it as an opportunity to compose dirty limericks.' I looked across at the recompression chamber. 'I'd like to have that thing a bit nearer the scene of the accident—maybe on the raft. I'll see what Rudetsky can do.'

IV

The work went on, week after week, and I nearly forgot about Gatt. We were in radio contact with Camp One which relayed messages from Pat Harris and everything seemed to be calm. Gatt had gone back to Mexico City and was living among the fleshpots, apparently without a care in the world, although his band of thugs was still quartered in Merida. I didn't know what to make of it, but I really didn't have time to think about it because the diving programme filled all my time. I kept half an eye on Halstead and found him to be working even harder than I was, which pleased Fallon mightily.

Every day discoveries were made—astonishing discoveries. This was indeed Uaxuanoc. Fallon's teams uncovered building after building—palaces, temples, games arenas and a few unidentifiable structures, one of which he thought was an astronomical observatory. Around the cenote was a ring of stelae—twenty-four of them—and there was another line of them right through the centre of the city. With clicking camera and busy pen Fallon filled book after book with data.

Although no one was trades-union inclined, one day in every week was a rest day on which the boffins usually caught up with their paper work while Rudetsky's men skylarked about in the cenote. Because safe diving was impossible under those conditions I used the free day to rest and to drink a little more beer than was safe during the working week.

On one of those days Fallon took me over the site to show me what had been uncovered. He pointed to a low hill which had been denuded of its vegetation. 'That's where Vivero nearly met his end,' he said. 'That's the Temple of Kukulkan —you can see where we're uncovering the steps at the front.'

It was a bit hard to believe. '*All* that hill?'

'All of it. It's one big building. In fact, we're standing on a part of it right now.'

I looked down and scuffled the ground with my foot. It didn't look any different from any other ground—there was just thin layer of humus. Fallon said, 'The Mayas had a habit of building on platforms. Their huts were built on platforms to raise them from the ground, and when they built larger structures they carried on the same idea. We're standing on a platform now, but it's so big you don't realize it.'

I looked at the ground stretching levelly to the hill which was the Temple of Kukulkan. 'How big?'

Fallon grinned cheerfully. 'Rudetsky went around it with a theodolite and transit. He reckons it's fifteen acres and averages a hundred and thirty feet high. It's an artificial acropolis —90 million cubic feet in volume and containing about six and a half million tons of material.' He produced his pipe. 'There's one something like it at Copan, but not quite as big.'

'Hell's teeth!' I said. 'I didn't realize it would be anything like this.'

Fallon struck a match. 'The Mayas . . .' puff—puff '. . . were an . . .' puff '. . . industrious crowd.' He looked into the bowl of his pipe critically. 'Come and have a closer look at the temple.'

We walked over to the hill and looked up at the partly excavated stairway. The stairs were about fifty feet wide. Fallon pointed upwards with the stem of his pipe. 'I thought I'd find something up there at the top, so I did a bit of digging, and I found it all right. You might be interested.'

Climbing the hill was a heavy pull because it was very steep. Imagine an Egyptian pyramid covered with a thin layer of earth and one gets the idea. Fallon didn't seem unduly put out by the exertion, despite his age, and at the top he pointed.

162

'The edge of the stairway will come there—and that's where I dug.'

I strolled over to the pit which was marked by the heap of detritus about it, and saw that Fallon had uncovered a fearsome head, open-mouthed and sharp-toothed, with the lips drawn back in a snarl of anger. 'The Feathered Serpent,' he said softly. 'The symbol of Kukulkan.' He swept his arm towards a wall of earth behind. 'And that's the temple itself—where the sacrifices were made.'

I looked at it and thought of Vivero brought before the priests on this spot, and shivering in his shoes for fear he'd have the heart plucked out of him. It was a grim thought.

Fallon said objectively, 'I hope the roof hasn't collapsed; it would be nice to find it intact.'

I sat down on a convenient tree stump and looked over the site of the city. About a fifth of it had been cleared, according to Fallon, but that was just the vegetation. There were great mounds, like the one we were on then, waiting to be excavated. I said, 'How long do you think it will take? When will we see what it was really like?'

'Come back in twenty years,' he said. 'Then you'll get a fair idea.'

'So long?'

'You can't hurry a thing like this. Besides, we won't excavate it all. We must leave something for the next generation—they might have better methods and find things that we would miss. I don't intend uncovering more than half the city.'

I looked at Fallon thoughtfully. This was a man of sixty who was quite willing to start something he knew he would never finish. Perhaps it was because he habitually thought in terms of centuries, of thousands of years, that he attained a cosmic viewpoint. He was very different from Halstead.

He said a little sadly, 'The human lifespan is so short, and man's monuments outlast him generation after generation, more enduring than man himself. Shelley knew about that, and about man's vanity. "My name is Ozymandias, king of kings: Look on my works, ye Mighty, and despair!" ' He waved his hand at the city. 'But do we despair when we see this? I know that I don't. I regard it as the glory of short-lived men.' He held out his hands before him, gnarled and blue-veined and trembling a little. 'It's a great pity that this flesh should rot so soon.'

His conversation was becoming too macabre for my taste, so I changed the subject. 'Have you identified the King's Palace yet?'

He smiled. 'Still hoping for plated walls of gold?' He shook his head. 'Vivero was mixed up, as usual. The Mayas didn't have kings, in the sense that we know them, but there was an hereditary chief among them called Halach uinic whom I suppose Vivero called king. Then there was the nacom, the war chief, who was elected for three years. The priesthood was hereditary, too. I doubt if the Halach uinic would have a palace, but we have found what we think is one of the main administrative buildings.' He pointed to another mound. 'That's it.'

It was certainly big, but disappointing. To me it was just another hill and it took a great deal of imagination to create a building in the mind's eye. Fallon said tolerantly, 'It isn't easy, I know. It takes a deal of experience to see it for what it is. But it's likely that Vivero was taken there for the judgement of the Halach uinic. He was also the chief priest but that was over Vivero's head—he hadn't read Frazer's *Golden Bough*.'

Neither had I, so I was as wise as Vivero. Fallon said, 'The next step is to get rid of these tree boles.' He kicked gently at the one on which I was sitting.

'What do you do? Blast them out?'

He looked shocked. 'My God, no! We burn them, roots and all. Fortunately the rain forest trees are shallow-rooted—you can see that much of the root system on this platform is above ground. When we've done that there is a system of tubes in the structure where the roots were, and we fill those with cement to bind the building together. We don't want it falling down at this late stage.'

'Have you come across the thing Vivero was so excited about? The golden sign—whatever it was?'

He wagged his head doubtfully. 'No—and we may never do so. I think that Vivero—after twelve years as a captive—may have been a little bit nuts. Religious mania, you know. He could have had a hallucination.'

I said, 'Judging by today's standards any sixteenth-century Spaniard might be said to have had religious mania. To liquidate whole civilizations just because of a difference of opinion about God isn't a mark of sanity.'

Fallon cocked an eye at me. 'So you think sanity is comparative? Perhaps you're right; perhaps our present wars will be looked on, in the future, as an indication of warped minds. Certainly the prospect of an atomic war isn't a particularly sane concept.'

I thought of Vivero, unhappy and with his conscience tearing him to bits because he was too afraid to convert the heathen to Christianity. And yet he was quite prepared to counsel his sons in the best ways of killing the heathen, even though he admitted that the methods he advised weren't Christian. His attitude reminded me of Mr. Puckle, the inventor of the first machine-gun, which was designed to fire round bullets at Christians and square bullets at Turks.

I said, 'Where did Vivero get the gold to make the mirrors? You said there was very little gold here.'

'I didn't say that,' contradicted Fallon. 'I said it had been accumulated over the centuries. There was probably quite a bit of gold here in one way and another, and a goldsmith can steal quite a lot over a period of twelve years. Besides, the mirrors aren't pure gold, they're tumbago—that's a mixture of gold, silver and copper, and quite a lot of copper, too. The Spaniards were always talking about the red gold of the Indies, and it was copper that gave it the colour.'

He knocked his pipe out. 'I suppose I'd better get back to Rudetsky's map and plot out next week's work schedule.' He paused. 'By the way, Rudetsky tells me that he's seen a few chicleros in the forest. I've given instructions that everyone must stay in camp and not go wandering about. That includes you.'

That brought me back to the twentieth century with a bang. I went back to camp and sent a message to Pat Harris via the radio at Camp One to inform him of this latest development. It was all I could do.

V

Fallon was a bit disappointed by my diving programme. 'Only two hours a day,' he said in disgust.

So I had to put him through a crash course of biophysics as it relates to diving. The main problem, of course, is the nitrogen. We were diving at a depth of about a hundred feet, and the absolute pressure at the depth is four atmospheres—about sixty pounds a square inch. This doesn't make any dif-
165

ference to breathing because the demand valve admits air to the lungs at the same pressure as the surrounding water, and so there is no danger of being crushed by the difference of pressure.

The trouble comes with the fact that with every breath you're taking four times as much of everything. The body can cope quite handily with the increase of oxygen, but the extra nitrogen is handled by being dissolved in the blood and stored in the tissues. If the pressure is brought back to normal *suddenly* the nitrogen is released quickly in the form of bubbles in the bloodstream—one's blood literally boils—a quick way to the grave.

And so one reduces the pressure slowly by coming to the surface very carefully and with many stops, all carefully calculated by Admiralty doctors, so that the stored nitrogen is released slowly and at a controlled safe rate.

'All right,' said Fallon impatiently. 'I understand that. But if you spend two hours on the bottom, and about the same time coming up, that's only half a day's work. You should be able to do a dive in the morning and another in the afternoon.'

'Not a chance,' I said. 'When you step out of the water, the body is still saturated with nitrogen at normal atmospheric pressure, and it takes at least six hours to be eliminated from the system. I'm sorry, but we can do only one dive a day.'

And he had to be satisfied with that.

The raft Rudetsky made proved a godsend. Instead of my original idea of hanging small air bottles at each decompression level, we dropped a pipe which plugged directly into the demand valve on the harness and was fed from big air bottles on the raft itself. And I explored the cave in the cenote wall at the seventy-foot level. It was quite large and shaped like an inverted sack and it occurred to me to fill it full of air and drive the water from it. A hose dropped from the air pump on the raft soon did the job, and it seemed odd to be able to take off the mask and breathe normally so deep below the surface. Of course, the air in the cave was at the same pressure as the water at that depth and so it would not help in decompression, but if either Katherine or myself got into trouble the cave could be a temporary shelter with an adequate air supply. I hung a light outside the entrance and put another inside.

Fallon stopped complaining when he saw what we began to bring up. There was an enormous amount of silt to be cleared first, but we did that with a suction pump, and the first thing I found was a skull, which gave me a gruesome feeling.

In the days that followed we sent up many objects—masks in copper and gold, cups, bells, many items of jewellery such as pendants, bracelets, rings both for finger and ear, necklace beads, and ornamental buttons of gold and jade. There were also ceremonial hatchets of flint and obsidian, wooden spear-throwers which had been protected from decay by the heavy overlay of silt, and no less than eighteen plates like that shown to me by Fallon in Mexico City.

The cream of the collection was a small statuette of gold, about six inches high, the figure of a young Mayan girl. Fallon carefully cleaned it, then stood it on his desk and re-garded it with a puzzled air. 'The subject is Mayan,' he said. 'But the execution certainly isn't—they didn't work in this style. But it's a Mayan girl, all right. Look at that profile.'

Katherine picked it up. 'It's beautiful, isn't it?' She hesitated. 'Could this be the statue Vivero made which so impressed the Mayan priests?'

'Good God!' said Fallon in astonishment. 'It *could* be—but that would be a hell of a coincidence.'

'Why should it be a coincidence?' I asked. I waved my hand at the wealth of treasure stacked on the shelves. 'All these things were sacrificial objects, weren't they? The Mayas gave to Chac their most valued possessions. I don't think it unlikely that Vivero's statue could be such a sacrifice.'

Fallon examined it again. 'It *has* been cast,' he admitted. 'And that wasn't a Mayan technique. Maybe it is the work of Vivero, but it might not be the statue he wrote about. He probably made more of them.'

'I'd like to think it is the first one,' said Katherine.

I looked at the rows of gleaming objects on the shelves. 'How much is all this worth?' I asked Fallon. 'What will it bring on the open market?'

'It won't be offered,' said Fallon grimly. 'The Mexican Government has something to say about that—and so do I.'

'But assuming it did appear on the open market—or a black market. How much would this lot be worth?'

Fallon pondered. 'Were it to be smuggled out of the country and put in the hands of a disreputable dealer—a man such as Gerryson, for instance—he could dispose of it, over a period of time, for, say, a million and a half dollars.'

I caught my breath. We were not halfway through in the

cenote and there was still much to be found. Every day we were finding more objects and the rate of discovery was consistently increasing as we delved deeper into the silt. By Fallon's measurement the total value of the finds in the cenote could be as much as four million dollars—maybe even five million.

I said softly, 'No wonder Gatt is interested. And you were wondering why, for God's sake!'

'I was thinking of finds in the ordinary course of excavation,' said Fallon. 'Objects of gold on the surface will have been dispersed long ago, and there'll be very little to be found. And I was thinking of Gatt as being deceived by Vivero's poppycock in his letter. I certainly didn't expect the cenote to be so fruitful.' He drummed his fingers on the desk. 'I thought of Gatt as being interested in gold for the sake of gold—an ordinary treasure hunter.' He flapped his hand at the shelves. 'The intrinsic value of the gold in that lot isn't more than fifteen to twenty thousand dollars.'

'But we know Gatt isn't like that,' I said. 'What did Harris call him? An educated hood. He isn't the kind of stupid thief who'll be likely to melt the stuff down; he knows its antiquarian value, and he'll know how to get rid of it. Harris has already traced a link between Gatt and Gerryson, and you've just said that Gerryson can sell it unobtrusively. My advice is to get the stuff out of here and into the biggest bank vault you can find in Mexico City.'

'You're right, of course,' said Fallon shortly. 'I'll arrange it. And we must let the Mexican authorities know the extent of our discoveries here.'

VI

The season was coming to an end. The rains would soon be breaking and work on the site would be impossible. I daresay it wouldn't have made any difference to my own work in the cenote—you can't get wetter than wet—but we could see that the site would inevitably become a churned-up sea of mud if any excavations were attempted in the wet season, so Fallon reluctantly decided to pack it in.

This meant a mass evacuation back to Camp One. Rudetsky looked worriedly at all the equipment that had to be transported, but Fallon was oddly casual about it., 'Leave it here,' he said carelessly. 'We'll need it next season.'

Rudetsky fumed about it to me. 'There won't be a god-damn thing left next season,' he said passionately. 'Those chiclero vultures will clean the lot out.'

'I wouldn't worry,' I said. 'Fallon can afford to replace it.'

But it offended Rudetsky's frugal soul and he went to great lengths to cocoon the generators and pumps against the weather in the hopes that perhaps the chicleros would not loot the camp. 'I'm wasting my time,' he said gloomily as he ordered the windows of the huts to be boarded up. 'But, god-damn it, I gotta go through the motions!'

So we evacuated Uaxuanoc. The big helicopter came and went, taking with it the men who had uncovered the city. The four young archeologists went after taking their leave of Fallon. They were bubbling over with enthusiasm and pro-mised fervently to return the following season when the real work of digging into the buildings was to begin. Fallon, the father figure, smiled upon them paternally and waved them goodbye, then went back to his work with a curiously grave expression on his face.

He was not taking any part in the work of the evacuation and refused to make decisions about anything, so Rudetsky tended to come to me for answers. I did what I thought was right, and wondered what was the matter with Fallon. He had withdrawn into the hut where the finds were lined up on the shelves and spent his time painstakingly cleaning them and making copious notes. He refused to be disturbed and neither would he allow the precious objects to be parted from him. 'They'll go when I go,' he said. 'Carry on with the rest of it and leave me alone.'

Finally the time came for us all to go. The camp was closed down but for three or four huts and all that was left would just make a nice load for the two helicopters. I was walking to Fallon's hut to announce the fact when Rudetsky came up at a dead run. 'Come to the radio shack,' he said breathlessly. 'There's something funny going on at Camp One.'

I went with him and listened to the tale of woe. They'd had a fire and the big helicopter was burned up—completely de-stroyed. 'Anyone hurt?' barked Rudetsky.

According to the tinny voice issuing waveringly from the loudspeaker no one had been seriously injured; a couple of minor burns was all. But the helicopter was a write-off.

Rudetsky snorted. 'How in hell did it happen?'

The voice wavered into nothingness and came back again, hardly more strongly. '. . . don't know . . . just happened . . .'

'It just happened,' said Rudetsky in disgust.

I said, 'What's the matter with that transmitter? It doesn't seem to have any power.'

'What's the matter with your transmitter?' said Rudetsky into the microphone. 'Turn up the juice.'

'I receive you loud and clear,' said the voice weakly. 'Can't you hear me?'

'You're damned right we can't,' said Rudetsky. 'Do something about it.'

The transmission came up a little more strongly. 'We've got everyone out of here and back to Mexico City. There are only three of us left here—but Mr. Harris says there's something wrong with the jet.'

I felt a little prickling feeling at the nape of my neck, and leaned forward over Rudetsky's shoulder to say into the microphone, 'What's wrong with it?'

'. . . doesn't know . . . grounded . . . wrong registration .'. . . can't come until . . .' The transmission was again becoming weaker and hardly made sense. Suddenly it cut off altogether and there was not even the hiss of a carrier wave. Rudetsky fiddled with the receiver but could not raise Camp One again.

He turned to me and said, 'They're off the air completely.'

'Try to raise Mexico City,' I said.

He grimaced. 'I'll try, but I don't think there's a hope in hell. This little box don't have the power.'

He twiddled his knobs and I thought about what had happened. The big transport helicopter was destroyed, the jet was grounded in Mexico City for some mysterious reason and Camp One had gone off the air. It added up to one thing—isolation—and I didn't like it one little bit. I looked speculatively across the clearing towards the hangar where Rider was polishing up his chopper as usual. At least we had the other helicopter.

Rudetsky gave up at last. 'Nothing doing,' he said, and looked at his watch. 'That was Camp One's last transmission of the day. If they fix up their transmitter they'll be on the air again as usual at eight tomorrow morning. There's nothing we can do until then.'

He didn't seem unduly worried, but he didn't know what

I knew. He didn't know about Jack Gatt. I said, 'All right; we'll wait until then. I'll tell Fallon what's happened.'

That proved to be harder than I anticipated. He was totally wrapped up in his work, brooding over a golden plate and trying to date it while he muttered a spate of Mayan numbers. I tried to tell him what had happened but he said irritably, 'It doesn't sound much to me. They'll be on the air tomorrow with a full explanation. Now go away and don't worry me about it.'

So I went away and did a bit of brooding on my own. I thought of talking about it to Halstead but the memory of what Pat Harris had said stopped me; and I didn't say anything to Katherine because I didn't want to scare her, nor did I want her to pass anything on to her husband. At last I went to see Rider. 'Is your chopper ready for work?' I asked.

He looked surprised and a little offended. 'It's always ready,' he said shortly.

'We may need it tomorrow,' I said. 'Get ready for an early start.'

VII

That night *we* had a fire—in the radio shack!

I woke up to hear distant shouts and then the closer thudding of boots on the hard ground as someone ran by outside the hut. I got up and went to see what was happening and found Rudetsky in the shack beating out the last of the flames. I sniffed the air. 'Did you keep petrol in here?'

'No!' he grunted. 'We had visitors. A couple of those goddamn chicleros got in here before we chased them off.' He looked at the charred remains of the transmitter. 'Now why in hell would they want to do that?'

I could have told him but I didn't. It was something else to be figured into the addition which meant isolation. 'Has anything else been sabotaged?' I asked.

'Not that I know of,' he said.

It was an hour before dawn. 'I'm going down to Camp One,' I said. 'I want to know what's happened down there.'

Rudetsky looked at me closely. 'Expecting to find trouble?' He waved his hand. 'Like this?'

'I might be,' I admitted. 'There may be trouble here, too.

Keep everyone in camp while I'm away. And don't take any backchat from Halstead; if he makes trouble you know what to do about it.'

'It'll be a pleasure,' said Rudetsky feelingly. 'I don't suppose you'd like to tell me what's really going on?'

'Ask Fallon,' I said. 'It's a long story and I have no time now. I'm going to dig out Rider.'

I had a bite to eat and then convinced Rider he had to take me to Camp One. He was a bit uncertain about it, but since Fallon had apparently abdicated all responsibility and because I was backed up by Rudetsky he eventually gave way and we were ready for take-off just as the sun rose. Katherine came to see me off, and I leaned down and said, 'Stick close to the camp and don't move away. I'll be back before long.'

'All right,' she promised.

Halstead came into view from somewhere behind the helicopter and joined her. 'Are you speeding the hero?' he asked in his usual nasty way. He had been investigating the Temple of Yum Chac above the cenote and was chafing to really dig into it instead of merely uncovering the surface, but Fallon wouldn't let him. The finds Katherine and I had been making in the cenote had put his nose out of joint. It irked him that non-professionals were apparently scooping the pool—to make a bad pun—and he was irritable about it, even to the point of picking quarrels with his wife.

He pulled her away from the helicopter forcibly, and Rider looked at me and shrugged. 'We might as well take off,' he said. I nodded, and he fiddled with the controls and up we went.

I spoke to Rider and he merely grinned and indicated the intercom earphones, so I put them on, and said into the microphone 'Circle around the site for a bit, will you? I want to see what it looks like from the air.'

'Okay,' he said, and we cast around in a wide sweep over Uaxuanoc. It actually looked like a city from the air, at least the part that had been cleared did. I could see quite clearly the huge platform on which was built the Temple of Kukulkan and the building which Fallon referred to jocularly as 'City Hall'. And there was the outline of what seemed to be another big platform to the east along the ridge, but that had only been partially uncovered. On the hill above the cenote Halstead had really been working hard and the Temple of Yum Chac was unmistakable for what it was—not just a

172

mound of earth, but a huge pyramid of masonry with a pillared hall surmounting it.

We made three sweeps over the city, then I said, 'Thanks, Harry; we'd better be getting on. Do you mind keeping low— I'd like to take a closer look at the forest.'

'I don't mind, as long as you don't want to fly too low. I'll keep the speed down so you can really see.'

We headed east at a height of about three hundred feet and at not more than sixty miles an hour. The forest unreeled below, a green wilderness with the crowns of trees victorious in their fight for light spreading a hundred and sixty feet and more from the ground. Those crowns formed scattered islands against the lower mass of solid green, and nowhere was the ground to be seen.

'I'd rather fly than walk,' I said.

Harry laughed. 'I'd be scared to death down there. Did you hear those goddamn howler monkeys the other night? It sounded as though some poor guy was having his throat cut—slowly.'

'The howlers wouldn't worry me,' I said. 'They just make a noise, nerve-racking though it is. The snakes and pumas would worry me more.'

'And the chicleros,' said Harry. 'I've been hearing some funny stories about those guys. Just as soon kill a man as spit, from what I hear.' He looked down at the forest. 'Christ, what a place to work in! No wonder the chicleros are tough. If I was working down there I wouldn't give a damn if I lived or died—or if anyone else did, either.'

We crossed a part of the forest that was subtly different from the rest. I said, 'What happened here?'

'I don't know,' said Harry, and sounded as puzzled as I was. 'That tree looks dead. Let's have a closer view.'

He manipulated the controls, and the chopper slowed and wheeled around the treetop. It was one of the big ones whose crown had broken free of the rest to spread luxuriantly in the upper air, but it was definitely leafless and dead, and there were other dead trees all about. 'I think I get it,' he said. 'Something has happened here, probably a tornado. The trees have been uprooted, but they're so damned close packed they can't fall, so they've just died where they are. What a hell of a place—you gotta die standing up!'

We rose and continued on course. Harry said, 'It must have been a tornado: the dead trees are in a straight line. The

173

tornado must have cut a swathe right through. It's too local-
ized to have been a hurricane—that would have smashed trees
over a wider area.'

'Do they have hurricanes here?'

'Christ, yes! There's one cutting up ructions in the Caribbean right now. I've been getting weather reports on it just in
case it decides to take a swing this way. It's not likely, though.'

The helicopter lurched in the air suddenly and he swore.
'What's wrong?' I asked.

'I don't know.' He was rapidly checking his instruments.
After a while he said, 'Everything seems okay.'

No sooner had he said it than there was a hell of a bang
from astern and the whole fuselage swung around violently.
The centrifugal force threw me against the side of the cockpit
and I was pinned there, while Harry juggled frantically with
the controls.

The whole world was going around in a cock-eyed spin;
the horizon rose and fell alarmingly and the forest was suddenly very close—too damned close. 'Hold on!' yelled Harry,
and slammed at switches on the instrument panel.

The noise of the engine suddenly stopped, but we continued to spin. I saw the top of a tree athwart our crazy path
and knew we were going to crash. The next thing—and last
thing—I heard was a great crackling noise ending in a smash.
I was thrown forward and my head connected violently with
a metal bar.

And that was all I remember.

Nine

My head hurt like hell. At first it was a distant throb, no
worse than someone else's hangover, but it grew in intensity
until it felt as though someone was using my skull for a snare-
drum. When I moved something seemed to explode inside
and everything went blank.

The next time I came round was better—but not much. I was
able to lift my head this time but I couldn't see. Just a lot of
red lights which danced in front of my eyes. I leaned back
and rubbed at them, and then was aware of someone groan-
ing. It was some time before I could see properly and then
everything was green instead of red—a dazzle of moving green
174

something-or-other showing through the transparent canopy.

I heard the groan again and turned to see Harry Rider slumped forward in his seat, a trickle of blood oozing from the side of his mouth. I was very weak and couldn't seem to move; besides which, my thought processes seemed to be all scrambled and I couldn't put two consecutive thoughts together. All I managed to do was to flop my head to the other side and stare through the window.

I saw a frog! He was sitting on a broad leaf staring at me with beady and unwinking eyes, and was quite still except for the rapid pulsation of his throat. We looked at each other for a very long time, long enough for me to repeat to myself twice over that poem about the frog who would a-wooing go—*Heigh Ho, says Rowley*. After a while he blinked his eyes once, and that broke the spell, and I turned my head again to look at Harry.

He stirred slightly and moved his head. His face was very pale and the trickle of blood from his mouth disturbed me because it indicated an internal injury. Again I tried to move but I felt so damned weak. *Come on*, I said; *don't be so grey and dim. Bestir yourself, Wheale; act like a man who knows where he's going!*

I tried again and managed to sit up. As I did so the whole fabric of the cabin trembled alarmingly and swayed like a small boat in a swell. 'Christ!' I said aloud. 'Where *am* I going?' I looked at the frog. He was still there, but the leaf on which he sat was bobbing about. It didn't seem to worry him, though, and he said nothing about it.

I spoke again, because the sound of my voice had comforted me. 'You must be bloody mad,' I said. 'Expecting a frog to talk back! You're delirious, Wheale; you're concussed.'

'Wha . . . wha . . .' said Harry.

'Wake up, Harry boy!' I said. 'Wake up, for Christ's sake! I'm bloody lonely.'

Harry groaned again and his eye opened a crack. 'Wa . . . wat . . .'

I leaned over and put my ear to his mouth. 'What is it, Harry?'

'Wa . . . ter,' he breathed. 'Water be . . . hind seat.'

I turned and felt for it, and again the helicopter trembled and shuddered. I found the water-bottle and held it to his lips, uncertain of whether I was doing right. If he had a busted gut the water wouldn't do him any good at all.

175

But it seemed all right. He swallowed weakly and dribbled a bit, and a pink-tinged foam ran down his jaw. Then he came round fast, much faster than I had done. I took a sip of water myself, and that helped a lot. I offered Harry the bottle and he swilled out his mouth and spat. Two broken teeth clattered on the instrument panel. 'Aagh!' he said. 'My mouth's cut to bits.'

'Thank God for that,' I said. 'I thought your ribs were driven into your lungs.'

He levered himself up, and then paused as the helicopter swayed. 'What the hell!'

I suddenly realized where we were. 'Take it easy,' I said tightly. 'I don't think we're at ground level. This is a case of "Rock-a-bye baby, on the tree top".' I stopped and said no more. I didn't like the rest of that verse.

He froze in his seat and then sniffed. 'A strong smell of gas. I don't particularly like that.'

I said, 'What happened—up there in the sky?'

'I think we lost the rear rotor,' he said. 'When that happened the fuselage started to spin in the opposite direction to the main rotor. Thank God I was able to declutch and switch off.'

'The trees must have sprung our landing,' I said. 'If we'd have hit solid ground we'd have cracked like an eggshell. As it is, we seem to be intact.'

'I don't understand it,' he said. 'Why should the rear rotor come off?'

'Maybe a fatigue flaw in the metal,' I said.

'This is a new ship. It hasn't had time to get fatigued.'

I said delicately, 'I'd rather discuss this some other time. I propose to get the hell out of here. I wonder how far off the ground we are?' I moved cautiously. 'Stand by for sudden action.'

Carefully I pressed on the handle of the side door and heard the click as the catch opened. A little bit of pressure on the door swung it open about nine inches and then something stopped it, but it was enough open for me to look down. Directly below was a branch, and beyond that just a lot of leaves with no sign of the ground. I looked up and saw bits of blue sky framed between more leaves.

Fallon had wandered about in the forest for many years and, although he wasn't a botanist, he'd taken an interest in it and on several occasions he had discussed it with me. From what he had told me and from what I was able to see I thought that we were about eighty feet up. The main run of rain forest is built in three levels, the specialists call them galleries; we had bust through the top level and got hooked up on the thicker second level.

'Got any rope?' I asked Harry.

'There's the winch cable.'

'Can you unwind it all without too much moving about?'

'I can try,' he said.

There was a clutch on the winch drum which he was able to operate manually, and I helped him unreel the cable, coiling it as neatly as I could and putting it behind the front seat out of the way. Then I said, 'Do you know where we are?'

'Sure!' He pulled out a clipboard to which was attached a map. 'We're about there. We hadn't left the site more than ten minutes and we weren't moving fast. We're about ten miles from the camp. That's going to be a hell of a walk.'

'Do you have any kind of survival kit in here?'

He jerked his thumb. 'Couple of machetes, first aid kit, two water-bottles—a few other bits and pieces.'

I took the water-bottle that was lying between the seats and shook it experimentally. 'This one's half empty—or half full—depending on the way you look at things. We'd better go easy on the water.'

'I'll get the rest of the stuff together,' said Harry, and turned in his seat. The helicopter sagged and there was the rending cry of torn metal. He stopped instantly and looked at me with apprehensive eyes. There was a film of sweat on his upper lip. When nothing else happened he leaned over gently and stretched his hand for the machetes.

We got all we needed into the front, and I said, 'The radio! Is it working?'

Harry put his hand out to a switch and then drew it back. 'I don't know that I want to try it,' he said nervously. 'Can't you smell gas? If there's a short in the transmitter, one spark might blow us sky high.' We looked at each other in silence for some time, then he grinned weakly. 'All right; I'll try it.'

He snapped down the switch and listened in on an earphone. 'It's dead! No signal going out or coming in.'

'We won't have to worry any more about that, then.' I opened the door as far as it would go, and looked down at the branch. It was about nine inches thick and looked very solid. 'I'm getting out now. I want you to drop the cable to me when I shout.'

Squeezing out was not much of a problem for me, I'm fairly slim, and I eased myself down towards the branch. Even going as far as I could, my toes dangled in air six inches above it, and I'd have to drop the rest of the way. I let go, hit the branch squarely with my feet, teetered sickeningly and then dropped forward, wrapping my arms about it and doing a fair imitation of a man on a greasy pole. When I got in an upright position astride the branch I was breathing heavily.

'Okay—drop the cable.'

It snaked down and I grabbed it. Harry had tied the water-bottles and the machetes on to the harness at the end. I left them where they were, for safety, and snapped the harness around the branch. 'You can come out now,' I yelled.

More cable was paid out and then Harry appeared. He had tied a loop of cable around his waist, and instead of coming down to the branch he began to climb up on top of the helicopter canopy. 'What the hell are you doing?' I shouted.

'I want to look at the tail assembly,' he said, breathing heavily.

'For Christ's sake! You'll have the whole bloody thing coming down.'

He ignored me and climbed on hands and knees towards the rear. As far as I could see, the only thing holding the helicopter in position was one of the wheels which was jammed into the crotch formed by a branch and the trunk of a tree and, even as I looked, I saw the wheel slipping forward infinitesimally slowly.

When I looked up Harry had vanished behind a screen of leaves. 'It's going!' I yelled. 'Come back!'

There was only silence. The helicopter lurched amid a crackle of snapping twigs, and a few leaves drifted down. I looked at the wheel and it had slipped forward even more. Another two inches and all support would be gone.

Harry came into view again, sliding head first back towards the canopy. He climbed down skilfully and let himself drop on to the branch. It whipped as his boots struck it, and I caught him around the waist. We'd have made a good circus turn between us.

He manoeuvred until he, too, was astride the branch facing

178

me. I pointed to the wheel which had only an inch to go. His face tautened. 'Let's get out of here.'

We untied the machetes and water-bottles and put the sling around our shoulders, then hauled the rest of the winch cable out of the chopper. 'How long is it?'

'A hundred feet.'

'It ought to be enough to reach the ground.' I started to pay it out until it had all gone. I went first, going down hand over hand. It wasn't so bad because there were plenty of branches lower down to help out. I had to stop a couple of times to disentangle the cable where it had caught up, and on one of those stops I waited for Harry.

He came down and rested on a branch, breathing heavily. 'Imagine me making like Tarzan!' he gasped. His face twisted in a spasm of pain.

'What's the matter?'

He rubbed his chest. 'I think maybe I cracked a couple of ribs. I'll be all right.'

I produced the half-empty water-bottle. 'Take a good swallow. Half for you and half for me.'

He took it doubtfully. 'I thought you said go easy on the water.'

'There's some more here.' I jerked my thumb at the scum-covered pool in the recess of a rotting tree. 'I don't know how good it is, so I don't want to mix it with what's in the bottle. Besides, water does you more good in your stomach than in the bottle—that's the latest theory.'

He nodded, and swallowed water convulsively, his Adam's apple jerking up and down. He handed the bottle to me and I finished it. Then I dipped it into the murky pool to refill it. Tadpoles darted away under the surface; the tree frogs bred up here in the high forest galleries, and lived from birth to death without ever seeing ground. I rammed the cork home, and said, 'I'll have to be *really* thirsty before I'll want to drink that. Are you ready?'

He nodded, so I grasped the cable and started down again, getting a hell of a fright when I startled a spider monkey who gave a squawk and made a twenty-foot leap to another tree, then turned and gibbered at me angrily. He was a lot more at home in the forest than I was, but he was built for it.

At last we reached bottom and stood in the humid green-ness with firm ground underfoot. I looked up at the cable. Some Maya or chiclero would come along and wonder at it,

179

and then find a use for it. Or maybe no human eyes would ever see it again. I said, 'That was a damnfool stunt you pulled up there. What the devil were you doing?'

He looked up. 'Let's get out from under the chopper. It's not too safe here.'

'Which way?'

'Any goddamn way,' he said violently. 'Just let's get out from under, that's all.' He drew his machete and swung it viciously at the undergrowth and carved a passage through it. It wasn't too bad—what Fallon would call a twenty-foot forest, perhaps, and we didn't have to work very hard at it.

After going about two hundred yards Harry stopped and turned to me. 'The chopper was sabotaged,' he said expressionlessly.

'What!'

'You heard me. That crash was rigged. I wish I could get my hands on the bastard who did it.'

I stuck my machete in the earth so that it remained upright. 'How do you know this?'

'I did the day-to-day maintenance myself, and I knew every inch of that machine. Do you know how a helicopter works?'

'Only vaguely,' I said.

He squatted on his heels and drew a diagram in the humus with a twig. 'There's the big rotor on top that gives lift. Newton's law says that for every action there's an equal and opposite reaction, so, if you didn't stop it, the whole fuselage would rotate in the opposite direction to the rotor. The way you stop it is to put a little propeller at the back which pushes sideways. Got that?'

'Yes,' I said.

'This helicopter had one engine which drove both rotors. The rear rotor is driven by a long shaft which runs the length of the fuselage—and there's a universal coupling here. Do you remember that bang we heard just before the crash? I thought it was the rear rotor flying off. It wasn't. It was this coupling giving way so that the shaft flailed clean through the side of the fuselage. Of course, the rear rotor stopped and we started to spin.'

I patted my pockets and found a half-empty packet of cigarettes. Harry took one, and said, 'I had a look at that coupling. The retaining screws had been taken out.'

'Are you sure about that? They couldn't have broken out?'

He gave me a disgusted look. 'Of course I'm goddamn sure.'

180

'When did you last inspect that coupling?'

'Two days ago. But the sabotage was done after that, because I was flying yesterday. My God, we were lucky to get ten minutes' flying without those screws.'

There was a noise in the forest—a dull *boom* from overhead—and a bright glare reflected through the leaves. 'There she goes,' said Harry. 'And we're damned lucky not to be going with her.'

II

'Ten miles,' said Harry. 'That's a long way in the forest. How much water have we got?'

'A quart of good, and a quart of doubtful.'

His lips tightened. 'Not much for two men in this heat, and we can't travel at night.' He spread out his map on the ground, and took a small compass from his pocket. 'It's going to take us two days, and we can't do it on two quarts of water.' His finger traced a line on the map. 'There's another cenote—a small one—just here. It's about three miles off the direct track, so we'll have to make a dog-leg.'

'How far from here is it?'

He spread his fingers on the map and estimated the distance. 'About five miles.'

'That's it, then,' I said. 'It's a full day's journey. What time is it now?'

'Eleven-thirty. We'd better get going; I'd like to make it before nightfall.'

The rest of that day was compounded of insects, snakes, sweat and a sore back. I did most of the machete work because Harry's chest was becoming worse and every time he lifted an arm he winced with pain. But he carried both water-bottles and the spare machete, which left me unencumbered.

At first, it wasn't too bad; more of a stroll through pleasant glades than anything else, but with the occasional tussle with the undergrowth. Harry navigated with the compass and we made good time. In the first hour we travelled nearly two miles, and my spirits rose. At this rate we'd be at the cenote by two in the afternoon.

But suddenly the forest closed in and we were fighting through a tangled mass of shrubbery. I don't know why the forest changed like that; maybe it was a difference in the soil which encouraged the growth. But there it was, and it slowed us up painfully. The pain came not only from the knowledge that we wouldn't get to water as quickly as we expected, but also very physically. Soon I was bleeding from a dozen cuts and scratches on my arms. Try as I would I couldn't help it happening; the forest seemed imbued with a malevolent life of its own.

We had to stop frequently to rest. Harry started to become apologetic because he couldn't take his turn with the machete, but I soon shut him up. 'You concentrate on keeping us on course,' I said. 'How are we doing for water?'

He shook a bottle. 'Just a swallow of the good stuff left.' He thrust it at me. 'You might as well have it.'

I uncorked the bottle, then paused. 'What about you?'

He grinned. 'You need it more. You're doing all the sweating.'

It sounded reasonable but I didn't like it. Harry was looking very drawn and his face had a greyish pallor under the dirt. 'How are you doing?'

'I'm okay,' he said irritably. 'Drink the water.'

So I finished off the bottle, and said wearily, 'How much further?'

'About two miles.' He looked at his watch. 'It's taken us three hours to do the last mile.'

I looked at the thick green tangle. This was Fallon's four-foot forest, and it had been steadily getting worse. At this rate it would take us at least six hours to get to the cenote, and possibly longer. 'Let's get on with it,' I said. 'Give me your machete; this one is bloody blunt.'

An hour later Harry said, 'Stop!' The way he said it made the hairs on the back of my neck prickle, and I stood quite still. 'Easy now!' he said. 'Just step back—very quietly and very slowly.'

I took a step backwards, and then another. 'What's the matter?'

'Back a bit more,' he said calmly. 'Another couple of steps.'

So I went back, and said, 'What the hell's wrong?'

I heard the sigh of his pent-up breath expelled. 'There's nothing wrong—now,' he said. 'But look there—at the base of that tree.'

Then I saw it, just where I had been standing—a coiled-up horror with a flat head and unwinking eyes. One more step and I'd have trodden on it.

'That's a bushmaster,' said Harry. 'And God help us if we get bitten by one of those.'

The snake reared its head, then slid into the undergrowth and vanished. I said, 'What a hell of a place this is,' and wiped the sweat from my forehead. There was a bit more wetness there than my exertions had called for.

'We'll take a rest,' said Harry. 'Have some water.'

I groped in my pocket. 'I'll have a cigarette instead.'

'It'll dry your throat,' Harry warned.

'It'll calm my nerves,' I retorted. I inspected the packet and found three left. 'Have one?'

He shook his head. He held up a flat box. 'This is a snake-bite kit. I hope we don't have to use it. The guy that gets bitten won't be able to travel for a couple of days, serum or no serum.'

I nodded. Any hold-up could ruin us. He took a bottle from his pocket. 'Let me put some more of this stuff on those scratches.' Harry cleaned up the blood and disinfected the scratches while I finished the cigarette. Then again I hefted the machete but a little more wearily this time, and renewed the assault on the forest.

The palm of my hand was becoming sore and calloused because sweat made the skin soft and it rubbed away on the handle of the machete. This was bladework of a different order than I was used to; the machete was much heavier than any sporting sabre I had used in the salle d'armes, and although the technique was cruder more sheer muscle was needed, especially as the blade lost its edge. Besides, I had never fenced continually for hours at a time—a sabre bout is short, sharp and decisive.

We continued until it was too dark to see properly, and then found a place to rest for the night. Not that we got much rest. I didn't feel like sleeping at ground level—there were too many creepie-crawlies—so we found a tree with out-spreading branches that were not too high, and climbed up. Harry looked inexpressibly weary. He folded his hands over his chest and, in the dimming light, again I saw a dark trickle of blood at the corner of his mouth.

'You're bleeding again,' I said, worriedly.

He wiped his mouth, and said, 'That's nothing. Just the cuts in my mouth where the teeth broke.' He lapsed into silence.

The forest at night was noisy. There were odd rustlings all about, and curious snufflings and snortings at the foot of the

183

tree. Then the howler monkeys began their serenade and I awoke from a doze with a sense of shock, nearly falling out of the tree. It's a fearsome sound, like a particularly noisy multiple murder, and it sets the nerves on edge. Fortunately, the howlers are harmless enough, despite their racket, and even they could not prevent me from falling asleep again.

As I dozed off I had a hazy recollection of hearing voices far away, dreamlike and inconsequential.

III

The next day was just a repetition. We breakfasted on the last of the water and I drank the noisome dregs with fervent appreciation. I was hungry, too, but there was nothing we could do about that. A man can go a long time without food, but water is essential, especially in tropic heat.

'How far to the cenote?' I asked.

Harry gropingly found his map. All his movements were slow and seemed to pain him. 'I reckon we're about here,' he said croakingly. 'Just another mile.'

'Cheer up,' I said. 'We ought to make it in another three hours.'

He tried to smile and achieved a feeble grin. 'I'll be right behind you,' he said.

So we set off again, but our pace was much slower. My cuts with the machete didn't have the power behind them and it was a case of making two chops when only one had been necessary before. And I stopped sweating, which I knew was a bad sign.

Four hours later we were still not in sight of the cenote, and the bush was as thick as ever. Yet even though I was leading and doing the work I was still moving faster than Harry, who stopped often to rest. All the stuffing seemed to be knocked out of him, and I didn't know what was the matter. I stopped and waited to let him catch up, and he came into view almost dropping with exhaustion and sagged to the ground at my feet.

I knelt beside him. 'What's wrong, Harry?'

'I'm all right,' he said with an attempt at force in his voice. 'Don't worry about me.'

'I'm worried about both of us,' I said. 'We should have

reached the cenote by now. Are you sure we're heading the right way?'

He pulled the compass from his pocket. 'Yes; we're all right.' He rubbed his face. 'Maybe we should veer a bit to the north.'

'How far, Harry?'

'Christ, I don't know! The cenote's not very big. We could quite easily miss it.'

It dawned upon me that perhaps we were lost. I had been relying on Harry's navigation, but perhaps he wasn't in a fit state to make decisions. We could even have overshot the cenote for all I knew. I could see that it would be up to me to make the decisions in the future.

I made one. I said, 'We'll head due north for two hundred yards, then we'll take up a track parallel to this one.' I felt the edge of the machete; it was as dull as the edge of a poker and damned near useless for cutting anything. I exchanged it for the other, which wasn't much better, and said, 'Come on, Harry; we've got to find water.'

I carried the compass this time and changed direction sharply. After a hundred yards of hewing, much to my surprise I came to an open space, a sort of passage through the bush—a trail. I looked at it in astonishment and noted that it had been cut fairly recently because the slash marks were fresh.

I was about to step on to the trail when I heard voices and drew back cautiously. Two men passed within feet of me; both were dressed in dirty whites and floppy hats, and both carried rifles. They were speaking in Spanish, and I listened to the murmur of their voices fade away until all was quiet again.

Harry caught up with me, and I put my finger to my lips. 'Chicleros,' I said. 'The cenote must be quite near.'

He leaned against a tree. 'Perhaps they'll help us,' he said.

'I wouldn't bet on it. No one I ever heard has a good opinion of chicleros.' I thought about it a bit. 'Look, Harry: you make yourself comfortable here, and I'll follow those two lads. I'd like to know a bit more about them before disclosing myself.'

He let himself slip to a sitting position at the bottom of the tree. 'That's okay with me,' he said tiredly. 'I could do with a rest.'

So I left him and entered the trail. By God, it was a relief to be able to move freely. I went fast until I saw a disappearing flick of white ahead which was the hindermost of the chicleros, then I slowed down and kept a cautious distance. After I'd gone about a quarter of a mile I smelled wood smoke and heard more voices, so I struck off the trail, and found that the forest had thinned out and I could move quite easily and without using the machete.

Then, through the trees, I saw the dazzle of sun on water, and no Arab, coming across an oasis in the desert, could have been more cheered than I was. But I was still careful and didn't burst into the clearing by the cenote; instead I sneaked up and hid behind the trunk of a tree and took a good look at the situation.

It was just as well I did because there were about twenty men camped there around a blue and yellow tent which looked incongruously out of place and seemed more suited to an English meadow. In front of the tent and sitting on a camp stool was Jack Gatt, engaged in pouring himself a drink. He measured a careful amount of whisky and then topped it with soda-water from a siphon. My throat tightened agonizingly as I watched him do it.

Immediately around Gatt and standing in a group were eight men listening attentively to what he was saying as he gestured at the map on the camp table. Four of them were obviously American from the intonation of their voices and from their clothing; the others were probably Mexican, although they could have come from any Central American country. To one side, and not taking part in Gatt's conference, were about a dozen chicleros lounging by the edge of the cenote.

I withdrew from my position and circled about the cenote, then went in again to get a view from a different angle. I had to get at that water somehow, without drawing attention to myself, but I saw that anyone going to the cenote would inevitably be spotted. Fortunately, this cenote was different from the others I'd seen in that it wasn't like a well, and the water was easily accessible. It was more like an ordinary pond than anything else.

I watched the men for a long time. They weren't doing anything in particular; just sitting and lying about and talking casually. I had the idea they were waiting for something. Gatt, sitting with his men under the awning in front of his elegant tent, seemed quite out of place among these chicleros, although if Harris was to be believed, he was worse than any of them.

There was nothing I could do there and then, so I drew away and continued to make the full circle around the cenote and so back to the trail. Harry was asleep and moaning a little, and when I woke him up he gave a muffled shout.

'Quiet, Harry!' I said. 'We're in trouble.'

'What is it?' He looked around wildly.

'I found the cenote. There's a crowd of chicleros there—and Jack Gatt.'

'Who the hell is Jack Gatt?'

Fallon, of course, hadn't told him. After all, he was only a chopper jockey in Fallon's employ and there was no reason why he should know about Gatt. I said, 'Jack Gatt is big trouble.'

'I'm thirsty,' said Harry. 'Can't we go along there and get water?'

'Not if you don't want your throat cut,' I said grimly. 'Look, Harry: I think Gatt is ultimately responsible for the sabotage to the helicopter. Can you stick it out until nightfall?'

'I reckon so. As long as I don't have to keep putting one foot in front of the other.'

'You won't have to do that,' I said. 'You just lie here.' I was becoming more and more worried about Harry. There was something wrong with him but I didn't know what it was. I put my hand to his forehead and found it burning hot and very dry. 'Take it easy,' I said. 'The time will soon pass.'

The afternoon burned away slowly. Harry fell asleep again or, at least, into a good imitation of sleep. He was feverish and moaned deliriously, which wasn't at all a good sign for the future. I sat next to him and tried to hone the machetes with a pebble I picked up. It didn't make much difference and I'd have given a lot for a proper whetstone.

Just before nightfall I woke Harry. 'I'm going down to the cenote now. Give me the water-bottles.' He leaned away from the tree and unslung them. 'What else have you got that will hold water?' I asked.

'Nothing.'

'Yes, you have. Give me that bottle of disinfectant. I know it will only hold a couple of mouthfuls, but water is important right now.'

I slung the water-bottles over my shoulder and got ready to go. 'Stay awake if you can, Harry,' I said. 'I don't know how long I'll be away, but I'll make it as quick as I can.'

187

I wanted to get down to the cenote before nightfall. It was quicker moving when you could see where you were going, and I wanted to get into a good position while the light held. As I came out on to the trail I took a scrap of paper from my pocket and spiked it on a twig as an indication of where to find Harry.

The chicleros had lit a fire and were cooking their evening meal. I manoeuvred into a strategic place—as close to the water as I could get yet as far from the camp as possible. The fire was newly built and the leaping flames illuminated the whole of the cenote and I settled down to a long wait.

The fire burned down to a red glow and the men clustered around it, some cooking meat held on sticks, and others making some sort of flapjacks. Presently the scent of coffee drifted tantalizingly over the cenote and my stomach tightened convulsively. I hadn't eaten for nearly two days and my guts were beginning to resent the fact.

I waited for three hours before the chicleros decided to turn in for the night although it was still quite early by city standards. Gatt, the city man, stayed up late, but he remained in his tent, no doubt under mosquito netting, and I could see the glow of a pressure lantern through the fabric. It was time to go.

I went on my belly like a snake, right to the water's edge. I had already taken the corks from the bottles and held them in my teeth, and when I put the first bottle in the water it gurgled loudly. Just then the first howler monkey let loose his bloodcurdling cry, and I praised God for all his creations, however weird. I withdrew the bottle and put it to my lips and felt the blessed water at the back of my parched throat. I drank the full quart and no more, although it took a lot of willpower to refrain. I filled both bottles and corked them, and then washed out the disinfectant bottle and filled that.

I daresay that anyone with keen eyes could have seen me from the chiclero camp. The sky was clear and the moon was full, and a man, especially a moving man, would be easily spotted. But I managed to get back into the cover of the forest without any outcry, so probably the chicleros hadn't a guard.

I found my way back to Harry without much difficulty and gave him a bottle of water which he drank thirstily. I had a problem—we had to get on the other side of the cenote under cover of darkness and that meant that Harry would have to move immediately, and I didn't know if he was up to it. I waited until he had satisfied his thirst, and said, 'We'll have to move now. Are you fit?'

'I'm okay, I guess,' he said. 'What's the hurry?'

'This cenote lies between us and Uaxuanoc and we want to get around it without being seen. I've discovered a trail on the other side which heads the right way. We'll be able to make better time tomorrow.'

'I'm ready,' he said, and hoisted himself slowly to his feet. But he had to clutch the tree trunk for support and that I didn't like. Still, he moved fast enough when we got going, and stuck close on my heels. I think the water had done him a lot of good.

I had a choice of making a wide sweep around the cenote and going through thick forest, or going straight down the trail and crawling around the chiclero camp. I chose the latter because it would be less strain on Harry, but I hoped he'd be able to keep quiet. We managed it without trouble—the dying embers of the camp fire gave good orientation—and I picked up the trail on the other side of the cenote. Once out of sight of the camp I checked the map and the compass and it seemed that the trail led pretty much in the direction of Uaxuanoc, which was all to the good.

After a mile of stumbling in the darkness Harry began to flag, so I made the decision to stop, and we pulled off the side of the trail and into the forest. I got Harry bedded down—he wasn't in any shape to climb a tree—and said, 'Have some more water.'

'What about you?'

I thrust the bottle into his hands. 'Fill up; I'm going back to get some more.' It had to be done—if we didn't get more water we'd never make it to Uaxuanoc, and since we only had the two bottles we might as well drink what we had.

I left him again and marked the place by thrusting a machete into the middle of the trail. Anyone moving along the trail would be certain of falling over it, including me. I didn't think anyone else would be moving around at night. It took me an hour and a half to get to the cenote, fifteen minutes to fill up, and another hour to get back and bark my shins on that damned machete. I swore at it but at least I was certain that Harry hadn't been discovered. He was asleep and I didn't wake him, but dropped into an uneasy doze beside him.

Harry woke me at daybreak. He seemed cheerful enough, but I felt as though I had been doped. My limbs were stiffened and I was one big ache from head to foot. I had never been a hearty camping type and this sleeping on the ground didn't agree with me. Besides, I hadn't had too much sleep at all and had been stumbling around in the forest for most of the hours of darkness.

I said, 'We have a decision to make. We can stick to the forest, which is safer—but slow. Or we can go up that trail with the likelihood of meeting one of Gatt's chicleros. What do you say, Harry?'

He was brighter this morning and not so disposed to mere acceptance. 'Who is this guy, Gatt?' he asked. 'I've never heard of him before.'

'It's a bit too involved to go into right now, but as far as we're concerned, he's sudden death. From what I've seen, he's allied himself with the chicleros.'

He shook his head. 'Why should a guy I've never heard of want to kill me?'

'He's a big-time American ganster,' I said. 'He's after the loot from Uaxuanoc. It's a long story, but that's the gist of it. There's a lot of money involved, and I don't think he'll stop at much to get it. He certainly won't stop short of killing us. In fact, he's already had a damned good try at it. I can't think of anyone else who'd sabotage your chopper.'

Harry grimaced. 'I'll take your word for it, but I hate like hell the idea of tackling the forest.'

So did I. An inspection of the map showed that we were a little more than five miles from Uaxuanoc. As we already knew, the forest in the immediate vicinity of Uaxuanoc was exceptionally thick and, in our present condition, it might take us two days to hack our way through. We couldn't afford two days, not on our limited supply of water. True, we had filled ourselves up, but that would be soon expended in sweat, and we only had the two quarts' reserve.

Then there was Harry. Whatever was wrong with him wasn't getting any better. The trail was easy travelling and we could do at least a mile an hour, or even more. At that rate we could be in Uaxuanoc in about five hours. It was very tempting.

Against it was the fact that the trail existed in the first place. The only place Gatt could comfortably camp was at the cenote we had just left—he had to stick near a water supply. So it followed that if he were keeping an eye on Uax-uanoc then the trail must have been made by his chicleros, and the likelihood of bumping up against one was high. I didn't know what would happen if we did, but all those I had seen were armed and, from Fallon's account, they were quite pre-pared to use their weapons.

It was a hell of a decision to make, but finally I opted for the trail. The forest was impossible and we *might* not en-counter a chiclero. Harry sighed in satisfaction and nodded his head in agreement. 'Anything but the forest,' he said.

We entered the trail cautiously, found nothing to worry us, and went along it away from Gatt's camp. I kept my eyes down and found plenty of evidence that the trail was in frequent use. There were footprints on patches of soft earth; twice I found discarded cigarette butts, and once an empty corned beef can which had been casually tossed aside. All that was in the first hour.

It worried me very much, but what worried me even more was Harry's slow pace. He started off chirpily enough, but he couldn't keep it up, and he lagged behind more and more. And so I had to go along more slowly because I didn't feel like getting too far ahead of him. It was evident that his con-dition was deteriorating very rapidly; his eyes were sunk deep into his head, and his face was white under the dark bristle of his beard. All his movements were slow and he kept one arm across his chest as he staggered along as though to stop himself from falling apart.

The trail was just as wide as was necessary for the passage of men in single file, otherwise I would have helped him along, but it was impossible for us to walk side by side and he had to make his own way, stumbling blindly behind me. In that first hour we only went about three-quarters of a mile and I began to get perturbed. It seemed that we would be a long time getting to Uaxuanoc by trail or forest.

It was because of our slowness that we were caught. I had expected to encounter a chiclero head on—one coming down the trail the other way—and I kept a very good lookout. Every time the trail bent in a blind corner I stopped to check the trail ahead and to confirm that we weren't going to run into trouble.

We didn't run into trouble—it caught up with us. I suppose a chiclero had left Gatt's camp at daybreak just about the time we had set out on the trail. He wasn't weak with hunger and sickness and so he made good time and came up on us from behind. I couldn't blame Harry for not keeping a good watch on our back trail; he had enough difficulty in just putting one foot in front of the other. And so we were surprised.

There was a shout, 'He, compañero!' and then a startled oath as we turned round, which was accompanied by the ominous rattle of a rifle bolt. He wasn't a very big man, but his rifle made him ten feet tall. He had put a bullet up the spout and was regarding us warily. I don't think he knew who we were—all he knew was that we were strangers in a place where no strangers should be.

He rattled out a few words and brought the muzzle of the rifle to bear on us. 'Aguarde acqui! Tenga cuidado!'

It all happened in a split second. Harry turned and cannoned into me. 'Run!' he said hoarsely, and I turned and took off up the trail. There was a shot which clipped a splinter from a tree and ricocheted across the trail in front, and a shout of warning.

I was suddenly aware that I could only hear the thud of my own boots and I turned to see Harry sprawled on the ground and the chiclero running up to him with upraised gun. Harry tried weakly to struggle to his feet but the chiclero stood over him and raised the rifle to ram the butt at his skull.

There wasn't anything else I could do. I had the machete in my hand, so I threw it. If the machete had hit with the hilt or the flat of the blade, or even with that damned blunt edge, it would have served enough to knock the man off balance. But it struck point first, penetrating just under his rib cage, sinking in deep.

His mouth opened in surprise and he looked down at the broad blade protruding from his body with shock in his eyes. He made a choked sound which throttled off sharply and the upraised rifle slipped from his hands. Then his knees buckled under him and he fell on top of Harry, arms outstretched and scrabbling at the rotting leaves on the ground.

I didn't mean to kill him—but I did. When I ran back he was already dead and blood was spurting from the wound with the last dying beats of his heart, reddening Harry's shirt. Then it stopped and there was just an oozing trickle. I rolled him away and bent down to help Harry. 'Are you all right?'

Harry wrapped his arms about his chest. 'Christ!' he said. 'I'm beat!'

I looked up and down the trail, wondering if anyone had heard the shot, then said, 'Let's get off this trail—quickly!' I grabbed the machete which Harry had dropped and slashed at the bush by the side of the trail, penetrating about ten yards into the forest, then I helped Harry, and he collapsed helplessly on to the ground.

His mouth was opening and closing and I bent down to hear him whisper, 'My chest—it hurts like hell!'

'Take it easy,' I said. 'Have some water.' I made him as comfortable as I could, then went back to the trail. The chiclero was indubitably dead and was lying in a puddle of rapidly clotting blood. I put my hand under his armpits and hauled the body off the trail and into cover, then went back and tried to disguise the evidence of death, scuffing up earth to cover the blood. Then I picked up the rifle and went back to Harry.

He was sitting with his back against a tree and his arms still hugged about his chest. He lifted lacklustre eyes, and said, 'I think this is it.'

I hunkered down next to him. 'What's wrong?'

'That fall—it's finished me. You were right; I think my ribs have got into my lungs.' A trickle of blood oozed from his mouth.

I said, 'For Christ's sake! Why didn't you tell me? I thought you were just bleeding from the mouth.'

He gave a twisted grin. 'Would it have made any difference?'

Probably it wouldn't have made any difference. Even if I had known about it I couldn't see that we could have done any different than we had. But Harry must have been in considerable pain marching through the forest with punctured lungs.

His breath came with a curious spasmodic whistling sound. 'I don't think I can make it to Uaxuanoc,' he whispered. 'You get out of here.'

'Wait!' I said, and went back to the body of the dead man. He was carrying a big water-bottle that held about a half-gallon, and he had a knapsack. I searched the pockets and came up with matches, cigarettes, a wicked-looking switchblade knife and a few other odds and ends. The knapsack contained a few items of clothing, not very clean, three tins of bully beef, a round, flat loaf about the size of a dinner plate, and a hunk of dried beef.

I took all this stuff back to Harry. 'We can eat now,' I said.

He shook his head slowly. 'I'm not hungry. Get out of here, will you? While you still have time.'

'Don't be a damned fool,' I said. 'I'm not going to leave you here.'

His head dropped on one side. 'Please yourself,' he said, and coughed convulsively, his face screwed up in agony.

It was then I realized he was dying. The flesh on his face had fallen in so that his head looked like a skull and, as he coughed, blood spurted from his mouth and stained the leaves at his side. I couldn't just walk away and leave him, no matter what the danger from the chicleros, so I stayed at his side and tried to encourage him.

He would take no food or water and, for a time, he was delirious; but he rallied after about an hour and could speak rationally. He said, 'You ever been in Tucson, Mr. Wheale?'

'No, I haven't,' I said. 'And my name is Jemmy.'

'Are you likely to be in Tucson?'

I said, 'Yes, Harry; I'll be in Tucson.'

'See my sister,' he said. 'Tell her why I'm not going back.'

'I'll do that,' I said gently.

'Never had a wife,' he said. 'Nor girl-friends—not seriously. Moved around too much, I guess. But me and my sister were real close.'

'I'll go and see her,' I said. 'I'll tell her all about it. '

He nodded and closed his eyes, saying no more. After half an hour he had a coughing fit and a great gout of red blood poured from his mouth.

Ten minutes later he died.

Ten

They chased me like hounds chase the fox. I've never been much in favour of blood sports and this experience reinforced my distaste because it gave me a very good idea of what it's like to be on the wrong end of a hunt. I also had the disadvantage of not knowing the country, while the hounds were hunting on their home ground. It was a nerve-racking and sweaty business.

It began not long after Harry died. I couldn't do much about
194

Harry although I didn't like just leaving him there for the forest scavengers. I began to dig a grave, using Harry's machete, but I came across rock close to the surface and had to stop. In the end I laid him out with his arms folded across his chest and said goodbye.

That was a mistake, of course, and so was the attempt at a grave. If I had left Harry as he was when he died, just a tumbled heap at the foot of a tree, then I might have got clean away. The body of the dead chiclero was found, and so was Harry's body, a little further in the forest; if I had left him alone then Gatt's men might not even have suspected that I existed. But dead men don't attempt to dig their own graves, nor do they compose themselves for their end in such a neat manner, and the hunt was on.

But maybe I'm wrong, because I did take as much loot from the dead chiclero as I could. It was too precious to leave behind. I took his rifle, his pack, the contents of his pockets, a bandolier stuffed with cartridges and a nice new machete, as sharp as a razor and much better than those I had been using. I would have taken his clothing too, for use as a disguise, had I not heard voices on the trail. That scared me off and I slipped away into the forest, intent on putting as much distance between me and those voices as I could.

I don't know if they discovered the bodies then or at a later time because, in my hurry to get away, I got thoroughly lost for the rest of the day. All I knew was that Gatt's trail to Uaxuanoc was somewhere to the west, but by the time I'd figured that out it was too dark to do anything about it, and I spent the night up a tree.

Oddly enough, I was in better shape than at any time since the helicopter crashed. I had food and nearly three quarts of water, I was more accustomed to moving in the forest and did not have to do as much useless chopping with the machete, and one man can go where two men can't—especially when one of the two is sick. Without poor Harry I was more mobile. Then again, I had the rifle. I didn't know what I was going to to do with it, but I stuck to it on general principles.

The next morning, as soon as it was light enough to see, I headed west, hoping to strike the trail. I travelled a hell of a long way and I thought I'd made a terrible mistake. I knew if I didn't find that trail then I'd never find Uaxuanoc, and I'd probably leave my bones somewhere in the forest when my food and water ran out, so I was justifiably anxious. I didn't find the trail, but I nearly ran into a bullet as someone raised a shout and took a shot at me.

The bullet went high and clipped leaves from a bush, and I took to my heels and got out of there fast. From then on there was a strange, slow-motion chase in the humid green dimness of the forest floor. The bush was so thick that you could be standing right next to a man and not know he was there if he were quiet enough. Imagine putting the Hampton Court maze into one of the big tropical houses at Kew, populating it with a few armed thugs with murder in their hearts, and you in the middle, the object of their unloving attentions.

I tried to move as quietly as I could, but my knowledge of woodcraft dates back to Fenimore Cooper and I wasn't so good at the Silent Savage bit. But then, neither were the chicleros. They crashed about and shouted one to the other, and a couple of shots were loosed off at random but nowhere near me. After a while I began to get over my immediate fright and the conviction grew upon me that if I chose a thick-ish bit of forest and just stood still I was as likely to get away with it as if I kept on running.

So I did that and stood screened by leaves with my hands sweaty on the rifle until the noise of pursuit disappeared. I didn't move out immediately, either. The greatest danger was the man more brainy than the others who would be doing the same as me—just standing quietly and waiting for me to come into view. So I waited a full hour before moving, and then, again, I headed west.

This time I found the trail. I burst into it unexpectedly, but luckily there wasn't anyone in sight. I hastily withdrew and looked at my watch to find it was after five in the afternoon, not far from nightfall. I debated with myself whether or not to take a chance and use the trail. I was tired, and perhaps my judgement wasn't as keen as it ought to have been, because I said out loud, 'The hell with it!' and boldly stepped out. Again it was a relief to have unhampered freedom of movement. There was no need for the machete, so I unslung the rifle and took it in both hands, and made good time, conscious that every step brought me nearer Uaxuanoc and safety.

This time *I* surprised a chiclero. He was standing in the trail with his back to me and I could smell the smoke of the foul cigarette he was puffing. I was retreating cautiously when, apparently by some sixth sense, he became aware of me and turned fast. I popped off a shot at him and he promptly fell flat and rolled into cover. The next thing was an answering shot, so close that I felt the thrill of air on my cheek.

I ducked for cover and, hearing shouts, pushed into the forest. Again, there was a fantastic game of hide-and-seek. I found another hidey-hole and froze in it like a hare in its form, hoping that the hunt would go around me. I listened to the chicleros plunging about and shouting to each other and there was something about the quality in their voices which made me think their hearts weren't in it. After all, one of their number was dead, stabbed in a very nasty way, and I had just taken a pot-shot at another. It can't have been very encouraging; after all, I'd shown definitely murderous tendencies, they didn't know who I was and I could be standing in wait to garrotte any one of them. No wonder they stuck together and shouted at each other—there was comfort in numbers.

They gave up at nightfall and retreated to wherever they had come from. I stayed where I was and put in a bit of solid thought on the problem, something which I'd been neglecting to do in the hurry-scurry of the day's events. I'd run into two lots of them during the day, and as far as I could make out, they were moving in groups of three or four. Whereas the first chiclero—the one I had killed—had been alone.

Again, this last lot was neither spying on Uaxuanoc nor staying at Gatt's camp, and it seemed to me that its sole purpose was to hunt for me, otherwise why would they have been staked out on the trail? It was very likely that Gatt had identified the body of Harry Rider and he had a shrewd suspicion of who Rider's companion was. Anyway, every time I tried to make a break for Uaxuanoc there had been someone placed to stop me.

Apart from all that, I had no illusions about what would happen to me if I were caught. The man I had killed would have friends, and it would be useless to expostulate that I hadn't intended killing him and that I was merely dissuading him from splitting Harry's skull. The fact was that I *had* killed him and there was no getting away from it.

Remembering how he had looked with the machete obscenely sticking from his body made me feel sick. I had killed a man and I didn't even know who he was or what he thought. Still, he had started it by shooting at us and he had

197

got what he deserved, yet, oddly, that didn't make me feel any better about it. This primitive world of kill or be killed was a long way from Cannon Street and the bowler-hatted boys. What the hell was a grey little man like me doing here?

But this was no time for indulging in philosophy and I wrenched my mind back to the matter at hand. How in hell was I going to get back to Uaxuanoc? The idea came to me that I could move along the trail at night—that I had already proved. But would the chicleros be watching at night? There was only one thing to do and that was to find out the hard way.

It was not yet dark and I had just time to get back to the trail before the light failed. Moving in the forest at night was impossible, and movement on the trail wasn't much better but I persevered and went slowly and as quietly as I could. It was very depressing to see the fire. They had hewn out a little clearing, and the fire itself was built right in the middle of the trail. They sat around it talking and obviously wide awake. To go round was impossible at night, so I withdrew regretfully and, as soon as I thought I was out of hearing, I hacked into the forest and found myself a tree.

The next morning the first thing I did was to go further into the forest away from the trail and find myself another tree. I chose it very carefully and established myself on a sort of platform forty feet above the ground with leaf cover beneath so thick that I couldn't see the ground at all and no one on the ground could see me. One thing was certain—these boys couldn't possibly climb every tree in the forest to see where I was hiding, and I thought I'd be safe.

I was tired—tired to death of running, and fighting this bloody forest, tired of being shot at and of shooting at other people, tired because of lack of sleep and because too much adrenalin had been pumped into my system, tired, above all, of being consistently and continually frightened.

Maybe the grey little man inside me was intent on running away. I don't know—but I rationalized it by saying to myself that I wanted a breathing space. I was staking everything on one last throw. I had a quart of water left, and a little food—enough for a day if I didn't have to run too much. I was going to stay in that tree for twenty-four hours—to rest and sleep and get my wind back. By that time I'd have eaten all the food and drunk all the water, and I'd bloody well have to make a move, but until then I was going to take it easy.

Maybe it's a trait of little grey men that they only go into action when pushed hard enough, and perhaps I was unconsciously putting myself into such a position that hunger and thirst would do the pushing; but what I consciously thought was that if the chicleros saw neither hair nor hide of me for the next twenty-four hours then they might assume that I'd either quit cold or gone elsewhere. I hoped, rather futilely, than when I came down out of that tree they'd have gone away.

So I made myself comfortable, or as comfortable as I could, and rested up. I split the food up into three meals and marked the water-bottle into three portions. The last lot was for breakfast just before I left. I slept, too, and I remember thinking just before I dozed off that I hoped I didn't snore.

Most of the time I spent in a somnolent condition, not thinking about anything much. All the affairs of Fallon and Uaxuanoc seemed very far away, and Hay Tree Farm could just as well have been on another planet. There was just the clammy green heat of the forest enfolding me, and even the ever-present danger from the chicleros seemed remote. I daresay if a psychiatrist could have examined me then he'd have diagnosed a case of schizophrenic retreat. I must have been in a bad way and I think that was my nadir.

Night came and I slept again, this time more soundly, and I slept right through until daybreak and awoke refreshed. I think that night's sleep did me a lot of good because I felt remarkably cheerful as I munched the tough dried beef and ate the last of the bread. I felt devilish reckless as I washed it down with the last of the water from the bottle. Today was going to be make or break for Jemmy Wheale—I had nothing left to fall back on, so I might as well push right ahead.

I abandoned the water-bottles and the knapsack and all I retained were the switchblade knife in my pocket, the machete and the rifle. I was going to travel light and fast. I didn't even take the bandolier, but just put a half-dozen rounds in my pocket. I didn't see myself fighting a pitched battle, and all the ammunition in the world wouldn't help me if I had to. I suppose the bandolier and the water-bottles are still up in that tree—I can't imagine anyone finding them.

I came out of the tree and dropped on to the ground, not worrying too much whether anyone saw or heard me or not, and made my way through the forest to the trail. When I got to it I didn't hesitate at all, but just turned and walked along as though I hadn't a care in the world. I carried the rifle at the trail and held the machete in the other hand, and I didn't bother to slow at the corners but just carried straight on.

When I arrived at the clearing the chicleros had chopped out for their little camp I stopped and felt the embers of the fire. It never occurred to me to be cautious in my approach; I just marched into the clearing, found no one there, and automatically bent to feel the heat of the embers. They were still warm and, as I turned them over with the point of the machete, there was a glow of red. It was evident that the chicleros were not long gone.

But which way? Up-trail or down-trail? I didn't particularly care and set off again at the same pace, striding out and trying to make good time. And I did make good time. I had examined the map and tried to trace the course of my wanderings during the days I had been harried. It was something of an impossibility, but as near as I could reckon I thought I was within three miles of Uaxuanoc, and I was damned well going to keep to that trail until I got there.

Fools may rush in where angels fear to tread, but there is also something called Fool's Luck. All the time those bastards had been chasing me and I'd been scared out of my wits, I had run into them, twist and turn as I would. Now, when I didn't give a damn, it was I who saw them first. Rather, I heard them nattering away in Spanish as they came up the trail, so I just stepped aside into the forest and let them pass.

There were four of them, all armed and all pretty villainous-looking, unshaven and dressed in the universal dirty whites of the chicleros. As they passed I heard a reference to Señor Gatt and there was a burst of laughter. Then they were gone up the trail and I stepped out of cover. If they'd had their wits about them they could easily have spotted me because I hadn't gone far into cover, but they didn't even turn their heads as they went by. I'd reached the stage when I didn't give a damn.

But I was heartened as I went on. It was unlikely that any more of them would be coming up the trail and I lengthened my stride to move faster so that I'd outpace any possible chicleros coming up behind. It was hot and strenuous work and the precious water I had drunk filmed my body in the form of sweat, but I drove myself on and on without relenting and kept up a killing pace for the next two hours.

Suddenly the trail took a sharp turn to the left, went on a hundred yards, and petered out. I stopped, uncertain of where to go, and suddenly became aware of a man lying on top of a hillock to my right. He was staring at something through field glasses, and as I convulsively brought up the rifle, he half-turned his head and said casually, 'Es usted, Pedro?'

I moistened my lips, 'Si!' I said, hoping that was the right answer.

He put the glasses to his eyes again and resumed his contemplation of whatever was on the other side of the hillock. 'Tiene usted fosforos y cigarrillos?'

I didn't know what he was saying, but it was obviously a question, so I repeated again, 'Si!' and climbed up the hillock boldly until I was standing over him, just a little behind.

'Gracias,' he said. 'Que hora es?' He put down the glasses and turned to look at me just as I brought the rifle butt down on his head. It hit him just above the right eye and his face creased in sudden pain. I lifted the rifle and slammed it down harder in a sudden passion of anger. This is what would have happened to Harry. The sound that came from him was midway between a wail and a grunt, and he rolled over down the hillock and was still.

I gave him a casual glance and stirred him with my foot. He did not move, so I turned to see what he had been looking at. Spread out below was Uaxuanoc and Camp Three, not a quarter of a mile away across open ground. I looked at it as the Israelities must have looked upon the Promised Land; tears came to my eyes and I took a few stumbling steps forward and shouted in a hoarse croak at the distant figures strolling about the huts.

I began to run clumsily and found that all the strength seemed to have suddenly drained from my body. I felt ridiculously weak and, at the same time, airy and buoyant and very light-headed. I don't know if the man I had stunned—or killed, for all I knew—was the only chiclero overlooking the camp, or whether he had companions. Certainly it would have been a simple matter for a man with a rifle to shoot me in the back as I stumbled towards the huts, but there was no shot.

I saw the big figure of Joe Rudetsky straighten as he turned to look at me and there was a faint shout. Then there was a bit of a blankness and I found myself lying on the ground looking up at Fallon, who wore a concerned expression. He

201

was speaking, but I don't know what he said because someone was beating a drum in my ear. His head shrank and then
ballooned up hugely, and I passed out again.

II

Water—clean, cold, pure water—is a marvellous substance.
I've used it sometimes to make those packet soups; you get
the dry, powdery stuff out of the packet which looks as un-
appetizing as the herbs from a witch doctor's pouch, add water
and hey presto!—what were a few dry scrapings turn into
luscious green peas and succulent vegetables.

I was very dehydrated after my week in the forest, and
I'd lost a lot of weight, but within a few hours I felt remarkably chirpy. Not that I drank a lot of water because Fallon
wouldn't let me and rationed it out in sips, but the sight of
that water jug next to my bed with the cold condensation
frosting the outside of the glass did me a world of good because I knew that all I had to do was to stretch my arm and
there it was. A lovely feeling! So I was feeling better although,
perhaps, like the packet soup I had lost a bit of flavour.

Fallon, of course, wanted to know what had happened in
more detail than in the brief incoherent story I told when
I stumbled into camp. He pulled up a chair and sat by the
edge of the bed. 'I think you'd better tell me all of it,' he said.

'I killed a man,' I said slowly.

He raised his eyebrows. 'Rider? You mustn't think of it like
that.'

'No, not Harry.' I told him what had happened.

As I spoke the expression on his face changed to startled
bewilderment, and when I finally wound down he said, 'So
we're under observation—and Gatt's out there.'

'With an army,' I said. 'That's what Pat Harris was trying
to tell you—but you wouldn't listen. Gatt has brought his
own men from the States and recruited chicleros to help him
in the forest. And the fire in the radio shack wasn't an accident—nor was the crash of the chopper.'

'You're certain it was sabotage?'

'Harry was,' I said. 'And I believe him. I also think the other
chopper—the big one at Camp One—was sabotaged. Your jet
is stranded in Mexico City, too. We're isolated here.'

Fallon looked grim. 'How many men did you see with Gatt?'

'I didn't stop to count—but from first to last I must have seen twenty-five. Some of those I might have bumped into more than once, of course, but I'd say that's a fair reckoning.' I stretched my hand and laid it against the coolness of the water jug. 'I can make a fair guess at what they'll do next.'

'And what's your guess?'

'Isn't it obvious? They're going to hi-jack us. Gatt wants the stuff we've brought up from the cenote and any other trinkets we may have found. It's still here, isn't it?'

Fallon nodded. 'I should have sent it out before.' He stood up and looked out of the window. 'What puzzles me is how you—and Gatt—can be certain of this.'

I was too tired to yell at him but I made an effort. 'Damn it, I've been bringing the stuff out of the water, haven't I?'

He turned. 'But Gatt doesn't know that. How can he know, unless someone told him? We haven't broadcast it.'

I thought about that, then said softly, 'I was in the forest for nearly a week after the sabotage and Gatt still hasn't made a move. He's out there and he's ready, so what's holding him up?'

'Uncertainty, perhaps,' suggested Fallon. 'He can't really *know* that we've found anything valuable—valuable to him, that is.'

'True. But all he has to do is to walk in here and find a million and a half dollars that's here for the taking.'

'More than that,' said Fallon. 'Paul made a big find in the Temple of Yum Chac. He wasn't supposed to start excavating, but he did, and he stumbled across a cache of temple implements. They're priceless, Jemmy; nothing like this has been found before.'

'Nothing is priceless to Gatt,' I said. 'What would it be worth to him?'

'As a museum collection you couldn't put a price on it. But if Gatt split it up and sold the pieces separately, then maybe he could pick up another million and a half.'

I looked at Fallon sourly. 'And you had the nerve to tell me there wouldn't be any gold in Uaxuanoc. We know Gatt can recognize the value, and we know he can dispose of it through Gerryson. So what do we do! Just hand it to him when he comes calling with his goons?'

'In all fairness I think we'd better talk it over with the others,' said Fallon. 'Do you feel up to it?'

'I'm all right,' I said, and swung my legs out of bed.

It was a gloomy and depressing conference. I told my story and, after a few minutes of unbelieving incomprehension, I managed to ram it down their throats that we were in trouble. Fallon didn't need convincing, of course, but Paul Halstead was as contrary a bastard as ever. 'This whole thing sounds very unlikely,' he said in his damned superior way.

I bristled. 'Are you calling me a liar?'

Fallon put his hand on my arm warningly. Halstead said, 'No, but I think you're exaggerating—and using your imagination.'

I said, 'Take a walk out into the forest. If you run into a bullet it won't harm you if it's imaginary.'

'I certainly think you could have done more to help poor Rider,' he said.

I leaned over the table to grab him but he pulled back sharply. 'That's enough!' barked Fallon. 'Paul, if you haven't anything constructive to say, keep your mouth shut.'

Katherine Halstead unexpectedly attacked her husband for the first time. 'Yes—shut up, Paul,' she said curtly. 'You make me sick.' He looked at her in bewildered astonishment. 'You're not taking Wheale's side again?' he said in a hurt voice.

'There are no sides—there never have been,' she said in an icy voice. 'If anyone uses his imagination, it's not Jemmy.' She looked across at me. 'I'm sorry, Jemmy.'

'I won't have you apologizing for me,' he blazed.

'I'm not,' she said in a voice that would cut a diamond. 'I'm apologizing to Jemmy on my own behalf—for not listening to him earlier. Now just shut up as Professor Fallon says.'

Halstead was so surprised at this attack from an unexpected quarter that he remained silent and somewhat thoughtful. I looked across at Rudetsky. 'What do you think?'

'I believe you,' he said. 'We had some trouble with those goddamn chicleros back at Camp One. They're a murderous lot of bastards, and I'm not surprised they took a shot at you.' He squared his big shoulders and addressed himself to Fallon. 'But this guy, Gatt, is something else again. We didn't know about him.'

'It wasn't necessary for you to know,' said Fallon colourlessly.

Rudetsky's face took on a stubbornness. 'I reckon it was, Mr. Fallon. If Gatt has organized the chicleros it means big trouble. Getting shot at wasn't in the contract. I don't like it—and neither do Smitty and Fowler here.' The other two men nodded seriously.

I said, 'What are you trying to do, Rudetsky? Start a trade union? It's a bit late for that. Whether or not Mr. Fallon misled you is beside the point. In any case I don't think he did it deliberately. The point at issue now is what do we do about Gatt?'

Fallon said wearily, 'There's only one thing we *can* do. Let him have what he wants.'

Smith and Fowler nodded vigorously, and Rudetsky said, 'That's what I think too.' Katherine Halstead's lips tightened, while Halstead twisted his head and looked about the table with watchful eyes.

'Is that a fact?' I said. 'We just give Gatt three million dollars, pat him on the head and hope he'll go away. A fat chance of that happening.'

Rudetsky leaned forward. 'What do you mean by that?'

'I'm sure you're not as stupid as that, Joe. Gatt is committing a crime—he's stealing three million dollars of someone else's property. I don't know who this stuff legally belongs to, but I'm sure the Mexican Government has a big claim. Do you really think that Gatt will allow anyone to go back to Mexico City to put in an official complaint?'

'Oh, my God!' said Fallon as the reality of the situation hit him.

'You mean—he'll knock us off—all of us?' said Rudetsky in a rising voice.

'What would you do in his position?' I asked cynically. 'Given, of course, that you don't have too much regard for the sanctity of human life.'

There was a sudden babble of voices, above which rose Rudetsky's bull-like tones cursing freely. Smith yelled, 'I'm getting out of here.'

I thumped the table and yelled, 'Belt up—the lot of you!' To my surprise they all stopped suddenly and looked towards me. I hadn't been used to asserting myself and maybe I over-did it—anyway, it worked. I stabbed my finger at Smith. 'And where the hell do you think you're going to go? Move ten yards into that forest and they've got you cold. You wouldn't stand a chance.'

Smith's face went very pale and he swallowed nervously. Fowler said, 'Jeez; he's right, Smitty! That's out.'

There was a sudden strength in Fallon's voice. 'This is impossible, Wheale; you're dragging up bogies. Do you realize what a stink there would be if Gatt went through with this . . . this mass murder? Do you think that a man can disappear with no questions asked? He'd never go through with it.'

'No? Who else but us knows that Gatt is here? He's experienced—he has an organization. I'll bet he can whistle up a hundred witnesses to prove he's in Mexico City right now. He'll make damned sure that there is no one to tie him up with this thing.'

Katherine's face was pale. 'But when they find us . . . find our bodies . . . they'll know that . . .'

'I'm sorry, Katherine,' I said. 'But they won't find us. You could bury an army in Quintana Roo and the bodies would never be found. We'll just disappear.'

Halstead said, 'You've put your finger on it, Wheale. Who else but us knows that Gatt is here? And the only reason we know is because of your say-so. *I* haven't seen him, and neither has anyone else—except you. I think you're trying to stampede us into something.'

I stared at him. 'And why the devil should I want to do that?'

He shrugged elaborately. 'You pushed your way into this expedition right from the start. Also, you've been very interested in the cash value of everything we've found. I don't think I have to say much more, do I?'

'No, you bloody well don't,' I snapped. 'And you'd better not or I'll ram your teeth down your throat.' All the others were looking at me in silence, letting me know that this was a charge that had to be answered. 'If I wanted to stampede you why would I prevent Smith going off? Why would I want to keep us together?'

Rudetsky blew out his breath explosively and looked at Halstead with dislike. 'Jesus! For a minute this guy had me going. I ought to have known better.' Halstead stirred uneasily under the implied contempt, and Rudetsky said to me, 'So what do we do, Mr. Wheale?'

I was about to say, 'Why ask me?' but one look at Fallon made me change my mind. He was oddly shrunken and stared blindly in front of him, contemplating some interior vision. What he was thinking I don't know and I'd hate to guess, but it was evident that we couldn't rely on him for a lead. Halstead couldn't lead a blind man across a street, while Rudetsky was a good sergeant type, super-efficient when told what to do—but he had to be told. And Smith and Fowler would follow Rudetsky.

I have never been a leader of men because I never particularly wanted to lead anyone anywhere. I was always of the opinion that a man should make his own way and that if he used the brains God gave him, then he didn't have to follow in anyone's footsteps and, by the same token, neither should he expect anyone to follow him. I was a lone wolf, a rampant individualist, and it was because of that, perhaps, I was labelled grey and colourless. I didn't take the trouble to convert anyone to my point of view, an activity which seems to be a passionate preoccupation with others, and it was put down to lack of anything worthwhile to say—quite wrongly.

And now, in the quiet hut, everyone seemed to be waiting for me to take over—to do something positive. Everyone except Fallon, who had withdrawn, and Halstead, of course, who would be actively against me for whatever peculiar reasons occurred to his warped mind. Rudetsky said in a pleading voice, 'We gotta do something.'

'Gatt will be moving in very soon,' I said. 'What weapons have we?'

'There's a shotgun and a rifle,' said Rudetsky. 'Those are camp stores. And I have a handgun of my own packed in my kit.'

'I have a revolver,' said Fowler.

I looked around. 'Any more?'

Fallon shook his head slowly and Halstead just regarded me with an unwinking stare. Katherine said, 'Paul has a pistol.'

'A shotgun, a rifle and three pistols. That's a start, anyway. Joe, which hut do you think is most easily defendable?'

'Are you thinking of having a battle?' asked Halstead. 'If Gatt *is* out there—which I doubt—you won't stand a chance. I think you're nuts.'

'Would you prefer to let Gatt cut your throat? Offer your neck to the knife? Well, Joe?'

'Your hut might be best,' said Rudetsky. 'It's near to the cenote, which means they can't get close in back.'

I looked at the empty shelves. 'Where's all the loot?'

'I packed it all up,' said Fallon. 'Ready to go when the helicopter came in.'

'Then you'll have to unpack it again,' I said. 'We've got to get rid of it.'

Halstead jerked upright. 'Goddamn it, what are you going to do? That material is priceless.'

'No, it's not,' I said bluntly. 'It has a price on it—seven lives! Gatt may kill us for it, if he can get it. But if we can put it out of his reach he may not consider seven murders worth the candle.'

Fowler said, 'That figures. But what are you going to do with it?'

'Dump the lot back into the cenote,' I said brutally. 'He'll never get it out without a lengthy diving operation, and I don't think he'll stick around to try.'

Halstead went frantic. 'You can't do that,' he shouted. 'We may never be able to retrieve it.'

'Why not? Most of it came out of the cenote in the first place. It won't be lost forever. Come to that—I don't give a damn if it is; and neither do these men here. Not if it saves our lives.'

'Hell, no!' said Rudetsky. 'I say dump the stuff.'

Halstead appealed to Fallon. 'You can't let them do this.'

Fallon looked up. 'Jemmy appears to have taken charge. He'll do what he must.' His mouth twisted into a ghastly simulacrum of a smile. 'And I don't think you can stop him, Paul.'

'The cave,' said Katherine suddenly. 'We can put it in the cave.'

Halstead's head jerked round. 'What cave?' he demanded suspiciously.

'There's an underwater cave about sixty-five feet down in the cenote,' I said. 'That's a good idea, Katherine. It'll be as safe and unavailable there as anywhere else.'

'I'll help you,' she said.

'You'll do no such thing,' snapped Halstead. 'You'll not lend a hand to this crazy scheme.'

She looked at him levelly. 'I'm not taking orders from you any more, Paul. I'm going my own way for a change. I'm going to do what *I* think is right. Uaxuanoc has destroyed you, Paul; it has warped you into something other than the man

I married, and I'm not going to be used as a tool for your crazy obsessions. I think we're finished—you and I.'

He hit her—not a slap with an open palm, but with his clenched fist. It caught her under the jaw and lifted her clean across the hut to fall in a tumbled heap by the wall.

I wasted no time in thoughts of fair fights and Queensberry Rules, but grabbed a bottle from the table and crowned him hard. The bottle didn't break but it didn't do him any good. He gasped and his knees buckled under him, but he didn't go down, so I laid the bottle across his head again and he collapsed to the floor.

'All right,' I said, breathing hard and hefting the bottle, 'has anyone else any arguments?'

Rudetsky grunted deep in his chest. 'You did all right,' he said. 'I've been wanting to do that for weeks.' He helped Fowler to lift Katherine to her feet, and brought her to a chair by the table. Nobody worried about Halstead; they just let him lie where he fell.

Katherine was dizzy and shaken, and Fallon poured out a stiff drink for her. 'I pleaded with you not to have him along,' he said in a low voice.

'That's water under the bridge,' I said. 'I'm as much to blame as anyone.' Rudetsky was hovering solicitously behind Katherine. 'Joe, I want his gun. I don't trust the bastard with it.'

'It's in the box by the bed,' said Katherine weakly.

Rudetsky made a sign with his hand. 'Go get it, Smitty.' He looked down at Halstead and stirred him with his foot. 'You sure got him good. He's going to have one hell of a headache.'

Katherine choked over the whisky. 'Are you all right?' I asked.

She fingered the side of her jaw tenderly. 'He's insane,' she whispered. 'He's gone mad.'

I stood up and took Rudetsky on one side. 'Better get Halstead back into his hut. And if it can be locked, lock it. We have enough on our plate without having to handle that lunatic.'

His grin was pure enjoyment. 'I'd have done the same long ago but I thought Fallon would can me. Oh, boy, but you tapped him good!'

I said, 'You can have a crack at him any time you like, and

you don't have to worry about being fired. It's open season on Halstead now; I've stopped being so bloody tolerant.'

Rudetsky and Fowler bent to pick up Halstead, who was showing signs of coming round. They got him to his feet and he looked at me blankly with glazed eyes, showing no sign of recognition, then Fowler pushed him out of the hut.

I turned to Katherine. 'How are you doing?'

She gave me a wry and lop-sided smile. 'As well as might be expected,' she said gently. 'After a public brawl with my husband.' She looked down at the table. 'He's changed so much.'

'He'll change a lot more if he causes trouble,' I said. 'And not in a way he likes. His credit's run out, Katherine, and you can't do anything more for him. You can't be a barrier between him and the rest of the world any more.'

'I know,' she said sombrely.

There was a shout from outside the hut and I spun around to the doorway. A single shot sounded in the distance, to be followed by a fusillade of rifle fire, a ragged pattering of shots. I left the hut at a dead run and made for the outskirts of the camp, to be waved down by Rudetsky who was sheltering behind a hut.

I went forward at a crouch and joined him. 'What the hell's going on?'

'Halstead made a break for it,' he said, breathing heavily. 'He ran for the forest and we tried to follow him. Then they opened up on us.'

'What about Halstead? Did they fire on him?'

'I reckon he's dead,' said Rudetsky. 'I saw him go down as he reached the trees.'

There was a muffled sound from behind and I turned to see Katherine. 'Get back to the hut,' I said angrily. 'It's dangerous here.'

Two big tears squeezed from beneath her eyelids and rolled down her cheek as she turned away, and there was a dispirited droop to her shoulders.

I waited there at the edge of the camp for a long time but nothing happened; no more shots nor even the sound or sight of a living thing. Just the livid green of the forest beyond the cleared ground of the city of Uaxuanoc.

Everything we did was under observation—that I knew. So I had a problem. We could take all the valuables down to the cenote quite openly and sink them, or we could be underhand about it and do it in secret. On balance, I thought that secrecy was the best bet because if we did it openly Gatt might get worried and jump us immediately with the job only begun. There was nothing to stop him.

That meant that all the packages Fallon had made up had to be broken open and the contents smuggled down piece by piece to my hut next to the cenote. Probably it would have been best to have just dumped the stuff as I had first suggested, but it seemed a pity to do that when the cave was available, so we used the cave. That meant going down there while Rudetsky lowered the loot, and that was something better left for after nightfall when prying eyes would be blinded.

For the rest of the daylight hours we contrived to give the camp an appearance of normality. There was a fair amount of coming and going between the huts and gradually all the precious objects were accumulated on the floor of my hut, where Rudetsky filled up the metal baskets we had used for bringing them from the bottom of the cenote in the first place.

Also on the agenda was the fortification of the hut, another task that would have to wait until after darkness fell, but Smith and Fowler wandered about the camp, unobtrusively selecting materials for the job and piling them in places where they could be got at easily at night. Those few hours seemed to stretch out indefinitely, but at last the sun set in a red haze that looked like dried blood.

We got busy. Smith and Fowler brought in their baulks of timber which were to be used to make the hut a bit more bullet-proof and began to hammer them in position. Rudetsky had organized some big air bottles and we hauled the raft into the side and loaded them aboard. It was tricky work because they were heavy and we were working in the dark. We also loaded all the treasure on board the raft, then Katherine and I went down.

The cave was just as we had left it and the air was good. I rose up inside, switched on the internal light I had installed and switched off my own light. There was a broad ledge above water-level on which the loot could be stored, and I sat on it and helped Katherine from the water. 'There's plenty of room to stash the stuff here,' I said.

She nodded without much interest, and said, 'I'm sorry Paul caused all this trouble, Jemmy. You warned me, but I was stupid about it.'

'What made you change your mind?'

She hesitated. 'I started to think—at last. I began to ask myself questions about Paul. It was something you said that started it. You asked me what it was I had for Paul—love or loyalty. You called it misplaced loyalty. It didn't take me long to find the answer. The trouble is that Paul hasn't—wasn't—always like this. Do you think he's dead?'

'I don't know; I wasn't there when it happened. Rudetsky thinks he is. But he may have survived. What will you do if he has?'

She laughed tremulously. 'What a question to ask at a time like this! Do you think that what we're doing here will do any good?' She waved her hand at the damp walls of the cave. 'Getting rid of what Gatt wants?'

'I don't know,' I said. 'It depends on whether we can talk to Gatt. If I can point out that he hasn't a hope in hell of getting the stuff, then he might be amenable to a deal. I can't see him killing six or seven people for nothing—not unless he's a crazy-mad killer, and I don't think he's that.'

'Not getting what he wants might send him crazy-mad.'

'Yes,' I said thoughtfully. 'He'll be bloody annoyed. He'll need careful handling.'

'If we get out of this,' she said, 'I'm going to divorce Paul. I can't live with him now. I'll get a Mexican divorce—it will be valid anywhere because we were married in Mexico.'

I thought about that for a bit, then said, 'I'll look you up. Would you mind that?'

'No, Jemmy; I wouldn't mind.' She sighed. 'Perhaps we can begin again with a fresh start.'

'Fresh starts don't come so easily,' I said sombrely. 'We'll never forget any of this, Katherine—never!' I prepared to put on my mask. 'Come on; Joe will be wondering what has gone wrong.'

We swam out of the cave and began the long job of transferring the treasure from the basket which Rudetsky had lowered into the cave. Basket after basket of the damned stuff came down, and it took us a long time, but finally it was all put away. We had been under for two hours but had never gone below sixty-five feet so the decompression time was just under an hour. Joe lowered the hose which dangled alongside the shot line and we coupled the two valves at the end to the demand valves on our scuba gear. During the hour it took us to go up he fed us air from the big bottles on the raft instead of using the air compressor which would have made too much noise.

When we finally reached the surface, he asked, 'Everything okay?'

'Everything is fine,' I answered, and swore as I stubbed my toe on an air bottle. 'Look, Joe: tip all these bottles over the side. Gatt might start to get ideas—he might even be a diver himself. He won't be able to do a damned thing without air bottles.'

We rolled the bottles over the side and they splashed into the cenote and sank. When we got ashore I was very tired but there was still much to do. Smith and Fowler had done their best to armour the hut, but it was a poor best although no fault of theirs. We just hadn't the material.

'Where's Fallon?' I asked.

'I think he's in his own hut.'

I went to look for Fallon and found him sitting morosely at his desk. He turned as I closed the door. 'Jemmy!' he said despairingly. 'What a mess! What a godawful mess!'

'What you need is a drink,' I said, and took the bottle and a couple of glasses from the shelf. I poured out a couple of stiff tots and pushed a glass into his hand. 'You're not to blame.'

'Of course I am,' he said curtly. 'I didn't take Gatt seriously enough. But who would have thought this Spanish Main stuff could happen in the twentieth century?'

'As you said yourself, Quintana Roo isn't precisely the centre of the civilized world.' I sipped the whisky and felt the warmth in my throat. 'It's not out of the eighteenth century yet.'

'I sent a message out with the boys who left,' he said. 'Letters to the authorities in Mexico City about what we've found here.' He suddenly looked alarmed. 'You don't think Gatt will have done anything about them, do you?'

I considered that one, and said at last, 'No, I shouldn't think so. It would be difficult for him to interfere with them all and it might tip off the authorities that something is wrong.'

'I should have done it sooner,' said Fallon broodingly. 'The Department of Antiquities is goddamn keen on inspection; this place will be swarming with officials once the news gets out.' He offered me a twisted smile. 'That's why I didn't notify them earlier; I wanted the place to myself for a while. What a damned fool I was!'

I didn't spare him. 'You had plenty of warnings from Pat Harris. Why the hell didn't you act on them?'

'I was selfish,' he said. He looked me straight in the eye. 'Just plain selfish. I wanted to stay while I could—while I had time. There's so little time, Jemmy.'

I drank some whisky. 'You'll be back next season.'

He shook his head. 'No, I won't. I'll never be back here. Someone else will take over—some younger man. It could have been Paul if he hadn't been so reckless and impatient.'

I put down my glass. 'What are you getting at?'

He gave me a haggard grin. 'I'll be dead in three months, Jemmy. They told me not long before we left Mexico City— they gave me six months.' He leaned back in his chair. 'They didn't want me to come here—the doctors, you know. But I did, and I'm glad I did. But I'll go back to Mexico City now and go into a hospital to die.'

'What is it?'

'The old enemy,' said Fallon. 'Cancer!'

The word dropped as heavy as lead into the quiet hut and there was nothing I could say. This was the reason he had been so preoccupied, why he had driven so hard to get the job done, and why he had stuck to one purpose without deflection. He had wanted to do this last excavation before he died and he had achieved his purpose.

After a while I said softly, 'I'm sorry.'

He snorted. '*You're* sorry! Sorry for me! It seems as though I'm not going to live to die in hospital if you're right about Gatt—and neither is anyone else here. I'm sorry, Jemmy, that I got you into this. I'm sorry for the others, too. But being sorry isn't enough, is it? What's the use of saying "Sorry" to a dead man?'

'Take it easy,' I said.

He fell into a despondent silence. After a while, he said, 'When do you think Gatt will attack?'

'I don't know,' I said. 'But he must make his move soon.' I finished the whisky. 'You'd better get some sleep.' I could see
214

Fallon didn't think much of that idea, but he said nothing and I went away.

Rudetsky had some ideas of his own, after all. I bumped into him in the darkness unreeling a coil of wire. He cursed briefly, and said, 'Sorry, but I guess I'm on edge.'

'What are you doing?'

'If those bastards attack, they'll be able to take cover behind those two huts, so I took all the gelignite I could find and planted it. Now I'm stringing the wire to the plunger in our hut. They won't have any cover if I can help it.'

'Don't blow up those huts just yet,' I said. 'It would come better as a surprise. Let's save it for when we need it.'

He clicked his tongue. 'You're turning out to be quite a surprising guy yourself. That's a real nasty idea.'

'I took a few lessons out in the forest.' I helped him unreel the wire and we disguised it as much as we could by kicking soil over it. Rudetsky attached the ends of one set of wires to the terminals of the plunger box and slapped the side of it gently with an air of satisfaction. I said, 'It'll be dawn fairly soon.'

He went to the window and looked up at the sky. 'There's quite a lot of cloud. Fallon said the rains break suddenly.'

It wasn't the weather I was worried about. I said, 'Put Smith and Fowler on watch out at the edge of the camp. We don't want to be surprised.'

Then I had an hour to myself and I sat outside the hut and almost nodded off to sleep, feeling suddenly very weary. Sleep was something that had been in short supply, and if I hadn't had that twenty-four hour rest in the forest tree I daresay I'd have gone right off as though drugged. As it was I drowsed until I was wakened by someone shaking my shoulder.

It was Fowler. 'Someone's coming,' he said urently.

'Where?'

'From the forest.' He pointed. 'From over there—I'll show you.'

I followed behind him to the hut at the edge of the camp from which he had been watching. I took the field glasses he gave me and focused on the distant figure in white which was strolling across the cleared land.

The light was good enough and the glasses strong enough to show quite clearly that it was Gatt.

Eleven

There was an odd quality in the light that morning. In spite of the high cloud which moved fast in the sky everything was crystal clear, and the usual heat haze, which lay over the forest even at dawn, was gone. The sun was just rising and there was a lurid and unhealthy yellow tinge to the sky, and a slight breeze from the west bent the branches of the trees beyond the cleared ruins of Uaxuanoc.

As I focused the glasses on Gatt I found to my disgust that my hands were trembling, and I had to rest the glasses on the window-sill to prevent the image dancing uncontrollably. Gatt was taking his time. He strolled along as unconcernedly as though he were taking his morning constitutional in a city park, and stopped occasionally to look about at the uncovered mounds. He was dressed as nattily as he had been when he flew into Camp One, and I even saw the tiny point of whiteness that was a handkerchief in his breast pocket.

Momentarily I ignored him and swept the glasses around the perimeter of the ruins. No one else showed up and it looked as though Gatt was alone, a deceptive assumption it would be wise to ignore. I handed the glasses to Rudetsky, who had come into the hut. He raised them to his eyes, and said, 'Is that the guy?'

'That's Gatt, all right.'

He grunted. 'Taking his time. What the hell is he doing? Picking flowers?'

Gatt had bent down and was groping at something on the ground. I said, 'He'll be here in five minutes. I'm going out there to talk to him.'

'That's taking a risk.'

'It has to be done—and I'd rather do it out there than back here. Can anyone use that rifle we've got?'

'I'm not too bad,' said Fowler.

'Not too bad—hell!' rumbled Rudetsky. 'He was a marksman in Korea.'

'That's good enough for me,' I said with an attempt at a grin. 'Keep your sights on him, and if he looks like pulling a fast one on me, let him have it.'

Fowler picked up the rifle and examined the sights. 'Don't

go too far away,' he said. 'And keep from between me and Gatt.'

I walked to the door of the hut. 'Everyone else keep out of sight,' I said, and stepped outside, feeling like a condemned man on his way to the gallows. I walked towards Gatt across the cleared ground, feeling very vulnerable and uncomfortably aware that I was probably framed in someone's rifle sights. Obeying Fowler's instructions, I walked slowly so Gatt and I would meet a little more than two hundred yards from the hut, and I veered a little to give Fowler his open field of fire.

Gatt had lit a cigar and, as he approached, he raised his elegant Panama hat politely. 'Ah, Mr. Wheale; lovely morning, isn't it?' I wasn't in the mood for cat-and-mouse chit-chat so I said nothing. He shrugged, and said, 'Is Professor Fallon available?'

'No,' I said shortly.

He nodded understandingly. 'Ah, well! You know what I've come for, of course.' It wasn't a question, but a flat statement.

'You won't get it,' I said equally flatly.

'Oh, I will,' he said with certainty. 'I will.' He examined the ash on the end of his cigar. 'I take it that you are doing the talking for Fallon. I'm surprised at that—I really am. I'd have thought he was man enough to do his own talking, but I guess he's soft inside like most people. But let's get down to it. You've pulled a lot of stuff out of that cenote. I want it. It's as simple as that. If you let me have it without trouble, there'll be no trouble from me.'

'You won't harm us in any way?' I queried.

'You just walk out of here,' he assured me.

'What guarantees do I have of that?'

He spread his hands and looked at me with honesty shining in his eyes. 'My word on it.'

I laughed out loud. 'Nothing doing, Gatt. I'm not that stupid.'

For the first time anger showed in him and there was a naked, feral gleam in his eyes. 'Now, get this straight, Wheale. I'm coming in to take that loot, and there's nothing you or anyone else can do to stop me. You do it peaceably or not—it's your choice.'

I caught a flicker of movement from the corner of my eye and turned my head. Some figures in white were emerging from the forest slowly; they were strung out in a straggling

217

line and they carried rifles. I swung my head around to the other side and saw more armed men coming across from the forest.

Clearly the time had come to put some pressure on Gatt. I felt in my shirt pocket for cigarettes, lit one and casually tossed the matchbox up and down in my hand. 'There's a rifle sighted on you, Gatt,' I said. 'One wrong move and you're a dead man.'

He smiled thinly. 'You're under a gun, too. I'm not a fool.'

I tossed the matchbox up and down, and kept it going. 'I've arranged a signal,' I said. 'If I drop this matchbox, you get a bullet. Now, if those men out there move ten more yards, I drop this box.'

He looked at me with the faintest shadow of uncertainty. 'You're bluffing,' he said. 'You'd be a dead man, too.'

'Try me,' I invited. 'There's a difference between you and me. I don't particularly care whether I live or die, and I'm betting that you do. The stakes are high in this game, Gatt—and those men have only five more yards to go. You had my brother killed, remember! I'm willing to pay a lot for his life.'

Gatt looked at the matchbox with fascination as it went up into the air, and winced involuntarily as I fumbled the next catch. I was running a colossal bluff and to make it stick I had to impress him with an appearance of ruthlessness. I tossed the box again. 'Three more yards and neither of us will have to worry any more about the treasure of Uaxuanoc.'

He broke! 'All right; it's a stand-off,' he said hoarsely, and lifted both arms in the air and waved them. The line of men drifted to a halt and then turned to go back into the forest. As I watched them go I tossed the matchbox again, and Gatt said irritably, 'For Christ's sake, stop doing that!'

I grinned at him and caught the box, but still held it in my fingers. There was a slight film of sweat on his forehead although the heat of the day had not yet started. 'I'd hate to play poker with you,' he said at last.

'That's a game I haven't tried.'

He gave a gusty sigh of exasperation. 'Listen, Wheale: you don't know the game you're in. I've had tabs on Fallon right from the beginning. Christ, I laughed back there at your air-strip when you all played the innocent. You really thought you were fooling me, didn't you? Hell, I knew everything you did and everything you thought—I didn't give a damn what

218

action you took. And I've had that fool Harris chasing all over Mexico. You see, it's all come down to one thing, one sharp point—I'm here and I'm on top. Now, what about it?'

'You must have had some help,' I said.

'Didn't you know?' he said in surprise, and began to laugh. 'Jesus! I had that damned fool, Halstead. He came to me back in Mexico City and made a deal. A very eager guy, Halstead; he didn't want to share this city with Fallon—so we made the deal. He could have the city and I'd pick up the gold and get rid of Fallon for him.' The corners of his mouth downturned in savage contempt. 'The guy was too chicken to do his own killing.'

So it had been Halstead, just as Pat Harris suspected, and when we found Uaxuanoc he had tipped off Gatt. No wonder Pat had been running round in circles when Gatt knew our every move. It made me sick to realize how ambition could so corrupt a man that he would throw in his lot with a man like Gatt. The funny part about it was that Halstead had meant to cheat Gatt all along; he had never expected anything of value to turn up for Gatt to get his hands on.

I said in a hard voice, 'Where is Halstead now?'

'Oh, the guy's dead,' said Gatt casually. 'When you chased him out my chicleros got a little trigger-happy and he caught one.' He grinned. 'Did I save you the trouble, Wheale?'

I ignored that. 'You're wasting your time here. You're welcome to come and take your loot, but you'll get wet doing it.'

'Not me,' said Gatt. 'You! Oh, I know what you've done with it. Halstead didn't die right away and he told me where the stuff was—after a bit of persuasion. It took time or I'd have been here sooner before you put the stuff in the water. But it doesn't matter, not really.' His voice was calm and soft and infinitely menacing. 'You can get it back, Wheale; you're a diver, and so is that Halstead bitch. You'll swim down and get it back for me.'

'You don't know much about deep diving. It's not a five-minute job.'

He made a slashing motion with his hand. 'But you'll do it all the same.'

'I don't see how you can make me.'

'Don't you? You'll learn.' His smile was terrible. 'Let's say I get hold of Fallon and go to work on him, hey? You'll watch what I do to him and then you'll go down. I promise you.' He dropped the stub of his cigar and tapped me on the

219

chest. 'You were right when you said there's a difference between you and me. I'm a hard man, Wheale; and you just think you're hard. You've been putting up a good imitation lately and you had me fooled, but you're like all the rest of the common punks in the world—soft in the middle, like Fallon. When I start taking Fallon apart slowly—or the girl, maybe—or that big ox, Rudetsky—then you'll dive. See what I mean?'

I saw. I saw that this man used cruelty as a tool. He had no human feeling himself but knew enough to manipulate the feelings of others. If I really had made an arrangement with Fowler I'd have dropped that matchbox there and then and taken my chance on being killed as long as he was eliminated. And I cursed my thoughtlessness in not bringing a pistol to shoot the bastard with.

I caught my breath and strove to speak evenly. 'In that case you must be careful not to kill me,' I said. 'You've heard of the goose and the golden eggs.'

His lips curled back from his teeth. 'You'll wish I had killed you,' he promised. 'You really will.' He turned and strode away and I went back to the hut—fast.

I tumbled in the door and yelled, 'Shoot the bastard!' I was in a blind rage.

'No good,' said Fowler from the window. 'He ducked for cover.'

'What gives?' asked Rudetsky.

'He's mad—staring stone mad! We've balked him and he's done his nut. He can't get his loot so he is going to take it out in blood.' I thought of that other madman who had shouted crazily, 'Weltmacht oder Niedergang!' Like Hitler, Gatt had blown his top completely and was ready to ruin us and himself out of angry spite. He had gone beyond reason and saw the world through the redness of blood.

Rudetsky and Fowler looked at me in silence, then Rudetsky took a deep breath. 'Makes no difference, I guess. We knew he'd have to kill us, anyway.'

'He'll be whipping up an attack any minute,' I said. 'Get everyone back in the hut by the cenote.'

Rudetsky thrust a revolver into my hand. 'All you gotta do is pull the trigger.'

I took the gun although I didn't know if I could use it effectively and we left the hut at a dead run. We had only got halfway to the cenote when there was a rattle of rifle fire and bits of soil fountained up from the ground. 'Spread out!' yelled Rudetsky, and turned sharply to cannon into me. He bounced off and we both dived for cover behind a hut.

A few more shots popped off, and I said, 'Where the hell are they?'

Rudetsky's chest heaved. 'Somewhere out front.'

Gatt's men must have gone on to the attack as soon as Gatt had gone into cover, probably by pre-arranged signal. Shots were popping off from all around like something in a Western movie and it was difficult to tell precisely where the attack was coming from. I saw Fowler, who was crouched behind an abandoned packing case on the other side of the clearing, suddenly run in the peculiar skittering movement of the experienced soldier. Bullets kicked up dust around him but he wasn't hit and he disappeared from sight behind a hut.

'We've gotta get outa here,' said Rudetsky rapidly. His face was showing strain. 'Back to the hut.'

He meant the hut by the cenote and I could see his point. There wasn't any use preparing a hut against attack and then being caught in the open. I hoped the others had had the sense to retreat there as soon as they heard the first shots. I looked back and cursed Rudetsky's neat and tidy mind—he had built the camp with a wide and open street which was now raked with bullets and offered no cover.

I said, "We'd better split up, Joe; two targets are more difficult than one.'

'You go first,' he said jerkily. 'I might be able to cover you.'

This was no time to argue so I ran for it, back to the hut behind us. I was about two yards from it when a chiclero skidded around the corner from an unexpected direction. He was as surprised as I was because he literally ran on to the gun which I held forward so that the muzzle was jammed into his stomach.

I pulled the trigger and my arm jolted convulsively. It was as though a great hand plucked the chiclero off his feet and he was flung away and fell with all limbs awry. I dithered a bit with my heart turning somersaults in my chest before I recovered enough from the shock to bolt through the doorway of the hut. I leaned against the wall for a moment, gasping for breath and with the looseness of fear in my bowels, then

I turned and looked cautiously through the window. Rudetsky was gone—he must have made his break immediately after I had moved.

I looked at the revolver; it had been fully loaded and there were now five shots left. Those damned thugs seemed to be coming from all directions. The man I had shot had come from *behind*—he had apparently come up from the cenote. I didn't like the implications of that.

I was wondering what to do when the decision was taken from me. The back door of the hut crashed open under the impact of a booted foot. I jerked up my head and saw, framed in the doorway, a chiclero just in the act of squeezing off a shot at me with a rifle. Time seemed frozen and I stood there paralysed before I made an attempt at lifting the revolver, and even as my arm moved I knew I was too late.

The chiclero seemed to *flicker*—that movement you see in an old film when a couple of frames have been cut from the action producing a sudden displacement of an actor. The side of his jaw disappeared and the lower half of his face was replaced by a bloody mask. He uttered a bubbling scream, clapped his hands to his face and staggered sideways, dropping his rifle on the threshold with a clatter. I don't know who shot him; it could have been Fowler or Rudetsky, or even one of his own side—the bullets were flying thick enough.

But I wasted no time wondering about it. I dived forward and went through that doorway at a running crouch and snatched for the fallen rifle as I went. Nobody shot at me as I scurried hell for leather, angling to the left towards the edge of camp. I approached the hut by the cenote at a tangent, having arrived by a circuitous route, and I could not tell if the door was open or even if there was anyone inside. But I did see Fowler make a run for it from the front.

He nearly made it, too, but a man appeared from out of nowhere—not a chiclero but one of Gatt's elegant thugs who carried what at first I thought was a sub-machine-gun. Fowler was no more than six paces from the hut when the gangster fired and his gun erupted in a peculiar double *booom*. Fowler was hit by both charges of the cut-down shotgun and was thrown sideways to fall in a crumpled heap.

I took a snap shot at his killer with no great hope of success and then made a rush for the door of the hut. A bullet chipped splinters from the door frame just by my head, and one of them drove into my cheek as I tumbled in. Then someone slammed the door shut.

When I looked out again I saw it was useless to do anything for Fowler. His body was quivering from time to time as bullets hit it. They were using him for target practice.

II

The rifle fire clattered to a desultory stop and I looked around the hut. Fallon was clutching a shotgun and crouched under a window; Smith was by the door with a pistol in his hand—it was evidently he who had shut it. Katherine was lying on the floor sobbing convulsively. There was no one else.

When I spoke my voice sounded as strange as though it came from someone else. 'Rudetsky?'

Fallon turned his head to look at me, then shook it slowly. There was pain in his eyes.

'Then he won't be coming,' I said harshly.

'Jesus!' said Smith. His voice was trembling. 'They killed Fowler. They shot him.'

A voice—a big voice boomed from outside. It was Gatt, and he was evidently using some sort of portable loudhailer. 'Wheale! Can you hear me, Wheale?'

I opened my mouth, and then shut it firmly. To argue with Gatt—to try to reason with him—would be useless. It would be like arguing against an elemental force, like trying to deflect a lightning bolt by quoting a syllogism. Fallon and I looked at each other along the length of the hut in silence.

'I know you're there, Wheale,' came the big shout. 'I saw you go in the hut. Are you ready to make a deal?'

I compressed my lips. Fallon said creakily, 'A deal! Did he mention a deal?'

'Not the kind you'd appreciate,' I said grimly.

'I'm sorry that guy was killed,' shouted Gatt. 'But you're still alive, Wheale. I could have killed you right there by the door, but I didn't. You know why.'

Smith jerked his head and looked at me with narrowed eyes. There was a question in them which he didn't put into words. I closed my hand tighter round the butt of the revolver and stared him down until his glance slid away.

'I've got another guy here,' boomed Gatt. 'Big Joe Rudetsky. Are you prepared to deal?'

I knew very well what he meant. I moistened my lips and shouted, 'Produce him alive—and I might.'

There was a long pause. I didn't know what I'd do if he were still alive and Gatt carried out his threats. Whatever I did would be useless. It would mean putting the four of us into Gatt's hands and giving him all the aces. And he'd kill us all in the end, anyway. But if he produced Joe Rudetsky and began to torture him, could I withstand it? I didn't know.

Gatt laughed. 'You're smart, Wheale. You sure are smart. But not tough enough. Is Fallon still alive?'

I motioned to Fallon to keep quiet.

'Oh, I suppose he's there—with maybe one or two more. I'll leave *them* to argue with you, Wheale, and maybe you'll be ready to make a deal. I'll give you one hour—and no more. I don't think you'll be tough enough for that, Wheale.'

We stood there, quite still, for two full minutes and he said nothing more. I was thankful for that because he'd already said enough—I could see it in Smith's eyes. I looked at my watch and realized with a sense of shock that it was only seven o'clock in the morning. Less than fifteen minutes earlier I'd been talking to Gatt outside the camp. His attack had come with a ruthless suddenness.

Fallon eased himself down until he was sitting on the floor. He laid the shotgun aside carefully. 'What's the deal?' he asked, looking at his feet. The voice was that of an old man.

I paid far less attention to Fallon than I did to Smith. Smith held an automatic pistol; he held it loosely enough, but he could still be dangerous. 'Yeah, what's this deal?' he echoed.

'There's no deal,' I said shortly.

Smith jerked his head towards the window. 'That guy says there could be.'

'I don't think you'd like to hear it,' I said coldly.

I saw his gun hand tighten up and I lifted my revolver. He wasn't standing very far away but I don't even know if I could have hit him. They tell me that revolvers are very inaccurate in inexperienced hands. Still, Smith wasn't to know I wasn't a gunman. I said, 'Let's all kill each other and save Gatt the trouble.'

He looked at the gun in my hand which was pointed at his stomach. 'I just want to know about this deal,' he said steadily.

'All right; I'll tell you—but put the gun down first. It makes me uneasy.'

The thoughts that chased through Smith's mind were reflected on his face and were as clear as though he had spoken them, but at last he made his decision, stooped and laid the pistol at his feet. I relaxed and put my revolver on the table, and the tension eased. Smith said, 'I guess, we're all jumpy.' It was an apology of sorts.

Fallon was still regarding the tips of his bush boots as though they were the most important things in the world. He said quietly, 'Who does Gatt want?'

'He wants me,' I said. 'He wants me to go down and retrieve the loot.'

'I thought he might. What happened to Rudetsky?'

'He's dead. He's lucky.'

Smith hissed in a sudden intake of breath. 'What's that supposed to mean?'

'Gatt's way of persuading me to dive isn't pretty. He'll take any of us—you, Fallon or Mrs. Halstead, it doesn't matter—and torture him to put pressure on me. He's quite capable of doing it, and I think he'd relish using his imagination on a job like that.' I found myself looking at it in a detached manner. 'He might burn your feet off with a blowlamp; he might chop you up joint by joint while you're still alive; he might—well, there's no end to that kind of thing.'

Smith had averted his face. He jerked nervously. 'And you'd *let* him do it? Just for the sake of a few lousy trinkets?'

'I couldn't stop him,' I said. 'That's why I'm glad Rudetsky and Fowler are dead. You see, we got rid of the air bottles, and diving without them would be bloody difficult. All we have are a few charged aqualung bottles—the big bottles are at the bottom of the cenote. If you think I'm going to dive in those conditions, with someone screaming in my ears every time I come up, then you're even crazier than Gatt.'

Smith whirled on Fallon. 'You got me into this, you crazy old man. You had no right—do you hear me? You had no right.' His face collapsed into grief. 'Jesus, how am I going to get out of this? I don't wanna be tortured.' His voice shook with a passion of self-pity and tears streamed from his eyes. 'Good Christ, I don't want to die!' he wept.

It was pitiful to watch him. He was disintegrating as a man. Gatt knew very well how to put pressure on a man's innermost core, and the hour's grace he had given us was not intended to be a relief. It was the most sadistic thing he had done and he was winning. Katherine had collapsed; Fallon was eaten up with cancer and self-recrimination, and Smith had the pith taken out of him by the fear of death by torture.

I was all knotted up inside, tormented by my sheer impotence to do anything about it. I wanted to strike out and tear and smash—I wanted to get at Gatt and tear his bloody heart out. I couldn't, and the sense of helplessness was killing me.

Smith looked up craftily. 'I know what we'll do,' he whispered. 'We'll give him Fallon. Fallon got us into this, and he'd like to have Fallon, wouldn't he?' There was a mad gleam in his eyes. 'He could do things with Fallon—and he'd leave us alone. We'd be all right, then, wouldn't we?'

'Shut up!' I yelled, and then caught hold of myself. This was what Gatt wanted—to break us down with a calculated cold cruelty. I pushed down the temptation to take out my frustrations on Smith with an awful violence, and spoke, trying to keep my voice firm and level. 'Now, you look here, Smith. We're all going to die, and we can die by torture or by a bullet. I know which I prefer, so I'm going to fight Gatt and I'm going to do my best to kill *him*.'

Smith looked at me with hatred. 'It's all right for you. He's not going to torture you. You're safe.'

The ridiculousness of what he'd just said suddenly struck me, and I began to laugh hysterically. All the pent-up emotions suddenly welled up in laughter, and I laughed uncontrollably. 'Safe!' I cried. 'My God, but that's funny!' I laughed until the tears came and there was a pain in my chest. 'Oh, safe!'

The madness in Smith's eyes was replaced by a look of astonishment and then he caught on and a giggle escaped him, to be followed by a more normal chuckle. Then we both dissolved in gales of laughter. It was hysterical and it hurt in the end, but it did us good, and when the emotional spasm was over I felt purged and Smith was no longer on the verge of madness.

Even Fallon had a grim smile on his face, remarkable in a man whose life and manner of death had just been debated by a semi-lunatic. He said, 'I'm sorry I got you into this, Smith; but I'm in it myself, too. Jemmy is right; the only thing to do is to fight.'

'I'm sorry I kicked off like that, Mr. Fallon,' said Smith awkwardly, 'I guess I went nuts for a while.' He stooped and picked up the pistol, took out the magazine and flipped the action to eject the round in the breech. 'I just want to take as many of those bastards with me as I can.' He examined the magazine and inserted the loose cartridge. 'Five bullets—four for them and one for me. I reckon it's best that way.'

'You may be right,' I said and picked up the revolver. I wasn't at all certain whether I'd have the guts to put a bullet into my own head if it came to the push. 'Keep a check on what's happening outside. Gatt said he'd give us an hour but I don't trust him that far.'

I crossed over to Katherine and dropped to my knees beside her. Her eyes were now dry although there were traces of tears on her cheeks. 'How are you doing?' I asked.

'I'm sorry,' she whispered. 'I'm sorry I broke down—but I was afraid—so afraid.'

'Why shouldn't you be afraid?' I said. 'Everyone else is. Only a damn fool has no fear at a time like this.'

She swallowed nervously. 'Did they really kill Rudetsky and Fowler?'

I nodded, then hesitated. 'Katherine, Paul is dead, too. Gatt told me.'

She sighed and her eyes glistened with unshed tears. 'Oh, my God! Poor Paul! He wanted so much—so quickly.'

Poor Paul, indeed! I wasn't going to tell her everything I knew about Halstead, about the ways he went in getting what he wanted so quickly. It would do no good and only break her heart. Better she should remember him as he was when they married—young, eager and ambitious in his work. To tell her otherwise would be cruel.

I said, 'I'm sorry, too.'

She touched my arm. 'Do we have a chance—any chance at all, Jemmy?'

Privately I didn't think we had a snowball's chance in hell. I looked her in the eye. 'There's always a chance,' I said firmly.

Her gaze slipped past me. 'Fallon doesn't seem to think so,' she said in a low voice.

I turned my head and looked at him. He was still sitting on the floor with his legs outstretched before him and gazing sightlessly at the toe-caps of his boots. 'He has his own problems,' I said, and got up and crossed over to him.

At my approach he looked up. 'Smith was right,' he said wanly. 'It's my fault we're in this jam.'

'You had other things to think about.'

He nodded slowly. 'Selfishly—yes. I could have had Gatt deported from Mexico. I have that much pull. But I just let things slide.'

'I don't think that would have worried Gatt,' I said, trying to console him. 'He would have come back anyway—he has quite a bit of pull himself, if what Pat Harris says is correct. I don't think you could have stopped him.'

'I don't care for myself,' said Fallon remorsefully. 'I'll be dead in three months, anyway. But to drag down so many others is unforgivable.' He withdrew almost visibly and returned into his trance of self-accusation.

There wasn't much to be done with him so I arose and joined Smith at the window. 'Any sign of action?'

'Some of them are in those huts.'

'How many?'

He shook his head. 'Hard to say—maybe five or six in each.'

'We might give them a surprise,' I said softly. 'Any sign of Gatt?'

'I don't know,' said Smith. 'I wouldn't even know what he looks like. Goddamn funny, isn't it?' He stared across at the huts. If they open fire from so close, the bullets will rip through here like going through a cardboard box.'

I turned my head and looked at the plunger box and at the wires which led to it, wondering how much explosive Rudetsky had planted in the huts and whether it had been found. As a kid I'd always been overly disappointed by damp squibs on Guy Fawkes Night.

The hour ticked away and we said very little. Everything that had to be said had been torn out of us in that explosive first five minutes and we all knew there was little point in piling on the agony in futile discussion. I sat down and, for want of something better to do, checked the scuba gear, and Katherine helped me. I think I had an idea at the back of my mind that perhaps we would give in to Gatt in the end, and I would have to go down into the cenote again. If I did, then I wanted everything to work smoothly for the sake of the survivors in Gatt's hands.

Abruptly, the silence was torn open by the harsh voice of Gatt magnified by the loudhailer. He seemed to be having trouble with it because it droned as though the speaker was overloaded. 'Wheale! Are you ready to talk?'

I ran at a crouch towards the plunger box and knelt over

it, hoping that our answer to Gatt would be decisive. He shouted again. 'Your hour is up, Wheale.' He laughed boomingly. 'Fish, or I'll cut you into bait.'

'Listen!' said Smith urgently. 'That's a plane.'

The droning noise was much louder and suddenly swelled to a roar as the aircraft went overhead. Desperately I gave the plunger handle a ninety-degree twist and rammed it down and the hut shook under the violence of the explosion. Smith yelled in exultation, and I ran to the window to see what had happened.

One of the huts had almost literally disappeared. As the smoke blew away I saw that all that was left of it was the concrete foundation. White figures tumbled from the other hut and ran away, and Smith was shooting fast. I grabbed his shoulder. 'Stop that! You're wasting bullets.'

The plane went overhead again, although I couldn't see it. 'I wonder whose it is,' I said. 'It could belong to Gatt.'

Smith laughed excitedly. 'It might not—and, Jeez, what a signal we gave it!'

There was no reaction from Gatt; the loud voice had stopped with the explosion and I desperately hoped I'd blown him to hell.

III

It was too much to hope for. Everything was quiet for another hour and then there came a slow and steady hail of rifle fire. Bullets ripped through the thin walls of the hut, tearing away the interior insulation, and it was very dangerous to move away from the cover of the thick baulks of timber Rudetsky had installed. The chief danger was not from a direct hit but from a ricochet. From the pace of the firing I thought that not more than three or four men were involved, and I wondered uneasily what the others were doing.

It was also evident that Gatt was still alive. I doubted if the chicleros would still keep up the attack without him and his bully boys behind them. They wouldn't have the motive that drove Gatt, and, besides, an unknown number had been killed in the hut. I was reasonably sure that none of the men in that hut could have survived the explosion, and it must have given the rest a hell of a shock.

The fact that the attack had been resumed after an hour also demonstrated that Gatt, no matter what else he was, could lead—or drive—men. I knew personally of three chicleros that had died; say another four, at a low estimate, had been killed in the hut, and add to that any that Fowler or Rudetsky had killed before being slaughtered themselves. Gatt must be a hell of a man if he could whip the chicleros into another attack after suffering losses like that.

The aircraft had circled a couple of times after the hut blew up and then had flown off, heading north-west. If it belonged to Gatt then it wouldn't make any difference; if it belonged to a stranger then the pilot might be wondering what the hell was going on—he'd certainly been interested enough to overfly the camp a couple of times—and he might report it to the authorities when he got to wherever he was going. By the time anything got done about it we'd all be dead.

But I didn't think it was a stranger. We'd been in Quintana Roo for quite some time and the only aircraft I'd seen were those belonging to Fallon and Gatt's little twin-engined job that had landed at Camp One. There's not much call for an air service in Quintana Roo, so if it wasn't Gatt's plane then it might be someone like Pat Harris, come down to see why Fallon had lost communication with the outer world. And I couldn't see that making any difference to our position either.

I winced as a bullet slammed through the hut and a few flakes of plastic insulation drifted down to settle on the back of my hand. There were two things we could do—stay there and wait for it, or make a break and get killed in the open. Not much of a choice.

Smith said, 'I wonder where all the other guys are? There can't be more than four of them out front.'

I grinned tightly. 'Want to go outside and find out?'

He shook his head emphatically. 'Uh-uh! I want them to come and get *me*. That way *they're* in the open.'

Katherine was crouched behind a thick timber, clutching the revolver I had given her. If she had not lost her fear at least she was disguising it resolutely. Fallon worried me more; he just stood there quietly, grasping the shotgun and waiting for the inevitable. I think he had given up and would have welcomed the smashing blow of a bullet in the head which would make an end to everything.

Time passed, punctuated by the regular crack of a rifle and the thump of a bullet as it hit thick timber. I bent down and applied my eye to a ragged bullet hole in the wall, working on the rather dubious principle that lightning never strikes twice in the same place. The marksmen were hidden and there was no way of finding their positions; not that it would have done us any good if we knew because we had but one rifle, and that had only two rounds in the magazine.

Fowler's body was lying about thirty feet from the hut. The wind plucked at his shirt and rippled the cloth, and tendrils of his hair danced in the breeze. He lay quite peacefully with one arm outflung, the fingers of the hand half-curled in a natural position as though he were asleep; but his shirt was stained with ugly blotches to mark the bullet wounds.

I swallowed painfully and lifted my eyes higher to the ruined hut and the litter about it, and then beyond to the ruins of Uaxuanoc and the distant forest. There was something about the scene which looked odd and unnatural, and it wasn't the ugly evidence of violence and death. It was something that had changed and it took me a long time to figure what it was.

I said, 'Smith!'

'Yeah?'

'The wind's rising.'

There was a pause while he looked for himself, then he said tiredly, 'So what?'

I looked again at the forest. It was in motion and the tree-tops danced, the branches pushed by moving air. All the time I had been in Quintana Roo the air had been quiet and hot, and there had been times when I would have welcomed a cool breeze. I turned carefully and strained my head to look out of the window without exposing my head to a snap shot. The sky to the east was dark with thick cloud and there was a faint and faraway flicker of lightning.

'Fallon!' I said. 'When does the rainy season start?'

He stirred briefly. 'Any time, Jemmy.'

He didn't seem very interested in why I had asked.

I said, 'If you saw clouds and lightning now—what would you think?'

'That the season had started,' he said.

'Is that all?' I said, disappointed.

'That's all.'

Another bullet hit the hut and I swore as a wood splinter drove into my calf. 'Hey!' shouted Smith in alarm. 'Where the hell did that one come from?' He pointed to the ragged hole in the wooden floor.

I saw what he meant. That bullet had hit at an impossible angle, and it hadn't done it by a ricochet. Another bullet slammed in and a chair jerked and fell over. I saw a hole in the *seat* of the chair, and knew what had happened. I listened for the next bullet to hit and distinctly heard it come through the roof. The chicleros had got up on the hillside behind the cenote and were directing a plunging fire down at the hut.

The situation was now totally impossible. All our added protection was in the walls and it had served us well, but we had no protection from above. Already I could see daylight showing through a crack in the asbestos board roofing where a bullet had split the brittle panel. Given enough well-aimed bullets and the chicleros could damn near strip the roof from the top of us, but we'd most likely be dead by then.

We could find a minimum shelter by huddling in the angle of the floor and the wall on the side of the hut nearest the hill, but from there we could not see what was happening at the front of the hut. If we did that, then all that Gatt would have to do was to walk up and open the door—no one would be in a position to shoot him.

Another bullet hit from above. I said, 'Smith—want to break for it? I'll be with you if you go.'

'Not me,' he said stubbornly. 'I'll die right here.'

He died within ten seconds of uttering those words by taking a bullet in the middle of his forehead which knocked him back against the wall and on to the floor. He died without seeing the man who killed him and without ever having seen Gatt, who had ordered his death.

I stooped to him, and a bullet smacked into the wall just where I had been standing. Fallon shouted, 'Jemmy! The window!' and I heard the duller report of the shotgun blasting off.

A man screamed and I twisted on the ground with the revolver in my hand just in time to see a chiclero reel away from the already long-shattered window and Fallon with the smoking gun in his hand. He moved right to the window and fired another shot and there was a shout from outside.

He dropped back and broke open the gun to reload, and I

leaped forward to the window. A chiclero was jumping for cover while another was staggering around drunkenly, his hands to his face and crying in a loud keening wail. I ignored him and took a shot at a third who was by the door not four feet away. Even a tyro with a gun couldn't miss him and he grunted and folded suddenly in the middle.

I dropped back as a bullet broke one of the shards of glass remaining in the window, and shuddered violently as two more bullets came in through the roof. Any moment I expected to feel the impact as one of them hit me.

Fallon had suddenly come alive again. He nudged me with his foot and I looked up to find him regarding me with bright eyes. 'You can get out,' he said quickly. 'Move fast!'

I gaped, and he swung his arm and pointed to the scuba gear. 'Into the cenote, damn it!' he yelled. 'They can't get at you there.' He crawled to the wall and applied his eye to a bullet hole. 'It's quiet out front. I can hold them for long enough.'

'What about you?'

He turned. 'What about me? I'm dead anyway. Don't worry, Gatt won't get me alive.'

There wasn't much time to think. Katherine and I could go into the cenote and survive for a little longer, safe from Gatt's bullets, but then what? Once we came out we'd be sitting targets—and we couldn't stay down forever. Still, a short extension of life meant a little more hope, and if we stayed where we were we would certainly be killed within the next few minutes.

I grabbed Katherine's wrist. 'Get into your gear,' I yelled. 'Get a bloody move on.'

She looked at me with startled eyes, but moved fast. She ripped off her clothes and got into the wet-suit and I helped her put on the harness. 'What about Fallon?' she said breathlessly.

'Never mind him,' I snapped. 'Concentrate on what you're doing.'

There was a diminution in the rate of rifle fire which I couldn't understand. If I'd have been in Gatt's place now was the time when I'd be pouring it on thick and heavy, but only one bullet came through the roof while Katherine and I were struggling with the harnesses and coupling up the bottles.

I turned to Fallon. 'How is it outside?'

He was looking through the window at the sky in the east and a sudden gust of wind lifted his sparse hair. 'I was wrong, Jemmy,' he said suddenly. 'There's a storm coming. The wind is already very strong.'

'I doubt if it will do us any good,' I said. The two-bottle pack was heavy on my shoulders and I knew I couldn't run very fast, and Katherine would be even more hampered. There was a distinct likelihood that we'd be picked off running for the cenote.

'Time to go,' said Fallon, and picked up the rifle. He had assembled all the weapons in a line near the window. He shrugged irritably. 'No time for protracted farewells, Jemmy. Get the hell out of here.' He turned his back on us and stood by the window with the rifle upraised.

I heaved away the table which barricaded the door, then said to Katherine, 'When I open the door start running. Don't think of anything else but getting to the cenote. Once you are in it dive for the cave. Understand?'

She nodded, but looked helplessly at Fallon. 'What about. . .?'

'Never mind,' I said. 'Move . . . now!'

I opened the door and she went out, and I followed her low and fast, twisting to change direction as soon as my feet hit the soil outside. I heard a crack as a rifle went off but I didn't know if that was the enemy or Fallon giving covering fire. Ahead, I saw Katherine zip round the corner of the hut and as I followed her I ran into a gust of wind that was like a brick wall, and I gasped as it got into my mouth, knocking the breath out of me. There was remarkably little rifle fire—just a few desultory shots—and no bullets came anywhere near that I knew of.

I took my eyes off Katherine and risked a glance upwards and saw the possible reason. The whole of the hillside above the cenote was in violent motion as the wind lashed the trees, and waves drove across as they drive over a wheatfield under an English breeze. But these were hundred-foot trees bending under the blast—not stalks of wheat—and this was something stronger than an English zephyr. It suddenly struck me that anyone on the hillside would be in danger of losing his skin.

But there was no time to think of that. I saw Katherine hesitate on the brink of the cenote. This was no time to think of the niceties of correct diving procedure, so I yelled to her,

'Jump! Jump, damn it!' But she still hesitated over the thirty-foot drop, so I rammed my hand in the small of her back and she toppled over the edge. I followed her a split-second later and hit feet first. The harness pulled hard on me under the strain and then the water closed over my head.

Twelve

As I went under I jack-knifed to dive deeper, keeping a lookout for Katherine. I saw her, but to my horrified astonishment she was going up again—right to the surface. I twisted in the water and went after her, wondering what the hell she thought she was doing, and grabbed her just before she broke into the air.

Then I saw what was wrong. The mask had been ripped from her head, probably by impact with the water, and the airline was inextricably tangled and wound among the bottles on her back in such a position that it was impossible for her to even touch it. She was fast running out of air, but she kept her head, and let it dribble evenly and slowly from her mouth just as she had done when I surprised her in Fallon's swimming pool back in Mexico City. She didn't even panic when I grabbed her, but let me pull her under water to the side of the cenote.

We broke into air and she gasped. I spat out my mouthpiece and disentangled her airline, and she paused before putting the mask on. 'Thanks!' she said. 'But isn't it dangerous here?'

We were right at the side of the cenote nearest the hill and protected from plunging fire by the sheer wall of the cenote, but if anyone got past Fallon we'd be sitting ducks. I said, 'Swim under water for the shot line, then wait for me. Don't worry about the shooting—water is hard stuff—it stops a bullet dead within six inches. You'll be all right if you're a couple of feet under; as safe as behind armour plate.'

She ducked under the water and vanished. I couldn't see her because of the dancing reflections and the popple on the water caused by the driving wind, but the boys on the hillside evidently could because of the spurts of water that suddenly flicked in a line. I hoped I was right about that bit of folklore about bullets hitting water, and I breathed with relief as there was

235

a surge of water at the raft as she went beneath it and was safe.

It was time for me to go. I went down and swam for the raft, going down about four feet. I'll be damned if I didn't see a bullet dropping vertically through the water, its tip flattened by the impact. The folklore was right, after all.

I found her clinging to the shot line beneath the raft, and pointed downwards with my thumb. Obediently she dived, keeping one hand in contact with the rope, and I followed her. We went down to the sixty-five-foot level where a marker on the rope indicated that we were as deep as the cave, and we swam for it and surfaced inside with a deep sense of relief. Katherine bobbed up beside me and I helped her climb on to the ledge, then I switched on the light.

'We made it,' I said.

She took off her mask wearily. 'For how long?' she asked, and looked at me accusingly. 'You left Fallon to die; you abandoned him.'

'It was his own decision,' I said shortly. 'Switch off your valve; you're wasting air.'

She reached for it mechanically, and I turned my attention to the cave. It was fairly big and I judged the volume to be in excess of three thousand cubic feet—we'd had to pump a hell of a lot of air into it from the surface to expel the water. At that depth the air was compressed to three atmospheres, therefore it contained three times as much oxygen as an equal volume at the surface, which was a help. But with every breath we were exhaling carbon dioxide and as the level of CO_2 built up so we would get into trouble.

I rested for a while and watched the light reflect yellowly from the pile of gold plate at the further end of the ledge. The problem was simple; the solution less so. The longer we stayed down, the longer we would have to decompress on the way up —but the bottles in the back-packs didn't hold enough air for lengthy decompression. At last I bent down and swished my mask in the water before putting it on.

Katherine sat up. 'Where are you going?'

'I won't be long,' I said. 'Just to the bottom of the cenote to find a way of stretching our stay here. You'll be all right— just relax and take things easy.'

'Can I help?'

I debated that one, then said, 'No. You'll just use up air.

There's enough in the cave to keep us going, and I might need what you have in that bottle.'

She looked up at the light and shivered. 'I hope that doesn't go out. It's strange that it still works.'

'The batteries topside are still full of juice,' I said. 'That's not so strange. Keep cheerful—I won't be long.'

I donned my mask, slipped into the water and swam out of the cave, and then made for the bottom. I found one of our working lights and debated whether or not to switch it on because it could be seen from the surface. In the end I risked it—there wasn't anything Gatt could do to get at me short of inventing a depth charge to blow me up, and I didn't think he could do that at short notice.

I was looking for the air cylinders Rudetsky and I had pushed off the raft and I found them spread out to hell and gone. Finding the manifold that had followed the cylinders was a bit more tricky but I discovered it under the coils of air hose that spread like a huge snake, and I smiled with satisfaction as I saw the spanner still tied to it by a loop of rope. Without that spanner I'd have been totally sunk.

Heaving the cylinders into one place was a labour fit for Hercules but I managed it at last and set about coupling up the manifold. Divers have very much the same problem of weightlessness as astronauts, and every time I tried to tighten a nut my body rotated around the cylinder in the other direction. I was down there nearly an hour but finally I got the cylinders attached to the manifold with all cocks open, and the hose on to the manifold outlet with the end valve closed. Now all the air in the cylinders was available on demand at the end of the hose.

I swam up to the cave, pulling the hose behind me, and popped up beside the ledge holding it triumphantly aloft. Katherine was sitting at the further end of the ledge, and when I said, 'Grab this!' she didn't do a damn thing but merely turned and looked at me.

I hoisted myself out of the water, holding the end of the hose with difficulty, and then hauled in a good length of it and anchored it by sitting on it. 'What's the matter with you?' I demanded.

She made no answer for some time, then said cheerlessly, 'I've been thinking about Fallon.'

'Oh!'

'Is that all you can say?' she asked with passion in her voice, but the sudden violence left her as soon as it had come. 'Do you think he's dead?' she asked more calmly.

I considered it. 'Probably,' I said at last.

'My God, I've misjudged you,' she said in a flat voice. 'You're a cold man, really. You've just left a man to die and you don't care a damn.'

'What I feel is my business. It was Fallon's decision—he made it himself.'

'But you took advantage of it.'

'So did you,' I pointed out.

'I know,' she said desolately. 'I know. But I'm not a man; I can't kill and fight.'

'I wasn't brought up to it myself,' I said acidly. 'Not like Gatt. But you'd kill if you had to, Katherine. Just like the rest of us. You're a human being—a killer by definition. We can all kill, but some of us have to be forced to it.'

'And you didn't feel you had to defend Fallon,' she said quietly.

'No, I didn't,' I said equally quietly. 'Because I'd be defending a dead man. Fallon knew that, Katie; he's dying of cancer. He's known it ever since Mexico City, which is why he's been so bloody irresponsible. And now it's on his conscience. He wanted to make his peace, Katie; he wanted to purge his conscience. Do you think I should have denied him that—even though we're all going to die anyway?'

I could hardly hear her. 'Oh, God!' she breathed. 'I didn't know—I didn't know.'

I felt ashamed. 'I'm sorry,' I said. 'I'm a bit mixed up. I'd forgotten you didn't know. He told me just before Gatt's attack. He was going back to Mexico City to die in three months. Not much to look forward to, is it?'

'So that's why he could hardly bear to leave here.' Her voice broke in a sob. 'I watched him looking over the city as though he were in love with it. He'd *stroke* the things we brought up from here.'

'He was a man taking farewell of everything he loved,' I said.

She was quiet for a time, then she said, 'I'm sorry, Jemmy; I'm sorry for the things I said. I'd give a lot not to have said them.'

'Forget it.' I busied myself with securing the hose, then began to contemplate what I'd do with it. The average diver

238

doesn't memorize the Admiralty diving tables, and I was no exception. However, I'd been consulting them freely of late, especially in relation to the depths in the cenote, and I had a fairly good idea of the figures involved. Sooner or later we'd have to go to the surface and that meant decompressing on the way up, the amount of decompression time depending on the depth attained and the length of time spent there.

I had just spent an hour at nearly a hundred feet and came back to sixty-five and I reckoned if I spent another hour, at least, in the cave, then I could write off the descent to the bottom of the cenote as far as decompression went. The nitrogen would already be easing itself quietly from my tissues without bubbling.

That left the ascent to the surface. The longer we spent in the cave the more decompression time we'd need, and the decompression time was strictly controlled by the amount of air available in the big cylinders at the bottom of the cenote. It would be unfortunate, to say the least, to run out of air while, say, at the twenty-foot decompression stop. A choice between staying in the water and asphyxiation, and going up and getting the bends. The trouble was that I didn't know how much air was left in the cylinders—Rudetsky had been doing the surface work on the raft and he wasn't available to tell me.

So I took a chance and assumed they were half full and carried on from there. My small back-pack bottles were nearly empty, but the ones on Katherine's harness were nearly full, so that was a small reserve. I finally figured out that if we spent a total of just over three hours in the cave I would need an hour and three-quarters, decompression—a total of five hours since we had dived under the bullets. There could possibly have been a change up on top in five hours. I grinned tightly. There wasn't any harm in being optimistic—Gatt might even have shot himself in frustration.

I consulted my watch and considered it lucky that I'd made a habit of wearing the waterproof and pressureproof diver's watch all the time. We'd been down an hour and a half, so that left about the same time to go before vacating the cave. I stretched out on the hard rock, still weighing down the hose, and prepared to wait it out.

. 'Jemmy!'

'Yes.'

'Nobody ever called me Katie before—except my father.'

239

'Don't look upon me as a father-figure,' I said gruffly.

'I won't,' she promised solemnly.

The light went out—not with a last despairing glimmer as the batteries packed in, but suddenly, as though a switch had been turned off. Katherine gave a startled cry, and I called out, 'Take it easy, Katie girl! Nothing to worry about.'

'Is it the batteries?'

'Probably,' I said, but I knew it wasn't. Someone had turned the light off deliberately or the circuit had been damaged. We were left in a darkness that could be felt physically—a clammy black cloak wrapped around us. Darkness, as such, had never worried me, but I knew it could have peculiar effects on others, so I stretched out my hand. 'Katie, come here!' I said. 'Let's not get too far away from each other.'

I felt her hand in mine. 'I hope we'll never be that.'

So we talked and talked in the blackness of that cave—talked about every damned thing there was to talk about—about her father and his work at the college, about my sports of fencing and swimming, about Hay Tree Farm, about the Bahamas, about my future, about her future—about our future. We were forgetful enough in that darkness to believe we had a future.

Once she said, 'Where did the wind come from so suddenly?'

'What wind?'

'Just before we ran for the cenote.'

I came back to the real and bloody world with a jerk. 'I don't know. Rider was telling me there was a hurricane off-coast. Maybe it swung inland. He was keeping an ear open for the weather forecasts, I do know that.' The crash of the chopper and the chase in the forest seemed to have happened an aeon before.

I looked at my watch and the luminous dial swam ghostlike in the darkness. It was just about time to go and I said so. Katherine was practical about it. 'I'll get ready,' she said.

My mouth was dry and I could hardly get the words out. 'You're not coming,' I said.

There was a brief gasp in the darkness. 'Why not?'

'There's only enough air to take one of us to the top. If we both go we'll both die. You can't go because God knows what you'd find up there. Even if Gatt has given up you'd still have to find the compressor parts which Rudetsky hid away and get the compressor going again. Could you do that?'

'I don't think so,' she said. 'No, I couldn't.'

240

'Then I must do it. God knows I don't like leaving you here, but it's the best way.'

'How long will you be?'

'Nearly two hours going up and maybe another hour to get the compressor going. You won't run out of air here, Katie; you should have enough for another seven or eight hours.'

'Seven hours will be too late, won't it? If it's as much as seven hours you won't be coming back at all. Isn't that right, Jemmy?'

It was—and I knew it. 'I'll be back long before then,' I said, but both of us knew the chances against it.

Her voice was pensive. 'I'd rather drown than just run out of air slowly.'

'For God's sake!' I burst out. 'You'll stay in this bloody cave until I get back, do you hear me? You'll stay here—promise me!'

'I'll stay,' she said softly, and then she was suddenly in my arms. 'Kiss me, darling.' Her lips were on mine and I held her tight, despite those damned clammy and unromantic rubber wet-suits we wore.

At last I pushed her away. 'We can't waste time,' I said, and bent down, groping for the hose. My fingers encountered something metallic which clattered on the rock, and I grasped it, then found the hose with my other hand. I pulled down the mask and whatever I was holding was in my way so I thrust it impatiently under the harness straps. 'I'll be back,' I promised, and slipped into the water, dragging the hose.

The last thing I heard before going under the water was Katie's voice echoing desolately round the cave. 'I love you— love you.'

II

I was holding the weight of about seventy feet of hose which tended to drag me down and I lost some height before I reached the shot line, but once there I was able to hold on to it while I hauled up more hose. When I felt resistance I stopped, and fastened the hose to the line with one of my fin-fasteners. I wouldn't need the fins from now on and the hose needed to be fastened so as to take the weight off me. That done, I went up slowly to the thirty foot mark, letting the air bubble from my mouth as it expanded in my lungs due to the lessening pressure and holding down my speed to less than that of the rising bubbles.

At thirty feet I climbed into the slings on the shot line and plugged the air hose into the demand valve on the harness, thus taking air from the big bottles at the bottom of the cenote and leaving the smaller harness bottles as a reserve. Then I looked at my watch. I would have to wait fifteen minutes at thirty feet, thirty-five minutes at twenty feet, and fifty minutes at ten feet.

Decompression is a slow and wearisome business at the best of times but this time the uncertainty of what I was about to meet when out of the water made it much worse. At the ten-foot level the suspense was awful because I knew I would be perfectly visible to anyone standing on the edge of the cenote. To make matters more nerve-racking the air gave out after only ten minutes at ten feet and I had to switch on to reserve; there had not been as much in the big cylinders as I thought and I was cutting things damned fine. And Katherine had been a little wasteful with the air from her bottles because it ran out fifteen minutes before my time was up, and I was forced to the surface.

I came up under the raft and hoped it wouldn't matter, pleased to be able to gulp in mouthfuls of sun-warmed air. I clung on to the underside of the raft with my head in the air space and listened intently. There was nothing to be heard apart from the soughing of the wind, which seemed to have dropped considerably in strength while we had been under water. I certainly heard no voices or anything human.

After a while I swam from under the raft and wearily climbed on board and shook off the scuba harness. Something clattered to the deck of the raft and I looked around in alarm for fear that it might have been heard before I bent to pick it up. It was a gold piece from the cave—the little statue of the Mayan maiden that Vivero had cast. I thrust it into my belt and then listened again and heard nothing of consequence.

I swam ashore to the rough dock that Rudetsky had made and trudged up the steps that had been hewn in the cifflike side of the cenote. At the top I stood in shaken amazement. The camp was a total wreck—most of the huts had disappeared completely, leaving only the foundations, and the whole area was a tangle of broken branches and even whole tree trunks from God knows where. And there was not a man in sight.

I looked towards the hut where we had made our stand and saw it was crushed and smashed under the weight of a big tree whose roots pointed skywards incongruously. Twigs cracked underfoot as I picked my way towards it and, as I got near, a brightly coloured bird flew out of the wreckage with a flutter of wings that momentarily alarmed me.

I prowled around, then stepped inside, climbing with difficulty over branches as thick as my own body. Somewhere among this lot were the spare scuba bottles I needed to bring Katherine to surface.

And somewhere among this lot was Fallon!

I found two machetes lying crossed as though someone had laid them down for sword dancing and took one to cut away at the smaller branches near where I would expect to find Fallon. After ten minutes of chopping I disclosed a hand and an arm outflung in death, but a few more cuts revealed the blood-smeared face of Smith. I tried again a little further along the line of the wall and this time I found him.

He was pinned to the ground by the branch that had struck him down, and when I put my hand on his arm I found, to my astonishment, that he was still warm. Quickly, I felt the pulse at his wrist and detected the faintest pulsation. Fallon was still alive! He had died neither by the hand of Gatt nor of the ancient enemy, but, incredibly, was still alive in spite of the violence of nature that had crashed a whole tree on to the hut.

I swung the machete and began to chop him free, which was not too difficult because he lay in the angle between floor and wall which had protected him from the tree in the first place, and I was soon able to drag him free and to put him in better comfort out of the sun. When I had done that he was still unconscious but his colour had improved and there didn't seem much wrong with him apart from the dark bruise on the side of his head. I thought he would presently regain consciousness naturally, so I left him for more important work.

The compressor parts had been hidden in a hole near the hut and covered with earth, but the whole area was covered with torn tree branches and other debris, including whole tree trunks. I wondered momentarily where they had come from and looked across the cenote to the hillside behind, and the sight of it took my breath in sharply. The ridge had been wiped clean of vegetation as if Rudetsky's gang had worked on it with power saw and flame-thrower.

There had been a wind—a big wind—that had assaulted the shallow-rooted forest trees and torn them clean out. I turned to look again at the hut and saw that the tree whose roots stuck up so ridiculously into the air must have been hurled from high on the hillside to strike downwards like some strange spear. And that was why the whole camp area, as far as I could see, was a wreck of timber and leafage.

The hillside was scraped clean to reveal the bare rock that had been hidden beneath the thin soil and, on top of the ridge, the temple of Yum Chac stood proudly against the sky very much as it must have looked when Vivero first saw it. I stepped back to get a better view of the whole ridge and looked past the ruined hut, and a great feeling of awe came upon me.

Because I saw Vivero's sign written in burning gold in the side of the ridge. I am not, in any sense, a religious man, but my legs turned to water and I sank down upon my knees and tears came to my eyes. The sceptic, of course, would write it off as a mere trick of the sun, of light and shade, and would point to parallels in other parts of the world where some natural rock formations are famous and well known. But that sceptic would not have gone through what I had gone through that day.

It may have been a trick of light and shade, but it was undeniably real—as real as if carved by a master sculptor. The setting sun, shining fitfully through scudding clouds, shed a lurid yellow light along the ridge and illuminated a great figure of Christ Crucified. The arms, spread along the ridge, showed every tortured muscle, and the nail heads in the palms of the hands cast deep shadows. The broad-chested torso shrank to a hollow stomach at the foot of the ridge, and there was a gaping hole in the side, just under the rib cage, which a sceptic would have dismissed as a mere cave. All the rib structure showed as clearly as in an anatomical drawing, as though that mighty chest was gasping for breath.

But it was the face that drew the attention. The great head lolled on one side against a shoulder and an outcrop of spiky rocks formed the crown of thorns against the darkening sky. Deep shadows drew harsh lines of pain from the nose to the corners of the mouth; the hooded eyes, crow-footed at the corners, stared across Quintana Roo; and the lips seemed about to part as though to bellow in a great voice of stone, 'Eloi! Eloi, Lama Sabacthani!'

I found my hands trembling and I could imagine what impression this miracle would have made on Vivero, a child of a simpler, yet deeper, faith than ours. No wonder he wanted his sons to take the city of Uaxuanoc; no wonder he had kept it secret and had baited his letter with gold. If this had been discovered in Vivero's time, it would have been one of the wonders of the Christian world, and the discoverer might even have been revered as a saint.

Probably this effect was not a daily occurrence and might depend on certain angles of the sun and, perhaps, times of year even. The Mayas, brought up in a different pictorial tradition and with no knowledge of Christianity, might not even have recognized it for what it was. But Vivero certainly had.

I knelt entranced in the middle of that devastated camp and looked up at this great wonder which had been hidden for so many centuries under a curtain of trees. The light changed as a cloud passed over the sun, and the expression of that huge and distant face changed from a gentle sorrow to inexpressible agony. I suddenly felt very afraid, and closed my eyes.

There was a crackle of twigs. 'That's right; say your prayers, Wheale,' said a grating voice.

I opened my eyes and turned my head. Gatt was standing just to one side with a revolver in his hand. He looked as though the whole forest had fallen on top of him. Gone was the neat elegance of the morning; he had lost his jacket, and his shirt was torn and ragged, revealing a hairy chest streaked with bloody scratches. His trousers were ripped at the knees and, as he walked around me, I saw that he had lost one shoe and was limping a little. But even so he was in better shape than I was—he had a gun!

He rubbed his hand over one sweaty cheek, streaking it with dirt, and lifted the other which held the revolver. 'Just you stay right there—on your knees.' He walked on a little further until he was directly in front of me.

'Have you seen what's behind you?' I asked quietly.

'Yeah, I've seen it,' he said tonelessly. 'Some effect, hey? Better than Mount Rushmore.' He grinned. 'Expecting it to do you some good, Wheale?'

I said nothing, but just looked at him. The machete was at my side and within reach of my fingers if I stooped a little. I didn't think Gatt would let me get that far.

'So you been praying, boy? Well, you gotta right.' The cultivated accent had vanished along with the elegance of his clothes; he had gone back to his primitive beginnings. 'You got every right because I'm gonna kill you. You wanna pray some more? Go right ahead—be my guest.'

I still kept my mouth shut, and he laughed. 'Cat got your tongue? Got nothing to say to Jack Gatt? You were pretty gabby this morning, Wheale. Now, I'll tell you something—confidential between you and me. You got plenty time to pray because you're not going to die quick or easy. I'm going to put a hot slug right in your guts and you'll take a long, long time to join our pal over there.' He jerked his thumb over his shoulder. 'You know who I mean—Holy Jesus up in the sky.'

There was a maniac gleam in his eyes and a tic convulsed his right cheek. He was now right round the bend and beyond the reach of reason. Gone was any idea he might have had of making me dive for the treasure—all he wanted was the violence of revenge, a booby prize for being cheated.

I looked at the gun he was holding and couldn't see any bullets in it. What I don't know about firearms would fill a library of books, but the revolver I'd used had rotated the cylinder when the trigger was pressed to bring a cartridge under the hammer, and before the gun was fired that cartridge would be visible from the front. I couldn't see any such cartridge in Gatt's gun.

'You've caused me a lot of trouble,' said Gatt. 'More trouble than any man I knew.' He laughed raucously. 'Get it? I put that in the past tense because guys who cause me *any* kind of trouble don't stay alive. And neither will you.' He was relaxed and enjoying his cat-and-mouse game.

I was anything but relaxed. I was about to stake my life on there not being two kinds of revolver. Slowly I stooped and curled my fingers around the handle of the machete. Gatt tensed and jerked the gun. 'Oh, no,' he said. 'Drop it!'

I didn't. Instead, I started to get to my feet. 'All right, buster,' shouted Gatt. 'Here it comes!' He squeezed the trigger and the hammer fell on an empty chamber with a dry click. He looked at it with startled eyes, and then backed away fast as he saw me coming at him with the upraised machete, turned tail and ran with me after him.

He scrambled over a tree trunk and became entangled in branches. I took a swing at him and a spray of leaves and twigs flew up into the air. Gatt yelped in fear and broke free, trying to make for the open ground and the forest beyond, but I ran around the tree, cutting him off, and he backed away towards the cenote.

He was still holding the useless gun which he raised and tried to fire again, giving me another bad moment, but it clicked harmlessly. I stepped forward again, manoeuvring him backwards, and he stepped back cautiously, not daring to take his eyes off me until he stumbled over the concrete foundations of the hut.

I will say he was quick. He threw the gun at me with an unexpected movement and I ducked involuntarily, and when I recovered he also was armed with a machete, which he had picked up from the floor of the hut. He squared his shoulders and a new confidence seemed to come over him as he hefted the broad-bladed weapon. His lips parted and his mouth broke into a grin, but there was no humour in his watchful eyes.

I automatically fell into the sabre stance—the classic 'on guard' position. As from a great distance seemed to come the ghostly voice of the maître d'armes crying. 'Use your fingers on the cut, Wheale!' I hefted the machete. This was no light sporting sabre to be twitched about by finger action as the Hungarian masters have taught; it could be more appropriately compared with a naval cutlass.

Gatt jumped and took a swipe at me and I instinctively parried with a clash of steel, then jumped back six feet and felt the sweat start out on my chest beneath the rubber suit. I had used the wrong parry, forgetting the machete had no guard for the hand. Gatt had used a sideways slash and I had parried in seconde, catching his blade on mine. If I hadn't jumped back his blade would have slid along mine and chopped my hand off—something that couldn't happen with a sabre.

I feinted at him to gain time to think and to watch his reaction to an attack. He tried to parry clumsily, missed my blade, jumped back and nearly fell. But he was agile for his age, and recovered quickly, successfully parrying again. I gave ground, well satisfied with what I had learned. Gatt was definitely no fencer. As a young mafioso he may have been an adept with a knife, but a machete is more like a sword than an overgrown knife, and I had the advantage.

247

So here we were, fulfilling the hypothetical prophecy of Pat Harris—Gatt and I alone in Quintano Roo with Gatt separated from his bodyguards. I was determined to make it as quick and as short as possible; I was going to kill Gatt as soon as I could. I didn't forget, however, that he was still highly dangerous, and advanced on him with due caution.

He had the sense to manoeuvre sideways so he would not have the wreckage of the hut behind him. That suited me because he could not retreat very far without coming to the edge of the cenote. He was sweating and breathing heavily, standing square on with his feet apart. He moved again, fast, and chopped down in a swing that would have cleaved my skull had it connected. I parried in quinte and stood my ground, which he didn't expect. For a split second he was very close and his eyes widened in fear as I released his blade and cut at his flank. It was only by a monstrous leap backwards that he avoided it, and the point of my machete ripped his shirt away.

I took advantage and pressed home the attack and he gave way slowly, his eyes looking apprehensively at my blade which is the wrong thing to watch—he ought to have been looking at my sword hand. In desperation he attacked again and I parried, but my foot slipped on a branch which rolled under the instep and I staggered sideways. I lost contact with his blade and it sliced downwards into my side in a shallow cut.

But I recovered and engaged his blade again and drove him back with a series of feints. He parried frantically, waving the machete from side to side. I gave ground then and put my hand to my side as though tiring and he momentarily dropped his guard in relief. Then I went in for the kill—a flèche and a lunge in the high line; he parried and I deceived his parry and chopped at his head.

The edge of the machete hit the side of his head just below the ear and I instinctively drew it back into a cut as I had been taught, and the blade sliced deep into his neck. He was dead before he knew it because I had damn near cut his head off. He twisted as he fell and rolled to the edge of the cenote, then slowly toppled over to fall with a thump on the wooden dock.

I didn't bother to look at him. I just staggered to the nearest support, which was a fallen tree, and leaned on the trunk. Then I vomited and nearly brought my heart up.

I must have passed out for a while because the next thing I knew was that I was lying on the ground, staring sideways at a column of industrious ants that looked as big as elephants from that angle. I picked myself up wearily and sat on the trunk of the tree. There was something nagging at the back of my head—something I had to do. My head ached abominably and little pointless thoughts chittered about like bats in an attic.

Oh, yes; that's what I had to do. I had to make sure that Jack Edgecombe didn't make a balls-up of the farm; he wasn't too enthusiastic in the first place and a man like that could make an awful mess of all the Mayan ruins. There was that pillar I'd found right next to the oak tree great-grandfather had planted—Old Cross-eyes I'd called him, and Fallon had been very pleased, but I mustn't let Jack Edgecombe near him. Never mind, old Mr. Mount would see to everything—he'd get a farm agent in to see to the excavation of the Temple of Yum Chac.

I put my hands to my eyes and wiped away the tears. Why the devil was I crying? There was nothing to cry about. I would go home now and Madge Edgecombe would make me tea, with scones spread thick with Devonshire cream and homemade strawberry jam. She'd use the Georgian silver set my mother had liked so much, and it would all be served on that big tray.

That big tray!

That brought it all back with a rush and my head nearly burst with the terror of it. I looked at my hand which was covered with drying blood and I wondered whose blood it was. I had killed a lot of men—I didn't know how many—so whose blood was this?

There and then I made a vow. That I would go back to England, to the sheltered combes of Devon, and I would never leave Hay Tree Farm again. I would stick close to the land of my people, the land that Wheales had toiled over for generations, and never again would I be such a damned fool as to look for adventure. There would be adventure enough for me in raising fat cattle and sinking a pint in the Kingsbridge Inn, and if ever again anyone called me a grey little man I would laugh, agree that it was so, and say I wouldn't have it otherwise.

My side hurt and I put my hand to it and it came away sticky with blood. When I looked down I saw that Gatt had cut a slice from my hide, chopping through the wet-suit as cleanly as a butcher with a cleaver. Bone showed—the bones of my ribs—and the pain was just beginning.

I suddenly thought of Katherine in the cave. Oh, God, I didn't want to go into the cenote again! But a man can do anything he has to, particularly a grey little man. Gatt wasn't a grey man—more like red in tooth and claw—but the grey men of the world are more than a match for the Gatts of this world—for one thing, there are more of them—and the grey men don't like being pushed around.

I pulled my weary bones together, ready to go looking again for those compressor parts and brushed the back of my hand across my eyes to rid them of the trace of those tears of weakness. When I looked across the city of Uaxuanoc there were ghosts there, drifting about in the ruins and coming closer—indistinct white figures with rifles.

They came soft-footed and looked at me with hard eyes, attracting each other with faint shouts of triumph, until there were a dozen of them in a big semi-circle surrounding me—the chicleros of Quintana Roo.

Oh, God! I thought desperately. Is the killing never going to end? I bent down and groped for the machete, nestled the hilt in the palm of my hands, then rose creakingly to my feet. 'Come on, you bastards!' I whispered. 'Come on! Let's get it over with!'

They closed in slowly, with caution and an odd respect in their eyes. I lifted the machete and one man unslung his rifle and I heard the metallic noise as he slammed home a round into the breech. There was a great throbbing sound in my ears, my vision darkened, and I felt myself swaying. Through a dark mist I saw the circle of men waver, and some began to run, and they shouted loudly.

I looked up to see a cloud of locusts descending from the sky, and then I pitched forward and saw the ground coming up at me.

'Wake up!' said the voice distantly. 'Wake up, Jemmy!'

I moved and felt pain. Someone, somewhere, was speaking crisp and fluent Spanish, then the voice said close to my ear, 'Jemmy, are you okay?' More distantly it said, 'Someone bring a stretcher.'

I opened my eyes and looked at the darkening sky. 'Who is the stretcher for?'

A head swam into view and I screwed up my eyes and saw it was Pat Harris. 'Jemmy, are you okay? Who beat you up? Those goddamn chicleros?'

I eased myself up on one elbow and he supported my back with his arm. 'Where did you come from?'

'We came in the choppers. The army's moved in.' He moved a little. 'Look, there they are.'

I stared at the five helicopters standing outside the camp, and at the busy men in uniform moving about briskly. Two of them were trotting my way with a stretcher. The locusts coming from heaven, I thought; they were helicopters.

'I'm sorry we couldn't get here sooner,' said Pat. 'It was that goddamn storm. We got a flick from the tail of a hurricane and had to put down half way.'

'Where have you come from?'

'Campeche—the other side of Yucatan. I flew over this morning and saw all hell breaking loose here—so I whistled up the Mexican army. If it hadn't been for the storm we'd have been here six hours ago. Say, where is everybody?'

That was a good question. I said creakily, 'Most of us are dead.'

He stared at me as I sat up. 'Dead!'

I nodded wearily. 'Fallon's still alive—I think. He's over there.' I grabbed his arm. 'Jesus! Katherine's down in the cenote—in a cave. I've got to get her out.'

He looked at me as though I had gone mad. 'In a cave! In the cenote!' he echoed stupidly.

I shook his arm. 'Yes, you damn fool! She'll die if I don't get her out. We were hiding from Gatt.'

Pat saw I was serious and was galvanized as though someone had given him an electric shock. 'You can't go down there

—not in your condition,' he said. 'Some of these boys are trained swimmers—I'll go see the teniente.'

I watched him walk across to a group of the soldiers, then I got to my feet, feeling every pain of it, and limped to the cenote and stood on the edge, looking down at the dark water. Pat came back at a run. 'The teniente has four scuba-trained swimmers and some oxygen bottles. If you'll tell them where the girl is, they can take oxygen down to her.' He looked down at the cenote. 'Good Christ!' he said involuntarily. 'Who's that?'

He was looking down at the body of Gatt which lay sprawled on the wooden dock. His mouth was open in a ghastly grin—but it wasn't really his mouth. 'It's Gatt,' I said unemotionally. 'I told you I'd kill him.'

I was drained of all emotion; there was no power in me to laugh or to cry, to feel sorrow or joy. I looked down at the body without feeling anything at all, but Harris looked sick. I turned away and looked towards the helicopters. 'Where are those bloody divers?'

They came at last and I explained haltingly what they were to do, and Pat interpreted. One of the men put on my harness and they jury-rigged an oxygen bottle and he went down. I hoped he wouldn't frighten Katie when he popped up in the cave. But her Spanish was good and I thought it would be all right.

I watched them carry Fallon away on a stretcher towards one of the choppers while a medico bandaged me up. Harris said in wonder, 'They're still finding bodies—there must have been a massacre.'

'Something like that,' I said indifferently.

I wouldn't move from that spot at the edge of the cenote until Katie was brought up, and I had to wait quite a while until they flew in proper diving gear from Campeche. After that it was easy and she came up from the cave under her own steam and I was proud of her.

We walked to the helicopter together with me leaning on her because suddenly all the strength had left me. I didn't know what was going to happen to us in the future—I didn't know if such an experience as we had undergone was such a perfect beginning to a marriage, but I was willing to try if she was.

I don't remember much about anything after that, not until I woke up in a hospital in Mexico City with Katie sitting by the bedside. That was many days afterwards. But I vaguely remember that the sun was just coming up as the chopper took off and I was clutching that little gold lady which Vivero had made. Christ was not to be seen, but I remember the dark shape of the Temple of Yum Chac looming above the water and drifting away forever beneath the heavily beating rotors.

Desmond Bagley

'Mr. Bagley is nowadays incomparable.' *Sunday Times*

The Tightrope Men

The Freedom Trap

Running Blind

The Spoilers

Landslide

The Golden Keel

Wyatt's Hurricane

High Citadel

The Vivero Letter

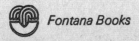 *Fontana Books*

Geoffrey Jenkins

Geoffrey Jenkins writes of adventure on land and at sea in some of the most exciting thrillers ever written. 'Geoffrey Jenkins has the touch that creates villains and heroes – and even icy heroines – with a few vivid words.' *Liverpool Post* 'A style which combines the best of Nevil Shute and Ian Fleming.' *Books and Bookmen*

A Cleft of Stars

A Grue of Ice

Hunter-Killer

The River of Diamonds

Scend of the Sea

A Twist of Sand

The Watering Place of Good Peace

 Fontana Books

Fontana Books

Fontana is a leading paperback publisher of fiction and non-fiction, with authors ranging from Alistair MacLean, Agatha Christie and Desmond Bagley to Solzhenitsyn and Pasternak, from Gerald Durrell and Joy Adamson to the famous Modern Masters series.

In addition to a wide-ranging collection of internationally popular writers of fiction, Fontana also has an outstanding reputation for history, natural history, military history, psychology, psychiatry, politics, economics, religion and the social sciences.

All Fontana books are available at your bookshop or newsagent; or can be ordered direct. Just fill in the form and list the titles you want.

FONTANA BOOKS, Cash Sales Department, G.P.O. Box 29, Douglas, Isle of Man, British Isles. Please send purchase price, plus 8p per book. Customers outside the U.K. send purchase price, plus 10p per book. Cheque, postal or money order. No currency.

NAME (Block letters)

ADDRESS
